Chas,
Thanks for your [...] [...]
friendship in [...]

The
Tesla
Testament

Eugene Ciurana

I hope that you enjoy
this story.
Best wishes,
Eugene
Ciurana

A CIMEntertainment Book
San Francisco, CA USA

San Francisco
21. Dec. 2007

Contact information:

Lynda Heinz
http://teslatestament.com
publicist@teslatestament.com

Library of Congress Catalog Card Number: Pending
ISBN: 1-4116-7317-4

Cover: Power transmitter by Nikola Tesla; CAD engineering by Rick Kraft; 3-D ray tracing by Stuart Dodgshon; layout and text by Charles Kiene

Produced in the United States of America

10 9 8 7 6 5 4 3 2 1

To Olga Dmitrievna "Varenka" Gavrilova
Are you ready for the next adventure?

The
Tesla
Testament

REBIRTH

CHAPTER 00

July, two years ago
World Affairs Council Gala Dinner
Speaker: Dr. Ferda Subidey, Nobel Prizewinner
Ft. Mason Festival Pavilion, San Francisco

Blam!

The gunshot blasted across the pavilion, shattering the festivities. Glamour gave way to fear, the ugly new reality mingled with the elegant men and women as they huddled by their tables. Francis Montagnet threw himself to the ground as the speaker's head exploded. A second shot reverberated through the air, then a third.

A woman screamed from the stage—it was his fiancée, Susan! He tried to make eye contact with her and to somehow get her to take cover.

Francis crouched and scanned the room. His table was next to the stage. Eight men, armed with AK-47s, had taken strategic positions throughout the pavilion. Three of them wore waiter's attire; the rest wore tuxedos. Their faces showed uniform resolve to fulfill their mission.

Francis looked back at the stage. Susan was petrified in her seat, her mauve dress was splattered with the murdered speaker's blood, her hands cradled her face; her mouth was open in an endless, shrill scream. She blinked, searching for him. "Stay down!" Francis yelled. She just sat there, her face set in a horrified grimace. At least she stopped screaming.

A ninth thug rushed to the stage brandishing a handgun. He was a tall, strong Middle Eastern man. Susan quivered when he got past her and snatched the microphone off the podium.

"Silence!" he barked. The terrorists fired their AK-47s into the air. The crowd hushed. "You are subject to the wrath of Allah for defying his infinite wisdom. All of you! On the floor, face down, or you'll be immediately shot."

Francis took mental note of the other eight terrorists' positions, covering about three hundred people. Sweat beaded on his forehead as he loosened his black tie. He reached slowly into his trouser pocket as he laid himself down and pulled his Tool Logic credit card multi-tool from it. He released the three-inch knife from the Tool Logic and concealed it under the palm of his right hand.

"I said get down!" a terrorist ordered someone. The loud crack following the shout told Francis that whoever hadn't complied had been shot.

"Oh, my God!" Susan screamed behind the thug on the stage. She started to get up from her chair, overtaken by hysterics.

Please don't move Susy, Francis pleaded mentally. *Get down.*

Too late.

The terrorist was jumpy. He turned around and walked toward Susan, who was halfway off her chair, paralyzed with fright. "Down!" he shouted, slapping her viciously, knocking her to the ground. A loud sob escaped her lips.

"You son of a bitch!" Francis growled.

"Quiet," the terrorist snapped, turning around and aiming the gun at him, "or you're next."

Francis clenched his teeth. No point in picking a fight with the bastard—yet. The odds were against him.

"We are members of *Enbeaath*, the Rebirth Alliance," Rayhan said into the microphone. "You are now prisoners of war. Your president authorized the detention of our Afghan, Philippine and Malaysian brothers, who are caged like animals in Guam and Guantanamo. Our demands are simple. We want their freedom. One of you will die every hour until they are released. The women will go first."

A man from the back of the room shouted something in what Francis guessed was Arabic. Another shot cut the harangue in mid sentence.

Think.

It's very doubtful that we'll get out of this alive, Francis thought. The government wasn't about to negotiate. They'd likely send a SWAT team to take the terrorists out. Casualties among the hostages would be chalked up as collateral damage.

Think.

He looked to his right. An older man laid flat on the ground, facing Francis, his eyes shut tight, mumbling a silent prayer. Neither he nor the other people with whom he'd shared the table would help. Francis turned his head slowly the other way. Two armed men guarded the entrance to the pavilion.

The terrorist on the stage shouted something in Arabic. Francis sensed the terrorists moving behind him. He couldn't raise his head without calling attention to himself.

"All the men will stay on the ground," Rayhan said over the mike. "All the women will slowly stand up and gather at the far end of the room. You! Move slower." A woman sobbed. "Better."

The terrorists herded the women to the back of the hall. A struggle broke off to Francis' left. A woman yelled, followed by the unmistakable sound of a hand slapping a face and the rattle of automatic fire. Screams of panic cut through the room.

"Get down!" a husky woman's voice yelled over the commotion, followed by the report of a gun.

Francis took the chance to look at the stage. The commotion caught the terrorist's attention; he fired a shot, then ducked behind the podium when a burst of automatic fire exploded across the stage.

Screams. Shooting. A struggle had begun.

Now!

Francis rolled on the floor under the stage. A skirt along its perimeter concealed him. The stage was propped on a portable steel assembly. He crawled his way to the back, where he could see a gap between the end of the stage and the wall. He freed himself of his jacket.

He guessed that a woman had started the row. Men and women shouted. Weapons were fired.

Francis made it to the back wall. He spied the stage and the room beyond it. A few men were rushing the terrorists. The brawl was fierce and it looked like the terrorists were losing.

The terrorist crouched next to the podium, aiming his gun left to right, undecided as to where to shoot. A shot buzzed past the terrorist and exploded in a rain of plaster a few inches from Francis' head. A tall, big boned woman in a red dress—probably the one who started the attack—took cover close to the entrance and was looking for her chance to shoot the terrorist on the stage with an AK-47.

Francis climbed onto the stage, trying to stay low and avoiding the speaker's corpse. The terrorist returned the woman's fire.

Move!

Francis clenched his three-inch blade with his right hand and vaulted toward the terrorist, knocking him down and grasping his gun hand. There! Francis head butted him as he turned his head; his nose made a wet cracking noise. Francis grabbed his gun hand and stabbed it in the back of his palm with the knife. The fingers sprung open. Francis snatched the GLOCK handgun.

Susan stirred on the stage. "Francis?" she sobbed, her voice tinged with confusion and hope.

"Roll yourself behind the stage! Go!"

The terrorist thrashed under Francis' weight, trying to free himself. Francis rolled off him and staggered to his feet. His opponent snarled and tried to jump him. Francis lurched to his left, rolled on the floor and snapped to his feet. The terrorist attacked again, but Francis was ready. He foot jabbed his solar plexus, knocking him back on his rear. Francis' knife was on the ground, a few feet from his opponent.

"Don't move!" Francis roared. "Your hands behind your head, now!"

The terrorist didn't move. He was sitting, propping himself with his hands, still looking for a chance to overcome Francis.

"Put your hands behind your head," Francis commanded once more and got closer.

Big mistake, Francis thought just as his enemy tried to swipe him down with his leg. Francis saw the terrorist's leg coming at his right shin. He blocked the blow by turning his shin 45 degrees; his Muay Thai training took over. The foot connected with Francis' shin with a loud thump. The terrorist grimaced and tried to spring to his feet but Francis was quicker. Francis snapped a roundhouse kick to his head, pivoting on his left leg, and stunning the terrorist.

"Enough," Francis said, aiming the gun before firing shots at the terrorist's upper left thigh and right shoulder. The man yelped in pain. The bastard was neutralized.

Francis was relieved when he saw Susan slide behind the stage. She was working her way toward the front of the pavilion, crouching low. Good girl.

The terrorist grunted. Francis ignored him and swiftly patted him down. He had no concealed weapons. Blood seeped from his wounds onto the stage.

The struggle was almost over. Of all the terrorists on the main floor, only two of them remained. They were back to back, swinging their weapons in a wide circle, preempting anyone from trying to rush them. Sweat ran down their bearded faces. They were getting ever closer to the exit.

Francis checked the magazine and chamber in the gun. Two shots left, and the fallen man did not have any spare magazines on him. He jumped off the stage, aiming his gun at the two terrorists, and got next to the woman in the red dress handling the AK-47.

"You're quite handy with that," Francis said, impressed. "I'm Francis."

"I'm Dana," her voice was low, husky. "First Marine expeditionary force out of Camp Pendleton. Before my sex change."

"Excellent. Do you think we can take those two clowns out?"

"We can try holding them back until the cavalry arrives. I'm low on ammo."

"So am I, but so are they. Otherwise they would've blasted their way out of here already."

A man at the far end of the pavilion had collected a rifle from one of the fallen terrorists and was making his way to the front of the room. The terrorists stopped to look around. They had three guns trained on them. A fourth man, whom Francis recognized as a professional football player, grabbed another AK-47 and closed in.

"You're surrounded," Dana commanded. "Put your weapons down."

"Never!" one of the terrorists yelled. "We would rather die."

"Put your weapons down!" Dana insisted and aimed.

Both terrorists aimed their weapons back at Dana and Francis. Francis stepped away from her. Two targets are harder to hit than one.

"Put the fucking rifles down!" yelled the man from the far end of the room. He was just a few yards away from the terrorists.

"No!" Susan's shriek rang in the room, followed by the loud bang of a spotlight falling onto the stage. Everyone's head whipped to look at her.

The terrorists fired, one aiming at Dana, the other one firing blindly at the stage.

The terrorist that Francis thought he'd neutralized had crawled to the edge of the stage and had managed to claw Susan's neck with his good hand. She had knocked the light from its stand as she struggled to free herself from him when a bullet struck her chest about the breastbone, knocking her back like a rag doll.

"No!" Francis shouted and fired his last two bullets at the terrorists.

Missed!

Both men made a run for the exit. Dana fired at them and caught the one on the left in mid stride. The taller one made it to the exit, gunshots rattled after him.

Francis ran to Susan's side. Someone by the stage found the guts to stand up and stabbed the terrorist's good hand with a fork. Three other men had jumped on the stage and hauled the terrorist away from Susan.

"Susan?" Francis called, "Susy? Please talk to me."

She opened her eyes. "It... hurts..." she whispered as Francis gently lay her down on the floor.

"Someone get a doctor!" Francis bawled. "She needs a doctor!"

"Francis... don't let me die!" She begged, clutching his arm. Blood accumulated at the corners of her mouth. "Please!"

"Don't talk, Susy, don't talk," tears welled in his eyes. "You're gonna be fine." Francis sat on the floor, coddling Susan's upper body. "Somebody help her, *please*," he cried in desperation. He wiped the blood splatters from her face.

"I'm cold, Francis..."

"Shush," Francis whispered.

"I..." she coughed, "I... love you. Kiss me..."

Francis kissed Susan's lips softly. Her body went limp. She closed her eyes.

Francis nuzzled his face against hers. He wailed until the paramedics finally arrived. Francis still held Susan tightly when the paramedics tried to pry them apart.

Susan's funeral had been more a celebration of her life than a mourning of her death. Francis now stood by her grave, reminiscing of their life together.

Francis had thought himself the luckiest man ever. He'd met Susan Marshall two years ago in Istanbul, where she had been working for the U.S. Department of Commerce. Francis had been marooned after a flight cancellation. He had met her the night when she had accepted a position with an advertising agency in San Francisco—Francis' hometown. They'd become lovers after her return. Susan chose him after fending off a long list of beaus. They became engaged three months earlier and a wedding was scheduled for the first week in December.

He missed her laughter and the way she looked at him. He missed her warmth.

And he had missed the chance to finally lead a normal life because a bastard's bullet had wrenched her away from him.

Francis stared at the headstone, his eyes inscrutable behind the dark sunglasses.

"Goodbye Susy," he said for the last time.

It was a chilly, windy afternoon in Colma, just a few minutes south of San Francisco. Adam Jones, Director of Operations for the National Security Agency, shivered as he ambled among the graves, searching for his friend through row after row. Montagnet's black car was parked outside.

Some of the graves at the Holy Cross Cemetery were over a hundred years old. Joe DiMaggio was buried here somewhere. The grounds were well kept, the inscriptions on the headstones told a million stories. Jones hated cemeteries but Francis Montagnet was his friend.

Jones spotted Francis standing at the end of the next row, his black coat flapping in the wind. He stood immobile by a new headstone, his body cast a long shadow in the setting sun. Jones approached him.

"Thanks for coming," Francis said in a low voice without turning to face him. "You didn't have to."

"My heart goes out to you, my friend," Jones said, reaching to the younger man and embracing him. "I know how you feel."

Francis returned the embrace, then separated. His expression was inscrutable behind the large black sunglasses. "No, you will never know how I feel, Adam," his voice was weary. "They say time will heal me. It's been two weeks, the longest two weeks of my life. I can't stand being at home. Her scent still floats in the air."

Francis looked thinner and paler than Jones remembered. "It wasn't your fault," Jones replied.

"I'm not blaming myself. Funny, quite a few people think I do. You're wrong. There is nobody to blame other than the bastard who killed her. The one who got away."

"That's what I wanted to talk to you about," Jones said. "They found the getaway boat. He ditched it south of Half Moon Bay. There were no prints, no clues to follow. According to the FBI, the terrorists bought the used boat in Scotts Valley. Paid cash. The FBI also raided two of their safe houses. They found some computers and what appears to be a one-time pad that they'll give to us for cracking."

"So he got away and will never get caught," Francis spat. "What a load of crap."

"You're wrong, Francis. Twenty-three civilians got injured or killed during this episode. These guys ain't common criminals. They'll be back. We'll be waiting for them."

"What about the agency?"

"The agency can't officially get involved, Francis. The FBI is all over it because all the casualties were civilians. We've got very little to go on. A couple of bad photographs, a few video stills. He's surely left our country by now. He'll make a mistake, talk about this to someone. Besides, Enbeaath can't be too happy that their hit team botched the operation. Our listening posts from Australia to Cape Town will come up with something. We'll get them. And I'll let you know when we do."

"I appreciate your efforts."

Jones put his hand on Francis' shoulder. "Pull yourself together, my friend. She would've wanted you to go on."

"I know, I know..." Francis said under his breath. "Let's go." Francis turned and began walking toward the entrance. "I miss her. I get home and I imagine her voice, I go to sleep and feel her body next to mine. I hate waking up because then I realize it's all a dream."

"Perhaps you'll consider working for us again," Jones said. "We could use your skills."

"No, Adam, I don't think I can work for you right now. I need to get away."

Jones and Francis walked side by side. Neither spoke until they reached the entrance to the cemetery.

"I understand."

"I'm leaving for a while, Adam," Francis suddenly announced. "I can't stand it here. All the vigilance, all the anti-terrorist rhetoric, meant nothing. These guys got through. What use is the current policy? In hindsight, why wasn't the speaker Subidey assigned a security detail? Every day the government makes a huge show of fighting terrorism, trampling over basic civil liberties, and yet the only ones affected are ordinary citizens and a few hoodlums low in the totem pole. The big cats still roam with impunity."

"That's why we need you Francis," Jones insisted. "You could help us track them down, put an end to all this suffering."

"That won't bring Susan back."

"No, but her death would have meaning."

"There is no meaning to it!" Francis snapped. "It was senseless. Telling it any other way is an insult to her memory. Please show her some respect." Francis sighed; Jones could tell he wouldn't budge. "I'm leaving the country tomorrow," Francis said.

"Where are you going?"

"Switzerland. I hitched a project there. I'll spend a few days in St. Moritz, then back to work."

"St. Moritz is a nice place. Where are you going to work?"

"Zurich. Long-term project with the Swiss Trust Bank. Network and application programs security and audit."

Jones figured that his friend had made up his mind. He offered his hand. Francis shook it; Francis' hand felt cold from exposure.

"Take care of yourself, my friend," Jones said simply. "I'll let you know if anything comes up."

"Thanks."

Jones watched Francis get into his black sports car. The engine fired, the car pulled onto El Camino Real and disappeared among the traffic heading to San Francisco. Jones just stood there, wondering if his friend's wounds would ever heal.

"See you soon, Francis," he said to himself before getting into his rental car. The groundkeeper closed the gate to the cemetery.

Jones drove south, to San Francisco International Airport, where he would catch a flight east. Tomorrow he'd be back to his office in Fort Meade, Maryland.

He had a job to do.

D-45

CHAPTER 01

April, this year
Tunguska Region, 100 km north of Vanavara, Siberia

It was the most desolate place colonel Sattar Reza Fakhri had ever visited. The flight from Vanavara had been at times uncomfortable and interesting. The snow piled high on the ground below, the trees looked dead way before they reached their destination. He and his escort, Dr. Fyodor Kaminsky, bounced back and forth as the helicopter flew through the cold, turbulent jet streams.

"It's like a desert," Fakhri yelled above the engine thumping, wiping the frosted passenger window with the back of his hand. "I've seen photographs before but nothing prepared me for this."

"Your Russian is very good, Fakhri," Kaminsky replied. "Yes, this is probably the most desolate place on Earth. It's been empty for almost a hundred years. Not that these marshes were densely populated before the event. Superstitious people believed the fields are haunted by *Agdy*, the spirits of destruction."

"I can see why. The devastation is mind-boggling."

"And we haven't gotten to the epicenter yet."

Neither spoke for another ten minutes. The pilot landed and cut power to the engine. He signaled his passengers that it was okay to jump off. Dr. Kaminsky swung the door open and exited the aircraft first.

The snow was only a half-meter deep, the charred trunks of endless fallen trees were semi-buried in many places, and others were bare.

The sky was blue and the sun peeked through above the horizon. It was late morning but they were north of 60 degrees latitude. Fakhri followed Dr. Kaminsky with difficulty. He wasn't used to strolling in the snow. He was warm but felt clumsy in the polar clothing supplied by his Russian partners. He would never feel comfortable in this environment; the hot desert was his home. The preternatural silence was daunting.

There were no birds, no standing trees. Only the occasional lichen stubbornly stuck out through the thinner snow layer.

"Amazing, don't you think?" Kaminsky asked.

"It is," Fakhri muttered. He was still trying to assimilate his surroundings. "The trees are most intriguing. They all fell in a radial pattern. The branches were stripped cleanly off them." Fakhri removed his right glove and touched the bark on a fallen trunk. "They feel like they're made of stone." He put the glove back on.

"We're close to ground zero. The blast generated by the event scorched the trees in a radius of 100 km. The shockwave knocked them over."

"You keep referring to it as 'the event'."

"There is no definitive way to describe it," Kaminsky adopted an almost professorial tone. "I worked here in the late eighties and through the nineties. The Gorbachev and Yeltsin governments wanted us to check for oil or exploitable minerals in the region. I led a team of geologists here. What we found—or rather, what we *didn't* find—was amazing."

"I read your original report. That's why your employer requested that you guide me here before we commit to buying the weapon."

"The conventional theory is that a meteorite collided with Earth. There are several clues that contradict that."

"Like what?"

"First, nobody saw even a shooting star that morning. An asteroid large enough to cause this much destruction should've left a fiery trail across the sky, visible for hundreds of miles, aiming like an arrow to the point of impact."

Fakhri wasn't impressed. "There were reports of a strange object falling from the sky. The sky glowed, according to some accounts."

"A glow isn't a trail," Kaminsky countered. "A glow conforms best with an electromagnetic disturbance, not a collision. The reports of a falling object are unreliable. Many people claimed they saw trails in the sky after the fact, but they can't agree as to their bearing. Various teams analyzed potential trajectories of a colliding celestial object since 1958. None coincide."

"I see."

"We're almost there," Kaminsky's breath was raspy. "Do you notice anything unusual?"

"Well, this area is almost completely flat," Fakhri looked around. It was like looking at the surface of the moon. "There are few rocks, or trees." Fakhri took a few steps forward. The ground felt mushy under his feet. "The ground is icy and crunchy. The few plants breaking through the snow seem very young."

"We're now at ground zero," Kaminsky announced. "Which reminds me of a second problem with the meteorite theory. We took all kinds of soil samples from here. We found various minerals, but few microspheres. That shatters the meteorite theory."

"What are microspheres?"

"They are the telltale clue left by a celestial collision. Small, almost round pebbles, made of silicates and metals, like iron, formed by fusion at very high temperatures. Sometimes they have gas bubbles inside. Other than a rock found by Khersonskyi, a geologist, in 1965, there is no evidence of meteorite chunks. And that rock was found three hundred kilometers from here. The analysis revealed that it came from a meteorite, but one that crashed four hundred years too early. Anyway, there should be microspheres all over this place. A couple of scientists from Los Alamos, Goda and Hill, ran a simulation in 1990 of an object breaking up in the atmosphere before impact. Even if only 10% of the mass of this purported meteorite had remained after entry, this area should have plenty of microspheres. Nobody can explain why there aren't any."

"And there is no impact crater...?"

"None."

"What about radiation?"

"It's at normal levels. The remaining plants and animals don't show mutations beyond what is statistically normal. Besides, radiation from what?"

Fakhri rocked on his feet uncomfortably before answering. "I have no idea."

"My point exactly. This area shows all the signs of a nuclear blast, except that there was no fallout, no residual radiation. A blast wiped out this region almost forty years before the first known atomic detonation."

"Could the Soviets or the current government have hidden evidence of an extraterrestrial device capable of doing this?" Fakhri felt like a fool asking.

"We looked into that," Kaminsky replied seriously. "Some lunatics have insisted on it for some time, like Alexander Kasantsev first proposed in 1946. Tales of a UFO crash surface from time to time. Burudinov, Cowan and Libby, scientists all, proposed a collision with a chunk of anti-matter or even a black hole. There are even wilder theories presented by other serious sources. I personally like thinking that the simplest explanation is the correct one."

"What supports your theory?"

"There is an article, published by a German, a professor Weber of the University of Kiel. The article was published almost a hundred years ago in a magazine called *Astronomische Nachrichten—Astronomical Messages*. Professor Weber observed periodic and unusual fluctuations of the needle of a compass for three consecutive nights, from June 27 through to the morning of the event. He was in Europe at the time."

"Did anyone else record those?"

"There was an intense magnetic storm recorded about one thousand kilometers from here at a Czarist military outpost in Irkoustk, later confirmed by five Soviet researchers. If this had been a meteorite impact, why were there electromagnetic disturbances for three nights prior to it? Why were they confined to this area? How did they influence the Earth's magnetic field to fluctuate? Why didn't the meteorite hit anywhere else? If the event had occurred in Belgium, the country would be gone."

"Are you serious?" Fakhri asked, the implications becoming clearer.

"This event would have obliterated New York City. Only places as far away as Boston or Philadelphia would have survived. The only concrete evidence, recorded throughout the world and corroborated at the time, is that of an electromagnetic disturbance as powerful as those caused by a 15 megaton atomic blast."

Fakhri slowly spun on his feet, scanning the desolate landscape. He finally asked, "Do you truly believe that this was caused by the prototype of our weapon?"

"That's exactly what I mean. This event, this *blast*, " Kaminsky waved his hand to the horizon, tracing an arc including everything they could see, "originated in Long Island, the United States, between midnight and two o'clock in the morning of June 30, 1908."

...

Byelaya Kryepast former Navy Base, a day later
Near Petropavlovsk Kamchatsky, Russian Far East

The White Fortress decommissioned Russian navy base was a small compound surrounded by snow, seemingly abandoned except for the lights shining from some of the scarce buildings. A dark blue Chevy Suburban approached the main compound, leading a caravan of six Kamaz all-terrain trucks over a snow-covered road. The blizzard had stopped a half hour earlier. The snow formed an endless blanket. The buildings ahead sprouted from the landscape like small islands at the border between the Sea of Okhuskt and the icy plains. Nobody was around except for a security guard who had checked on Fakhri and his men occupying the vehicles, more than a kilometer behind.

Fakhri marveled at the snow from his comfortable passenger seat in the Suburban. Thank goodness that their Russian host, Anatoly Kuryakin, had provided this vehicle for the highest-ranking members of the group. It represented comfort for its occupants and high status to the Russians at the compound. He imagined the miserable cold endured by his men, seeping through every crack in the vehicles behind. Fakhri and his men were tough, but they never imagined that the Rebirth Alliance would send them to a mission in the coldest place in the world.

"The entrance is on the other side of the building," their driver said in accented English. He'd been practicing with Fakhri since they met ten hours earlier. "My orders are to leave you at front of building..."

"Thank you," Fakhri replied after a pause. "I suppose we'll have to walk in the snow?"

"Just short distance. No more than 30 meters. I was told to drop you off as close to the entrance as possible."

"Where is the machine shop?"

"You are looking at it now. Is well camouflaged, though. We want to protect from spy _sputnik_—what is word? Ah, satellite."

Fakhri scanned the ground before him. He realized that the flat surface sloped ahead. He guessed the building faced the ocean, built on a natural ground dip.

They drove about the slope silently. Just as he had guessed, the huge white building doors were on the other side, the sea flowed inside the building beneath them. There was a fence on the side of the building, complete with barbed electric wire. A small security post stood between them and the building. A guard peered at them through frosted windows. The Suburban stopped right in front, the rest of the vehicles grouped closely. Fakhri checked his parka, adjusted his goggles, and fitted his gloves.

"I cannot go inside," the driver said. "You will be taken care of. Do you have papers?"

"I do," Fakhri replied, waving his plastic ID card at the driver. "Thank you." He opened the door and hopped off the vehicle before the driver responded. Captain Akhmar, his second in command, followed.

Fakhri shivered and clasped his hands behind his back to hide the shivering from his men. It was damn cold!

The team jumped off the vehicles and made their way to the security post. Everyone's discomfort was obvious. The hairs in his nostrils froze, annoying Fakhri. It was such an unnatural prickly feeling! Frost formed on his mustache. The snow was thigh deep. It took him some time getting used to walking in it. He reached the security post. The unsmiling guard had already opened a window.

"Daytie propusk," the gruff guard barked when they approached.

"Vot," Fakhri replied in Russian and showed his ID. "We all have similar tags. Akhmar?" he addressed his second in command in Arabic while the guard inspected his badge. "Ensure that our men stick together. I have a feeling these savages will shoot first and ask questions later if anybody drifts away from the group."

"I'll see to that, colonel," Akhmar replied and summoned his men to convey the orders.

The security guard swore at the weather under his breath and walked out of the booth. He opened the gate. Fakhri and the rest of his men entered the compound. The Russian guard watched them with a curious expression. The gate closed when they were all inside.

"Head straight for that door," the guard explained, pointing ahead. "Vassily Dmitrievich waits for you." He headed back to the warmth of his post before Fakhri replied.

The group approached the gigantic, featureless white wall. A small door opened to their right, close to the center of the structure. A man stood there, waving at them to hurry in. Fakhri led his men inside as fast as possible. One by one they entered. Fakhri removed his gloves and goggles.

"Welcome to White Fortress, colonel," the Russian said. "I'm Vassily Dmitrievich Volin."

"My pleasure, Dr. Volin," Fakhri replied and shook hands with his host. "Anatoly Petrovich's told us all about your work."

Volin seemed pleased. "Shall we proceed?"

"Please lead the way," Fakhri said absently. He and the rest of his group were looking at the giant contraption sitting in a pool of water built in the center of the hangar. A dock surrounded it on three of the four sides of the building.

They walked around the pool, their eyes fixed on the shiny, metallic globe raised atop a tower about two hundred feet tall. The top of the tower was a few feet short of scraping the roof.

"It's huge," Fakhri said. "What's that, sixty, seventy meters tall?"

"Fifty-seven, or one hundred and eighty seven feet."

"Incredible. And you were able to finish it in such a short time."

"We had the original plans," Dr. Volin said as they both walked around the tower. "The museum in Belgrade facilitated them to us."

Fakhri was silent for a few seconds, absorbing the qualities of the structure. "Are those beams made of wood?"

"Yes. It's made of a lightweight wood, with aluminum fasteners at the joints. A well trained crew can take it apart or assemble it, with minimum use of the crane, in about eighteen hours."

"Why wood?"

"We wanted to use the exact materials used in the original."

"How much training will my team need?"

"About twenty days, more or less."

"How many men?"

"Six. I would train eight, though, just in case."

"What about maintenance?"

"You can replace many of the beams without having to tear the structure apart at any time."

"What about the sway from the ocean?"

"There is no sway; pitch or roll are the appropriate terms. They're negligible. The platform designed for this takes that into account. It's based on the latest oilrig technology. Our derrick by itself is very sturdy."

"It would seem so. The tower has an octagonal base, with beams crisscrossing it for axial and lateral support," Fakhri replied.

"You will also notice that this is a pyramidal derrick. That distributes the stresses about the whole structure more efficiently. The globe at the top is quite heavy."

"It must be; after all it's filled with coils and other conducting materials."

"Actually, it's superconductive materials," Dr. Volin corrected. He pointed at the globe. "About five tons of special ceramics, cables, and coolant ducts. Using superconductors was our only innovation over the original design. Come with me."

Fakhri followed Dr. Volin to a hydraulic lift next to the tower. They entered the cage, and Dr. Volin pressed a button to begin their slow ascent. Volin released the button when they reached their height. Their heads were almost level with the steel beams supporting the roof and about ten feet above the top of the incomplete dome.

Fakhri felt a bit weak at the knees. He didn't like being this high above the ground.

"The hardest part," Dr. Volin said, pointing at the open globe, "will be installing the metallic plates. They were specially tooled for the dome. Their surface is very smooth, and they must be fastened with special bolts with exact force, to avoid distorting their shape."

"What about that maze of cables and conductors?" Fakhri asked, pointing at the superconductive tubes that would be encased by the dome.

"They are pre-built in discrete modules. Each module plugs into the next, closing the circuit. They all connect to that coil," Volin pointed to a shaft, "that in turn connects to a special rod dug into the earth about 40 meters. All your men will have to do is perforate a shaft for the rod, line it with the insulating material, and raise the shaft around the rod and coil all the way to the globe. The globe's proper name is 'terminal', by the way."

"That's why we needed the drilling equipment on board..."

"Indeed. The rod must carve into the earth at least a thirty meters. That's necessary for grounding the structure and for tapping the Earth's energy source."

"Amazing," Fakhri commented, a bit awestruck. "And the energy can be stored before it is transmitted, right?"

"That's really Dr. Ulyanova's field," Volin replied modestly. "She's designed the transformers and capacitors. Of course she doesn't know about the tower and the terminal. But her expertise is in high-yield electrical circuits. She will explain this much better than I can when you return to Moscow."

"I'm looking forward to speaking with her," Fakhri said, smiling.

"I bet you do," Dr. Volin replied with a smug smile. "Smart, beautiful and single. You two should be together."

"Not until after my mission is over," Fakhri snapped back. Yes, Dr. Varvara Ulyanova was definitely smart and beautiful, but he wasn't about to admit they'd been lovers for a while now. "Anyway, how do you channel the energy?"

"The current passes through the shaft in the center, all the way to the terminal on top. A microcontroller adjusts the focal point along the shaft depending on the distance to target. This focal point is independent of the amount of energy to transmit. The design uses the Earth as a giant spherical capacitor. The ionosphere and the surface of the Earth represent the plates, the atmosphere in between acts as a dielectric. The tower channels the energy accumulated by this capacitor to a specific geographical point. We must be able to control the focal point in the tower because the target and the power to transmit to that point are relative to distance, and to the electrical capacity relative to the ground and the differential with the ionosphere."

"You're over my head."

"What we're trying to do is simply create a focused conduit of high voltage electricity, not unlike a bolt of lightning. The thousands or even millions of volts involved in the discharge, and its location, are dependent on the placement of the focal point in relation to the energy accumulated in the terminal and the distance to target."

"And all of this is done with commonly available industrial components?"

"Indeed, it is," Dr. Volin pressed the button and they began their descent to the ground. "That's the whole point of our research. The tower, the terminal, and the capacitors and coils are all built with non-weaponized components. There aren't any restrictions on their movement across borders. Siemens produced some of our electrical components. The microcontrollers are based on off-the-shelf PC technology. This design works more effectively than most modern plants or weapons, yet it's extremely simple. Its simplicity, ironically, is what stopped its development for almost a century."

"How so?"

"This technology is simple but expensive, even at today's costs. The original data transmission intent was defeated by Marconi's dirt cheap but inelegant design. Engineers, scientists, and investors thought this design unworkable. The energy transmission properties were never independently confirmed before the prototype was torn down in 1917."

The lift reached the ground floor. Dr. Volin opened the cage and let Fakhri out first. Three Russians had organized his men in groups of ten, and were talking to them through interpreters. Good. Their training would begin immediately.

Another crew went to work. They used a crane to place the necessary plates on the terminal. Fakhri followed Dr. Volin to his office.

Dr. Volin pulled a keychain full of keys from his pocket, studied them for a second, and selected one to unlock the door. He opened it and allowed Fakhri in before entering and closing the door behind him.

"Tea?"

"Yes, thank you."

"Vodka? It's cold."

"No," Fakhri sneered. Didn't the Russian know that Islam prohibited alcohol?

Volin poured two mugs of tea and a half glass of vodka for himself. He and Fakhri sat down on opposite sides of Dr. Volin's desk.

Fakhri sipped his tea. It was hot and strong. "Dr. Volin, why hasn't anyone developed a similar device yet if the principles are so simple?"

"Similar devices have been developed in the past by hobbyists all over the world. They were incomplete toys. They lacked the technical information we possess, and even ours is incomplete. Also, the technology to control this energy transmitter was in diapers when the first prototype was created."

"Are you saying that while the prototype worked, it couldn't be controlled?"

"Indeed. Now we have better conductive materials, computers to control the system's behavior, and a hundred years of experience. The energy transmitter can handle the electromagnetic energy as long as the appropriate resonance conditions exist. Maintaining the balance between the earth and the ionosphere harmonic oscillations requires the sophisticated controllers, coils and capacitors developed by Dr. Ulyanova. All this equipment can thus tap and store the Earth's electromagnetic energy indefinitely, or discharge it on command at a rate and location of our choosing. Only a few problems remain. We don't have the complete plans and we don't have time to extrapolate what we need from the existing design in order to meet your deadline."

"I'm aware of that," Fakhri said. "My team in the United States is working on obtaining the missing documents as we speak."

"Indeed?" Dr. Volin said and slammed the vodka down his throat. "We'll need those documents soon or we won't be done on time. We have roughly thirty days if we're to meet your deadline. We don't know how to calibrate the focal point or the transformers."

"The documents will be here within ten days," Fakhri said. "They include the missing plans for the energy transmitter and for our defensive weapons."

"That's good to know," Dr. Volin said, pouring himself another half glass of vodka. "You'll need all the power you can muster from the transmitter to operate your defenses." A klaxon blared somewhere in the main building. "Time for our demonstration."

Dr. Volin opened the blinds shielding the large window. The klaxon blared again, all the men grouped at the far end of the building. Heavy machinery opened the gates facing the ocean. A portion of the roof above the energy transmitter slid back, exposing the tower to the gray sky.

Dr. Volin's telephone rang. He picked the receiver up.

"Da," he said, glancing through the window, "yes, start the count-down." He hung up. "Our demonstration is about to begin."

Fakhri nodded and said nothing. Volin handed him a pair of high-power binoculars.

"Our target is straight ahead."

"How far from us?" Fakhri said, peering through the objectives and adjusting the diopter. A solitary, battered fishing boat was anchored past the gates, bobbing in the cold waves.

"About one thousand meters," Dr. Volin said. "The vessel itself is about forty meters long." The klaxon blared at one-second intervals. "We're less than ten seconds from firing."

Fakhri looked to the sky above. The clouds swirled in an unnatural dance above the tower. The terminal glowed. A loud hum was heard above the insistent klaxon shrieks.

The flash of lightning was instantaneous. A column of light parted the heavens and hit the boat. It was straight, unlike natural lightning with its endless, spidery branches. The boat vaporized in the distance. Steam rose from the ocean. Fakhri searched the surface for flotsam. The boat had disappeared as if it had never existed. The shock wave reached them. The windowpane vibrated. Fakhri felt elated hearing the low rumble coming from the distance.

"Amazing," Fakhri whispered, placing the binoculars on Volin's desk.

"Indeed," Dr. Volin replied and clinked his glass against Fakhri's mug. "To our success! If all works as intended, we'll prove that the Tunguska event wasn't just a fluke." Volin gulped his drink and smiled. "We will possess the deadliest weapon ever created."

CHAPTER **02**

Central Intelligence Agency

Adam Jones, Deputy Director of Operations for the National Security Agency, always felt a bit self-conscious when he visited the CIA headquarters. He paced to the large window while he waited for Mitchell Kennedy, Director of Central Intelligence. A TOP SECRET GAMMA Signals Intelligence alert had summoned him to this meeting. What crisis had prompted it?

The CIA director's seventh floor office was large but not luxurious. An imposing, modern glass and stainless steel desk dominated the far end of the room, the director's executive chair was pushed against it. The desktop was neither messy nor ordered. Folders and binders were piled on it, a few scattered memos, a half-full mug of coffee, and some loose sheets contrasted sharply with the neat stacks of bound documents. Organized chaos, Jones thought. He looked out the window, musing that while most people had pinned Langley as the home of the CIA, in reality HQ was located in McLean, Virginia. Langley had been the name of a farm on the grounds where the CIA compound now stood.

Every aspect of the CIA had been sanitized after the scandals of recent years and the subsequent political finger pointing and press scrutiny. Director Kennedy had taken the reforms introduced by former DCIs and clamped on them after the terrorist attacks of 2001. DCI Kennedy engineered the hardest push against international terrorism after years of a somewhat complacent attitude in the agency.

The door opened behind Jones. He turned and met with his host in the middle of the room. Kennedy was a lanky six foot three. His salt-and- pepper hair was slicked back, further accentuating the receding line above his forehead. Clear, steady blue eyes held Jones' gaze as they shook hands. The CIA director had a firm, friendly grip.

"Hello, Adam," Kennedy said in his soft, thin voice. "Donna and Bancroft will be here any minute." He was referring to Donna Rogers, director of the Treasury Department Intelligence Agency, and Ken Bancroft, the FBI director.

"It's nice seeing you, Mitch," Jones said. "What's this really about?"

"Something big has come up with Enbeaath," Kennedy said and the door opened. "But perhaps we should start formally now that we're all here," he completed as a secretary admitted Donna Rogers and Ken Bancroft into the room.

Jones had never met the director of Treasury intelligence. She was a short, gaunt and commanding woman. Her teeth and fingertips were tinted yellow from the endless cigarettes she smoked, her wiry hair and total disdain of makeup gave her a dowdy appearance.

Bancroft was a middle aged, humorless man just over five feet tall. His expressionless eyes showed the whites all around the black irises, his pudgy face was pasty white under a mop of dark brown hair. He wore a cheap suit and smelled of cheaper aftershave. Jones had never met Bancroft before; he didn't like the first impression.

The four of them expressed their greetings and proceeded to a small table at the far end of the room. There were four seats. Jones sat with Kennedy to his left and Rogers to his right, facing Bancroft. A clean white board hung from the wall behind Kennedy. *Erase after use - Spies booked this room after you* read a sign in black bold letters across the top. A pitcher of water and four glasses were in the center of the table. Jones had placed his yellow pad and felt tip black pen on the table while he had been waiting for the DCI.

"I called this meeting upon receiving this news from Bern," Kennedy began. "One of our Swiss assets uncovered information about a burglary at the DARPA repository in Virginia less than a week ago."

"What happened?" Jones asked.

"A civilian employee named Miles Wood of the DARPA Defense Sciences Office was found dead in Zurich yesterday," Bancroft explained. "He disappeared from his post at DARPA three days ago. We believe that he stole a cache of documents and tried to sell them to a hostile bidder."

"What kind of documents are we talking about?"

"We don't know for sure. All we know is that the missing documents were stored in a vault. All of them were processed in microfiche in the late 1940s and early 1950s. Wood probably destroyed the indices because we can't find them."

"I don't understand what the big deal is," Jones shifted in his chair. "Whatever it was must have been old and almost useless by now."

"We thought that at first," Kennedy said. "However, there was evidence in the man's hotel room to contradict that assumption."

"There was a receipt for a large funds transfer," Donna Rogers said. "Wood had just opened an account with the Swiss Bank Trust three days ago, upon his arrival to Switzerland. Someone deposited two million dollars into the new account and set up a safety deposit box. We assume this is the payment for the info in the DARPA cache. The Swiss authorities are mum as to the origin of the funds because, in their view, they aren't related to the crime." She produced four sets of documents from her briefcase, kept one, and passed the rest to Jones, Bancroft and Kennedy. "The CIA intercepted these from the Swiss authorities and provided them to Langley. They forwarded them to us for analysis."

Jones examined the documents. There were four sheets of paper. A cover sheet was simply labeled *Sensitive Compartmentalized Information.* Next was a formal letter written in English on Swiss Trust Private Bank stationary. The note was short and businesslike, dated three days prior. It was an introduction from the bank's senior relationship manager to Miles Wood, detailing the services offered. All processing fees, including setting up a safety deposit box, had been waived as a courtesy. Next was a collage of typewritten pages, done by photocopying overlapped sheets from various documents. All the documents were old, judging from the typography. The last sheet showed the bank's logo and three columns of letters and numbers of encoded information. A vertical and a horizontal bar code were printed at the top of the page.

"Do you know what this is?" Bancroft asked Rogers showing her the cryptic page.

"We figured it's a receipt for the transaction. As you saw, the amount of the deposit is mentioned in the letter, but the rest is gibberish to us. We believe the rest of the columns break down the amount into smaller sums, each sent to a different account for investments, stocks, and so on."

Jones poured some water on his glass and took a couple of sips. "Yet there's no concrete evidence of foul play, is there?"

"The evidence is circumstantial. That's where we come in," CIA director Kennedy said. "So far the deceased is only guilty of leaving his post without notice, and perhaps of tax evasion." Kennedy clasped his hands in front of him, stared at them for a few seconds. "The real issue is the coded account and the safety deposit box. From the letter we gather that two different people have access to it. Wood was to set it up, but someone else has access to it. Think of it as a golden drop. We can't figure out who else has access to it, or what it contains, and the Swiss won't help."

"Can't we subpoena the bank? Is there some international law we can apply? After all, weren't secret accounts supposedly abolished more than fifteen years ago?"

"It's not that simple," Bancroft said. "Switzerland's banking laws override any action we might wish to take. The Swiss Bank Trust holding company doesn't own any assets in the United States where we could apply leverage. Customers must provide full disclosure to the bank when you open an account, but that doesn't mean that the bank will tell *us* who the account holders are, or even admit that this is Wood's account."

"I thought these laws were changed so that law enforcement and, er, friendly governments could better monitor illegal activity."

"The Swiss have their own ideas about that," Rogers spat with obvious disdain. Jones guessed she'd crossed swords with them before over similar issues. She continued. "Unlike our banks, their laws require a special search warrant, valid only for specific account numbers. We can't go to the Swiss with a statement like 'we're carrying out an investigation.' We must first produce a cross referenced list of accounts and their owners. Proof of illicit manipulation must be presented to a judge, and *in some cases* we'll be able to open the accounts only if a perpetrator is being tried for crimes directly related to the funds in those accounts. Wood was found at Platzpitz—typically called Needle Park by the locals. It's known by that name because the city tried to corral the heroin addicts there twenty years ago. Officially users don't have legal protection to use the park for shooting up anymore. Addicts still roam the park anyway. According to the Swiss authorities, Wood was looking for a fix and got killed in the process. The account in question isn't related to the crime, blah, blah, blah."

"Sneaky little bastards, aren't they?" director Kennedy said. "Are you sure about the laws?"

"Yes. Swiss privacy laws supersede international commerce laws. The Swiss government hasn't ratified them. Any time we pressure them they cry bullshit about their neutrality."

"So where does that leave us?" Jones asked.

"We must learn what was bought, and who bought it," Kennedy said, holding the encrypted page up. "Our guys took a shot at it. No score. Whatever they encrypted this with is very sophisticated."

"The longer we wait, the harder it'll be to trace the funds will be," director Rogers punctuated.

"Our forensic lab worked on this page," Bancroft said, holding the collage photocopy in his hands. "Notice here, here, and here," he pointed at three areas on the page. "They believe the first is part of the letterhead from the National Defense Research Committee, the next is part of the seal from the former Office of Alien Property, and the last is a portion of a letter signed by FBI director Hoover in the late 1940's."

Jones reached into his coat and pulled out his reading glasses. He put them on and peered intently at the page. "Interesting," he brought the page closer to his eyes. "I don't think I've heard of this National Defense Research Committee before."

"They were a dependency of a now defunct Office of Scientific Research and Development, which eventually became DARPA."

"Could the stolen documents be related to nuclear weapons?" Jones took another sip of water.

"That's the first thing we thought," Bancroft replied, rolling his eyes. "We believe it didn't. The document logs show very few references to their use since 1945. They were used by the Air Force on something called *Project Nick* in the late 1940's, and DARPA used them for a project code named *Seesaw* in the 60's. Both projects were about weaponization of high-energy transmissions. Both were killed before 1970."

Jones removed his glasses and massaged the bridge of his nose. "Sounds like precursors to the Strategic Defense Initiative. Did either effort succeed?"

"No, and we checked with both the Air Force and DARPA. Documents related to *Seesaw* and *Nick* were intact but the cross-reference index is missing."

"Why did Wood make this collage?"

"I believe he used this as proof that he managed to acquire the missing information," Kennedy replied. "The buyer wanted to make sure he had the goods."

"Where does the NSA fit in this?"

"We must learn who is the other account holder with access to the safety deposit box. Our cryptographers and the FBI's are working on this document," Kennedy pointed at his copy of the transaction receipt, "but that will take time."

"It's not only time," Jones said, looking at his copy. "There are too few groupings in this document for cryptanalysis. We need more data."

"I figured your people are the only ones who can crack this."

Jones scratched his chin, looked at the ceiling for a few moments, thinking. Yes, he thought, we could try getting our hands on more of these transmissions. He carefully worded his reply. "We'll have a better chance if we intercept a large number of similar documents to work with. Your guys can help us with that. Fax, phone and Internet links we have covered. Our COMINT guys can probably intercept the bank's communications."

"Sounds like a plan," Rogers said.

"When we started, though, you mentioned Enbeaath. What's their angle in all this?"

Kennedy opened a folder he had brought to the table with him, produced two photographs and passed them around.

Jones looked at the first photo. It was a black and white shot of someone's face —or what was left of it. "Wood?" he asked.

"Miles Wood," Kennedy replied. "Pointblank shot in the nose with a 12-gauge."

Jones passed the photo to Rogers, who barely looked at it before handing it to Bancroft. Kennedy gave him the second photo. It depicted a crime scene. There were a few markers on the ground, placed by the Swiss police to identify potential evidence. Wood's body was sprawled on the dirt, his arms and legs bent in unnatural positions, his head rested close to a tree trunk. Someone had circled the area by Wood's right hand with a red marker. The perpetrators had drawn a crude glyph on the ground, perhaps with a twig. A low whistle escaped Jones' lips.

Enbeaath. The word 'rebirth' written in Arabic.

"The Rebirth Alliance involvement is doubtless," Kennedy explained. "This is their SOP for dealing with traitors. A gunshot through the nose, aiming upward, is guaranteed to kill. Middle Eastern terrorist groups since the 70's employed this technique."

"Poor bastard," Rogers said. There was little sympathy in her voice.

"Whatever Wood sold them was important enough to have him killed," Bancroft said. "We must find out what Wood was selling, and who the buyers are."

Jones picked up the encrypted receipt and turned to Rogers. "Did your folks look at this?"

"Yes, to no avail."

"We probably can't decipher this particular document, and it will take time. There isn't enough data here for analysis. I wonder how long we have before all the pieces are in place."

Jones remained silent for a few seconds, thinking. He took a sip of water, removed his glasses and rubbed the bridge of his nose. "We can start work on this at once. What other efforts are running in parallel?"

"Our embassies and other sources in Europe, the Middle East and Southeast Asia are keeping an eye for sudden wealth befalling the usual suspects," Rogers replied.

"The Bureau is going over Wood's background," Bancroft said. "We'll establish his relationship with Enbeaath soon."

"We're trying to identify who of our people in Switzerland might be in a position to get first hand information," director Kennedy continued. "The Swiss are very cagey about disclosures, and most of our people are trained in dealing with diplomatic and military sources, not in banking. Bankers are notoriously conservative, especially in Switzerland. Even the things they confide to their lovers are extremely vague."

Jones put his glasses back on and leaned back on his chair, his eyes shifting from Kennedy to Rogers, then to the ceiling. He was sketching the outlines of a plan in his mind, but he needed to be sure.

"What's the profile for your ideal candidate?" Jones casually asked Kennedy.

"We need a NOC—"

"What's that?" Rogers demanded. "A 'knock'?"

"Non-official cover, Donna. That's a civilian, someone with access to the bank and in a position of trust. An employee would be perfect. NOCs can enter and exit countries, meet foreigners, and otherwise snoop around without raising alarms. Business people are ideal, but they usually resist working with us. A Swiss citizen would be perfect, but their nationalism runs deep and they know that penalties under Swiss law are very steep, so I think that's unlikely. Our asset must get hold of the originating account, confirm ownership, and unearth the destination for all transfers made from it. Any background materials, invoices, confirmation notices, receipts, and other documents that he can get his hands on are a plus."

"Putting your sexism aside," Rogers said cantankerously, "have you ruled out the possibility of this asset being a woman?"

"No," Kennedy replied, his tone of voice reflecting his lack of interest in pursuing the argument. "Whoever our asset is, he, she, or *it*," he said facetiously; Rogers ignored him, Bancroft chuckled, "must be fluent in Arabic and German or French. A combination of at least two of those languages might be fine. This person must have enough brains to analyze the data on site, and make a quick decision on its relevancy."

"We have a potential asset in place," Jones said softly.

"Who is this person?" Rogers asked with curiosity.

"You may have heard about him," Jones said. Careful, he thought. "Do you remember the terrorist incident in San Francisco a couple of years ago, where the Turk ideologue, Subidey, was killed?"

"I vaguely—" Rogers began and was interrupted by Kennedy.

"You're not seriously considering bringing that..." Kennedy was at a loss of words, "that... *maniac* to this!"

"Who are you two talking about?" Bancroft snapped impatiently. "Don't waste my time with guessing games."

"His name is Francis Montagnet," Jones replied slowly, carefully choosing his words. "He has a talent for finding himself in the right place at the wrong time. Two and a half years ago he helped us recover classified technology from a supposedly trusted defense contractor. It was a critical situation. He fits your profile almost perfectly, Mitch, and he has a grudge against Enbeaath."

Donna Rogers was about to ask something, but thought better of it. Bancroft shifted in his chair and stared hard at his batch of documents. Jones was sure neither had clearance for something this deep.

"He's also extremely unstable under pressure," Kennedy said. "You and I know he wouldn't pass our Asset Validation System tests, Adam. The man is a walking bomb. And he doesn't speak Arabic. Let's be reasonable here. During the incident in San Francisco Montagnet almost had himself and the hostages butchered."

"Can we afford being reasonable?" Jones countered. "What you said is true, though a bit exaggerated. On the other hand, during his last official assignment for us Montagnet managed to complete the mission, and unearthed more crap about our"—he looked at Rogers and Bancroft and changed his wording—"er, target than we could've otherwise. Besides, this assignment will be a piece of cake. Swiss banks don't go after moles with blazing guns. Most important, *he's already doing a project* for Swiss Trust Private Bank."

"You have one of your men in place?" Rogers asked incredulously.

"Well, Donna, he's actually not one of our guys. Just someone we've *recruited* before."

"I think this black bag op is a crazy idea," Bancroft interrupted the flow of the conversation, getting up.

"Ken," Jones said in an almost conspiratorial tone, "Mitch's being cagey because the Montagnet dossier is one of those Eyes Only files detailing stuff you're better off not knowing about."

"Sounds like this guy is a serial killer or something."

"That he is not, but he's a dangerous customer. Montagnet got away with making fools of the CIA, NSA, Interpol, FBI, Secret Service, and the IRS during his last caper. On the other hand, he delivered intelligence so explosive that not even the President knows all the details."

Director Rogers tapped the table with her bony fingers. She took a cigarette from her side pocket, twirled it in her fingers.

"What exactly did he do?" Bancroft demanded, returning to the table. The name Montagnet didn't ring any bells.

"I overstepped my bounds and recruited him to recover some files related to a US military project," Jones explained. "The contents are restricted, even today. He succeeded against incredible odds. He was out there for weeks without backup, running from one place to another. The bad guys were after him, and Montagnet almost lost his life on several occasions. He was double-crossed by the one person he trusted the most."

"But you think he can pull this off?" Rogers insisted.

"He's one more asset we'll use in this operation. We may decipher this before he tracks the money, or we may get to recover the items from the safety deposit box. Mitchell may find someone to complement or even help Montagnet."

Jones presented a couple of likely scenarios to Rogers and Bancroft while Kennedy paced to the window and back, listening to them.

"We can make this work, and he's already been employed by us in the past. He's a known quantity. Fits the NOC model perfectly," Jones finished.

"How so?" Rogers asked.

"NOCs are contractors. They carry out a job, we or the CIA pay them off, and life goes on."

"So you're giving this sensitive job to some... *mercenary*?" Rogers asked incredulously.

"Call him an agent, or an asset. We need someone on the inside," Jones replied. "We don't have enough data from this sheet to decrypt the information. If things get rough Montagnet won't need backup. He's got his own team."

"We have to be careful here, Adam." Kennedy returned to the table and sat on his chair. "There were two unexplained stiffs last time. We don't want that now, not in this political climate."

"Those two deaths couldn't be traced back to Montagnet either," Jones said. "Look, the scenario is different this time. First of all, he's not the only asset involved. The CIA is already tracking this. Second, COMINT might decode this," he held the money transfer up, "if he can produce the encryption key or other useful data. We then pay Montagnet a consulting fee and end the story. Think about the advantages as well. He might unravel this, being so close to the source. And the man has initiative."

"He has too much initiative, if you ask me," Kennedy said after a long pause. "Ken?"

"I don't know all of the details, but I agree with Adam. The sooner we find out what's up, the better."

"Mitch, if we run the operation from NSA, the CIA won't get involved. Unlike you, we don't have Congressional oversight. We're military. We can run this as an op under the Special Access Programs. Not even the President needs to know."

"Okay, Adam, you win. But no unexplained dead, no gun play, and no stunts landing in our lap."

"There shouldn't be any reason for them this time, Mitch."

"How do you suggest we approach him?" Bancroft asked.

"I'll take care of that myself," Jones said. "He doesn't have a high opinion of the CIA, and he'll be distrustful of anyone from FBI. I'm not even sure he'll do it, but if he does I'd like to keep an eye on him."

"We must assign someone to back you up," Kennedy said. "I'm thinking of someone in the Directorate of Operations, with experience in Europe, to become his case officer. You'll make the pitch, Adam, and we'll handle him."

"I know that you have jurisdiction," Jones said, "but he won't accept your guys handling him."

"Sounds like you gentlemen have some issues to work out," Bancroft said. "Just get us the missing documents."

The four discussed the scenarios for another two hours. The discussions led to the execution of operation ZEPHYR.

CHAPTER 03

Downtown Moscow

I'm very lucky, Dr. Varvara Dmitryevna Ulyanova thought. I'm thirty-one, have a great job, a tiny but beautiful apartment, and the chance to travel. Varvara—or Varenka, as her dear ones called her—had come a long way from Volgograd. What else could she want?

Varenka brushed some powder over the pale makeup base, put the brush down, and studied herself in the bathroom mirror. She approved of the effect, then blended a baby pink on the apples of her cheeks. She had a healthy glow without looking made up. She daubed her new Maybelline white eye shadow next, carefully blending the color down into the corners of her eyes. She applied a bit of mascara to draw attention to her deep blue eyes—her best feature—and a touch of super shiny, colorless lip-gloss. She removed the barrette holding her hair away from her face. Her dark brown, wavy hair fell to her shoulders. She squeezed a bit of straightening balm onto her left palm, rubbed it between her hands, and carefully applied it from the roots to the ends of her hair. She brushed it until she was satisfied.

Today she wanted to look her best because Sattar Fakhri was coming to visit. He was at least ten years older than her, and just what she needed. Her two-year marriage to Sasha had failed because he behaved like an adolescent. She had a man now. Sattar was scheduled to come to the office that morning. She could hardly wait before seeing him.

Varenka went from the tiny bathroom to her bedroom. She crooned in unison with the radio, which was playing BI-2's latest hit. BI-2 was her favorite Russian band. She looked at herself in the mirror. The white Sharagano shirt with thin black stripes went well with her black pants. Something was missing, though. She opened a box atop her dresser, chose a simple choker and put it on. Pretty!

Varenka was getting her tailored gray wool jacket from the armoire when the phone rang. She strode to the small living room and picked up the receiver.

"*Da,*" she said with a smile, knowing that only the dearest person in the world called her so early in the morning.

"Good morning, Varenka," her mother chirped. "How are you today?"

"I'm fine Mama, thank you. I must be brief. I don't want to be late for work."

"Thanks for the money you sent," her mother avowed. "I will save it for when I need it."

"You're welcome, Mama," Varenka replied. "But please buy something you like with it, promise? Your pension is not enough. It'll be fine if you splurge a little."

"Ay Varenka, you're very sweet. I don't want to spend the money you work so hard for."

Varenka held the phone against her head with her right shoulder and put her left earring on. "Anything new in Volgograd?" she asked, changing the subject. She shifted the phone to her left shoulder to attach the other earring.

"Spring is here, but it's still cold. This weekend I'll go to our dacha if it doesn't snow. The orchard needs work and I need exercise."

"That sounds fabulous, Mama. Are you going by yourself?"

"Your aunt Masha will come with me. She says hello, though she is a tad upset that you don't write to her very often."

"I have been really busy..." Varenka's voice trailed. She felt a twinge of guilt. "I'll send her a card next week, I promise."

"Are they keeping you so busy that you aren't eating well?"

"No, Mama, I'm fine."

"You were too skinny last time I saw you. You must eat better."

"I'm fine, Mama, really," Varenka smiled. Her mother was always trying to feed her. "And I feel great the way I am now. By the way, did I tell you I'm going to Vienna soon?"

"Vienna... A beautiful city. What will you do there?"

"I'm attending a conference. Technical stuff related to my work."

"Are you going by yourself?"

Varenka smiled mischievously. "No, I'm meeting Sattar there." She couldn't mask the excitement in her voice.

"Is that the Arab man you mentioned?"

"Yes, Mama."

"You sound cheerful."

"Yes, Mama," she laughed. "I'm happy. He's very intelligent and handsome."

"Is he treating my Varenka well?"

"Very well, Mama. He's a real gentleman. He's very *kulturnyi*."

"Have fun in Vienna then. Anyway, you're old enough to know what you're doing."

Varenka glanced at her watch. 08:27. "Mama, I must go or I'll be late for work. Talk to you this Friday?"

"Yes, but call me up in the morning. We're heading to the dacha early afternoon."

"I will, Mama. Take care until then. I love you."

"Love you too, *Varenka malenkaya*, little Varenka"

Varenka hung up and rushed in and out of her bedroom to snatch her white purse. She stopped in the foyer to change her slippers into her white loafers. She grabbed her keys and let herself out.

Varenka locked only the sturdy top and bottom dead bolts. The middle one, a relic from Soviet times, was so old and clunky that it often got stuck. She was too busy to call a locksmith to replace it, so she usually left it unlocked. It wasn't the wisest thing to do in Moscow these days, but she didn't own anything really valuable anyway. Varenka put the keys in her purse, walked four flights of stairs to the street and headed for the metro.

Varenka rushed out of the station and headed to the office after the half hour crush. She arrived at work, identified herself to the security guard, and took the lift to her office on the fifth floor. Alona, her secretary, was busy preparing the handouts for her nine-thirty meeting. Varenka greeted her and went into her cramped office, zigzagging between her credenza and her desk after setting her purse atop the filing cabinet by the door. She sat down and powered her workstation on.

"Dr. Ulyanova, I've brought your tea," Alona said from the door.

"Come in," Varenka replied, waiting for the computer to boot up. "Anything new I should know about?"

"Nothing. Everyone confirmed attendance to the meeting except for Mr. Kuryakin." Anatoly Kuryakin was their boss and owner of Teknoil, the largest oil exploration equipment manufacturing firm in the Russian Federation. Varenka had worked for Teknoil for two years after stints at Gazprom in Russia and International Refinery Equipment in the UK.

"I didn't think he'd bother, to be honest," Varenka said. She brought the tea glass to her lips by its nickel holder. She relished the exquisite aroma before sipping carefully. "Excellent tea, thank you. Anything else?"

"Dr. Volin called. He wants you to call him back. He had some questions but they were too technical for me."

"Dr. Volin should learn to use email," Varenka grumbled. "His old school habits cost us money, plus we have a significant time zone difference." Her workstation was up and she logged on.

"I'll go finish the handouts for the meeting," Alona said.

Varvara nodded and turned her attention to the screen. She opened her email. There were a couple of messages from German and Swedish vendors wanting an appointment to offer their equipment, a note from a friend, and a note from Sattar Fakhri. She clicked on the latter with mounting excitement.

```
Dear Varvara Dmitryevna,


The team here made significant progress. Unfortunately I won't
be able to arrive in Moscow today as planned because our team
from   Switzerland   hit   a   snag.   The   documentation   on   the
transformers array was lost on its way to us and I must travel
to Zurich to recover it. I will stop in Moscow on my way to
Switzerland   to   speak   with   Anatoly   Petrovich   about   business
issues the day after tomorrow. I would be honored if you would
join me for dinner that evening.


Regards,
Sattar
```

She blushed. Fortunately nobody was around! Any disappointment she'd felt for him not coming today was erased by the invitation. He was so formal! She accepted with an equally polite reply. She skimmed over the other messages, replied appropriately, and reviewed the document that Alona had left on her desk. It was fine for the meeting.

Teknoil teams in Moscow and at the decommissioned Navy base of White Fortress were building what Kuryakin and Sattar described as "the most unique oilrig in the world." They weren't joking. The rig's design was unlike any Varenka had ever been involved with. It implemented a number of cutting edge technologies that, in many ways, puzzled Varenka's experienced mind. It seemed almost as if the team in White Fortress, many of them former defense engineers, were assembling something completely unrelated to drilling for oil on the high seas.

Varenka gathered her pen and the copy of the handout and walked to the conference room. Misha and Vladimir, two lead engineers who reported to her, were discussing the rig when she walked in.

"The rig is extremely lightweight," said the pockmarked Misha, nodding to Varenka in acknowledgment as she entered the room. "Every component is made of carbon fiber, specially treated woods or lightweight alloys most commonly used in aerospace. Take the moorings," Misha insisted to a slack jawed Vladimir while Varenka sat at the head of the table. "They are made of a special polyester fibers, not steel. This means a weight reduction of about 80 percent for the mooring system without compromising its integrity."

"The first storm to hit the platform will blow it hundreds of miles away," the pessimistic Vladimir said in his squeaky voice. "It's so light it'll float away like a feather."

"Or they can simply pack and move it elsewhere quickly. What do you think, Dr. Ulyanova?"

"The design is unlike anything I've seen before," Varenka conceded. "I can't understand where they'll install the top drive systems, the finger boards, and all the other heavy machines. They don't have enough space."

"Perhaps our colleagues from White Fortress have come up with new, space age drilling equipment?"

"Perhaps."

"I don't know," Vladimir squirmed in his chair. "Those people scare me. They all used to work for the military."

"You're paranoid, Vladimir," Misha chided.

"I wish I understood how the thing works," Varenka said. "We're asked to design components to spec without understanding the whole puzzle. We're plugging our designs into a black box."

"You know that they're keeping a tight lid on the whole project until the patents are filed," Misha said.

"That doesn't make sense; we're all under nondisclosure. Still," Varenka insisted, "I would like to understand how they plan to make this thing work. Why is the hoisting system designed for loads of only 15,000 pounds, while the industry standard for oil drilling equipment is about 200,000 pounds? Why doesn't the platform have any pumps? What are those turbines for?"

"What I would like to know," Vladimir squeaked, "is where do they intend to get the power to drive all the equipment they *do* have on board. Have you two calculated the electrical load? The generators they have can't produce that much electricity."

"Perhaps that's one of the things the team at White Fortress is designing," Varenka said. "Like those strange 'bladeless' turbines they had our shop build for them."

"Or what drives them," Vladimir insisted. "Energy can't be produced out of nothing."

"Maybe they have a design for harnessing the ocean waves," Varenka commented. "A few teams in England and the United States are working on that. Maybe Dr. Volin and his people figured out how to make it work."

"Maybe, though I don't understand how they intend to generate two megawatts of power from waves alone. Even the most advanced experiments to date produced a maximum of 20 kilowatts. The systems relied on channeling the surf from shore. How could they intend to make it work from an oilrig sitting in the middle of the ocean? It's physically impossible. And don't get me started with the design of the rig itself."

"What about it?" Misha asked.

"Last time Dr. Volin was here I got a chance to look at the documents he'd brought with him. Mr. Kuryakin called me to his office, where he was meeting with Dr. Volin..." Vladimir's voice trailed.

"And?" Misha scolded him. "We don't have all day to hear this story."

"And, well, I glanced at the plans for the rig. What I saw surprised me."

"How so?"

"It seems like most of the machinery, whatever it is, sits inside a big metallic globe atop a pyramidal derrick."

"That's different," Varenka frowned. "What did the rig look like again?"

"It looked almost like a giant, metallic mushroom. Strange stuff, really. I couldn't see the scale but my guess is that it was at least 50 meters tall."

Alona the secretary interrupted their discussion, leading the rest of the staff of ten to the meeting. Varenka waited until they all greeted one another, then work began on her agenda. Alona took notes for the minutes while Varenka and her staff discussed the issues at hand, such as efficiency factors in an array of electrical transformers they'd designed.

Varenka couldn't help but wonder about the purpose of the rig. Vladimir's description of a "giant, metallic mushroom" nagged at her subconscious. She vaguely remembered seeing something like that somewhere, many years ago. I'll research it later, she thought. We're behind schedule and I can't worry about this right now. I know! I'll ask Sattar when we go out. It's time someone told us how the whole thing works. Why is our design so different from every oil drilling platform ever built?

CHAPTER **04**

Baden, Switzerland

Green. Francis sat on the grass covering the western side of the hill. A cobblestone road snaked its way through the gorge between him and the hill beyond it. Several houses were built on the opposite side, the gardens bloomed with the colors of spring. Francis savored the clean air with a sigh. The town of Baden was on his right, beyond the casino at the foot of the hill. The sun was setting, its fiery red light reflected by the Alps far to the south on this unusually clear day.

I miss you Susy, Francis thought.

Francis understood it was time to move on. Susan's death felt more distant with every passing day. He'd loved her, and she'd loved him back. They had shared many interests, from skydiving to classical theater. He missed her laughter and the way she tilted her head when she looked at him. He'd been ready to share with her his most intimate fears and secrets.

No more brooding, Francis thought bitterly. Time to move on.

The sun was below the horizon, the cool breeze caressed his face. A few cars went by in both directions of the road below. Two pedestrians came to view on his right, treading along the sidewalk.

Francis recognized his friend Adam Jones as the baldpate. The guy with him was a new face. Francis got up, dusted himself off, and grabbed his black shoulder bag before walking down hill to meet the two men.

"You really haven't changed," Francis said as he approached Jones and his companion. "How are you doing?"

"So-so, keeping busy," Jones replied. "You lost some weight since we saw each other last."

"It's the climate and the food. Besides, I don't use a car here that often, with all the public transportation. It's amazing what walking everywhere will do for you." Francis held Jones's right hand in both of his, let go, and looked his companion up and down. "Who's your date?" he teased.

"This is Stanley Wright," Jones replied, "Deputy Trade Representative of the US."

"Nice meeting you," Wright said, extending his hand to Francis.

"Oh, a CIA man. The pleasure is all yours," Francis said acidly. Wright was a thin man about his age, plus or minus a couple of years. Dark blue suit, white shirt, dark blue tie. Short blond hair. Fidgety. His voice rang of sincerity but his cold, slightly bulging eyes betrayed him. Francis guessed Wright to be a good liar, all in the interest of national security of course, or in Wright's interests when it suited him. Francis had met slimy characters like him before and had learned his lesson the hard way. Francis turned to Jones. "I thought this was a private meeting."

"Our friends by the river insisted on Stan joining us," Jones said. "We don't have resources like they do over here."

"Bringing unexpected guests is hardly my idea of a trusting relationship, though," said Francis. He looked at his watch. "Shall we go? We have a reservation."

"I thought we'd talk here," Wright whined, baffled.

"The view is breathtaking but I made plans to talk elsewhere. I just like this place because there isn't a place to park, and you can spot anyone coming from several hundred meters away. You never know who you'll run into, right?"

"Right," said Wright with a thin, humorless smile.

Francis led his companions to the center of town. They passed the casino, headed up a few alleys then down the street to a plateau at Kurplatz.

"This is Kur square," Francis said, pointing to a small stone carved fountain placed next to the entrance to an odd looking building. A thin stream of water flowed from a spout in the fountain. There were courtesy paper cups by it.

"Help yourself," Francis said, taking a paper cup and filling it with water. He put the cup to his lips and drank slowly, watching his companions do the same. He didn't care for the smell of rotten eggs rising from the water but helped himself to a second serving.

Jones wrinkled his nose at the smell but braved drinking the stuff. Wright was more of a sissy and immediately refused.

"The Romans thought these waters were the best for your health," Francis explained. "The sulfur in them is reputed to cure everything from arthritis to colds. It has a foul stink but you grow used to it after a while."

"Never tried anything quite like this before," Wright said. Francis was testing him and he'd flunked.

Francis had another serving before dumping the paper cup in a nearby recycling bin. His companions imitated him and followed to the building.

"Where exactly are we going?" Jones inquired.

"A bit of relaxation will do you good," Francis said as they approached a reception desk. *Thermalkurort* read a sign above it. He approached the older female clerk. "*Grüezi*," Francis greeted in Swiss German, then continued in English. "I have a reservation for two. Montagnet and Jones."

"Of course, Mr. Montagnet. That'll be 300 francs," the woman said, handing him two towels and two keys attached to a security pin that doubled as a key chain.

"*Merci*," Francis thanked her, and handed a key to Jones. He opened his shoulder bag while he spoke. "This is the most exclusive resort in Baden. It takes months to book a room here and at least three weeks advanced notice to use the pools. Fortunately for us, a couple from Zug canceled so we're able to get in." Francis turned to Wright. "Too bad you can't join us," Francis shrugged and turned to Jones. "Besides, I only brought swimming gear for two. Do you want boxers or Speedos, Adam?" Francis held two new black garments to Jones, who was doing his best not to laugh.

"I'd never fit in the others," Jones replied, grabbing the black boxers.

"Wait a minute," Wright protested. "This is unacceptable and—"

"And whatever Adam and I discuss will remain private for now," Francis snapped. "We'll meet you here in an hour."

"Stan, I warned you guys that things would happen this way," Jones continued. "Go check out the casino, enjoy the view. Time flies when you're having fun, right?"

"Right," Wright fumed. "If there is no choice."

"See you later," Francis said, walking past the reception desk with Jones in tow.

"Sometimes you're too much, Francis," Jones chuckled. "You didn't have to humiliate him."

"And you didn't have to bring him."

"Rules of the game. He's your contact if you chose to play ball."

"Contact or case officer?" Francis asked. They entered the dressing room.

"Contact. This whole operation is handled by Fort Meade, not by the Agency."

"You can change in any empty dressing room," Francis explained. "The number on your key matches your locker's. I'll wait for you by the scale over there."

Jones nodded and went to change, chuckling.

Francis changed in his stall. Of course he'd had an extra pair of trunks, but he wasn't about to invite Wright to join. Francis put the black trunks on, then rolled his clothes and put them into the shoulder bag. He stepped out of the dressing room, found his locker and put his stuff away. Jones was already waiting for him.

Francis and Jones rinsed the day's dust off their bodies in the showers, then followed several German-speaking tourists to the pool in the back.

Francis entered the hot pool first.

It was 114 degrees Fahrenheit, he remembered from the brochure. It took him a while to get used to it. It felt wonderful after the initial shock was over.

The pool was shaped like a mirrored L, its floor covered with old, light blue tiles. Francis and Jones entered it close to the intersection of the short and long stretches. Each side of the pool was about 20 feet wide and at least a hundred feet long. The scalding water had a strong smell of sulfur. Sweat beaded on his forehead.

"We're heading over there," Francis turned to Jones, pointing to a place a few meters in front. The German tourists waited in line for their turn at the water jet.

"What are those people waiting for?"

"We're all taking turns around the pool. As you can see, there's a person every two meters or so," Francis pointed at several men and women equally spaced along the pool ledges. "There's a jet at each of those locations. The jets begin at the bottom of the pool, and at different heights along the wall. The first one massages your feet. After a minute or so you'll hear a bell and everyone will shift to the next jet, which will massage your calves, and so on until you get a water massage on your neck."

"Sounds relaxing."

"It is. At the end, we'll step into that circular tub at the center of the pool for a Jacuzzi-like body massage. The whole process takes about twenty minutes. More than enough time to talk business."

"This is too much of a public place," Jones said. Francis glanced at him. He didn't like the look in his friend's eyes.

"I know. That's why I chose it. The gurgling makes an excellent white noise screen. No eavesdroppers. Besides, there isn't much of a place for you to hide a wire now, is there?"

"Very ingenious..."

"Don't take it personally. It's business."

"I won't, Francis."

"Any chance you can lose the spook?"

"Can't say I will. We're supposed to work together."

"Do you trust him?"

"He's a lawyer or something. International business, that's why he got assigned to Switzerland. I trust him to do his job."

"So be it," Francis said. The first bell tolled. He yielded the jet to Jones and moved to the next one. The water felt good against his calves.

"Are you feeling all right?" Jones asked, tapping his head.

"Most of the time I do." The bell clanged and they scooted over to the next jet. "Susan's loss just saddens me, nothing more. What does this have to do with what you want me to do this time?"

"Nothing. I just want to make sure you're okay. This will be strictly a white-collar op, no muscle. I need you to get a hold of some files for Uncle Sam."

"Understood."

Francis listened to Jones' brief for several minutes. It was no wonder Jones himself had come looking for him personally. Montagnet listened without interrupting. He spoke twice to nudge his friend to the next jet, but remained silent otherwise.

This is a hell of a situation, Francis thought.

"So? Are you on board?" Jones asked when finished.

"Very tricky business, Adam. I'm not sure I want to do it."

"God knows what's in that safety deposit box, or who is paying for it."

"That's my point," Francis said, almost whispering. Jones was probably straining to hear him over the gurgling noise. "You can't take Swiss banking privacy laws lightly. This is not the United States. Even this conversation could land me in jail."

"Aren't you involved in building the Swiss Trust Private Bank infrastructure? Could you at least sneak a Trojan horse to snatch the account information we're looking for?"

"Leaving any technological safeguards aside, there's still the issue of accountability. The bank's auditors will put two and two together, faster than you can say ZEPHYR, if I go after the account. They're ferocious. They'll find me out. Thoroughness is the Swiss national trait, remember?"

"You can cover your tracks."

"What kind of backup will I get this time."

"None. You'll be a NOC."

"Some things never change, do they?" Francis uttered. "Let me think about it." The bell tolled, Francis and Jones moved to the last and next to last jets.

What is really at stake? Francis thought. Who are the bad guys?

"There is something you should know," Jones interrupted his reverie.

"What's that?"

Jones leaned closer to Francis. "We have evidence that Enbeaath is involved in this."

Francis clenched his jaw. "Are you sure?" Francis demanded, his voice icy.

"We're positive."

The bell clanged once more. Francis and Jones entered the central tub. A middle aged Swiss woman and her daughter shared it with them for a minute, then left after the next bell clanged. Francis stayed put. Skipping one turn along the jets gave them a couple of extra minutes in private.

"Who else knows about this?" Francis asked.

"The Director of Central Intelligence and a Deputy Director of Operations for them. The head of Treasury's Office of Intelligence Support. Bancroft of the FBI. You, me, and Wright."

"I see. What about supplies, expenses, that sort of thing?"

"Give me a list. I'll provide anything you need."

"Timeframe?"

"Yesterday."

Montagnet smiled. "Okay, let's talk business then." It was time for them to leave the pool. "Let's go. We can finish this conversation over dinner."

Francis and Jones joined Stan Wright by the fountain when they emerged from the bathing house, then they walked a few blocks to a typical Swiss restaurant on Todistrasse. The restaurant was busy, yet the host sat them immediately.

"I'm a regular," Francis explained.

They ordered dinner. Francis asked for spaghetti with finely shredded white truffles. His companions ordered sausages and rösti, the traditional Swiss grated, pan fried potatoes. Francis forced a bottle of 1997 Amarone Cesari over Jones' and Wright's protests that they were working.

"Would you join us?" Wright asked.

"I don't drink, thank you," Francis replied politely. "I understand that Valpolicella wines are delicious, though."

Wright briefed Francis during the meal. Francis listened politely. Jones occasionally intervened to clarify some point. They spoke until dessert was over. Francis ordered a tisane after his pastry. Jones and Wright ordered coffee. They were clearly not used to the European custom of drinking their coffee after dessert.

"The scenario holds water," Francis said after Jones and Wright ordered coffee. "I'll do it."

"I don't think this is as potentially dangerous as previous missions you ran for us," Jones replied.

"I accept, but you'll have to back me up if anything goes wrong," Francis countered. "It all comes down to this: will you guys exfiltrate me from Switzerland if this blows up in my face?"

"Here's a number," Wright responded, handed him a card from his shirt pocket. "Memorize it and destroy the card. Anything you need, just call and we'll get it for you."

"You realize that this implies getting me anything from a plane ticket to a lawyer?"

Wright hesitated a few seconds before answering. "Yes, I understand."

The herbal infusion and coffee arrived. Francis sipped his. It was strong.

"I want one million dollars available to me through three separate accounts in Swiss, Dutch, and British banks," Francis said. "You must provide me with credit and debit cards in three separate names. I'll also need three separate passports."

"What?" Wright almost choked on his coffee. "That's too much."

"It's my neck. I must have the ability to bail if things go wrong. Open joint accounts; your investment will be safe. I just need to make sure I have ready access to cash if I must scram."

"I'll see what I can do," Wright grumbled. "I can't get you American passports, though. It's against the rules to—"

"Spare me the civics lesson," Francis snapped. "I already have two American passports anyway. I don't care which countries or names you choose, as long as they hold water. Anything that I can pass for will do. Ideally I'd like a Swiss, a Russian and a Spanish passport. Just make sure that I speak the language from the country I'm supposed to be from and that I look the part."

"I'll see what I can do," Wright said non-committal. "What other languages do you speak?"

Huh? Francis thought, looking quizzically at Jones. Hasn't the spook read my dossier? "Adam? Is this guy for real?"

"This whole operation is deep, deep cover, Francis," Jones replied. "Eyes only, restricted access. Your file is handled by senior officers only, much to Stan's annoyance."

"They took need-to-know a bit far," Wright whined.

Jones turned to Wright and said, "Francis also speaks Russian, Spanish and French. Bits of almost every European language. Common courtesy phrases, right?" Francis nodded, amused. Jones continued. "Get him a EU passport. Issued in Spain or France."

Wright nodded slowly.

Francis drank the last of his tisane, its sweet taste lingered on his palate for a few seconds. "I won't start working on this until I get those conditions met. I must plan for a quick getaway if I'm caught."

"It's done, Francis," Jones said. Wright was about to protest but Jones raised his hand and continued. "We'll arrange several drops for you.

Entry visas into Switzerland, if appropriate, will be stamped on the passports."

"Thanks Adam, I knew I could count on you." Francis faced Wright. "Don't worry, Stan. You'll get the passports back when this is over. I won't have use for them. This is why I don't like career bureaucrats like you involved in our dealings. They're too fond of red tape."

"Hey, wait a minute—" Wright protested.

"You guys almost got me killed during our last op," Francis snapped. "We'll run this my way or no way." He got up, ignoring Wright. "I look forward to hearing from you again, Adam. It was nice meeting you, Stan." Francis made to leave before either man had a chance to respond.

Can I trust Jones? Francis asked himself. Jones had kept a close, watchful eye on Francis during their last adventure together, and had helped tidy things up when it was over. "Are you involving me again in something I'd have to count on my guardian angel for, Adam?"

Jones' expression betrayed nothing when he answered. "I'm sure your guardian angel will be there if you need him. Just get this done."

Francis smiled and left the restaurant. "Guardian angel" were their panic code words.

An attractive, thin blonde woman left the restaurant immediately behind Francis. She took the sidewalk across the street at roughly his same pace. She, like him, headed for the train station. Francis ignored her until they were both inside. He looked over his shoulder, searching for a tail. They weren't followed.

"*Hej*," Francis greeted her in Swedish. She was another foreigner like him and 20% of the Swiss population. He continued in English. "Hi! Did you capture our conversation?"

"It was hard at first," Erika Vacker replied. Francis loved her deep voice and Scandinavian accent. "The clanking silverware covered the sound sometimes, yes? I compensated using digital filters." She handed him a small bundle that, Francis knew, contained the directional microphones and videotapes of the evening's conversation.

"You're the best, Erika. Thanks." He put the package into his shoulder bag.

"You're welcome, Francis. It was fun. Watch your behind out there, yes?"

"Of course." They pecked each other's cheeks three times in the Swiss traditional way—right, left, right—and Erika left the platform. He waited alone for the 22:42 train back to Zurich.

CHAPTER **05**

Moscow

A restless Sattar Fakhri watched for his ride from the lobby of the Marriott Tverskaya Yamskaya. A few businessmen, most of them European, also waited for their rides or were settling their bills at the registration desk. A group of American tourists emerged from one of the twin elevators and strolled to the entrance on Tverskaya Yamskaya Street.

Pigs, he thought. No, they were worse than pigs. Pigs at least had the excuse of not being able to think. Fakhri had sworn that he would rid the Middle East of Israel, the United States, and their western allies. They were all like a cancer that had to be extirpated.

A black Mercedes limousine roared into the hotel's passenger loading zone across from the lobby. Fakhri recognized it immediately. It was an armored version of the 600 SL, black and ominous with its reinforced suspension, puncture-safe tires and bulletproof windows. The car stopped next to the glass doors. An obsequious chauffeur jumped out of the limousine and rushed to open the door for him. Fakhri walked to the vehicle, nodded to the chauffeur and climbed in.

"*Dobroye utro,*" greeted a deep, humorless voice inside the vehicle.

"Good morning to you, Kurok," Fakhri replied in Russian, seating himself opposite to Anatoly Kuryakin. The car pulled away from the hotel and headed down to Tverskaya, then veered toward the Kremlin and Okhotny Ryad.

"Was your journey from Kamchatka a pleasant one?"

"Most comfortable, thank you. The airplane you sent was lonely, for I was the only one on board."

"It was nothing more than a taste of Russian hospitality. Vodka?"

"No, thank you."

Kurok opened the mini-bar to produce a cut crystal bottle and a tumbler. It was only nine o'clock in the morning. No wonder the man looked like he did.

Anatoly Petrovich Kuryakin was an imposing figure, even sitting down. His bald, oversized head rested on massive shoulders developed in his younger, Soviet Army days. Quasi-varicose veins crisscrossed his red, bloated face, permanent reminders of the alcohol excesses he indulged in. He didn't smile often, and when he did his mouth was a sinister patch of gold teeth. He had even had a diamond put on one of his front teeth. Kuryakin's once powerful shape had surrendered to the hedonistic pleasures bought by newfound riches. His chest expanded to a gigantic belly, evidence of the constant bacchanals Kuryakin and his circle threw for themselves, their clients, and those they wanted to impress—or to bribe.

"I'm still getting used to this," Fakhri said, "watching someone drink so early in the day, I mean."

"It's never too early for vodka. You should try it sometime. Was your trip successful?"

"Couldn't have been better. The energy transfer tower performed well in the test, and my men are quickly learning the ins and outs of its assembly and operation. They'll start drills in about a week, using old boats as targets."

"Your progress is impressive, colonel."

"We still have a problem with long range targeting. Our agent managed to fetch the documents from the DARPA vault but he had an accident before delivery was possible."

"How long a delay does that mean?"

"A day or two, maximum. The documents we're missing provide the clue for properly targeting over a long distance. The flow of electrical current through the energy transmitter and to the particle beam cannons must be precisely controlled by varying the current circulating through the coils and capacitors. It all boils down to getting the mathematical formulas. We don't have time for trial and error."

"You must remember that I have as much riding on your progress as you do," Kuryakin said, pointing a finger thick as a sausage at Fakhri.

Fakhri looked out the window to buy time before answering. He'd anticipated this discussion, but was inwardly fuming with frustration. The giant red slug in front of him cared for nothing other than money and power. The same ruthlessness that had earned Kuryakin the nickname Kurok, or Trigger, was coldly applied to everything the man did. Even his self-destruction was ruthless.

"Kurok, we'll get the documents. We had *wet business* to take care of."

"So you killed him."

"The operative got greedy. My men acted hastily. Unfortunately the operative had already locked the documents in a shared deposit box that only he and I have access to. I have less than forty days to get ready. I'm aware of the pressure."

"Yes," Kurok said, swilling his vodka. "Remember that, shall this prototype succeed, I'll be in a position to dictate policy in Russia. I always wanted to be president. That's why I agreed to participate in this harebrained enterprise."

The limousine stopped at a traffic light. An old beggar peered inside, her lips moving in silent pleas, her voice muted beyond the tinted window.

"We want to execute the operation during the San Francisco United Nations anniversary, at the Summit of the Nations. It will serve to showcase our point and further humiliate the Americans."

"What if you wait a few more days? Killing all the industrialized world's leaders in one morning will make your point and will benefit my *biznis*. Chaos emerges in a vacuum, giving rise to new opportunities. However, my affairs will undoubtedly prosper regardless of that, and you can equally horrify the world by vaporizing the population of San Francisco or Washington D.C."

The traffic light changed to green, the vehicle headed southeast on Moskoryetzkaya quay.

"This will be as much a political statement as it will be a tactical strike," said Fakhri.

"And your zeal can be your undoing. Using force to achieve political goals seldom works. My country," Kurok waved his hands encompassing everything outside the limousine, "tried that for many years. We succeeded only in pushing it back twenty years. Moral decay, economic ruin are still with us. *Biznis* now flourishes, but many are hungry for each of us with a roof over our heads."

"Don't lecture me about misery," Fakhri hissed. "Children all over the Middle East are hungry, disease spreads quickly."

"And your anger blinds you, colonel."

"You're so removed from reality, trapped in your gilded cage, that you've forgotten what you believed in for so long."

"Are you referring to Lenin's fantasies? Please, I wrote some of the speeches for Andropov and Chernenko. And many times I've refuted them, so I won't waste my time on that. Opportunities are everywhere. Were it not for *razoruzheniye*, you wouldn't be able to carry out your revenge."

"What's that word again?"

"Disarmament. We're more liberal in its interpretation nowadays. We sell the weapons we have no use for, you benefit from them. To us it's all trade. We don't care about your ideology anymore. And we'd like seeing those weapons outside of the *Rodina*—the Motherland, beyond the reach of those who wish to return to the days of old. What you do with them, how you execute your revenge, is up to you unless you threaten us."

"This isn't about revenge, this is about Allah's justice."

"And I'm sure you believe that, colonel Fakhri. But that's just a fiction. Take this advice from an older, wiser man." Kurok poured himself another shot of vodka and gulped it down. "I hold the purse strings so I do what I want. Those fools, Zhirinovsky, Lipov and Lebed were as zealous in their beliefs as you are in yours. And that was their undoing. Lipov changed his idealism for greed, and his greed for martyrdom. He forgot that it was people like me who financed his political career. And where is he now? In some obscure post in Krasnoyarsk? Will he die in a mysterious accident like Lebed? Remember this: money is everything."

The limousine stopped in front of a new gray building off Volgogradsky prospekt. Eight armed men dressed in gray uniforms stood guard at the entrance. Four of them promptly approached the car and one opened the door. All of them looked around, their eyes darting from one pedestrian to the next. Security around Kurok was tight because of the constant fear of an assassination attempt. These men would kill or maim instantly at their boss' biding. Private Security Services read the badges pinned to their uniforms below their nametags. He stepped out of the limo and walked through the entrance just as the four guards formed a human shield around Kurok's waddling mountain of flesh.

The Spartan building lobby was decorated with only a few steel and glass fixtures. The windows were reflective on the outside to prevent anyone from peering in. The floors sparkled. A large door opened to Fakhri's right, another guard appeared and headed for him. There were several more men in the room adjoining this one.

"Follow me, please."

Fakhri followed him to a glass elevator in the back of the building. They entered and patiently waited for Kurok to waddle in. The man made his way to them, but now and then his frown betrayed the pain he felt. Gout? Didn't the man see what his excesses brought him? Kurok and two guards squeezed in, one of them pressed the button for the tenth floor. The door closed.

It was like a ride to a different universe. The door opened to a lavishly decorated corridor. Kurok was the first one out, guards in tow. Fakhri followed them down the wood paneled corridor a couple of steps behind, tailed by his silent escort. The corridor opened to a large reception area with a single desk at its center. A gorgeous blonde woman worked the computer and compact telephone system. Her makeup was a tad heavy, her lips a bright crimson. She wore a very tight silk blouse that outlined her breasts and slim waist. Her hands were carefully manicured. Her skills were undoubtedly better at satisfying her boss' fantasies than at typing or filing.

Kurok barked a few orders, the woman flinched and busily typed something into her computer. Kurok walked to his office on the left. The tall double doors opened automatically as they all approached, perhaps in response to a switch pressed behind them by the secretary. The guards stayed outside, the doors closed behind them.

"Sit down," Kurok bellowed as he sat at his own desk.

Fakhri sat on a plush leather chair directly in front of Kurok's desk.

"Dr. Volin and his team will begin construction of prototype number 2 immediately," Kurok said. "Both weapons should be completed at roughly the same time. The key for us is to coordinate our attack with yours."

Fakhri studied Kurok for a few seconds before answering. "All I can do is give you a date and a time. The rest you will learn from CNN. Is the Russian president attending the summit?"

"He is. My sources confirmed it. We shall be ready," Kurok coughed loudly. "We also want a commitment from your people guaranteeing a ceasefire in Chechnya, and surrender of a few Chechen leaders. Something that will look good on the press when my cabinet takes over. In the meantime, doctors Volin and Ulyanova need the missing specs. This is just idle speculation unless you deliver them."

"I've got a meeting with her in a few minutes," Fakhri replied. "I will check on her team's progress and will explain the situation to her. Either way she will get the documents within the next three days."

"She's attending a conference in Vienna. Is there any chance you could get the documents and interpret them before she leaves?"

"A slim chance at best," Fakhri said. "I don't leave for Zurich until tomorrow. Then we must translate the documents and convert them to a useful format for Dr. Ulyanova's and Dr. Volin's teams. That's why this will take at least a day or two."

"I suppose you're right. Why don't you hand the documents as they are to her team?"

"I don't believe it's a good idea," Fakhri confidently said. "The sample provided by our contact included various papers from the FBI and the US Department of Defense along with our documents. It will be better if neither team is exposed to the originals. Dr. Volin is aware of the background, since he worked on the Soviet particle beam weapons systems in the eighties. Dr. Ulyanova, on the other hand, is still under the impression that we're building a revolutionary new offshore oil-drilling platform. I would like to keep that fiction alive for as long as possible."

The Praga Restaurant had a tradition going back to the times of Czar Nikolai II. Varenka was impressed that Sattar Fakhri had chosen it for their date.

Sattar came to pick her up at seven thirty in a Mercedes limo. It was her first time in one. Varenka helped herself to a shot of chilled Stolichnaya Krystal from the bar. She'd never met a man who didn't drink before. That felt strange to her. She was fidgety with anticipation, killing time by making small talk during the ride from her apartment.

The driver dropped them off at the entrance to the Praga, an old but beautiful three story building at number 2 Old Arbat. The yellow building's architecture was that blend of Russian and French styles so popular in the late 19th century, when it was erected. A uniformed doorman helped her out of the car, the host led them past the palatial entrance to the elevator.

"I hope you don't mind," Sattar said as the elevator took them to the topmost floor, "but I made reservations for the international court. There are nine different dining areas in here, each with its own unique style. I thought I'd play it safe. The Russian court is probably full of tourists anyway."

"That was a good idea," Varenka said as the elevator doors opened to a corridor with black and white marble floors lined with neoclassical statues.

Another host checked their reservations and led them left to a room with a view of the New and Old Arbat streets. The room was sparsely decorated, the tables were made of solid wood and beautifully set. They arrived at their table, the host took her overcoat and Sattar's.

"This is very elegant, Sattar," Varenka said after a waiter took their order for drinks.

"I thought you may like this, Varenka."

"I want to have fun tonight. It's been a long time since I've been out. You were gone for too long."

"Believe me, I wanted to get back sooner," Sattar said, reaching across the table to caress her hand.

"I believe you," she smiled, enjoying his touch. "I was beginning to wonder if there wasn't a Mrs. Fakhri keeping you away from me."

Varenka regretted her tease as soon as she finished speaking the words. Sattar's expression darkened. The air between them chilled.

"Mrs. Fakhri died a long time ago," Sattar said with unexpected solemnity.

The waiter returned with their drinks—mineral water for Sattar, a cosmopolitan cocktail for her—and Sattar ordered the Mediterranean combination for two.

"I didn't mean to pry," Varenka apologized after the waiter left.

"You didn't know," Sattar replied. "My wife Umayma and my newborn son died in Lebanon in 1983."

"I'm sorry to hear that. Do you feel like talking about it?"

Sattar's brown eyes honed on hers, his handsome features darkened. Varenka knew he was struggling with a painful memory, and trying to decide whether to share it with her or not.

"It has been a long time," Sattar said. "My family died during an attack by the US Marines in retaliation for the deaths of several of their men at the hands of Palestinian revolutionaries. They bombed the hospital where Umayma had given birth to our son. I didn't even have a chance to say goodbye to her."

"That's... that's horrible," Varenka stuttered.

"It's all in the past. That's one of the reasons why I approached Teknoil for our project. I didn't want to deal with an American or English company for our project."

"I understand completely," Varenka said and reached for his hand across the table. He felt warm to her touch. "I'm sorry I asked."

"Don't be. You had nothing to do with it." He gently pulled his hand away and reached into his coat pocket. "This is for you," he said, handing her a small parcel.

Varenka opened the box. There was a small gold pendant shaped like a tree. It was attached to an elegant chain. "This is beautiful, Sattar! I... I can't accept it."

"I would be honored if you would," Fakhri insisted. "It's a cedar, the national tree of Lebanon."

"Thank you," she contemplated it for a bit. "May I put it on?"

"Please do."

"I didn't know you were Lebanese," Varenka said as she fastened the chain behind her neck.

"I was born in Iran. My mother is Lebanese, my father was Iranian."

"Sounds very exotic to me."

"It was a bit unusual growing up. I was lucky to grow up in Iran, Saudi Arabia, and Lebanon. Beirut was my home until 1976, then I went to university in Spain, then England. I've been working all over the Middle East since 1983."

"Anatoly Petrovich and Dr. Volin call you colonel..."

"I... I served with the Iranian military many years ago," Sattar said, avoiding her eyes. "I received an honorary rank."

Their food arrived. The waiter placed a tray full of exotic delicacies on the table. Sattar described the more unfamiliar ones to her. They all had strange but delicious sounding names: moussaka, hummus, tabbouleh, a soup called molokhia. There were familiar items like tomatoes, olives and cucumbers. Varenka recognized dolmas because people from the

Caucasus ate them and they'd become an occasional part of the Russian diet, especially among people from the now independent Georgia.

Varenka helped herself to small portions of everything. She enjoyed the tabbouleh the most. She shared the water with Sattar; the food was so good she didn't want to numb her palate with more vodka. The mineral water had a subtle salty flavor that worked perfectly for clearing her taste buds.

The busboy removed the dishes and utensils from the table after they finished eating.

"Would you care for dessert?" the waiter asked.

"I believe we're fine," Sattar replied after Varenka looked at him and shook her head. "Please bring us two espressos. Would you care for some cognac?"

"No, thank you. I'm fine."

"Varenka," said Sattar after the waiter left, "I would like seeing more of you when the project is over."

"I would enjoy that," she replied, gazing into his eyes. "I think it would be a good idea to wait until the project finishes. It's best to be discreet in these matters."

"Of course."

"Which reminds me: the sooner I get the rest of the documentation from your engineers, the sooner I can wrap up our part of the project. When will the White Fortress team finish?"

"They don't have the information. That's why I'm going to Switzerland tomorrow." He averted his eyes.

"Do you think we'll get them before my trip to Vienna?"

"I will try getting them to you as soon as possible, I promise."

"Sattar, I would like to ask you a few questions about the rig and the equipment on board. We don't understand why it's so different from anything we've done before."

Sattar gave her an obviously uncomfortable look before answering. "Go ahead."

"The array of capacitors and transformers for the rig, for one. They could be arranged to produce direct current in the millions of volts. Why aren't we using polyphase alternating current for driving the machine tools? And what are the machine tools anyway?"

"I can't go into details on that yet," Sattar said before she continued. "We have patent issues."

"It would help us enormously if you told us what is it we're building our components for. The electrical power necessary for running the rig is more in line with uses in particle physics, like an atom smashing cyclotron, than with machine tools. And the few machines we understand appear to run on direct, not alternating, current. How could you possibly get such an amount of power for transmission and operation if there isn't a single generator on board the rig of that capacity? Scientists have problems generating potentials of 5 million volts. Our system, in theory, could generate over *50 million* volts!"

"Someone achieved that a long time ago," Sattar said softly. "You will have to trust me when I say that this will all be clear when the time comes to fully disclose our designs."

The waiter came in with the coffee. He placed the cups in front of them and left.

"Excellent aroma," Varenka said after sipping a bit of espresso. "I suppose you can't tell us about the turbines..."

"I'm sorry, but I can't speak about that either."

Varenka was disappointed. It would probably be better not to show it. She'd find out soon enough anyway. "Very well," she said and drank the last of her espresso. "I'll wait for your team to give us all the data."

Sattar settled the bill. They got up, got their coats, and headed for the entrance, where Sattar's driver already waited for them. Varenka played with Sattar's gold pendant around her neck. She felt special. She put her arm through his on the way to the car. She could feel his strong muscles through the fabric.

It was a quick ride back to her home. They arrived, the driver opened the door and helped her out. Sattar followed her.

"Walk me upstairs?"

"Of course."

They climbed the stairs to her apartment. She could feel Sattar's body close behind.

They reached Varenka's apartment. She unlocked the door. "Do you want to come in?"

"I... I think I'd better go," Sattar said nervously. "I fly to Zurich very early tomorrow morning."

"It's a shame. I could make us some tea," Varenka said.

Sattar was about to say something when Varenka stood on tiptoes and placed her arms around his neck. He was so tall! He put his hands around her slim waist, sending a shiver through her body. She felt so ready for him!

"It... it's time for me to go..." he stuttered.

Varenka pulled his handsome face down and gently kissed his lips. His black mustache tickled her. At first he didn't respond, then he parted his lips and his tongue gently probed hers.

Bozhe moi! Varenka thought. He was a good kisser.

He pulled her body against his, the kisses became urgent. She could feel his hard member struggling against his pants fabric to get free. She pushed the door open. They entered the apartment and kicked the door shut. They left a trail of clothes from the entrance to Varenka's bedroom.

Varenka and Sattar urgently caressed each other atop her bed. She put a condom on him before letting her passion run free. She made love to this beautiful, mysterious man with wild abandon. She melted in his arms, crying out his name as both bodies exploded in ecstasy.

"I love you, Varenka," he whispered into her ear after they calmed down, cradling her in his powerful arms.

"I love you too, Sattar." Varenka fell asleep with her head on his chest, listening to his heartbeat, holding in her right hand the gold pendant that her lover had bestowed upon her.

CHAPTER **06**

Zurich

Duck!

Francis bent his knees but kept his back almost straight from the waist up and quickly covered the right side of his head with his right forearm. Erika's fist crashed against it, the padding of the 16-ounce boxing glove barely cushioning the blow. Francis snapped back to fighting stance and foot-jabbed his opponent to increase the distance between them, following immediately with a right kick to her head. Erika effortlessly avoided the kick and countered with two right kicks to his body. He painfully blocked them with his left shin, stepped in with his left leg, and swung a right kick at her. Missed!

"Come on Francis, you can do better than that against a 110 pound girl!" she teased him through her mouthpiece.

Francis recovered his stance. His boxing gloves felt heavy. He jabbed twice quickly, forcing her to step back. Erika and Francis circled around each other. She jabbed back and surprised him with a jab straight left hook straight combination, sending him against the ropes. He protected his face with his gloves, his chest and upper abdomen with his forearms as Erika savagely delivered blows to his head and body in a flash. All Francis could see were Erika's agile legs and lower body, too stunned to respond to her attack.

The bell rang. The round and match were over.

"Good workout, yes?" Erika mouthed through the dental protector while returning to her corner.

"Yes," Francis hissed, catching his breath and going back to his corner.

Their trainer Suvit, the Thai master, had a look of disapproval when Francis approached him.

"Francis, you big guy," Suvit scolded, "you fast, you hit heavy, but you no look."

"She's too fast—"

"No excuse! You fast too. You no look. Look her body. And relax. Body too tense—you tired quick." Suvit stepped through the ropes onto the canvas. "Muay Thai is martial art like dancing. Too much effort, you fight yourself, not opponent. Relax shoulders, better rhythm, and look eyes. Jab, jab, straight, left kick, two right kick, she no stop you. Erika! Stay ring."

They all walked to the center of the ring. Francis caught his breath during the brief pause. "One minute, fight," Suvit ordered.

Jab, jab, jab… Erika and Francis went at it like dancers. Step, step, step…

"Francis, you too tight, you like robot. Relax! Make body like noodle. Breath nose, relax, *ayie*... good, much better."

He was lost in the hypnotic quality of Suvit's voice, half listening to him yet wholly focused on Erika. She attacked him swiftly, but this time his gaze never left hers. Her attack was reflected in her eyes. Straight, right kick, right kick.

Sidestep, block, block. Francis countered fluidly, effectively returning her attack with a left foot jab double right kick combination. She blocked the first kick, the second one he connected against her ribs. Pain flashed in her eyes when his right shin hit her upper body. She recovered her stance, kicked twice and Francis blocked her. She stepped in and hesitated in throwing a jab straight combo.

Now!

Francis clenched Erika's neck with both hands, locking her head with his forearms. She struggled, failing to straighten her body. He pulled her toward him and delivered two knees to her ribcage, one on each side.

Suvit stopped them. He'd only been trying to make a point for both of them.

"*Aiye*... see? Look eyes, you do better. Now, sit ups, pushups. Then you two go showers."

Francis and Erika saluted their trainer in the traditional Wai Kru, hands together as if in prayer. They jumped out of the ring after briefly stopping at their corners to spit out their mouthpieces. One of the fighters waiting his turn on the ring helped Francis out of his gloves and headgear. He removed himself his sweaty shin pads.

Taking them off felt good.

He cleaned and packed his mouthpiece, headgear and gloves, and spent the next fifteen minutes doing sit ups, pushups, and squats, three sets of fifty each. He was drenched in sweat and exhausted when he went to the locker room.

Francis took a scalding shower followed by a cold spray. He discovered a small bruise under his left eye while shaving, undoubtedly Erika's doing. It wasn't serious. He dressed, packed his gear, and met Erika on his way out.

They walked together. He enjoyed training in the mornings before starting his day at the office. It keeps me focused, he told others when asked. The early morning air was pleasantly cool, people rushed on their way to work. Francis put his Cébé sunglasses on to guard his eyes from the glare. They walked down the Lowenstrasse to Paradeplatz, where they would catch their train.

"How was training for you?" Erika asked.

"Great," he said. "You got me good a couple of times."

"You lost concentration, yes?"

"Maybe. Too much on my mind."

"How is your eye?"

"It doesn't hurt, if that's what you're asking."

"You should focus more, relax more. Your mind was elsewhere, yes? Something bothering you?"

"I've been thinking about ZEPHYR, that's all."

"That's too risky, Francis. You shouldn't expose yourself. You've already got a bad reputation as a troublemaker."

"I don't think that's relevant any longer."

"More than you think, yes? The last thing you need is getting caught prying in a customer's account."

"This isn't an ordinary customer, Erika," Francis replied as they arrived at the train stop on Paradeplatz.

"But why do you get involved in this? It's too risky! And it's not because of patriotism."

"Let's say I'm just hedging my bets. We can't afford to let the bad guys run loose, and I have a score to settle with Enbeaath."

"I don't believe you. I think you just get your kicks from doing this, yes?"

"Well, maybe a little," Francis smiled. "Jones himself asked me to jump in. That means this is truly serious. You don't get the head of operations of the most sophisticated intelligence agency in the world asking for your help every day. It's the CIA guy, Wright, who I don't trust."

"Francis, if you don't trust them, why will you do this?"

"I'm in a position to help."

"That's no answer."

"Look, Erika, Adam wouldn't have come to me unless the situation was really desperate. Remember also that the Rebirth Alliance killed my fiancée."

"So? Does that justify risking your freedom here, yes?" She leaned closer and whispered: "You're looking at a minimum of ten years in a Swiss jail without a chance to appeal if you get caught."

"I won't."

"*Gud I himlen!* You're stubborn! You're reckless. You were not this reckless before. This is stupid. You underestimate the Swiss police."

"They aren't any better than the FBI or the CIA. All of them rely on tracing back your steps. I will ensure there aren't steps to trace back. This... this is necessary."

"I just don't want to see you in trouble, yes? I... I care about you. As a friend."

"Not this again. Please."

"Francis, you're a great friend, and very sweet when you're not being so troublesome. Why do you do this, though? I care for you, and I'd hate to see you hurt, yes?"

"Erika, I also like you a lot," he looked into her lively blue eyes. "Most importantly, I trust you. I'd like to count on your help, if you're willing. But don't pass judgment on this, or try to figure out why I do it. I don't know the answers myself. I guess it's the rush."

"What do you mean, 'the rush'?"

"The adrenaline rush, the rush I get from doing something I'm not supposed to do."

"I wish I understood your death wish. Why you do the things you do? Some suicidal mania?"

"I'm not suicidal. I just enjoy the rush when I get to do something exciting. And what's a bigger rush than saving the world?"

"Your modesty is overwhelming," she said sarcastically.

"I did it once already," Francis smirked, then continued when Erika didn't respond. "Okay, that's a stupid answer. Sorry about that. But please don't worry about me. I can take care of myself."

"Francis, my darling—" Erika kissed his cheek. "Just be careful. The train is here."

"I'll be fine," he said just as train number 13 turned right off Banhofstrasse. The blue and white car stopped and its doors opened after a couple of seconds. A few people exited the train, then Francis followed Erika inside. They sat in a couple of empty seats up front. Francis asked casually, "What have you found out about the document?"

"It was issued by a private banking office here in Zurich. The receipt in question doesn't actually hold the transfer information. It just has a list of references to the real data, yes?"

"What do you mean?"

"The number sequences are duplicate public keys for some authentication algorithm, possibly MAC. The data is stored at the bank, and you use those keys to access the real data."

"So all I have to do is log on to one of the bank's back end systems to gain access to it?"

"Yes, but it's not that easy. The public keys are only a part of it. Relationship managers handle private banking accounts. The relationship manager is a combination of salesman and investment advisor, yes?"

"So?"

"Private banking customers are busy people. The relationship manager is responsible for entering the data and ensuring that things are executed. Customers are catered to, not expected to do anything on their own. This is also done for security purposes. Accountability, more than anything."

"I would assume that the relationship manager handles the account from the customer's premises, right?"

"Yes, or from his office at a branch. They use modems when they visit customers. They also have a VeriCard pseudo random number generator. Do you know the ones I'm talking about?"

"Like a pocket calculator?"

"*Ja, ja...* The card is synchronized with a special clock, and the central computer and the card generate the same pseudo random number at the same time, with a tolerance of only two tenths of a second. When logging in, the relationship manager must enter a user ID, password, and the VeriCard eight digits code valid for the current minute. The session is rejected if the user makes any typos, and the system won't offer another login prompt for another two minutes. Three consecutive rejections on a given ID and the system shuts the relationship manager out for good and erases the local hard drive's allocation tables. The computer becomes useless."

"Isn't that a bit too harsh?"

"That's Swiss Trust Bank's security policy. The bank issues a new machine and VeriCard to the relationship managers if they blow it, and the incident goes into their personnel file. They get fired if they report too many mishaps."

"What if I were inside the bank's corporate network? How would the verification take place?"

"A bit differently. You'd only have to authenticate yourself against the transaction processor and the database."

"Which are what?"

"CICS," 'kicks' she said in techie jargon, "MQ Series and DB2. There is also a front end application that validates you against both."

"So, theoretically, all I have to do is gain access to the application, provide the keys, and I'm in?"

"Well, you need a copy of the receipt. There are additional authentication data in the bar codes on the page."

"And that means I need a scanner to do that."

"Exactly."

The train climbed the hill slowly. They reached a stop across from a street mall. Francis had bought some fruit and Perrier at the Migros supermarket there several times. They were just a few blocks away from their stop at the bank's technology center off Schweighofstrasse.

"You can use any full page scanner for this, yes?" Erika continued. "The software interprets the bar code, then presents the data to you."

"What access levels do I need?"

"Yellow will show you the data, green will also let you modify it."

"You're a sweetheart," Francis said earnestly. "How can I make it up to you?"

"By being careful, yes?"

"You got it, Erika."

She likes me, Francis realized by the look she gave him. Her blue eyes looked at him warmly, even expectantly.

Francis had become a loner after Susan's death. He had friends, of course, but other than a few one-night stands he had avoided getting involved with any woman. Half of his soul craved intimacy, the other half recoiled from it when offered. He wasn't sure the wound had healed.

"You're sweet, Erika," he said finally. "Please don't worry about me."

"Oh, you crazy man," Erika replied warmly as if reading his thoughts. "I wonder if you'll one day want to come home and find something other than an empty flat, yes?"

"One day, perhaps."

"You must take care of yourself so that you get to see that day, yes? Also, I am selfish in asking you to be careful."

"How so?" Francis was oddly—but pleasantly—excited about this turn in the conversation.

The train arrived at their stop; Erika looked him straight in the eye before standing up.

"Francis, it took me a long time to find the right sparring partner. I wouldn't want to start all over again."

Francis smiled and followed her out of the train.

Francis took off his sunglasses as he hurried across the promenade on his way to the office. Erika had walked to a newspaper kiosk at the far end of the promenade; Francis said goodbye and headed to the security check in.

The Swiss Trust Bank data center was a thirteen-story building, skillfully camouflaged as a squat, boring, two story structure. Only the topmost two floors were visible from street level. The rest of the building was carved *into* the mountain. From top to bottom, the first eight hidden floors were home to information technology executives, system analysts, other various technology types, and the bank's mainframe computers. He'd overheard a couple of bank employees mention the existence of a cash vault on one of the lowest floors, with a secret entrance at the foot of the mountain. Armored cars shuttled currency back and forth from the vault to the bank's business clients. He'd also heard, but had been unable to confirm, that a huge valuables vault occupied the lowest level. It was rumored that a large chunk of

Nazi loot still rested in this and other repositories scattered under Zurich.

Francis pondered these idle thoughts as he reached the security entrance. The employee lobby seemed warm and welcoming. There were a few scattered potted plants and modern artwork hung from the walls.

Appearances are deceiving, though.

Francis pulled his bank ID from the outside breast pocket of his leather jacket and clasped it to his belt before reaching the nearest entrance. The badge was also a radio transmitter. There was a security post to the left and seven glass passageways into the building. Each 10-foot long passage was equipped with sensors on its low ceiling that detected a badge's digital signal. The security system automatically opened the glass door at the end and closed the glass door behind the bearers if they were authorized to enter or leave the building. Otherwise both doors would remain closed and the intruder would be trapped in the bulletproof glass cage.

I hate these badges, he thought with contempt.

Francis knew there were radio and infrared sensors all over the building. If an infrared sensor picked up a heat signal from a person, the radio signal must confirm who that person was. He had once left his badge at his desk and wandered off to get a cup of tea. That action summoned the security hounds and earned him a harsh reprimand. The guards had arrived in less than two minutes, just as he'd finished pouring his tea.

Big Time Big Brother Syndrome.

Francis reached the bank of elevators.

"*Grüezi*," he greeted the three men and women waiting there.

"*Guten Morgen*," one responded, the rest used the Swiss greeting.

The elevator arrived; Francis ignored the rest of the passengers during his ride to the second floor from the top, counting ground level as zero.

"Good morning," the secretary greeted him in English from the desk across his office when he entered his work area.

"*Grüezi*, Ursula," Francis smiled. "Anything important for today?"

"You're expected at a meeting at fourteen hours with herr Koehler. Something to do with the review of the new object models. The rest of the day is open so far. The paperwork for the interns just came in, and you must sign and return it today."

"I will," Francis said. Having a couple of college kids around would be fun. "When are their interviews scheduled?"

"Next Monday at nine-thirty."

"Great; I'll be ready for them."

Ursula smiled sweetly and gave him a piece of paper. "This is for you."

He glanced at it. It was a shipping bill. "When did this arrive?"

"Just a few minutes ago. The mail delivery person wants to know when you'll be ready to accommodate the boxes here."

Francis read the sender's information. Heavenly Technology Ventures, in Redwood City, CA. *Electronic testing equipment* was the content's description. Three bundles.

Great, he thought. And he smiled when he saw the signature. G. Lange. Subtlety had always been one of Adam Jones' best traits.

"Please have them bring the boxes as soon as possible," he said. "Is there anything else?"

"No, Francis, that was all."

"Thanks, Ursula," Francis entered his office.

Francis powered his computer on. It was a top of the line, high-end color notebook. It ran a highly specialized version of Linux known as SE/RT. Most commercial computers used by corporations worldwide run either Windows or some version of Unix. Windows, in particular, is remarkably insecure; its main feature is ease of use and configuration. Linux SE/RT stood for Security Enhanced/Real Time, and it was a variation on a version of Linux produced and released to the public by the National Security Agency. Francis' computer was almost impossible to hack by an intruder. It also had all the bells and whistles installed in it for probing a variety of network systems. His computer could be used as a control station for large networks. Most importantly, he'd installed an encrypting file system that rendered his files completely unreadable to unauthorized users.

He logged on.

A number of windows appeared on his screen. He ignored them and clicked on the email icon. The NSA probably wanted to know if the boxes had arrived.

```
From:   pr3d4t0r@internet.lu
To:     guardian_an9el@yahoo.com
```

Subject: Packages arrived

The bundles arrived today without trouble. Thanks for paying for
all the import duties as well. I'm sure I will enjoy playing
with my new toys.

It's nice knowing that my Guardian Angel still flutters over me.
Regards,

FXM

Adam will be pleased, he thought as he clicked the *send* icon.

Francis responded to the rest of the messages in his email box. He would be busy with work the rest of the morning. It would be a while before he could continue his investigation.

It was late afternoon.

"Ursula?" Francis said on his way to his office.

"Yes?"

"Please hold all my calls. I'm going to be busy for the next hour or so."

"No problem."

He closed the door behind him and proceeded to work.

The three cardboard boxes had been brought to his office while he'd been gone to lunch. He opened them all and extracted their contents carefully, trying not to spill packaging material on the floor. The Styrofoam peanuts had a tendency to drift all over the place, and he'd be finding bits of it for the next two months.

I have a funny feeling I may not be working here that long, though.

The larger box contained what appeared to be an unremarkable computer of the same make and model as his. It was a black portable, apparently identical. The new one, however, was considerably heavier. The hard disk drive was missing. Francis understood he was to install his own disk in it.

So be it.

The other two boxes contained a new pair of VR9 glasses, cybergloves, an extra set of lithium batteries, a PCMCIA network analyzer, three small, nondescript black plastic boxes packed with unidentified electronics, a lightweight backpack explicitly intended to carry the computer with maximum comfort, something that looked like a pager, and a man's toiletry set including a razor, shaving cream, and a deodorant. It's all a ruse, he thought. Whatever the cans contain, I'm sure it isn't toiletries.

He turned his attention to the small black gadgets. Each mysterious black box appeared to be some kind of network adapter. *EviLink* was the brand, probably fictitious, though not without a sense of irony. Montagnet turned it in his hands, pressing on several surfaces and popping and retracting appendages. Obviously he could use the gadget for connecting to a network, almost certainly to spy on it without detection, and regardless of the technology employed for transmissions.

The NSA has the best toys, he thought.

Francis installed his hard disk on the new computer and stored the old one in a drawer. After verifying all connections, he powered the computer on.

The screen glowed, a message appeared on it.

```
Press your thumb against the Touch Pad.
```

The touch pad was the small, pressure sensitive flat square right below the keyboard, which was used in portable computers instead of a mouse. Normally, a person rubbed it up, down, left and right for moving the cursor on the screen, and tapped it to mimic the mouse button action. He placed his thumb over the square. Unlike a regular touch pad, this one also had a built in miniature scanner. A flash of light swept over the touch pad, his thumbprint was captured into the device.

```
Just a moment...
Identification complete: PR3D4T0R
JANAP/299: ZEPHYR
```

He smiled. Very slick. Taxes at work, he mused. He wondered how much this toy cost. He read the screen.

```
Good afternoon, Francis.
```

This is a TEMPEST grade computer. You can safely use it in all environments without having to worry about anyone eavesdropping on you. 98% of all electromagnetic emissions are effectively shielded. All network traffic can be encrypted on demand, and I know your data stores are also virtually immune to unauthorized use.

Please give these tools the best possible use. In case of emergency, press the DVD tray release button twice with the drive empty and get at least 10 feet away from it. The system will melt after thirty seconds, regardless of whether it is powered on or not.

This system is due back with us at the end of your mission. I cannot stress enough the urgency of this matter. Please report any progress as soon as possible.
Best of luck,

Adam Jones
Deputy Director, Operations
National Security Agency

Click here to continue

He clicked on the message. The screen blanked, the system started normally.

It was time to probe the network.

He ran a complete system test, then connected it to the bank's network using one of the *EviLink* boxes.

Francis poked the system in several places, queried the EviLink box itself and found that it acted like a router. It had built in SSH encrypted session terminal capabilities. Francis established his initial DSA passphrase using the secure shell key generator and logged on to the little black box.

The *EviLink* had instructions for setting up their unique address and other configuration data. All the devices were supposed to work in unison. Francis could assign one on his computer as a master control station, and the others would communicate with it as long as there was some physical path between them. Each box worked in "promiscuous mode", inspecting every piece of data routed through it then letting it flow. Francis had the option of modifying data packets, or to silently log their contents, source, and destination.

He picked up the phone and dialed a bank internal number.

"Gehrig," Thomas Gehrig answered, following the Swiss custom.

"Hello, this is Francis Montagnet, Thomas," he pronounced it stressing the A.

"Ah, hello, Francis. How can I help you?"

"We discovered some performance issues in mixing the traffic from the intranet with the outside world. I'd like to set up a couple of sniffers at the main routers feeding into the backend systems. We must profile the data to ensure that both internal and external systems offer transaction throughput within the specs."

"Has herr Eggenberger cleared this procedure?" Gehrig asked, a hint of bureaucratic fear in his voice.

"Not yet. He'll ask me to get your opinion first. He'll want you to review my plan anyway." Let's stroke the man's ego, Francis thought. "After all, you rule all network operations. Everyone knows that nothing happens without your approval."

"*Ja*, you are very correct," Gehrig replied, pleased. "What do you propose?"

"Nothing too obtrusive. I'd like to install the sniffers for a couple of weeks, watch the traffic, collect some data and crunch it for spikes."

"I don't have space for sniffers," Gehrig said. Francis sensed he was being difficult. Gehrig was a responsible system administrator. A sniffer running on the private bank's network was anathema to all the privacy policies and laws that Gehrig was contracted to protect.

"These babies are really small, Thomas. About the size of a cigarette pack. They record the data passively. We'll just let them sit there, then dump the data on a PC for analysis." Francis lied. Or rather, he'd said some half-truths. The *EviLink* devices could store a large amount of data indefinitely, but they would also communicate with one another over the network. Francis would be able to analyze the traffic regardless.

"So, no data leaves the data center without my supervision?"

"Not one bit, Thomas. You can personally dump the data from the sniffers to the target PCs."

"No, my assistant can do that. I just don't want anyone but you, me or him accessing the data, and all analysis should be done in a secure area."

"Absolutely," Francis smiled. "See? That's why I wanted to run this through you first."

"*Ja*, I can help you with that," Francis heard Gehrig shuffling papers on his desk, probably looking at his calendar. "I can see you tomorrow at fifteen thirty hours. Do you want me to come up?"

"No, I can meet you down in the control center. Would you please call security to let me in?"

"*Im fass haa*, see you tomorrow."

It took Francis three days to convince Gehrig and Markus Eggenberger, the CIO, but he finally got the green light to set the *EviLinks* up in the control center. One box was plugged to the concentrator for traffic coming from the Internet; the other was plugged to the internal network router. He was at his office, connecting his own *EviLink* to his computer and setting up a few parameters. Soon his computer was intercepting all traffic in the branches, the back office systems, and the bank's mainframes.

The computer was running while he studied the cryptic receipts for the money wires provided by Stanley Wright.

Francis created a software trap using a lexicographical analyzer. His trap basically read all traffic circulating through the *EviLinks*, scanning for references to the account number, the account holder's name and last name, and any references to the keywords safety deposit box, appointment, and the account holder's name within the same paragraph. He took mental note to buy flowers for Erika. He wouldn't have gotten this far without her help. He hacked his way into the database. He read all the account's data.

This is interesting, Francis thought, reading the account holder's name.

Romualdo Del Villar. A *Spanish* name. He had expected an Arabic sounding name.

No transactions were posted. Del Villar had no other accounts with the bank. The current balance was about 400 million Swiss francs, or over 250 million dollars.

There was nothing else to do but wait. He left the sniffer running in the background and password protected his screen and keyboard. Francis was hoping to catch a bank employee entering this information into the network, or Del Villar himself—or one of his minions—using NetDirect, the bank's Internet based on line banking system to request status or to carry out a transaction.

It's a long shot, but it may be worth it.

Billions of bytes circulated through the bank every day. Somewhere, somehow, someone was acting on Rebirth's behalf.

I will be ready, he thought, and opened the door to his office. Other things occupied his mind now, his usual work. Francis could completely dissociate his actions, compartmentalize them, and dissect them with cold precision and without remorse, not unlike the machines he worked with.

This is a trait of a sociopath or a genius, his shrink had said once.

He carried on with the rest of his day as if nothing unusual were going on.

"Gottlieb," a man answered the phone.

"This is Francis Montagnet, from IT services," Francis said, trying to contain his excitement. Del Villar had scheduled a meeting with Marcel Gottlieb, relationship manager, at ten thirty the following morning. Del Villar had requested the appointment to open his safety deposit box.

"Yes, herr Montagnet, how may I help you?"

"We're conducting some tests on the network and we'll need access to your branch tomorrow morning."

"Are those tests why the computer is running so slowly today?" Gottlieb asked.

"Yes, that's part of the reason." In reality, Francis had been delaying traffic flow to Gottlieb's computer all afternoon. He figured the bank executive may need some motivation for letting the technicians come over. "I can probably speed up your network connections while I'm there."

"At what time will you be here?"

"Around nine thirty."

"That's our busiest time," Gottlieb complained.

"I understand. This testing is necessary, though. The system must be at high load levels. We won't be in your way."

"How many people will work on this? Our offices are small. The fewer disruptions the better."

"I think I can run the tests by myself, if that works for you. And I can ensure that you don't have any more problems with your computer."

"That will be grand, herr Montagnet."

"Thank you, herr Gottlieb. See you tomorrow," Francis said and hung up.

This is it, Francis thought. There will be no dress rehearsal. Tomorrow is my one chance of getting the contents of that safety deposit box.

CHAPTER **07**

Zurich

"Good morning, please sit down," Marcel Gottlieb, the middle-aged Swiss Trust Bank relationship manager urged after they shook hands.

"Thank you," Fakhri replied and sat on the comfortable leather chair across from Gottlieb.

"May I offer you some coffee? Tea perhaps?"

"Coffee will be fine."

Fakhri scanned the room while Gottlieb called his assistant and requested a coffee service for two. The clock atop the church of Saint Peter dominated the view from the third floor window, the thick glass panes muffled the noise rising from Paradeplatz and Banhofstrasse. The office was ostentatious but tastefully decorated. It was the office a wealthy customer would expect when conducting business with one of the most successful private banks in the world.

Fakhri was there under an assumed identity. The Spanish passport in the breast pocket of his finely tailored dark gray suit identified him as Romualdo Del Villar, a resident of Madrid. His Spanish was good, and he played the part of the businessman well. As an added bonus, Gottlieb did not speak Spanish; they spoke English.

The mousy female assistant arrived with a small tray holding two cups of steaming coffee, cream and sugar, napkins, and two small silver spoons. The china was well crafted, possibly Bavarian. She placed a coffee cup next to each man and left the room.

"Mr. Gottlieb, I'd appreciate it if you can expedite these proceedings."

"I understand, Mr. Del Villar, that we are to transfer the funds from your account here to your foreign banks. All we need is the destination account information and the transfers will be done."

"Here," Fakhri said, producing a sheet of paper from his briefcase and pushing it across the desk. "Two banks in Gibraltar, the third one in Cyprus."

"Let me see," Gottlieb said, picking up the sheet and adjusting his bifocals over his nose. "Yes, we consistently do business with these banks. What are the amounts?"

"Seventy five million dollars to each bank in Gibraltar, the other fifty million goes to Cyprus," Fakhri sipped his coffee. It was good and strong.

"And the timeframe?"

"Today, if possible."

"Mr. Del Villar, I don't understand why you've chosen to deal with us in person. This is an unusual procedure."

"My company requires the funds immediately, and I must retrieve a few items from my safety deposit box," Fakhri explained. "We're in the middle of an infrastructure development project in the Caspian Sea, and you know how the Russians are. They won't lift a finger unless the funds are escrowed. My company decided that, for our own privacy, using those banks instead of your institution would make more sense."

"Yes, discretion is a rare commodity these days," Gottlieb agreed. Fakhri guessed that Gottlieb would agree to anything to keep a customer happy. "And what is your company's business?"

"Construction and civil engineering. Bridges, roads, hydroelectric dams, that sort of thing."

"I see. Very commendable."

"We believe so," Fakhri drank the rest of his coffee. "A lot of reconstruction is still pending. We'll start with the roads, then we'll advance to rebuilding schools and hospitals. At least that's the plan for now."

"Please give me a few moments," Gottlieb turned his chair to face his computer workstation. "I will access the appropriate accounts. I must get authorization from the central database before we move on."

"Please go ahead," Fakhri said. There was a copy of the Financial Times on top of the desk. He picked it up. It featured the usual news. Companies' fortunes; the effects of U.S. policies on the Euro; common speculation on the prices of certain stocks based on analysts' recommendations.

Gottlieb was typing at his workstation. The clicks resonated in the quiet office. He picked up the phone, dialed a number and had a brief exchange in German. He hung up.

"We'll receive the authorization in a few moments," Gottlieb said, still looking at his screen.

"That's fine," Fakhri replied casually.

Gottlieb's computer beeped four rapid digital sounds. The documents were signed and transmitted.

"The digital signature is here, Mr. Del Villar," Gottlieb said finally. "The transaction may proceed at once."

"Thank you."

Gottlieb looked at his screen, frowned, typed some more, read the screen, then clicked the mouse over some control.

"Is anything the matter?" Fakhri asked with forced disinterest. He could feel Gottlieb tensing slightly as he looked at his display.

"My computer is not working correctly," Gottlieb said, a puzzled tone in his voice. "I will restart it."

"No problem," Fakhri said, wondering if any flags had been raised and surreptitiously watching Gottlieb over the open newspaper.

Gottlieb shut the system down, waited a few seconds, then powered the machine back on. A few electronic beeps later the system was back on-line. Gottlieb navigated his screen with the mouse pointer, clicked on a few icons, and his application program came up.

"This is very strange," Gottlieb said, almost to himself. "There was an error when I accessed your account."

"What seems to be the problem?" Fakhri asked; his voice betrayed a hint of anxiety.

"The... the transaction is still not going through. At first I thought it was a problem with my computer—wait a moment, there is something else." A window popped open on the monitor displaying yellow letters over a red background. "I see... the problem is with the communications." Goettlieb's voice was soothing, diminishing the importance of the problem. "The bank is upgrading the backend systems. An engineer called yesterday to warn me about the upgrades to network communications from this branch."

"What does that mean?"

"A small delay, Mr. Del Villar, nothing to be concerned about. I have a contact number here," he pointed at the screen, "for the engineer in charge. I will resolve this immediately."

"Carry on."

Gottlieb picked his phone up and dialed a number.

"*Grüzi, Marcel Gottlieb am Apparat, Ja...* Marcel Gottlieb, private banking, Paradeplatz office, third floor. I'm having problems with my computer... I see... How soon can you come over?... Yes, thank you." Gottlieb turned to Fakhri. "The engineer is on his way. He shall be here shortly. An American chap I believe, this engineer. He's already in the building."

"How much longer will this take? We are on a very tight schedule."

"My apologies. It shan't be long, I assure you." There was a knock on the door.

"Come in," Gottlieb called. The door opened.

Fakhri swiveled around in his chair. A tall man with pale skin who looked to be in his thirties walked in. Fakhri's jaw almost dropped. It was the same man who had blown Enbeaath's San Francisco operation two years ago! He looked a bit different, but Fakhri wasn't mistaken. The man's dark brown hair was cut very short, his inquisitive green eyes were set over a longish, broken nose. The wide mouth bent upward at the corners with a hint of a smirk. The squared chin line, broad shoulders and flat stomach denoted a man in excellent shape. His walk was light and assured, his movements economical. He was dressed completely in black, with a Nehru collared shirt under a light alpaca blazer; light trousers and shiny black shoes completed his attire. He watched the man carefully.

"I apologize for this delay, herr Gottlieb," the newcomer said as he reached the desk. "We'll resolve the problem in no time. I may need to use your workstation."

"Of course," Gottlieb stood up and met with the man before Fakhri. "Perhaps I should introduce you first. This is Mr. Romualdo Del Villar."

Fakhri stood up and extended his hand. The newcomer gripped his hand firmly. Fakhri felt like someone kicked him in the stomach. This was the same man who had botched the operation in San Francisco, two years ago.

"It's nice meeting you, Mr. Del Villar," the man said, businesslike. "I'll take care of you shortly. My name is Francis Montagnet."

"My pleasure," the man called Del Villar replied.

Francis studied 'Del Villar' as they shook hands. He was a good five inches taller than Francis, and looked to be in his early to mid forties. He had a carefully groomed mustache. Olive skin. Deep, piercing brown eyes under slightly bushy eyebrows. The body was large and in shape and he carried himself with a certain military air. There was something familiar about the man that Francis couldn't quite put his finger on. 'Del Villar' sat down.

"*¿Del Villar? ¿Habla español?*" Francis asked casually, pronouncing the last name Del Vee-YAHR. "Where are you from?"

"*Sí, hablo español. Soy madrileño,*" Del Villar replied after hesitating, his eyes narrowing. "I'm from Madrid. How about you? Where are you from?"

Got you, you lying bastard, Francis thought. The accent, the inflections were wrong. This man spoke quickly and with good command of the language but was not a Spaniard, as he claimed. A Spaniard would have replied *I speak Castilian*, not *I speak Spanish*. Only non-native speakers and some Latin American people refer to the language as Spanish.

"Oh, some days I feel like I'm from everywhere," Francis replied evasively as he sat on Gottlieb's chair. "I'll be quick here."

Francis entered a few commands to unlock Gottlieb's workstation. He closed all the running applications and waited a few seconds. He started the financial planning program and stared at its startup reports, conscious that 'Del Villar'—or whatever his name was—and Gottlieb had their eyes fixed on him.

"Everything is back to normal, herr Gottlieb," Francis finally said in English after tapping a few keys. "You may continue your work. You won't have any more issues."

"Thank you, herr Montagnet," Gottlieb said and sat on his chair after Francis got up and made to leave the office.

"It was a pleasure meeting you, Mr. Del Villar," Francis said in Spanish. He tried to ignore the man's eyes, trained on him like gun barrels. "Perhaps we could get together later? There are very few Spanish speakers in this city. I miss the culture."

"I must pass on that," Del Villar replied. "Unfortunately I'm leaving tonight. I have business demands elsewhere."

"That's too bad. Maybe some other time."

"Maybe."

Francis bid his goodbye and walked out of the room, closing the door behind him, feeling uneasy. There was something about Del Villar that deeply unsettled him. What was it? He glanced at his watch. He would have to deal with that later.

Action!

Francis ran down the stairs to the ground floor. He didn't want to risk getting stuck in an elevator so close to his prize. His quarry was identified. Now he had to set the trap.

Fakhri finished his transaction with Gottlieb. What the hell was that man Montagnet doing in Switzerland? Was this a trap? He patted under his left armpit. His GLOCK handgun was there, reassuring, in its holster. Fakhri tried to relax. Montagnet didn't seem to suspect anything. Still, the sooner this deal was over, the better.

The female assistant came to fetch Fakhri and led him down to the ground floor, where the retail branch did business.

"This way please," she said, opening an unmarked door by the hallway into the branch. Fakhri followed. He glanced over his shoulder to check if they were followed. Nobody was back there.

They walked down a long, sterile corridor. There was no artwork on the walls, their steps clacked on the white marble floor, which sloped downward. Fakhri guessed they were well under street level when they reached the end of the corridor. They arrived at another door at the end.

"One moment, please," she said. "Please stand behind the gray line until I open the door."

Fakhri stepped back and waited for the assistant to complete her operation. A numeric keypad, similar to a calculator's or a phone's, was in place where a doorknob and lock would have been on a normal door. She pressed a button and the keypad lit up. The numbers, star and pound symbols were projected from behind the buttons, their random distribution changed every time someone wanted to activate the door. This prevented Fakhri from guessing the assistant's eight-digit personal identification number by following the position of the numbers she pressed. The numbers would be rearranged next time anyone tried opening the door. The relays clicked and the door popped open.

"Please come with me, Mr. Del Villar."

They entered a tastefully decorated chamber. The door closed. There were three rooms on the left, their doors open. A simple but elegant desk complete with a chair was in each. The chamber itself had a small reception area and a desk with a phone. A heavy steel door was on the right.

"Please leave your briefcase in the middle room and enter your account number and PIN, sir," she indicated, stepping aside after activating the pad on the wall by the door and entering her code.

Fakhri did as instructed and came by the door. He entered the numbers. The vault's door receded into the roof with a loud pneumatic hiss. The area past the threshold was pitch dark at first, then bright lights bathed it, blinding Fakhri for a few moments.

"This way," the assistant said and crossed into the vault. Fakhri followed.

There were seemingly endless rows of anonymous safes and boxes. They ranged in size from a few inches to four or five feet diagonally. Each was labeled with a combination of letters and numbers meaningful only to the bank's administrators and the account holder.

The assistant turned to the right and stopped in front of a bank of drawers.

"May I please have your key?" she asked. He gave her the key.

The assistant inserted his key on a lock to the right of Fakhri's letter-sized box and her own key to the left. She turned both keys simultaneously and the door popped open. She pulled a red metallic drawer from it, its front face the dimensions of a letter-sized envelope but at least two feet long. She handed the box to Fakhri.

"Thank you," he said as he inspected the lock on the box. It was intact. He grabbed a small handle from the side of the box and followed the assistant back to the reception chamber.

"Please take the box into the room with you," she indicated, sitting at the desk outside. "There is a switch by the desk lamp. Signal me when you're ready to exit."

Fakhri nodded and entered the room. The door automatically swung on its hinges as soon as he entered, locking him inside. He looked around the room. There weren't any cameras or windows. Swiss Trust Private Bank didn't take any chances when it came to its clients' privacy.

Fakhri placed the box on the table and opened the lock with his key. He released the latch and opened the drawer. Nested within it was a titanium container about seven inches square and three inches deep. The container opened on three sides, pivoting the two halves with a hinge along the fourth side. The rubberized insides were dry to the touch. A small stack of microfiche slides was inside. Fakhri produced a jeweler's magnifying glass from his briefcase, screwed it onto his right eye, and took a slide from the stack.

The slide was parceled in tiny rectangular areas, each corresponding to a page photographed long ago. He studied a few of the pages. Some were handwritten, some typed, a few showed hand drawn diagrams drafted sixty, eighty, a hundred years ago. He put the slide aside and grabbed another one from the bottom of the stack and repeated the inspection. Everything was in order.

An alarm sounded.

An alarm!

A voice announced something in German over a PA system. Fakhri was at a loss. He hurriedly stacked the slides in order, placed them into the titanium container, unscrewed the lens from his eye and placed everything in his briefcase, locking them safely inside by rolling the combination lock tumblers. The door popped open behind him.

"Mr. Del Villar, please hurry!" said the assistant. "There is a fire in the building. We must evacuate immediately!"

"Coming," Fakhri said, closing and locking the safety deposit box drawer. He dashed out of the room and handed the drawer and his key to the assistant. "Here, I'll wait while you put this back in my box," he yelled. The wailing alarm grew louder. "There is nothing inside it anyway."

The assistant grabbed the box and hurried into the vault. She returned forty-five seconds later and punched a button by the doorway. The door into the vault, propelled by compressed air, crashed instantly closed.

"We aren't safe in here," the assistant said, handing back his key. Fakhri was beginning to feel her anxiety. "The ventilation system should sustain us for a few minutes before the smoke overcomes it. Protocol indicates that we must evacuate immediately. After you!" She opened the door and let Fakhri out first, then followed him after closing the door. They both hurried up the corridor toward the entrance. The wailing grew louder. The assistant reached to open the door.

"Wait!" Fakhri said and shoved her back. He touched the door. It felt cool. The fire had not reached them. Perhaps only the upper floors were on fire? "Go ahead, but watch out for smoke or fire."

"Thanks," she said, and carefully opened the door.

Black, thick, acrid smoke rushed into the corridor. It stung the eyes and lungs. Fakhri knew they had to leave immediately.

"Go!" he said and pushed the girl ahead of him.

The black smoke engulfed them in almost total darkness. His eyes watered, his lungs burned. Dammit! The assistant sprinted away from his grasp, knowing her way out from habit, leaving him behind and stunned for a few seconds. Which was the way out? Oh, yes, to the right. He could barely see people rushing down stairs from the upper floors. Just a few more meters and he would reach the street.

Was someone walking next to him? He strained to see through the tears. Yes, someone was walking toward him. *Someone wearing something like a gas mask.* It was a man, his head encased in some kind of plastic bubble. Was this a fireman or a paramedic?

That was Fakhri's last thought before what looked like a deodorant aerosol container materialized in front of his face. He squinted. The oversized valve was depressed, squirting his eyes, mouth and nostrils with a calmative agent, knocking him unconscious.

Francis put the Halothane variable bypass vaporizer in his right hip pocket. Del Villar's body crumpled to the floor. The 5% Halothane dosage would knock him out for a few minutes.

Maybe I should leave you here, Francis thought.

Even though the smoke cloaked him entirely, there was always the small probability that one of the cameras was capturing his actions. He would have to play along. He inhaled deeply and removed the lightweight hood of the personal breathing equipment, rolled it and shoved it under his shirt. The PBE made hardly any bulk.

He grabbed Del Villar's briefcase with his left hand, the man's suit collar with his right, and dragged both toward the exit, just a few yards away.

Just in time, he thought as four firefighters rushed in.

"*Brauchen Sie Hilfe?*" one of the men asked him.

"I don't speak German," Francis said in a raspy voice.

"*Parlez-vous français?*"

"*Oui*," Francis coughed. "I found this guy unconscious back there."

"We'll take care of him," the fireman said. Two of them grabbed Del Villar's arms, put them over their shoulders, and carried him out. "Do you need help?"

"I can follow you out," Francis said.

Francis walked outside with the fireman. A large crowd of bank employees and gawkers had gathered in front of the bank and over by the train stop. Francis coughed a few times when the clean air rushed into his lungs. A few ambulances and other emergency vehicles were parked there, others were just arriving. An efficient female paramedic looked him over and gave him a thumbs up.

Francis thanked her. Del Villar was laying on a gurney a few feet away, his mouth and nose covered by an oxygen mask.

His eyes were open.

Del Villar was obviously trying to clear his vision. His eyes focused on the briefcase, then on Francis' face.

Shit.

Del Villar tried to get up but the paramedics pushed him down on the gurney.

Francis turned around and made his way through the crowd toward Banhofstrasse. Del Villar had finally propped himself up and was waving his hand at two Arabic-looking men on the other side of Paradeplatz. The men gave one another a puzzled look and rushed to Del Villar's side.

Francis turned left at the corner and trotted north, past Peterstrasse and Münzplatz. The briefcase handle felt slippery in his sweaty, nervous hand. He only had a few precious seconds to escape or Del Villar's goons would catch him.

CHAPTER **08**

NSA Headquarters
Fort Meade, MD

Adam Jones was in his office at the National Security Agency headquarters when the ZEPHYR NINE GAMMA transmission came through SPINTCOMM. He read it quickly, then picked up his gray secure phone to dial the CIA's CoS number in Zurich. Chief of Station Stan Wright answered on the first ring.

"Wright speaking."

"This is Adam Jones, Stan. I just read your cable."

"I'm glad you were at your office," the CIA man said. "Looks like I underestimated Montagnet."

"He came through with more than we expected, I agree. The real question is what to do with it."

"I already sent a copy of the report to Langley for analysis. The ultimate strategy will come—of course—from there but we have an immediate problem to solve. Montagnet must leave Zurich now."

"Can he hold the electronic funds transfers back for one night? We might be able to set up a trace."

"It's very unlikely. He is positive that the opposition spotted him already. He isn't returning to the bank. Montagnet is sure that nobody saw him set up the smoke bombs but sooner or later someone is bound to put two and two together and notice that he's been missing since the event. The police may want to hold him for questioning. A camera may have filmed him. He won't return to his office."

"If he can't delay the transaction, can someone intercept Del Villar?"

"We *could* try. Although Montagnet told us that Del Villar was leaving immediately, we didn't find a record of anyone by that name leaving Zurich within the next two days. Montagnet is positive that 'Del Villar' is an illegal anyway."

"An illegal?"

"Agency jargon," Wright explained. "An alias."

"I see," Jones tipped his chair back, staring at the ceiling. He didn't want this Del Villar character to slip through their fingers. "Is there any way we can nab Del Villar and take him to a NATO country? Germany perhaps?"

"I don't know if I can put such plan in action in just a few hours, Adam. We could catch a lot of flak if we make a move without notifying our Swiss friends. They won't lift a finger to help us unless they're sure that Del Villar is up to something illegal or unless his activities prove to be a threat to Swiss security."

"Perhaps we can snatch him on a false identity charge?"

"Tough to prove. He's laying low. For all we know he rented a car and is driving over the border instead of flying," Wright paused for a moment. Jones heard papers shuffling over the line. "We could try abducting him and taking him to a safe house for interrogation. We'd use the local talent. This is all wishful thinking until we find him."

"Use Montagnet," Jones suggested. "You'll discover he's even more resourceful as you get to know him."

"That's also something I want to talk to you about. Was he supposed to make contact with the mark in the first place?"

"Not necessarily. I figure he saw the opportunity and took it."

"He took too many risks for just meeting this Del Villar, Adam. He *exposed* himself."

"I'm sure he covered his tracks."

"We won't be able to exfiltrate him if he screws up."

"He knows that."

"Do you know anything I don't?"

"Only that Montagnet operates this way. He likes leaving open options. Now, back to the report. What have you guys found out?"

"We're looking for flags on the accounts. It will take at least until tomorrow before we get a break. One thing we're assuming, based on the transfer to the Cyprus bank, is that Del Villar represents, or is dealing with, the Russians. They have a predilection for Cypriot banks."

"He doesn't sound Russian from Montagnet's description. He ought to know better. What about the banks in Gibraltar?"

"Not much there. Gibraltar is mostly a financial haven for guys with huge profits and greedy ex-wives after fat alimony payments. Their banking privacy laws are just a tad less stringent than Switzerland's, so it would take us some time before we crack them open."

"With the information we have, though, we can trace the transactions as they move through the world financial networks."

"Hold on a moment," Jones said, pressing the MUTE button on his phone. He turned to his workstation and entered a query. No results. He picked up the phone again. "Stan? We don't have anything on anyone named Romualdo Del Villar either. Run with it. We're starting intercepts now on all COMINT channels with flags for Del Villar and the banks."

"How soon will you get results?"

"Can't say. It all depends on how nimble and quiet this Del Villar character is. So far he's managed to not catch our attention. Do you have anything else in Switzerland?"

"Not much," Wright answered. "The fund transfers Montagnet provided are our only lead."

Jones turned to his computer and entered another query. He would put the British GCHQ and a number of NSA and Echelon ground based stations throughout Europe on alert.

"I think Montagnet has done everything he could accomplish," Jones said. "I'm sure we'll fit the remaining pieces of this puzzle together through other sources. What happens next?"

"I will debrief Montagnet tonight and get the data over to you. He believes he's acquired the goods from the safety deposit box. It's a stack of microfiche slides, possibly the missing DARPA documents. In the meantime we put a call to our friends in CESID regarding Del Villar. You should have whatever we collect before you leave home for dinner, since our time zone is six hours ahead."

Jones knew that CESID was the ultra secret Spanish intelligence service or *Centro Superior de Información de la Defensa*. Their origins could be traced to the 1960's with General Franco's OCN, *Organisación Contrasubversiva Nacional,* or National Counter-subversive Organization. The advent of democracy in Spain and the end of the Cold War meant a new focus for them on counter terrorism and narcotics warfare. They hated the NSA because of the agency's constant quest to crack their codes but they were known to work well with the CIA.

"Then let's get on with it," Jones replied. "Talk to you tonight." He hung up.

. . .

GCHQ Morwenstow Listening Post
Cornwall, United Kingdom

It was a chilly evening in the southwestern coast of England. The air carried the salty smell of the Celtic Sea, the waves crashed against the cliffs of Sharpnose Point. Digital and analog microwaves pierced the perennial clouds shrouding the sky, reaching the dozen satellite dishes aimed at the heavens.

The signal contained a long watch list of keywords and names. Captain John Hooper ran it through his computer, generating a set of four digit numbers associated with them. He passed these four digit numbers, or groupings, on to the UKUSA listening posts in Cyprus and Vienna through the Echelon system. A customized supercomputer system ran at each location, connected to the rest of the Echelon network. These computers systems were code named Dictionaries.

Hooper had just come on duty when the signal came from the United States. The Government Communications Headquarters had a joint charter with the American NSA established under the UKUSA Communications Intelligence Agreement. Signals and communications intelligence resources were shared by both agencies in the pursuit of common goals, and for this reason the UKUSA agreement had divided the world into *spheres of interest*. The GCHQ monitored communications in most of Western Europe and the Middle East. The current signal had reached Captain Hooper because he was the supervising officer 98J (electronic intelligence interceptor/analyst) responsible for the Cyprus listening post. He read it and prepared it for distribution to the appropriate interception posts.

The Dictionary systems in Morwenstow, Cyprus and Vienna logged the watch list and sifted through SIGINT and COMINT intercepts. An avalanche of phone, fax, and digital transmissions flowing from Switzerland through the cables, international licensed carriers, and the INTELSAT system were automatically analyzed by Echelon. Hooper carried on with his regular duties after submitting the signal for analysis.

A half hour later the Dictionary flagged a message.

It was a transmission between a Swiss and a Cypriot bank. The transmission itself was encrypted but the signal analysis software was able to determine the origin and destination. Hooper attached the intercept to a SPINTCOMM message and sent it to Fort Meade for processing. The rest of the evening went by with no further events.

"Sir, we have a problem," Jones said. He was on the phone with USAF General Morgan Helmwood, Director of the National Security Agency. "ZEPHYR went haywire."

"Do we have the CIA report yet?"

"No sir. They're playing it close to their chest, as always," Jones loosened his tie. He felt flustered. Sticky sweat ran down his armpits. "The only reason I found out was because Wright was supposed to report back before the end of the day. I tried contacting him when the signal came up. My call was automatically bounced to Langley. A duty officer handled me. I expect an official communication later."

"What have we got? What about your asset?"

"The Cyprus RSOC (Regional SIGINT Operation Center) of GCHQ intercepted what we believe is the correct funds transfer flagged by Montagnet. I assigned two cryptanalytic experts and one cryptomaterial checker to extract the recipients from the signal. We'll try to crack the data before they launder the funds elsewhere. As for the DARPA documents cache I have no answer for you yet. Wright of the CIA is dead, and Montagnet is missing, sir. We have no idea where he is."

CHAPTER 09

Zurich

Angst.

Francis scanned the dwindling pedestrian traffic for signs of danger. He averted his sight whenever anyone tried to make eye contact. He had been on the run all day, having spent his time at various cafés, bookstores, and other public places, always vigilant against threats. None had materialized so far. He didn't go to his apartment; they'd look for him there first. His stomach growled; he ignored it. Other than consuming three bottles of Rhäzünser mineral water he had neither drunk nor eaten anything else that day. He wanted to stay sharp. A belly full of food would slow him down.

Francis was on his way to the rendezvous point with the CIA man. He hurried down Unterfeldstrasse in Oerlikon on his way back to Zurich. He got to the train station and looked at the clock. 20:31. He would meet Stan Wright in a half hour. He waited at the far end of the platform.

20:45.

The intercity train pulled into the station. Most cars were empty. Francis approached a second-class, non-smoking car, walked in, and sat close to the car entrance. The train began to move after about one minute. The next stop would be the Zurich Hauptbanhof—Main Train Station.

Francis leant back and rubbed his face with both hands. His eyes felt gritty. It had been a long day.

Getting away from Paradeplatz had been easy. Thank goodness Del Villar's thugs had been slow to react. He'd gone to a café off Uraniastrasse and immediately got to pry Del Villar's briefcase open with his ToolLogic knife.

Inside he found a metallic container holding what were undoubtedly the missing DARPA documents. There were also an Iranian passport and a Russian business visa issued in Madrid, an airplane ticket to Moscow for that afternoon, and a security badge that identified the carrier as colonel Sattar Fakhri in Cyrillic.

That name made more sense.

All the documents were safely stored for now, waiting for Montagnet and Wright to retrieve them. Francis couldn't afford carrying them around.

The train stopped. Francis stretched and left the train car, casually scanning his path. Nobody gave him nervous glances or signs of recognition. He walked at a leisurely pace from the platform to the south gate. Nothing was out of the ordinary.

Good.

Francis approached one of the many taxis parked by the entrance. He could walk there but figured that, the shorter the time he spent walking around, the better. The driver started the engine when Francis opened the door and climbed in.

"*Grüezi*," Francis said. "Please take me to Grossmünster Platz."

"Very well, sir," the driver replied, putting the car in gear and pulling away from the sidewalk.

"I want you to go past Zentral, up Seilergraben then down to Bellevue Platz. Turn right on Limmatquai. Take your time."

"That's a big loop."

"I'm early for my engagement."

"Very well, sir."

The ride to Bellevue Platz took about eight minutes. The taxi turned right.

"Please slow down," Francis instructed, scanning the road ahead. The driver obliged.

The Limmat river flowed south on their left, the traffic was light. The usual crowd returning home after dinner on the Niederdorfstrasse flowed from the crooked streets and alleys onto the Limmatquai. Many of them were looking for a cab.

"Stop right here," Francis commanded. He paid the driver and tipped him adequately. He left the cab and headed toward Grossmünster Platz.

There it was!

The silver Opel with a broken taillight was parked exactly where Wright had indicated.

Excellent!

He repressed the urge to run to the car.

Twenty yards.

Nobody paid attention to him.

Ten yards.

A drunken couple came down from Frankengasse; the Swiss man bumped into him. Francis tensed, ready to vault. The man and woman mouthed their apologies in between hiccups and giggles. They moved on.

Five yards.

Wright's head was clearly visible through the rear window. Francis strode the last few steps, opened the door and entered the car.

"I'm glad you're on time," Francis said, pulling the door closed. "I've been running around all day—"

Fuck.

Francis froze. The unmistakable feel of a high caliber handgun muzzle was pressing against the back of his head. Someone had been hiding in the backseat of the car.

"Put your hands on the dashboard," the man's voice ordered in accented English. "You make one *moov* I don't like, you're dead."

"Whatever you say," Francis obeyed. He stole a glance at Wright. "What's going on?"

Stan Wright had been dead for at least an hour. His bulging eyes were glazing already. His neck had been duct taped to the headrest to hold the head upright. The assassins had placed a plastic bib of sorts over the front of his shirt, concealing the hollowed out chest. It looked like a white smock to a casual observer. Wright's killer had slashed him from his navel to his collarbone and pulled his entrails out. The torture had produced the answers his captors wanted. He had probably begged to be killed to stop the excruciating pain. The nauseating smell of congealing blood rising from the body and trickling onto the driver's seat pervaded the car. Francis fought the urge to vomit.

"Don't play innocent, Montagnet. The Colonel wants his *beelongeengs*."

"I don't know what you're talking about ouch!" Francis mouthed. His captor whacked him with the pistol.

"*Shuddup.*"

A yellow, windowless delivery van double-parked next to them, its hazard lights blinking. The back double door opened and two men got out and surrounded the car.

"This is a .357 magnum," the voice behind him explained. "I can shoot you through the door if you try anything. Exit the car when my colleagues approach you."

The door opened. Francis kept his hands up, measuring the distances, looking for a chance to act.

None came.

Two men surrounded him as soon as he was out of the car. One of them jabbed his ribs with a gun, nudging him to the van. All of them climbed inside. Francis heard the man from the back seat slam Wright's car door shut and walk away.

The van doors closed, the vehicle merged with traffic. He was on his way to a rendezvous with destiny.

Colonel Sattar Fakhri sat behind the driver, looking at Francis. "Frisk him," he commanded.

The thug on Francis' right kneed him in the groin. Francis collapsed to the floor, writhing with pain. The two men knelt beside him. One flattened him against the steel floor of the van. The other man pulled Francis' jacket off his shoulders. They patted him down. They handed the contents of his pockets to Fakhri.

"What have we here?" Fakhri asked, opening Francis wallet.

Think.

"Nothing of interest, I see. What is this?" Fakhri pulled the various parts of the ToolLogic apart. He examined the three-inch knife, the screwdriver, the laser pointer.

What do I do? Francis thought. How should I play this? Let's see... Fakhri, two heavies, and the driver. Not good.

"Francis Montagnet," Fakhri hissed. "You have caused me many problems today. Who the hell do you think you are?"

Deceive them. That's how I should play it.

"I... I'm sorry..." he almost whimpered.

"Sorry? Sorry? You shall die quickly if you return my property."

"Mr. Del Villar, please don't kill me..." Francis said in a thin voice.

An excited exchange in Arabic between one of them and Fakhri followed.

They found the key.

"I don't have time for childish games, Montagnet," Fakhri growled, holding a key up. Francis had filed the number off earlier. "What is this key for?"

"It's a... it's a..." Francis feigned a stutter, "it's for a locker at the Hauptbanhof."

"Number?"

"I... I don't remember..."

Fakhri nodded to the thug on his right. The man hit the back of his left hand with the butt of his pistol. Pain shot up Montagnet's arm.

"Number?" Fakhri insisted.

"Really, I don't remember," Francis stuttered. "Please, let me show you where it is. It's on the second floor down, by... by... by the public showers."

Fakhri spoke to the driver. He caught the word 'Hauptbanhof' in the exchange.

"You will tell me which locker."

"Look, I don't know anything other than the Wright guy wanted me to swipe your briefcase. Really. I'll give you the money he paid me," Francis had not blinked for almost a minute; his eyes were tearful. He begged in a thin voice. "Please, just don't kill me!"

Fakhri appraised him as someone would appraise a steak at the supermarket. "How much did the CIA spook pay you?"

"CIA?" Francis cried. "He told me *you* owed him money! He said you guys were dealing drugs! Heroin! He gave me twenty-five thousand dollars, promised twenty-five more and a kilo of uncut smack when I produced your briefcase..."

The van stopped after a couple of minutes.

"For the last time, Montagnet, which locker?"

"Let me show you, I don't want any shit with you, honest. I'll leave the country tonight. Really. I don't want to die; all I wanted was some money. I'll work for you. I'll do anything you want. *Please!*"

Fakhri spoke quickly to his men. They replied. Francis heard the unmistakable click of cocking hammers. "Listen, you dumb, lying fuck," Fakhri threatened, "you will come with us and show us the locker. Baghel and Malik have their guns trained on you. You will die if you try anything."

"Look, Mr. Del Villar," Francis said, using the fake name. He didn't want them to know yet that he'd opened the briefcase, "whatever you say. I'm not up for any hero shit. I'll show you where it is."

Fakhri stared at him for a long time before nodding to his men. They pulled him up by his collar. His left hand still hurt a bit. He flexed his fingers. Nothing was broken. The van doors opened, Baghel and Malik stepped out, their guns concealed in their coat pockets, aimed at his body. Francis followed them out, then Fakhri.

The van had parked by the eastern entrance to the train station, across the street from the Landesmuseum. Fakhri shut the doors down, the driver pulled away, probably to go around the block.

"Lead the way," Fakhri commanded by his side.

The four men walked toward the boarding platforms. The Internet café to their left and a couple of bars were open; all the other stores were closed.

"Follow me," Francis said, heading for the escalators.

The group got to the second floor down. The Western Union office was on their right, the public baths in front, several rows of pay-per-use lockers were on the left. Francis walked to the third bank of lockers.

"This is it," he said, pointing at the first locker on the top row, next to the aisle.

Fakhri said nothing. Francis edged closer to Fakhri, the two thugs followed him like his shadow.

Fakhri opened the door. The briefcase looked small in the oversized locker. Fakhri pulled it out and examined the latches. He frowned when he realized that Francis had forced it open.

Fakhri pressed the releases. The latches popped up. Francis and the two thugs were standing right behind Fakhri when he opened the briefcase.

Now!

Francis dropped to one knee. He had rigged the fake shaving foam can sent by Jones to the hinges of the briefcase. The can was actually a disguised number 15 *stinger* grenade, manufactured by Defense Technology Corp. of Casper, Wyoming, and filled with OC and rubber balls. The grenade exploded in the confined space. 180 rubber pellets spread in a 50-foot radius, painfully hitting Fakhri and the two thugs in their face, stunning them. A few pellets hit Francis, but he was anticipating the sting and had cradled his face in his hands when he crouched.

Go!

The grenade dispersed OC, or oleoresin capsicum, along with the pellets. OC, the pepper spray active ingredient, compounded the pain inflicted on Fakhri and his men, blinding them just long enough for Francis to get away.

The few people on the upper floor screamed after the explosion, amplified by the empty locker.

Move!

A shot buzzed by Francis ear. One of Fakhri's men had the wherewithal to fire at him as he dashed toward the escalators. A second slug crashed against the sliding rubber banister just as Francis got there, missing his waist by a few inches.

"Help! Police! Terrorists!" Francis yelled at the top of his lungs, wanting to create chaos. He didn't want the police after *him*, but he certainly wanted to sic them on Fakhri and his cadre. Some of the other people on the floor panicked and ran after him, blocking Fakhri and his men, who were rubbing their eyes and face and trying to chase him.

The escalator traveled slowly, Francis leapt up the steps two and three at a time. He landed at the top just as several gendarmes ran up, blowing their whistles, their weapons ready. Francis dashed past the Banhof Meeting Point and off to the main entrance.

I have no money. I have no telephone. Damn!

The night was cold. Francis looked left toward the Banhof bridge, just in case Fakhri's support team were there. He didn't see the van. Excellent! What he did see, last in the row of taxis, was the same cab he'd taken to his fateful meeting with Wright. He ran to it. He reached it, opened the door, and jumped in.

"Hi," Francis panted, "Remember me?"

"Yes, sir, the ride to the Grossmünster Platz," the driver replied. "Where to this time?"

"I was mugged," Francis explained, rushing the words. "Drug addicts, I think. I don't have money with me but I can pay you when we get to our destination. Are you game?"

"Is that why the police were called? I saw them run into the station. Sure, I'll drive you, as long as we go within city limits."

"Thanks, I really appreciate it," Francis said earnestly. The driver pulled away from the station. "We're going to Schontalstrasse, off the Sihl river."

"Oh, my God," Erika said. "I'm so glad you got away."

"I'm fine," Francis said, still feeling a bit shaken as he collapsed on her living room sofa. "I'm going to need your help, though. May I have some mineral water and a small bite to eat? I'm famished. Nothing fancy, though; I don't want to get sluggish."

"Sure," she said and went into the kitchen.

Francis did a set of five breathing exercises. He calmed somewhat. He was weighing his options, which seemed rather bleak now that his CIA backup was dead.

I must get out of Zurich.

There is only one place where I can turn for help.

"Erika, may I use your phone? It'll be a long distance call."

"Go ahead," she said from the kitchen.

Francis picked the handset up and dialed a number. Thank goodness it wasn't a cordless phone. No point in risking local eavesdroppers on the conversation. Landlines were a bit more secure. He dialed a number in the 443 area code that he'd memorized long ago.

A male operator answered.

"This is Francis," he said. "I want to talk to Mr. Lange."

"Just a moment, sir," the impersonal male voice said. "I'll transfer you."

Francis knew that the operator had looked at his access phrase in the computer. *Mr. Lange* was an alias for Adam Jones. The line clicked.

"Francis?"

"Yes, Mr. Lange," Francis said.

"Where are you?"

"I'm still in Zurich, sir."

"Are you all right?"

"I'm fine sir. And I have the product samples you requested. The local sales rep, though, got very sick. He'll need a lot of rest."

"I know. The office called and told me earlier. How are you doing?"

"I had a couple of sneezes, but I shook them off. Just in time as well. The other firm knows I have the samples and wants to get in on the deal. I don't think there is anything else for me to do in Zurich, sir. I want to go to Stuttgart. I could drive into Germany in a few hours."

"No, the Stuttgart branch office is closed," Jones said. That meant that the NSA had no personnel able to help there. "We don't have a big presence in Germany. You'll have to get to Vienna."

"Vienna is a bit far, and I don't think flying is a good idea for me, with my sneezing and all. I may catch a cold."

"You can probably go by train, arrive there early in the morning. Call me when you get there and I'll have someone from the office pick you up at your hotel."

"What about offices in Geneva or Bern? Should I head there?"

"Negative. There is nothing for you to do in Switzerland since you already have the samples. Head to Vienna."

"Very well, sir. Talk to you tomorrow." He hung up.

"What was that all about?" Erika asked when she returned to the living room. She placed a plate with baby carrots, a cup of tea, and a bottle of mineral water on the coffee table.

"That was Jones. They know Wright is dead. They can't exfiltrate me from Switzerland or from Germany, so I get to go to Vienna."

"That's dangerous, yes?"

"Very much," he said after swallowing a couple of sweet baby carrots he'd chewed. "I'm sure that the bad guys and his gang are looking for me all over the city. He'll have people at the airport for sure. Bern and Geneva are off limits. Their top dog, a man named Fakhri, probably has people at the Hauptbanhof as well, and I'll have to go by train."

"Let me check the schedule," she said, getting up and walking to a bookshelf. She leafed through a booklet. "There is a train to Vienna at twenty three oh five tonight, yes?"

"That gives us barely an hour to gather my stuff and head to the station. Can we buy the tickets there?"

"Everything is closed now. You'll have to buy the tickets on the Internet or aboard the train itself, assuming they have room."

He sipped his water. "Will you help me get there on time?"

"Of course, Francis. What are friends for?"

"Let's go, then."

Francis laid low in the back of Erika's Alfa Romeo, peeking from under a dark blanket cloaking his shape. The car was parked half a block away from his flat. He watched Erika enter the building on Hufgasse. Nobody followed her in. After checking their available time, Francis had told her to wait at least ten minutes before returning, and to avoid turning any lights on, since his flat faced the narrow street. He had described the floor plan, and where his ready bag was stored.

Erika finally emerged from the building, hauling behind her a wheeled, black carry-on like a flight attendant's, but larger. Francis watched carefully. Nobody moved to intercept her. Good. She made it to the car, tossed the bag on the passenger seat, and drove off.

"We're going to the train station, yes?"

"Yes, darling. This is my final stop," Francis said from the back seat, pulling his carry-on to the back seat. It was uncomfortable as hell trying to change in the back of the car, but he wanted to be ready by the time they reached the Hauptbanhof. "Is anyone following you?"

"No, there is hardly any traffic."

"I want you to go to my office tomorrow and get my portable computer. The door is open. Ursula doesn't get there until eight-thirty, so you'll have no problems grabbing it if you come early. Take it to one of the quays. Press the DVD tray release button twice and toss it in the river—uff!"

"Very well," Erika said. "What are you doing back there?"

"Changing," Francis said, cutting the plastic bag open. All the clothing items inside the bag had been vacuum-sealed to reduce their volume. He took a leather jacket out of it. "What time is it?" Francis asked.

"It's twelve minutes until the train leaves."

"Hurry, then. I still have to pick up the item. Drop me off at the north entrance."

Erika steered the car past the Landesmuseum and parked in the passenger drop off area of the station. She kept the engine running.

"Well," Francis said from the back seat, "I guess this is it for now." He reached over the passenger seat and opened the door. He pushed the backrest forward and let himself out. Erika exited the car and came by his side as he pulled his black and silver Boblbee Megalopolis Ergo backpack from the back seat.

"Be careful out there," Erika said, looking into his eyes.

"Don't worry, I'll be fine."

Erika stood on tiptoes and kissed Francis in the Swiss manner, right-left-right cheek. He hugged her tightly. She embraced him back.

"I only have a few minutes," Francis said, letting her go. He hated goodbyes. "I'll see you soon."

Francis put his arms through the backpack harness. The Ergo was waterproof and anatomically fitted, had an impact resistant hard shell, and padded shoulder straps that made it comfortable to carry. It fit well over Francis' sleek black leather jacket. The jacket was intended for motorcycle riding, designed to prevent injury to the shoulders, lower back, elbows and forearms with its concealed high impact pads. The pads were invisible from the outside and detracted no mobility from the user. He zipped the front of his jacket up to his upper chest as he walked into the train station.

Five minutes to go.

Francis hurried past the boarding platforms for the last time. He felt comfortable in the black jeans, though his walking was made a bit harder by the steel-toed, steel-shanked combat boots he now wore. He looked at the arrivals and departures board above him. The train to Vienna was the last one departing that night. He stopped at the station's meeting point, casually glancing all around him.

None of Fakhri's thugs was in sight.

Francis walked to a potted plant next to a food kiosk and dug into the dirt around the plant's roots. Here it is, he thought, curling his fingers around the key. He pulled it out, scanned his surroundings once more, and hurried down the escalators while wiping the dirt off the key.

Three minutes.

The police had cordoned off the area around the locker where he'd hidden Fakhri's booby-trapped briefcase. A forensics technician worked behind the yellow tape. Francis walked past it to the last bank of lockers and opened the appropriate one. The metallic clamshell container was still there. He left Fakhri's passport and documents behind.

Two minutes.

Francis took the backpack off his shoulders, opened the top and shoved the clamshell inside. He closed the container and rushed up the escalators as he flung the backpack over his shoulders.

One minute.

He felt flustered. If nothing else, he knew that in Switzerland you could set your watch to the train arrivals and departures. He got to the ground floor, then turned toward the boarding platform and ran as fast as he could toward the train. He was about to reach the long platform when one of Fakhri's men walked toward him from the south entrance to the Hauptbanhof. It was Baghel.

The train whistle resonated throughout the empty train station.

Damn!

Francis charged the man at full speed. Baghel's eyes widened in surprised recognition.

Francis held his right hand up by his right shoulder, fingers curled back, and headed straight for the man, who was reaching inside his jacket—for a gun? Francis didn't care to find out. He shot his right hand up and out, catching the thug squarely in the chin with the ball of his hand, knocking him flat on his back. If he wasn't out cold by the sucker punch, he'd definitely passed out when his head bounced against the cold cement floor. Francis didn't stop.

The train is leaving!

A conductor three cars down saw him running at full speed. He yelled something in German at him and waved his hands, unmistakably signaling that the train wouldn't wait for him.

The train gained speed.

Francis pushed himself to the limit.

Ten meters.

Faster!

Five meters.

The incredulous conductor watched when Francis leapt off the platform and caught a handrail next to him. Francis' upper right arm muscles screamed with the effort, his body dangled precariously as the train sped faster. His sweaty hand slid down the handrail.

"Open the door!" Francis gasped. His grip would slip any moment.

The bewildered conductor pulled the door open and held his hand out. Francis grabbed it with his left, and the conductor helped him into the car.

The red faced, furious conductor was yelling at Francis in German.

"Sorry about that," Francis said in English. "I couldn't miss this train."

"Are you crazy? You can die doing that!" the man shouted.

"I couldn't miss this train," Francis said. "My mother is very sick in Vienna. She may not live past the night. Here," he unzipped the front of his jacket, produced his new wallet from the inside breast pocket, and handed him a two hundred Swiss francs bill, "thanks for your help. What's the cost of a ticket?"

The conductor opened his mouth, said nothing at first, then regained his composure. "This is a second class car, not a sleeping car. I believe all sleeping cars are sold out."

"That's fine. How much for a seat?"

"Two hundred and fifty francs." Francis paid the man, a ticket was handed back.

"There are open seats by the entrance."

"Thanks," Francis replied and went into the car.

Francis wiped his brow with the back of his hand. He was drenched in sweat from the run and the adrenaline rush. He felt hot in the leather jacket, but dared not take it off. He looked down the dimly lit car; nobody was even remotely interested in him. The car seemed full of people in their late teens or early twenties. A student trip, perhaps?

He chose an aisle seat, sat down, and shoved his backpack under the seat in front of him. Thank goodness this wasn't an old train. The seats had somewhat comfortable back and headrests, and they tilted back significantly farther than coach airplane seats. A young man sitting across the aisle greeted him before turning his face away to look out the window. The city lights faded in the distance.

Francis leaned his seat as far back as it went and stretched his legs in front of him, looping his left leg through the backpack's shoulder strap a couple of times. He pondered his escape. He had surely injured the man at the station. Francis doubted, however, that Fakhri or his men would report him to the authorities. They'd have too many questions to answer.

Francis closed his eyes and willed himself to sleep. For the time being he was out of Zurich, in one piece, and out of danger.

CHAPTER **10**

Zurich

"Imbecile!" Fakhri shouted, backhanding Baghel's face.

"That was the last train out of Zurich tonight," Malik informed. "He's going to Vienna."

"Get out of my sight, you son of a syphilitic whore," Fakhri growled. Baghel rubbed his jaw, got up and left the room.

The group was at a safe house by the Zurich airport, rented to Malik for over two years now. Malik was the lead Rebirth Alliance operative in Zurich. Fakhri led Malik to the large table in the living room. They sat down. Malik poured coffee for both of them.

"The train arrives in Vienna at eight-thirty in the morning tomorrow," Malik explained. "The first flight to Vienna is at seven-thirty."

"Why Vienna, Malik?"

"It was the last train out. He probably figured we'd be watching the airport, as we did."

"Your instincts are probably right," Fakhri said, almost to himself.

"I'd imagine that Montagnet is just improvising at this point. They couldn't have foreseen us taking the CIA pig out."

"Agreed. We should try intercepting him before he gets to Vienna and summon help."

"I think you can wait until he gets there. He might get off the train anywhere between here and there. I do think that is his final destination, though."

"Why is that?"

"If Montagnet is a CIA agent he's more likely to find help in a large city like Vienna. The U.S. embassy has a chief of station there. Also, remember what Wright said during the interrogation. Montagnet is not an officer, nor is he associated with the Agency directly. All they want from him is the documents he stole from you."

"We must intercept him before he hands them over then. Montagnet is a dangerous dog."

"That's my point, Colonel," Malik insisted. "Montagnet's liaison was Stan Wright. He probably doesn't know who to contact at the embassy yet. We can keep the embassy under surveillance. Other brothers from the Alliance will assist in catching him. Montagnet will need some time to identify himself to the local spooks before they bring him in. We'll catch him during that time."

Frakhri drank the rest of his coffee and stared at the bottom of the cup. Vienna. "I think you're right, Malik."

"Go to sleep, Colonel. I will make sure that our brothers expect you first thing in the morning. You will present our case to the Alliance no later than nine o'clock."

"Good night, then," Fakhri said.

Vienna

Fakhri had never been to the Austrian capital. The ride from the airport to the mosque felt too long. He admitted it was a beautiful city but the people seemed arrogant and rude.

Sheik Dogukan Yabuz was the Turkish leader of the local Rebirth Alliance cell. He led a virtuous public life as a prominent religious leader of the thriving Turkish population of Vienna. Yabuz and Fakhri had once trained together in Libya, in the early 1990's.

Fakhri arrived at the mosque. A young man in traditional garb met him. Fakhri removed his shoes, placed the soles against one another, and handed them to the young man for safekeeping. He was led to a room in the back of the building.

"The peace of Allah be with you," Yabuz greeted Fakhri upon entering his chambers.

"And with you," Fakhri replied, grasping Yabuz's right hand with his, left hand on Yabuz's right shoulder, and exchanging a kiss on each cheek.

"Please sit down," Yabuz pointed at some plush cushions on the carpeted floor of his chamber. "Malik informed me of your plight, Colonel."

"Malik is efficient," Fakhri said, sitting on a cushion, without crossing his legs, both feet firmly planted on the floor.

"Do you have a photograph of the man we're after?"

"Unfortunately I don't," Fakhri said. "We had no time for that. He is a sly one. He's managed to shake my men twice."

"And we shall not let that happen again, Colonel. What do you need from us?"

"Round the clock surveillance teams at the American embassy. All other ground troops must be on the lookout for this man. Montagnet is a dangerous terrorist and agitator. He must be captured and the documents he carries recovered."

"And they shall, Colonel."

"I also need a small team to work with me. Arabic speakers, preferably. I understand most of your team is Turkish."

"An Egyptian and two Pakistani men already asked to serve under your command, Colonel."

"Professionals?"

"You will find no better men."

"Can you procure weapons?"

"We have a wide range of side arms available. We are partial to GLOCK pistols, being Austrian made and extremely reliable. We can provide Czech or German weapons if you prefer."

"The GLOCKs will be fine, with plenty of ammunition," Fakhri said. "Dogukan, it's extremely important that this matter be addressed swiftly but quietly. I prefer if Montagnet dies, but there must be no witnesses, no flashy killings, no explosions. Our cause will gain no political advantage from a spectacular kill. Recovering the documents is the priority."

"I understand. I will convey your instructions."

Frakhri looked at his watch. "It's just after nine in the morning. Montagnet is already somewhere in the city. Malik provided his description. Find him. There is no time to lose."

Onan Baris' day had a wonderful start. His wife had made a delicious breakfast commemorating their first marriage anniversary. She hinted that other celebrations would follow that evening. He was smiling when he sat at his desk. The sky was clear above the city. The view from his seventh floor office was breathtaking. It would be a great day.

The phone rang.

"Baris," he answered.

"The peace of Allah be with you," said a male voice in Turkish.

Onan straightened up. "Yes?"

"We have a mission to accomplish, my friend. Your skills are required today."

"I understand," he replied formally. He had finally been called to action. He would have to cancel the plans with his wife that night. He opened his notebook and readied to take notes. "How may I assist?"

He was dreaming of a beach with impossible blue skies and beautiful sirens swimming in the ocean. There was a sailboat in the distance, seagulls and pelicans flew overhead. He knew it was a dream because the scene was so crisp and perfect. Nothing in real life was quite like that.

A golden crab walked sideways in front of him. He studied it carefully, engrossed in its beauty. Then the crab's shell exploded in a million sparkling pieces.

Zeki opened his eyes. The phone was ringing. Probably a wrong number or a salesman. He looked at the alarm clock by his bed. It was not even ten o'clock in the morning! He drove his taxi from four in the afternoon to four in the morning. He hated being awakened so early, especially in a morning after driving very few fares. Noon was more to his liking, one o'clock in the afternoon better.

"*Ja*," he answered the phone, expecting a German speaking sales pitch.

"The peace of Allah be with you," the voice said in Turkish.

Zeki sprang from the bed. "And with you," he replied, rubbing his eyes with his free hand.

"Your eyes and ears are wanted."

"They are yours day and night."

"An infidel has caused great problems for us and must be punished. He is on the loose in the city."

"You honor me with your request," Zeki replied. "I shall help you catch him."

"Colonel!" Rafik called. "They found him!"

It was late afternoon. Fakhri had spent the day briefing his team and readying them to move in when the time came. There had been no contacts at the American embassy or the train stations. They assumed that Montagnet was still in Vienna. The gamble was about to pay off.

"Where is he?" Fakhri demanded.

"We aren't sure of his current exact location," Rafik explained. "He was first spotted this morning leaving the area around the Opera on foot. Unfortunately our contact was in no position to follow, and summoning resources took too long."

"Who's the contact?"

"A Turkish woman named Afet. She manages the room cleaning crews at a downtown hotel. She spotted the mark this morning, when he checked in without a reservation. She knew nothing of our search at the time. She only noted this man's arrival because he was checking in too early and he was the only one checking in at that time other than a floor full of conventioneers."

"Is he at the hotel right now?"

"No, he came back and left again. During his second visit she identified him. She's rescheduled herself for the evening shift so she can keep an eye on him."

"Promote this woman. She sounds resourceful."

"Afet will personally turn his bed this evening so she can confirm his presence. His luggage, consisting of a small backpack, is still in the room. The documents you're looking for weren't in it."

"I didn't think Montagnet is that carefree," Fakhri said. "Rafik, I want ten armed men at or around that hotel at all times. Get cars for you, me and for the rest of your team. I want to be there when we close in on him. Montagnet will not get away alive this time."

D-25

CHAPTER 11

Vienna

"What a beautiful place!" Varenka exclaimed out loud. She had asked the taxi driver to take the long route to the hotel. It was barely nine o'clock in the morning; they were bound to fight the traffic anyway so she might as well enjoy the long ride. She'd heard that Vienna was nice, but nothing she'd ever seen—including Saint Petersburg and Kiev— prepared her for the majestic architecture of this city.

"How long will you stay?" the driver asked. He was an immigrant. He spoke Russian with typical Ukrainian inflections.

"Four days. I'll be trapped in meetings and seminars for the first three, though. What is this?" There was a beautiful palace on their right, overlooking a long, fabulously kept garden. They were driving downhill behind a red trolley car, and she caught glimpses of the palace through the gates along the wall. The garden must be at least 500 yards long.

"That's the Belvedere," he explained. "They've got a very large art collection, and a rich history. Prince Eugen built the palace, but he never lived in it. He thought it too ostentatious. He lived at the complex at the other end of the garden."

"Amazing."

"Did you know that the armistice for the Great War was signed there?"

"No, I didn't," Varenka replied, trying to remember her history lessons.

"Leave some free time to visit the Belvedere. There's a whole gallery on the Upper Belvedere devoted to Gustav Klimt that you must see. There are other works by artists like Schiele and Oskar Kokoschka."

"I don't know if I'll have time," she replied, already wishing she could stay longer. She wondered if Klimt's The Kiss, one of her favorite paintings, was on display there. She would have to find out. If so, she'd sneak out to see it. "Thanks for the tip."

"You must visit the Volksmuseum," the driver insisted enthusiastically. "And the Rathaus. And Saint Stephan's Cathedral is within walking distance of your hotel."

"Seems like I must spend a month here to see everything you mentioned," Varenka said. "Unfortunately I must get back home soon. Too much work."

Varenka looked out the window. It was a cloudy day. At least it wasn't cold. They were driving by a park, it's name written on a plate. Reading the Roman characters was a bit difficult. S-t-a-d-t-p-a-r-k—? Western visitors must have the same problem reading Cyrillic when they visit Moscow, she mused.

Moscow... lots of work pending. She sighed.

She had not heard from Sattar since their passionate interlude two nights ago. He had left for Switzerland only the day before and was probably back in Moscow already. At least he could have called. She missed him. If he made it to Vienna, perhaps they'd go to the Belvedere together. They were both too busy; a little R&R would do wonders for them. She would love to walk the Belvedere gardens hand in hand with him.

Varenka would call her office after checking in. She had to keep Misha and Vladimir on a short leash or their work slacked. She also had to check if Sattar had produced the remaining documentation they needed to complete the project. The pressure made for very hectic schedules, and Sattar and Anatoly Petrovich were adamant about finishing on time.

The taxi drove by an imposing building taking a whole block.

"What is this? A theater?" Varenka asked.

"This is the Opera. Your hotel is right behind it."

The taxi went around the building and stopped in front of a beautiful façade. She opened her purse and searched for the fare due, leafing through the unfamiliar bills of various colors and denominations. A uniformed porter opened her door and courteously helped her out after she paid the driver. A red clad bellboy rushed to get her medium-sized suitcase and garment bag from the boot.

Varenka looked at the magnificent entrance before going in, admiring the flags of Austria, the EU, England, Germany, Japan, and the United States flying above the red awnings. The four-story building reflected what she'd labeled traditional Viennese style. She was glad Kuryakin had insisted in her staying there for the conference, even though it was significantly costlier than other accommodations. It was a nice perk of her job. She entered the hotel.

The entrance hall was cozy, with wood paneling and a rich red carpet with an intricate gold pattern covering every inch of the floor. A professional and well dressed hostess met a couple at the entrance to the small café on her left and led them to their breakfast table. The aroma of coffee teased her nose as she walked to the front desk on the far right. Three people waited their turn before the single clerk. The bellboy approached and gave her a luggage claim ticket after saying something in German.

This was one of the most luxurious places Varenka had ever seen in her life. It would be like staying in a palace. She felt a little giddy.

Varenka looked around while she waited. There was a board announcing the day's events in German, English, and French. She spoke what she called "school English", and she had considerable difficulty listening to and conversing in the language, but she could read it well enough. *Complex Systems: Control and Modeling Problems* was the conference topic. The first session, Varenka noted, would begin at ten thirty and was titled *Information Interaction Models in Control Systems* and would be held in the hotel's Marble Room. She had a bit over an hour for freshening up, eat some breakfast, find the Marble Room, and register for the conference.

A second clerk came on duty, the two people in front of her were serviced. She'd be checked-in shortly.

Two men and a woman came out of the small lift beyond the registration desk. She was surprised that the hotel, clearly built over a hundred years ago, and with only four floors, had a lift. Russian building codes didn't require one on buildings with fewer than eight floors.

The man ahead of her finished his transaction. It was her turn with the clerk.

"Good morning madam, may I help you?" he asked in English.

"Yes, thank you," Varenka replied, approaching him. "I have reservation."

"Surname?"

"Ulyanova, Varvara."

"How do you spell that?"

"Er, slow, please?"

"How do you spell that?" the man repeated.

She spelled her name for him.

"May I have your card and passport?"

"Ah, excuse one moment," Varenka said, not sure about what he'd asked. *Passport* she understood. She searched her purse for her electronic pocket translator. She found it before handing him her passport.

"Can you write?" she said, offering the translator to the man.

"*Zdrastye*," the customer with the other clerk turned to her and spoke in Russian. His voice was rich but soft, self-confident. "Hello, perhaps I can be of assistance. He wants your credit card for room charges."

"Of course," she smiled at the man, a bit surprised. "Thank you." She handed her Sberbank Visa to the clerk.

The man removed his black sunglasses. His green eyes, set under straight eyebrows and above a longish, broken nose, reflected a playful, flirtatious quality when he returned her gaze. His mouth was parted in a friendly smile. His chin showed a day's stubble. He might have traveled all night to get here. He was unshaven but did not look scruffy. He dressed in leather and combat boots but his clothes looked of good quality. The man held himself still, yet he seemed to radiate a strong, almost threatening energy all around him. He was a man with a purpose. How old was he? Somewhere in his thirties, she guessed. It was hard to guess.

The clerk spoke, the man translated. "Do you have any luggage?"

"Yes; here," she said, handing her luggage tag. The clerk punched the number in the computer and returned the tag to her. "Thank you."

"You're in room 213," the clerk said, handing her a key attached to a heavy, ornate, brass key chain. "It's on the second floor."

The man next to her was done checking in as well. They walked together to the lift. He was comfortably taller than her, though not as tall as Sattar.

"Are you attending the conference?" Varenka asked.

"No, but I'm here on business," the man said, pushing the button to recall the lift. "I wish I could; it sounds interesting. I've done some work in mission critical, real time control systems. Mostly network control rooms. Automated factories, industrial robots. That kind of thing."

"Thanks for giving me a hand back there," she said when the lift arrived, "Mr., er, what's your name?"

"Francis," he offered his hand. "And you are?"

"Ulyanova, doctor Varvara Dmitrievna Ulyanova," she said, shaking his hand. He had a warm, firm grip.

They entered the lift. Both showed their keys to the liveried lift operator, who closed the door.

"*Varvara Krasna, Dlinnaya Kosa*," Francis said. "*The Beautiful Varvara of the Long Braid.*"

That caught her by surprise. "Do you know that fairy tale?"

"Of course. The movie wasn't that good, but the story was sweet. Anyway, I've always liked your name; it's very romantic," he smiled. Francis' voice had a curious lilt. His Russian was lightly accented—she couldn't place where he was from. His accent didn't sound Russian or American, yet he had spoken English fluently. "Didn't Tolstoy also write a character named Varvara in *War and Peace*?"

Varenka felt herself blush. "She was in Anna Karenina."

"Yes, I remember now. She inspired Kitty to be less selfish and then married Koznyshev, right?"

"Right," Varenka smiled.

The lift arrived at her floor.

"It was a pleasure meeting you, Varvara Dmitrievna. Have a great conference."

The door opened. Varenka stepped out and turned to look at Francis.

"The pleasure was mine, Francis; perhaps we'll meet again."

Francis gave her a somewhat longing smile and waved a casual good-bye as the lift door closed. Varenka turned to her right and walked down the long corridor searching for her room, feeling flattered and a bit intrigued. Who was this dangerous looking foreigner with knowledge of obscure characters in Russian literature, who had a twinkle in his eye, and who spoke with a soft, indefinite accent?

CHAPTER **12**

Vigilance. Francis reminded himself to stay alert. He found Dr. Ulyanova very attractive but this was no time for playing. She did have a beautiful name, and the way she pronounced his—*Friend-sees*—was very alluring. He caught a final glimpse of her slim figure treading down the corridor before the elevator doors closed. He knew he would remember her deep blue eyes for a long time, and he wondered what it would be like to kiss her pink lips. He sighed. He had not been romantically involved for a long time. On the other hand, fantasizing about a woman he'd probably never see again wasn't worth it.

The elevator stopped on the third floor, the doors opened. Francis thanked the operator and walked to his room. He found it, number 318, on his left. He unlocked the room, pleased that the hotel still used old-fashioned keys instead of magnetic cards. The latter would've shattered the illusion of going regally back in time.

The spacious room had a large window facing Philarmoniker Strasse and the Opera. His dainty room, like all others at the Sacher, was furnished with antiques. It was furnished with a small desk, a comfortable chair, an armoire. A painted portrait of an elegant woman, some forgotten Austrian bourgeois, dominated the wall above the desk. He opened the armoire. A TV had been ingeniously installed inside, with all its cables hidden from view. He was disappointed in the bed. He'd forgotten that requesting a single room normally resulted in getting a spacious one with a narrow, single bed.

Oh, well.

Francis took the backpack off and stripped. His neck felt stiff after the long train ride. The seat had looked much more comfortable than it had been. He went into the large bathroom at the far end of the room. It had a toilet and a bidet. The transition from the carpet to the bathroom's cold marble floor shocked him a bit. Probably a common occurrence. The hotel provided a white terrycloth robe that was "available for purchase at the front desk" and a pair of white complimentary slippers, both embroidered with a burgundy Sacher logo. He took the slippers out of the cellophane wrapper, put them on, and went to the room to get his toiletries from the backpack. He returned with a small, black wallet containing a can of shaving foam, a Gillette Mach 3 razor, and a sewing kit. He placed these items on the sink, poured some bubble gel (courtesy of the Sacher) in the bathtub, filled it up, and immersed to his neck in it after taking the slippers off.

What a night it had been. His body relaxed in the hot water. He rested his head against the wall, closed his eyes and began planning his next moves.

First, I need some quality rest, he thought. I can't function if I'm too sleep deprived. Didn't Napoleon say that fatigue had lost as many battles as a poor strategy?

Second, I must contact Adam Jones and figure out how the hell I'm getting out of here.

Fakhri and his thugs must know for sure that I'm in Vienna.

The realization sent a chill down Francis' spine.

I must outsmart them. I must be better than they are. If the way they ran things in Zurich is any indication, they must have a team here, perhaps one in every major European city. How can I turn that to my advantage? What would I do if I were Fakhri?

Francis stood up, drained the bathtub and opened the handheld shower. He sprayed himself with cold water, dried himself, then went to the sink and shaved. He put the terry cloth robe on.

What is this? He thought after sitting at the antique desk and taking the clamshell container from his backpack. A courtesy mini Sacher tort was placed on a small cardboard box atop the desk, with a note from the manager indicating that full size torts were sold downstairs. He gobbled the chocolate delicacy in two bites—it was delicious. He opened the container and took a microfiche out. He couldn't read any of the documents. The images were too small. Francis put it back in the container and closed it. He then produced one of his old twelve-inch Raider II knives from the backpack and unsheathed it. He took the container and the knife with him to the narrow bed, placed them under the pillow, and dialed the operator.

"May I help you?"

"Yes, I need a wake up call at eleven o'clock, in about two hours."

"Very well sir." The operator hung up.

Francis disrobed and got in bed. He lay on his side; his right hand griped the knife under the pillow. He closed his eyes, relishing the feel of the cool sheets against his naked skin. He fell asleep.

It took him a while but the old librarian finally understood him. Francis spoke no German and she spoke none of the languages he knew. It was a very funny situation. Finally he produced a microfiche slide and she understood what he wanted. She handed him a form, where he filled in his name. She completed the rest and asked him to sign it. Francis scribbled an unreadable squiggle and she led him to a back room.

He was at the Osterreichisches Staatsarchive on Nottendorfer Gasse. The concierge at the Sacher had recommended him to go there. The archive had a large collection of periodicals, many stored on microfiche.

The librarian led him to a GBC microfiche reader at the far end of the library, and mimed that he only had a half hour by pointing at the wall clock. He smiled, muttered "*Danke*," and got to work.

The clamshell container had been concealed under his leather jacket, tucked behind him in his waistband. He took it out, sat down, powered the microfiche reader on, chose a slide, and placed it in the reader.

There were 32 pages per slide, twenty-three slides total. The pages on the first slide were an eclectic collection of old drawings, typewritten pages, and handwritten documents. The handwritten ones caught Francis' attention because some of them were written in Cyrillic, but the language wasn't Russian, though it was Slavic. The handwriting was small and hard to read. He moved over to a different page.

The page was an old engineering diagram for an electrical circuit. It described a monophase transformer, with varying inductance coils in an array that Francis had never seen before. He was familiar with electrical machines like motors and transformers, having been required to study them for getting his computer engineering degree, but this didn't look like anything he'd seen before. He wasn't sure, but the handwritten notes and the formulas appeared to describe a direct current circuit; who would need a direct current transformer? That didn't sound right. An electrical engineer would probably make more sense of this. He moved on.

Some of the typewritten pages were nothing more than lists of materials: cables, wiring, pipes, wood, copper plates, and so on. Clearly there wasn't anything really interesting here. Or was there? What did Fakhri want with all this? Perhaps the real information was steganographically hidden in the collection of documents as a whole, rather than in the pages themselves. He would have to analyze them all before he could make sense of them. That was Jones' job anyway.

Francis turned the machine off and replaced the microfiche slide in the clamshell container. He inspected the reader and found what he was looking for: a sticker with the vendor's name, address, and phone number. He wrote them down, gathered his stuff, thanked the librarian, and left.

"So how much would it cost?" Francis asked the image conversion employee. He was at an office in the Oberdöbling neighborhood. It had taken him well over an hour to get here because he wanted to be sure that nobody was tailing him.

"It will be expensive, particularly if you want the conversion done today."

"I certainly do. I also want the data stored on a 128 megabyte memory card, not on CD-ROM."

"That shouldn't be a problem, herr Montagnet. Do you have the memory card with you?"

"I do," he said, handing the employee a plastic bag. He'd purchased a color handheld computer running the Palm OS, its traveling kit, a modem, and two compatible memory cards for it. He could carry the handheld in his shirt pocket. Each memory card was about as thick as a coin and had a surface of a bit over a square centimeter. "There are about seven hundred and fifty pages in there. Will they fit?"

"Let me check," the employee clicked some numbers in a desk calculator before answering. "Are there lots of graphics pages?"

"I'm not sure."

"They might fit, if there aren't too many graphics. It's all black and white anyway. Normally we'd fit about three thousand black and white text pages in that amount of memory."

"Do your best."

"We close every day at five thirty. Your documents should be done an hour before then. And we need a deposit."

Francis paid the man and got a receipt. He had things to do elsewhere.

. . .

"It's me, Mr. Lange," Francis said. "I'm glad I caught you so early in the morning, your time."

"I presume you made it to Vienna?"

"Yes, I'm here. I've been running around all day." He'd had lunch at Hawelka, a pub he loved on Dorotheergasse, owned by an old Polish family. The place had a lot of character and wasn't frequented by the tourists; the patrons were mostly local artists and bohemians. He had headed back to the hotel afterward to make this call.

"Where are you?"

"I'm in my room at the Sacher hotel."

"Fancy," Jones sounded a bit edgy. "What room number and under what name?"

"318, Richard Bishop," Francis said.

"Good," Jones replied. "We'll be ready to pick you up at eight o'clock this evening, your local time. Be ready to move."

"I will," Francis said. "Why can't I go to the main office in Vienna?" He was talking about the American embassy on Boltzmanngasse.

"Because this deal was worked out from headquarters. The local branch wouldn't be able to help you. Our reps will pick you up and escort you directly to an airplane back here. You'll get VIP treatment," Jones probably meant he'd be traveling under diplomatic cover, but unknown to the embassy and CIA staff. Plausible deniability.

"Have I met the guys coming for me?"

"No, you haven't. They're Vince and Paul. They'll be easy to recognize. They'll identify themselves to you properly, of course."

"So be it, Mr. Lange," Francis said. "I'm looking forward to closing this deal as soon as possible. There is too much competition."

"I understand. I'll see you first thing tomorrow morning, when you get to my office."

"'Bye then."

Francis hung up. He looked at his watch. It was past three in the afternoon. Time for him to pick up the converted documents. He smiled on his way out the room, noticing that his bed had been made in his absence. He just loved staying in this place.

. . .

Afet walked the third floor for the seventh time since noon. It was a few minutes past seven thirty in the evening and she was tired and grumpy after working two straight shifts. Sheik Yavuz had praised her effort. She wouldn't let him or the Rebirth Alliance down.

Afet didn't know anything about this man other than his name, Montagnet. Somehow he was tied to the injustices in the Middle East, the murders of innocents, the discrimination against her people in Austria, or the exploitation of Muslim men and women worldwide. Her hatred for such people ran deep, her devotion to Rebirth and to Sheik Yavuz guided her actions.

She went for the fifth time to room 318. She knocked on the door softly.

"Who is it?" a muffled voice said in English from within. Finally!

"Good evening, sir," she replied, "I'm here to turn your bed."

Afet saw the man's shadow under the door. He peered at her through the peephole, making sure she was whom she claimed. The door opened.

"Good evening," the man named Montagnet greeted, smiling at her. "Thanks for coming."

He went back to the desk, where he had a few items scattered on top. She noticed three knives in their sheaths, a few papers, his key. She closed the curtains, then went to the bed and readied it for him. She smiled inwardly. He'd probably never sleep on this bed again. She gave a cursory inspection to the bathroom and headed for the door. He thanked her before the door shut.

Afet pushed her cart to the service elevator at the far end of the corridor. She checked for other people on the deserted floor, found no one, and took her mobile phone from her apron. She dialed a number.

"May the peace of Allah be with you," a voice she didn't recognize answered.

"And with you," she replied. "This is Afet. The man Montagnet is in his room right now. I have visual confirmation, repeat, I have visual confirmation."

"Allah will bestow you with a long life, Afet," said the voice. "Remain on site and keep the mark under surveillance. The team shall be ready to move in just a few minutes."

The phone line clicked dead. Afet busied herself at an area between the escalators and the guests' elevator. Montagnet couldn't leave the floor without passing her.

CHAPTER **13**

Twilight. The sky was a deep velvet purple; a few stars peered through the occasional holes in the clouds hovering over the city. Francis was looking out the window, feeling increasingly anxious. It was almost eight, the exfiltration team had not arrived yet. He watched the elegantly dressed men and women leaving the hotel for dinner or heading to the casinos or the opera. He longed to have their carefree attitude. He would shortly be out of danger and leaving Vienna.

All his stuff was packed except for the clamshell container, which he would hand over to Paul and Vince as soon as they showed up. He didn't want the responsibility any longer. He had strapped his three sheathed daggers to each arm and to his right leg.

A bell in the distance tolled eight o'clock.

The phone rang, startling him. Dammit, calm down! He admonished himself.

"Yes?" he answered.

"Francis, this is Paul," a man's voice with a Texan accent said. "We're in the building. Get ready for evac."

"Identify yourself."

"I'm a cherubim sent by your guardian angel." That was all Francis needed to know. This guy had to be legit.

"Hurry up."

Francis hung up the phone, took his jacket from the chair and put it on, leaving the zippers on the sleeves open for easier access to the daggers. He paced back and forth, the few minutes until the rap against the door felt like ages. He looked through the peephole. A square jawed blonde guy with a crew cut was there. He stepped next to the door.

"Who is it?"

"It's Paul."

He grabbed the clamshell container and opened the door.

"Let's move," Francis said, shaking hands with Paul.

"Is that the item?" Paul pointed at the container as they walked toward the elevator and the door to Francis' room shut closed.

"Yes, this is it. Aw, damn," Francis said, turning around. "Let me get my backpack. I'll—"

He never completed the sentence.

Two Mediterranean looking men rushed down the corridor toward them, aiming their silenced guns at Francis and Paul. One of them fired. The slug penetrated the back of Paul's skull, splattering his brains out through a fist-sized hole on his forehead.

Move!

Francis dashed away from the pursuers, zigzagging in the confined corridor. It was a desperate race toward the emergency exit. He shoved the clamshell container in his waistband.

"Run for cover!" he yelled at the housekeeping lady who'd turned down his bed earlier as he approached her by the stairwell.

She didn't move.

Francis dodged her, two slugs crashed against the elevator door in front of him. Just two more meters and...

...and the bitch tripped him!

Francis rolled toward the stairs, narrowly avoiding her when she vaulted at him. She landed next to him. Both scrambled to their feet, the two men were closing fast. Francis was the first to get up and managed to push kick her face, knocking her arse-first against the wall. Three more shots followed.

Move!

Francis ran down the steps, struggling to zip up the front of the form fitting leather jacket. That would help hold the container in place. The men were approaching fast, their footsteps were louder. He got to the second floor, jumped over the banister to the next flight of stairs, gaining a precious few extra meters between him and his pursuers.

What now?

Francis reached the first floor. He opened the emergency exit door, ready to vault past the registration desk and to the waiting car outside, where Vince would take him to safety.

Damn!

He'd forgotten this was a European building. The first floor was a *lodging* floor. The registration desk and main entrance were on the *ground* floor.

He startled two more men guarding the stairwell and elevator. They sprung to chase after him.

I have four on my tail now, dammit!

Francis slammed the door shut, catching one of the men's arms against the frame. He dropped his pistol.

Excellent!

Francis snatched the silenced gun, a GLOCK, and fired blindly through the door. The other pursuers' steps clattered closer, a painful grunt came through the closed door.

I nailed at least one of them!

He barely had time to dash down the remaining flight of stairs to the ground floor before four shots tore through the door, missing him by inches.

Just a few more steps.

He jumped over the last few steps, landing next to the door. He tore it open and ran to the main entrance. He realized he didn't know what Vince looked like, but he guessed he'd have a car waiting.

He had not reached the front desk when the tall shape of Sattar Fakhri blocked that escape route.

They were expecting me!

Francis raised his gun, firing wildly at Fakhri, who ducked for cover. He missed! He ran in the opposite direction. If he remembered correctly, there was another exit to the pedestrian only Kärntner Strasse. He was running wildly when the emergency stairwell door burst open behind him and the two thugs from the third floor joined the chase.

Madness!

Francis felt the fury of the cornered animal swelling within him when he turned at the T intersection and saw a man guarding the glass door exit. He raised his gun, steadying his aim, and fired two shots, catching the man's body. The target crumpled to the floor. Another man, standing beyond the glass door, saw him and joined the chase.

Francis wasn't sure how many bullets the magazine held. There was an aisle leading in the opposite direction from the door. He ran away from the new attacker, fired almost blindly when he reached the intersection, catching the two pursuers in the front. Excellent! He wasn't sure but he thought he'd caught one in the chest and the other one in the head. The quasi-pointblank impacts sent both men flying in Fakhri's way.

I can't run away forever.

There were doors and side aisles in his way, but most of them seemed to be dead ends. The other aisle, leading to the small bistro by the main entrance, was at the end of this aisle. He turned left and sprinted once more, his gun ready.

Think.

He stopped in his tracks. Footsteps! One man was in pursuit. *Only* one. He turned around and ran back. He turned right and fired the gun three times. Only the first shot left the muzzle. The other two trigger squeezes produced nothing. He dropped the gun behind a potted plant.

The bullet caught his pursuer in the chest and he was stumbling backward. Francis jammed his shoulder against him hard, knocking him to the ground, and kept running toward the side exit. He spotted two men across the street, watching the hotel. That wasn't a way out.

Screams!

Someone was coming down the aisle; a woman working at the hotel. Francis turned into the aisle toward the emergency stairs, skipping over the fallen bodies and past the hysterical woman.

Men and women came running from the lobby. Pandemonium exploded.

"Help!" Francis yelled after catching his breath. "Someone's shooting people!"

More screams.

Francis knew they were waiting for him in the lobby. He ran toward the emergency stairs and yanked the door open. He unsheathed the dagger from his left forearm and held it in his right hand with the blade along his wrist. He ran upstairs. He had to recover his backpack and the goodies inside it. He was otherwise defenseless.

There has to be a way out!

He climbed the steps two and three at the time, his body fueled by adrenaline and fear. A fire alarm wailed. Someone had finally decided to bring some help. Great! The chaos would work to his advantage, if he played his cards right.

Francis was about reach the second floor door when it swung open. A number of guests rushed his way, most of them dressed in evening clothes. He peered over their heads and saw none of Fakhri's thugs. They'd probably gone to the first floor to assist in the pursuit.

That face!

Dr. Varvara Ulyanova came through the door, behind two men and a woman. She was by herself. Francis shoved the knife up his right sleeve.

"Dr. Ulyanova!" He called.

"Francis! What's happening?"

"I don't know," Francis lied. "A fire, I think. Dr. Ulyanova, I *need* your help."

"What?"

"A man is waiting for me outside, an American. He'll be in a car somewhere by the main entrance. Please go to him and tell him I'll be down in a minute. It's very important. He *must* wait for me."

"I... I can't..."

"Please," he begged. Every second counted. "I must retrieve my papers from my room, because if I lose them I'll be ruined. *Please!*"

She studied him for what seemed like an eternity.

I must look deranged, he thought, with my sweaty face and my eyes wild with excitement.

"Please," he insisted once more. "My life depends on it. Just tell him to wait for me."

"Is this something illegal?" she asked, making her way down the stairs.

"Of course not. But I'm heading upstairs and, if I lose those documents, I'll be ruined! The sirens, the fire may scare my driver off. You must catch him before he leaves!"

"Hurry up then," she said, rushing downstairs as he headed up.

Just a few more seconds and...

Francis bust through the door. The housekeeping lady was standing up, wiping a bloody nose, talking on a mobile phone in a foreign language and leaning against her cleaning cart. She shouted excitedly into the phone when she saw him, then grabbed a long metallic handle for a broom of some sort. She swung it at him. Francis ducked.

The woman jumped to fighting stance, wielding the broom handle expertly. Kendo training, perhaps. Francis instinctively jolted to his fighting stance, both fists up, left leg forward. The woman attacked, wielding the handle like a *shinai*, or Kendo sword. The handle gave her precious reach, and Francis could do nothing but avoid her rabid attack.

Kick!

Francis tried kicking the improvised sword off her hands. He missed. She spun around and stabbed forward with the handle. Francis half stepped back and parried the handle with his right forearm, deflecting the blow to his throat. She knocked the dagger out of his hand! The woman had anticipated the move and counterattacked, swinging the handle diagonally, aiming for his head. He put his arm up, catching the blow with his armored forearm and shoulder. The pads within the jacket absorbed the impact painlessly. Francis stepped in with his left leg at a forty-five-degree angle with respect to the woman's body. He turned his hips, throwing a roundhouse kick at her mid section. He caught her abdomen, knocking her breath out. Francis pulled his right leg back and immediately swung another kick, this time aiming for her head. His shin crashed against her neck, the woman fell unconscious next to Paul, her uniform soaked in Paul's blood. Another goon came running at him from the far end of the corridor.

I won't make it to my room. Damn!

He grabbed the broom handle and his knife from the floor, turned around and ran to the emergency stairs. He pulled the door closed behind him and jammed the door by sliding the long metallic rod through door handle and against the wall. The thug fruitlessly struggled to open the door. Nobody was coming this way.

Run!

Francis dashed down the stairs. He could hear the wailing emergency vehicles pulling in front of the hotel. Maybe there would be enough chaos on the ground floor to allow his escape.

Varenka reached the ground floor. The alarms screeched incessantly, people looked anguished as they scrambled for the exit. Two hotel employees were by the emergency stairs, politely but firmly directing people toward the main exit. A large crowd from the two restaurants flanking the entrance was herded out. She joined the human flow.

It probably wasn't a fire, she reasoned. The sprinklers weren't on. There was no smell of smoke. It had to be something else.

Varenka noted a hysterical woman wailing and stammering to a police officer who took copious notes as she followed the crowd outside.

Two police cars were parked by the entrance, other emergency vehicles approached from the distance, judging by the increasingly loud sirens. A police officer began waving the taxis, a couple of horse buggies for the tourists, and the few cars away. Varenka looked around for signs of Francis' driver. The cars pulled away from hotel. She didn't have a chance to talk to the drivers.

Varenka scanned the crowd for signs of Francis when her heart skipped a beat.

Was that Sattar?

Yes! Sattar was by the entrance, anxiously scanning the crowd. He was several meters away to her left, oblivious to her. He'd come to Vienna! She smiled. He *did* care for her. She figured Sattar was looking for her, her face lost in the sea of anguished mugs.

"Sattar! Over here!" she waved at him. He didn't hear her over the din. He was absorbed searching past the guards and into the lobby.

"Sattar!" she called again.

At least fifteen more people, mostly hotel employees, erupted from within the hotel. She could see Francis among them, though he was slouching for some reason. She started to make her way toward Sattar and called him again. Poor man, he looked so anxious! Sattar was probably worried about her! She must let him know she was fine.

"Dr. Ulyanova?" Francis called, from her right.

"Yes, Francis? Sorry, I couldn't find the person you asked me to—" she apologized.

"Thanks anyway," he cut her off, disappointed. "I gotta run," he said, rudely turning away from her. This man was not *kulturny*. At least he wasn't acting very civilized.

"You're welcome—" she began to speak.

"Varenka!" the yell cracked through the air like thunder. Sattar's voice!

She smiled and turned to face him. He was plowing his way through the crowd. She expected relief in his eyes at finding her; instead, a violent hatred burnt in the orbs, which were focused not on her but on Francis.

"Do you know that bastard?" Francis asked her incredulous.

"What?" she asked, suddenly afraid and confused.

"That man wants to kill me! Come!"

Francis grabbed her arm and roughly pulled her toward him. She tripped on her high heels.

"*Otpustyi menya!*" she screamed, "Let go of me!" He released her.

Fakhri produced a gun and aimed it at this crazy lunatic named Francis. Why? Why was Sattar wielding a gun?

Sattar fired two shots in succession, the bullets zoomed past her head like angry hornets. Varenka was almost in the line of fire, yet Fakhri didn't seem to care! What was going on?

The crowd was paralyzed for a few instants, unsure of what was happening, then almost everyone hugged the ground simultaneously. A police officer spotted Sattar brandishing his gun. Sattar yelled something back she couldn't understand and flashed what looked like a badge at him. He and the policeman started toward them. Sattar aimed his gun at them but screaming people running for cover blocked him.

"Get down, dammit!" Francis dragged her toward the curb, forcing her to crouch by him. A metallic, oblong box fell from the folds of Francis' clothes. He clawed at it like a drowning man to a lifesaver. A taxi was parked there. He yanked the door open and roughly pushed her inside. Another gunshot reverberated through the air.

Varenka was jammed between the floor of the car and the seat. Francis dove into the car and yelled something at the driver, throwing a wad of bills onto the passenger seat. The car shot forward, the open door banged shut with the momentum. She was terrified.

Francis sat behind the passenger's seat and helped her up.

"Are you crazy?" she screamed at him. "What do you think you're doing?"

"We need to talk!" Francis snapped. She straightened herself up. He grabbed her hand and twisted it down at the wrist.

It hurt!

"Why are you doing this to me?"

"Listen, doctor, I have nothing against you but you have to be honest with me. Are you one of them?"

"One of them *what*?"

Francis bent her wrist down further.

"I don't have time to fool around, doctor. You know Sattar Fakhri. He called your name! Did he send you after me?"

"That *hurts!* I don't know what you're talking about! Yes, I know him."

"He's been trying to kill me since yesterday!"

"What!?"

"Listen to me carefully, doctor," Francis' tone was threatening but he loosened the grip on her hand. "We're going to the American embassy. You'll be free to go after you drop me off. Afterward you can go to the authorities or to Fakhri and say anything you want about me. You can say I hurt you, or that I stole from you. I don't care. In the meantime, however, you'll behave like a good little girl or I'll break your arm. Is that clear?"

American embassy? Why was Francis acting like a maniac? "I... I don't understand. I... I helped you," she said.

"Did you really? Or were you there to lure me out in the open?"

He twisted her wrist, harder this time. She stifled a cry out of pride. Why did this man want to hurt her?

"Please, Francis, I don't know what you're talking about!"

He looked into her eyes. She was too afraid to think straight. "You'll do what I say until we get to the embassy."

"Yes! Don't hurt me!"

"Don't get any illusions about the driver assisting you. I know your English is terrible and he thinks you're hysterical after the shooting. Any doubts he might've had vanished with the money I gave him. Our friend here," Francis read the cab driver's ID attached to the dashboard, "Zeki, won't help you."

"I thought *you* were helping me when the shooting started!" Varenka cried, half scared, half angry.

Francis ignored her and turned to the driver. He spoke to him in English, articulating the words too quickly for her to understand. The door locks clicked shut. Francis glanced through the rear window, then back to her. He seemed satisfied.

"Dr. Ulyanova, I apologize if I'm wrong about you but my life is in danger. I don't know what that bastard Fakhri is to you, but you should probably stay away from him if you want to live," he placed the container on the seat between them. He continued. "I don't trust you. You're my hostage right now. No more games and no more drama, got it? Good. Now I want you to sit back and enjoy the ride."

Varenka turned her face away from him, looking out the window. A silent tear ran down her left cheek. She was frightened. What was going on? Why was Sattar trying to kill Francis?

CHAPTER **14**

Turmoil. Francis gazed at Varvara Ulyanova and the doubts crept into his mind again. She seemed genuinely scared and confused. Was she a Fakhri plant? What was she doing in Vienna? He didn't know what to believe. Was there a way for Fakhri and his thugs to anticipate he would be staying at the Sacher? Then again, Fakhri had called her by name...

They sat as far away from each other as they could in the confined space in the back of the taxi. Francis looked out his window. The evening traffic dwindled, there were almost no pedestrians on the street. He guessed they were heading south, though Francis didn't know the city well enough to be sure.

"How far is the embassy?" he asked the driver.

"Just a few more blocks, sir," the driver answered.

Francis looked out the rear window once more. Nobody seemed to be following them; there were hardly any cars on the streets.

The taxi circled around a park before noticeably slowing down. They turned right onto a dark, narrow, tree lined driveway.

Something is wrong, was Francis's last thought before the floodlights directed at the taxi blinded him. A chill ran up his spine.

"*Bozhe moi!*" Varvara screamed when the car stopped. "Oh my God!"

There were three cars, one in front of them and one on each side of the driveway among the trees. Their high beams shone onto them, a few silhouettes ran to the cab. He distinguished the shape of a couple of assault rifles against the piercing glare. They had short muzzles; possibly AK-102s.

Damn, he thought. Francis' eyes darted about, looking for a escape route. He glanced at their driver, who calmly powered the car off, got out, and mockingly opened Varvara's door. Francis barely had time to shove the clamshell container under the passenger seat before someone yanked his door open and a pair of hands roughly dragged him out. He saw from the corner of his eye that two more thugs were also pulling Varvara out of the car.

Four men surrounded Francis. One of them was much taller than everyone else. Francis recognized the man's contour. It was colonel Sattar Fakhri.

Oh shit, oh shit, oh shit, Francis thought, surrendering, placing his hands over his head, fingers intertwined, and with his legs slightly apart.

"Francis Montagnet," Fakhri said, his voice dripping a quiet rage threatening to explode at any instant. His face was obscured by the contrasting shadows. "Your luck ran out. Rafik," he turned to the man on his left, "pat him down."

The two men carrying the automatic rifles took positions at Francis' sides. Rafik was a short and stocky humorless man who went about his business briskly and efficiently. He patted Francis' neck, his back, his legs. He found the dagger attached to his right boot and removed it along with its sheath. He then opened the front zipper of the jacket and expertly ran his hands along Francis' torso and over his shoulders. He frowned when he felt the shoulder and back padding, then carefully probed those areas for concealed weapons. Rafik turned to Fakhri and said something in Arabic. Fakhri nodded and Rafik returned by his side.

Rafik overlooked my forearms!

Two men roughly pushed Ulyanova next to Montagnet. Black mascara streaks ran down the corners of her eyes, one of the men pinned her arms behind her back. She looked pale and petrified.

"What were you doing with this pig?" Fakhri demanded in Russian, approaching Ulyanova.

"Sattar...?" she cried. "You're here—what's going on?"

Fakhri's only response was a sharp slap across her face that sent her reeling to the ground.

"Why?" she asked after choking a sob.

"Leave her alone," Francis snapped. The man on his right hit his face with the stock of his rifle, knocking him to the ground. The whole right side of his face throbbed, particularly the cheekbone. Pure rage consumed Francis. He scrambled to his feet, ready to pounce on this bastard when the clicking noises of men cutting cartridges in their automatic weapons stopped him.

"You lying whore," Fakhri hissed, ignoring him. "I should have guessed that you were working for the Americans." He crouched next to her, harshly pulled her by her hair to face him. "That was the reason for your interest in me, wasn't it, bitch?"

"I don't know what you're talking about," Ulyanova sobbed. "Why are you doing this to me?"

"What were *you* doing with this," he pointed at Montagnet, "this piece of dog shit?"

"I just met him today!" Ulyanova cried. "He asked me to help him when the alarm at the hotel went off! Stop that!" she cried. Fakhri's hand squeezed her chin like a vise. "You're hurting me!"

Fakhri studied her for a few seconds, then let go of her. He said something to the men in Arabic. One of the men beside Francis pulled him roughly back on his feet. Fakhri approached him menacingly.

"You know damn well what I'm looking for," he said in English. "Where is it?"

"Let her go, motherfucker," Francis blurted. "I'm the one you want. She's telling the truth. I met her this morning."

"No, Montagnet, I can't afford that. We're too close to achieving our goal to risk having you or this bitch spoil it." He turned to Ulyanova and yelled in Russian, "I trusted you! Kuryakin trusted you!"

"Sattar, I don't understand. What are you doing? Why do you want to hurt me?"

"Cunt," Fakhri growled with disgust before spitting. The sputum hit the ground just inches from Ulyanova's dress. Ulyanova cowered away from it, her eyes wide with disbelief.

Francis realized that a new drama was unfolding before him. Fakhri was hurt, his *pride* was hurt. Ulyanova meant something to him. He was acting like a cuckold. That made him more dangerous to both of them.

"Leave her alone, Fakhri," Francis said softly but firmly. "You'll gain nothing from abusing her."

"You stay out of this!" Fakhri screamed enraged, pointing an accusing finger at him. Fakhri stepped closer to him, and Francis thought for a moment that Fakhri would poke his eye out. Francis held his breath, waiting for Fakhri's self control to return. The fury burning in his dark brown eyes dimmed. "Where are the documents, Montagnet?"

"I don't know," Francis insisted feebly.

Fakhri punched him in the gut. Francis barely had time to tighten his abdominal muscles. The punch hurt, but it wasn't so hard as to knock the breath out of him. Francis feigned more pain than he felt.

I've got to buy some time, find a way out!

"Ever since our new encounter yesterday I figured you'd be nothing but trouble," Fakhri said. "I never thought you'd cause me so many problems."

"Asshole," Francis hissed through clenched teeth.

Fakhri threw a right punch, this time hitting him on the left side of his face. Francis tensed but the men by his side quickly seized his arms and held him back.

"This isn't a game, Montagnet," Fakhri continued. "I want my documents. Now. I saw you drop and fetch the container before you got in the taxi."

"You must need glasses," Francis replied.

Fakhri stared at him hard for a few more seconds before turning to their driver. "You are Zeki, right? Go search the car. We're looking for a small metallic container, about the size of a book."

Zeki didn't respond; Francis heard his footsteps retreat, followed by the sound of the cab doors opening and closing behind him.

"The daring and lack of finesse shown by the American intelligence services never ceases to amaze me," Frakhri said. "You had a lot of gall mugging me at the Swiss bank."

"I'm glad I impressed you," Francis replied.

Fakhri's punch connected with his jaw. Francis saw stars, his head snapped back with the impact.

His jaw hurt like hell. He'd bitten the inside of his right cheek, a blood trickle tasted salty.

"You think you're funny?"

Careful now, Francis thought. I better keep my mouth shut. At least he's not abusing Ulyanova anymore.

The man named Zeki returned from the cab and handed the container to Fakhri after whispering something to him. Fakhri nodded and waved him away. The taxi driver got back in the car, fired the engine, and was gone in a few seconds.

Fakhri opened the container and counted the slides. He then produced a jeweler's magnifying glass from his coat pocket and checked three or four random slides from the set. He smiled. The documents set was complete.

"Well, Montagnet, your usefulness is at an end," Fakhri said, placing the container in his breast pocket.

"What about the woman?" Francis asked. His arms were getting numb after holding them for so long over his head.

"What about her?"

"Let her go. She had nothing to do with me. She spoke the truth."

Fakhri glanced at Ulyanova with disgust before answering in Russian. "I don't believe you. She isn't worth it anyway. She's a risk that must be eliminated."

"What...?" Ulyanova said, staring wide eyed at Fakhri.

"What harm does she represent to you? Look at her," Francis was about to point at Ulyanova with his left hand when the thug on that side pressed the muzzle of his gun against his ribs. Francis put the hand back above his head. "The woman is petrified. She isn't worth your trouble."

"She is the only person in the world outside our circle of trust who could actually figure out what these," Fakhri tapped the documents in his pocket, "are for. She may or may not be working with you; I don't care."

"Fakhri, you... are you going to kill me?"

Fakhri looked at her for a long time, then he turned to his henchman Rafik and barked a command in Arabic. The other men snapped to attention. Rafik headed for the car in front of them, jumped behind the wheel and turned the engine on.

"Good bye, Varvara Dmitrievna," Fakhri said before boarding Rafik's car as it pulled by the group. He slammed the door shut and nodded his head at the men guarding Francis and Ulyanova. The car went back to the main street, the engine roar faded away.

"You," the thug on his right jabbed him with his gun, "move over there. No running, no funny business."

The thug on Francis' left took the lead, as they moved past the car. The lights from the car parked opposite were turned off. Francis followed, the man behind him kept the muzzle of his rifle pressed right against his spine.

"Nyel'zya!" Ulyanova screeched behind them. "Stop it!"

Francis inched his right hand up the left wrist. His fingers were numb and the process seemed painfully slow. Any moment these bastards would shoot him in the back, and it would all be over.

The men said something to one another, the one behind him laughed. Francis touched the handle of his dagger with the tips of his index and middle fingers.

Ulyanova's hysterical cries stopped suddenly at the sound of a vicious slap. The night air in the deserted park carried the sound of her painful sobs.

"You," the man behind him commanded, "kneel."

Francis knelt slowly, the two men grouped in front of him.

They are smiling, Francis noted.

The two men exchanged a few words. They seemed to have a friendly disagreement. Francis realized they were arguing as to who should do the coup de grace.

Francis was pulling the dagger from his sleeve by the very tip of his fingers. All he needed was a few more seconds...

Ulyanova's scream could have awakened the dead. Francis' two guards were startled by it, both looked past him at the two cars and, presumably, at the two guys with of Ulyanova.

Now!

Francis used the momentary distraction to pull the dagger out. He took aim and threw the knife at the man on his right. The pointed blade punctured his throat, a horrified expression of surprise flashed on the man's eyes as he dropped his rifle and put both hands to his neck to pull the dagger out. Blood gushed from the wound.

Roll!

Francis rolled on the ground toward both men's legs. The one on the left was quicker and fired a shot.

I'm hit!

A hot, stinging sensation spread up Francis' right leg. He didn't care. He used his limited momentum to punch the man's groin with all his might.

The man doubled over, desperately trying to aim the assault rifle at him.

Attack!

Francis grabbed the barrel with his right hand and pointed it sideways as he grabbed the stock with his left. He swiped the man's right leg, tripping him to the ground, and both he and Francis struggled to get control of the rifle. Francis saw the other man clawing his neck with one hand, the blood gurgling as he tried to speak. He crouched and was feeling the ground for the rifle he dropped.

I only have a few seconds!

Francis struggled with his former captor. Both men rolled on the ground. The man was strong. The pain up Francis' leg became more severe. Francis summoned every ounce of strength and tried to twist the rifle out of the thug's hands.

He failed.

The man twisted back. Francis lost his right grip for an instant then frantically grabbed the barrel before the man had a chance to recover. His opponent used the momentum to try to get atop Francis. He failed, and Francis rolled him over until he was atop the man.

They stared into each other's eyes. It was a stare full of hate. The man's breath smelled of onions.

Fuck you!

Francis head-butted the man between the eyes, blinding him. Francis felt the man's body twitch under his, so he hit him again so hard that his own forehead hurt. His opponent's hands relaxed around the assault rifle.

Roll!

The other man had pulled Francis' knife from his throat and rushed Francis. He landed on top of his colleague, Francis tried snapping to his feet but his right leg didn't respond.

I'm hit, dammit!

Francis ignored the pain. He had the assault rifle. He had never fired such a weapon before, but he figured the thug had probably pressed the safety off and it would be ready to fire. He took aim and fired at the two fallen men, one, two, six, eight times. The man with the gouged throat was still, the other one's left leg rattled, his mouth gaped in a rictus.

Go!

Francis knew he had very little time. He grabbed his bloodied dagger from the ground, wiped it on the dead man's shirt, and put it in its sheath under his right sleeve. He limped back to where the two cars were parked, crouching low, trying to offer as small a target as possible.

Another scream!

Francis figured Ulyanova was somewhere about ten meters past the cars, to his right. At least they hadn't killed her. He went past the cars, weaving between the trees for cover, then he distinguished the shapes of three bodies ahead. He closed in.

Just a few more meters.

What he saw filled him with disgust. Beneath a huge tree, one of the captors was holding Ulyanova down, his body across her torso and neck, immobilizing her, suffocating her, and pinning her right arm with his hands. The other man had pushed Ulyanova's dress above her hips and forced himself between her legs, inching forward, struggling to keep Ulyanova's legs spread and pushing her pelvis down to steady it. Her white panties were curled around her left ankle.

"*You son of a bitch!*" Francis roared, dropping his dagger and opening fire.

He missed the first shot because of the rifle's recoil, the second one caught the rapist in the head or the upper torso. The injured man collapsed sideways with the impact. The other man rolled off Ulyanova and fired back repeatedly with his handgun.

The fusillade spread in an arc. One caught Francis on his left shoulder, spinning him around. The man kept firing, Francis rolled on the ground and desperately tried to find a good position for returning fire.

Francis flexed the fingers on his left hand. He didn't feel any pain. The bullet had gone through the jacket and had been absorbed or deflected by the padding.

Pounce!

Francis jumped to his feet, the rifle steady in his hands, and opened fire. The man ran for cover behind the tree, Ulyanova just lay on the earth, paralyzed with fright. It was dark. Francis fired blindly at the last place where he'd seen the man. There was no sound. Suddenly, a hand lashed out from the foot of the tree, snatched Ulyanova's mane of hair and dragged her back.

She screamed.

Francis aimed the rifle at the shadow behind Ulyanova. The terrorist hammer locked her neck, pointing his gun at her right temple. He pushed her toward Francis, who tried to aim the rifle at the thug's head peering from behind hers.

The man said something in German. Francis blinked, trying to clear his vision.

One clear shot, that's all I need.

The man waited expectantly for an answer. Francis had no clue as to what he said, but he figured he wanted him to drop his weapon. Francis held his ground.

The man yelled at him, pressing the gun against Ulyanova's temple. She yelped.

"Okay," Francis said, lowering the rifle. The man was merely five meters away. "You win," Francis crouched slowly, dropping the rifle at his feet. "Easy now."

The gun left Ulyanova's temple and its gaping muzzle stared at Montagnet. He was about to lurch away when the man swore. Francis realized that Ulyanova had bitten the man's gun hand.

A shot was fired. It whizzed past Francis into the night.

Francis jumped at the pair, swiftly shoving Ulyanova away and hitting the terrorist's face with his right elbow. The terrorist tried aiming the gun at Francis, who'd ensnared his wrist with his left hand and desperately tried to keep the gun away from him. Inch by inch, the gun turned inexorably toward Francis.

Both men fell. Francis tried head butting the man; he turned his face away and Francis' forehead and nose painfully thudded against the ground. He rolled to his left, placing all his weight on the man's gun arm. At least he wouldn't be able to fire at him.

The man's left hand sprung at Francis' throat, choking him. Francis grabbed the man's wrist and tried to get him off, but he was too strong. Francis tried pushing him away with both hands, to no effect. This maniac was winning. He would crush Francis' larynx unless he got out of his lock quickly.

Francis struggled to get his left hand around the man's right arm while he tried forcing the terrorist to release the death grip with his own right hand. It was then that a rock crashed against the terrorist's head.

The terrorist was startled; he dropped the gun. The impact angered him. He turned to Ulyanova, who had hit him with the rock. He unconsciously loosened his grip on Francis.

Francis took this chance to slide his right arm through the terrorist's left and to find his neck; he grabbed it and squeezed. They were both now trying to choke each other.

The two men rolled on the ground, struggling for survival. Francis puffed for air, his throat closing ever tighter in the man's vise like grip. His vision blurred.

Francis rolled with the man one, two, three times; they gained momentum. This was Francis' only chance. Francis forced himself away from the thug. Both men lost their grip on one another simultaneously.

Francis rolled back, desperately reaching up his right sleeve with his left hand. The terrorist jumped toward him, landing atop Francis, forcing the air from his already depleted lungs.

I got it!

The man tried pinning Francis' arms but was too late. Francis thrust the dagger forward, slicing the man's cheek. The man screamed. Francis pushed him off, gripping the dagger tightly, and stumbled to his feet. The other man also jumped to his feet. Both men circled around each other, waiting for a chance to attack. Francis tossed the knife to his right hand, holding it blade down in a reverse grip. The terrorist vaulted forward.

Francis, his right leg buckling, sidestepped the man. In a desperate move, Francis tried deflecting the man's attack with his left arm and plunged the dagger into his ribcage. The man screamed. Francis pressed his advantage and rolled over the thug.

There!

The terrorist's neckline was momentarily exposed. Francis savagely plunged the dagger to its hilt just under the man's collarbone, then twisted. The flesh made a sucking sound, blood spurted from the wound. Francis stumbled back, then fell backward, the knife still in his right hand. The thug shot him a look full of venom and panic. Both men knew that, if the artery had been severed, the man would bleed to death.

The thug started toward Francis. Francis tried getting up, panting, and failed. His leg hurt too much. His knuckles whitened, gripping the knife as hard as he could.

There was no need for that.

The thug tentatively stepped forward, his expression mutated from hatred to fear before toppling over. Blood gushed from the wound. Francis watched fascinated as the man lost consciousness. With a gasp, the man finally died.

Ulyanova slowly approached Francis. She gently removed the knife from his grip with her delicate hands. They looked at each other. Francis fell on his back, trying to catch his breath. The pain in his leg and the night air rushing into his lungs were more than he could handle. He felt sticky with sweat. Every breath he sucked burned his throat. Ulyanova knelt beside him and propped his head up with a cool, trembling hand.

At least I am alive, he thought, looking into her beautiful blue eyes. He tried to smile at her before fainting.

CHAPTER **15**

Fort Meade, MD

When the shit hits the fan, it splatters all over.

Adam Jones had received several tough calls. The news coming from Vienna worsened by the minute. Paul and Vince, the two men assigned to bring Montagnet back in, had been found dead, one at the hotel, the other in his parked car around the corner.

The small office felt stuffy. Jones loosened his tie and rolled his sleeves up.

There had been conflicting reports from the hotel. Jones had been talking with the Austrian authorities, who wasted no time raising hell and threatening a diplomatic incident. Paul and Vince were listed as American military attachés among the embassy personnel. The deaths of military attachés pointed to an undercover op on Austrian soil. Jones had contacted the Department of State, explained the situation in as simple terms as he could, and hoped the diplomats would pick up the pieces. The suits at State also wasted no time making a stink, and the whole thing was quickly spiraling out of control.

These were the "unexplained stiffs" that Mitch Kennedy of the CIA had warned him against when he floated the idea of retaining Montagnet. A potential witness, a hotel housekeeping employee, was hospitalized with a severe concussion. It was anybody's guess when she would wake up. She had been hit on the temple with a blunt object. Four Turks had been found dead at the Laaer Recreational Forest after the neighbors reported gunshots. The Austrian police were all over the case, though so far the deaths had been blamed on drug related gang warfare by the local news.

Jones had spoken with Rudolph Reisner, a colleague in the Austrian *Gendarmerieeinsatzkommando Cobra*, or GEK Cobra counter terrorism unit. How the hell did they pronounce that? Reisner had provided additional information about the killings. All the dead were Turkish immigrants, though there were no other links between them. All of them held steady jobs and were known for their diligence and professionalism. None was considered a risk factor, and none had an open dossier with Austrian or other European intelligence or law enforcement agencies. None even had had a traffic violation.

Reisner had mentioned something that piqued Jones' interest. A preliminary examination by the coroner showed that one of the dead men had a deep knife wound near his breastbone. The man had died of a gunshot, though the wound probably happened before the man was shot. No sharp weapons were found at the site.

Knives were Montagnet's signature.

Nobody knew where Montagnet was or what had happened to the documents. Neither the NSA, nor any diplomatic pressure, had been able to stop the money wires sent from Switzerland the day before. All NSA stations on the alert efficiently traced the funds transfers but the State Department had been too slow to react; the funds had been flushed from the target accounts, lost in the labyrinth of financial markets. The suits from State had sat on their hands for too long, the chance to pressure the governments hosting the receiving banks was lost.

Enbeaath had bilked them successfully, and there was nothing Jones could think of that would stop them now. The NSA didn't even know for sure who *they* specifically were. The Del Villar lead had been fruitless.

It had been a long, nightmarish day, and it wasn't over yet. He had to report his progress—or lack of it—to the Director of the NSA in just over thirty minutes. There was a high probability that Francis was captured or killed. Operation ZEPHYR had probably failed.

Where was his friend? What had happened to Francis Montagnet?

Moscow

It was one-thirty in the afternoon. The meeting between Anatoly Kuryakin and Fakhri wasn't going well. As expected, Kurok was angry at Varenka's elimination. Holding the meeting in Kurok's office made Fakhri feel particularly uncomfortable. Kurok was drinking a glass of vodka, Fakhri had been served a cup of black tea. He had not touched it yet.

"Why did you eliminate her, Colonel?" Kurok asked for the third time. "This could mean a significant setback."

"I beg to disagree, Kurok," Fakhri replied. "I had reasons to believe that she was a spy for the Americans."

"Nonsense. What would be her incentive?"

"Money, perhaps?"

"No, that doesn't wash. Dr. Ulyanova was professional and loyal. She made a more than comfortable living here in Moscow."

"How about blackmail?" Fakhri sipped his tea. It smelled delicious. "Any skeletons in the closet?"

"Other than a nasty divorce three years ago she was squeaky clean," Kurok said, shifting his massive weight in his chair. He swilled half of his glass of vodka. "All my employees in a position of trust are thoroughly investigated when they're hired. We run a tight ship."

"And yet I caught her with the very same bastard who stole the documents from me in Zurich," Fakhri said defensively. "Who knows what she shared with him? The whole enterprise might be at risk."

Kurok swallowed the rest of his vodka and stared hard at Fakhri for several seconds. The Russian's bloodshot eyes were like unblinking cameras.

"What's done, is done," Kurok said finally. "I'm sure you acted in what you thought were our best interests, Colonel. Whatever she told them wasn't enough to create a stir, or the FSB would already be at our doorstep. Do you have a contingency plan?"

"I spoke with Dr. Volin at White Fortress before flying out of Austria this morning. He believes he can take over Dr. Ulyanova's team and complete their work within schedule. My people are translating the remaining documents to Russian. We shall have bound document sets for everyone involved within forty-eight hours."

"We must further reduce potential vulnerabilities. We can't risk another leak, if your assumptions about Dr. Ulyanova are true. I will fly everyone in Dr. Ulyanova's team to White Fortress. They will work there until the project is complete."

"Thanks, Kurok."

"As for the death of Dr. Ulyanova, she won't be missed for several weeks, I'm sure." Kurok clasped his hands in front of him, relaxing. "She has very few friends in Moscow, and we know she doesn't have a close relationship with her family. Of course, we may have to answer a few questions to the authorities when the time comes, but the wheels of justice spin slowly across international borders. I hope that nothing ties you directly with whatever incident you concocted."

"Nothing whatsoever. My team in Vienna will make it look like a drug related quarrel between her and Montagnet. The appropriate props, such as traces of heroine and a few syringes, will be scattered around the crime scene. She'll be thought of a tourist looking for drugs in the wrong place."

"So sad," Kurok sighed, shaking his giant head. "Well, this wet business is over. We shall proceed."

Fakhri stood up and shook hands with Kurok before leaving. There was a certain sadness, a certain solemnity in Kurok's demeanor regarding Ulyanova. The Russian honcho had honestly liked the bitch.

Fakhri had spent what he considered as plenty of time mourning her death, clinically analyzing it, and finally dismissing it as necessary. Ulyanova had used him. He had loved her and she'd betrayed him. Her penalty fitted her offense against him and Rebirth Alliance. He had been thinking with his *kiri* instead of with his head. He was convinced that, like a succubus, she had tried to seduce him to his own destruction.

Bumping the bitch off had fully vindicated him.

CHAPTER **16**

Vienna

Pain. Francis Montagnet's leg ached, his right eye was almost shut, his jaw hurt. He stirred in his seat.

Seat?

He cursed as he propped himself up, trying to clear his head. He was in a car. The wipers quickly swiped the windshield back and forth, clearing the rain. The street lighting was poor, the traffic almost non-existent.

Varvara Ulyanova drove the car, white-knuckled grip on the wheel. She propped herself up, with her torso almost against the wheel. Her driving style was jerky; he figured that she didn't drive often. Thank goodness that the car had an automatic transmission.

They came to a red light. Ulyanova slammed on the breaks. Francis barely had time to brace himself; his face almost hit the top of the glove compartment.

"Ungh," he groaned.

"You're awake," Ulyanova said, looking at him blankly.

"Yes," Francis said, rubbing his eyes. His throat hurt a bit. "Where are we going?"

"I don't know. I've been driving for about ten minutes, trying to figure out what to do."

"Pull over there," Francis said, pointing past the intersection. "We need to talk."

The light turned green. Francis looked at the street names as they crossed the intersection. Raxstrasse and Neilreichgasse. He had no idea where they were. Ulyanova parked and powered the car and the headlights off.

"Thanks," Francis said, fighting a wave of nausea, "for taking me with you."

"I don't know if that was a good idea or the stupidest thing I've ever done."

"I'm sorry," Francis avowed. He shifted in his seat. He was very thirsty.

"You passed out after the fight was over," Ulyanova explained. "You're heavy. It was hard dragging you to the car."

"Why did you do that?"

"Because... because you saved my life."

"You could've left me back there," Francis said.

"No, I couldn't after what you did. You stopped those animals from raping me. A rape is the most awful thing that can happen to a woman. I wouldn't like that to be the last thing I experienced before dying." She bit her lip. "You almost got killed protecting me. The least I could do was bring you with me."

"Thanks, Dr. Ulyanova. I probably owe you my life," Francis said, touching the improvised tourniquet she'd made by wrapping his own belt around his upper right thigh. His leg felt numb.

"Call me Varenka," she said. "It's time for you to loosen that," she said pointing at the tourniquet. "It's been about twenty minutes since I did it."

"Sure," Francis said, loosening his belt. "I don't think I'm bleeding anymore," he struggled forward and ran his hand over the floor mat and along the car door. It was moist in places but it wasn't soaked. He brought his hand to his face. Surprisingly little blood was smeared on it. He wiped it off against the side of his seat. "I'm very thirsty, though."

"You lost quite a bit of blood," Varenka said. "At least a half-liter. It's a rather vicious wound. A bullet?"

"Yes, one of the men who dragged me away caused it."

"I don't think the bullet is in you. There were two wounds, on each side of your calf muscle. It looks like the bullet only damaged the muscle. You wouldn't be able to walk if it had shattered the bone."

"I don't think I can walk right now."

"You're probably in shock."

Francis inhaled as deeply as he could before exhaling slowly. "It feels good being alive."

"We need to find a doctor, call the authorities."

"No," Francis said as firmly as he could. "No authorities, and no doctors unless we can find someone we can bribe."

"Why?"

"Because we'll be sitting ducks for the bad guys if we're taken into custody while this mess is sorted out."

"You may die if you don't get medical attention."

"I will die for sure if Fakhri and his thugs get their paws on me," Francis looked at her. "And, by the looks of it, so will you."

Varenka's eyes filled with tears. They were tears of frustration, not sadness. She was probably reliving the trauma of the evening. Francis felt a wave of tenderness toward her, wondering if there was something he could do to help her feel better.

"I don't understand what's going on!" Varenka sobbed. "Why did he try to kill me?"

"What do you know about him?"

"He is someone I met through work," Varenka replied, stifling a sob. "We are—no, we *were* lovers."

Jesus Christ, Francis thought. Of all the people in the world, he had had to ask Fakhri's girlfriend for help. No wonder the guy was pissed.

"What do you mean you met him through work? You hardly look like a terrorist."

Varenka glared at him. "What is that supposed to mean?"

"Colonel Sattar Fakhri is probably a leader in *Enbeaath*, the Rebirth Alliance terrorist organization."

"He..." Varenka stopped, puzzled. Francis' words slowly sank in. "He claimed to be businessman. Arab oil interests. My company is building a new type of oil drilling offshore rig for his company."

"The men we ran into tonight were hardly oil executives. He's up to something sinister."

"I... I can't believe it," Varenka whimpered and quietly began to cry.

"Varenka," Francis said, tentatively holding her right forearm in his dirty left hand. She didn't pull away. "I'm really sorry you went through that tonight. The important thing is that we're alive."

"Yes, you're right," Varenka looked up, the blue wells of her eyes brimming with tears. "So what do we do now?"

"Let me think," Francis said. He couldn't concentrate because of the pain. "I have no idea where we are, I feel awful, and it's just a matter of time before someone comes looking for us."

"This is a rental car," Varenka took the keys from the ignition and showed them to Francis. The key chain was a Hertz tag with the car license number printed on it. "I took the keys from the man you were struggling with. I don't think anyone will miss the car for a while."

"You're probably right. Let me see something," he said, opening the glove compartment. There was a city map in it. "It's kind of dark in here," he said, unfolding the street map and squinting at the small print in the poor light coming from outside. "Don't turn the lights on, though. I don't want to attract attention."

"Very well. Do you know where we are?"

"I don't have a clue," Francis replied. He felt a bit lightheaded. "I don't know Vienna very well beyond downtown. Do you recognize anything?"

"I've never been here before," Varenka said, wiping her eyes with the back of her hand. "I just turned left at the street by the park, found a roundabout and kept going. I figured we'd get to a main street soon."

Francis thought they were somewhere south of downtown. He traced the streets with his finger. He looked around. It was hard to see through the rain but they were clearly on a wider street. He searched the map again.

There!

He found Rax Street. It ran east west. The battle must've happened at Laaer Wald. He traced the street again and found their current intersection.

"We must head north to get downtown, or at least to a busier street."

"Which way is that?"

"To the right," Francis said, wiping the sweat off his forehead with a tremulous hand. "I don't feel well."

"Then what? Are we going back to the hotel?"

"Yes, but I can't stay there," Francis said, patting his left breast pocket. Good. He still had his wallet. "Can you help me find a new hotel?"

"Let's go then," Varenka turned the engine and took off.

Varenka's driving was terrible. Eventually she gained confidence in controlling the car, though not before whipping both of them when starting and stopping. Francis felt worse by the minute. Finally they reached their destination. Francis was barely conscious when Varenka put some sunglasses on him and dragged him out of the car. She was fussing over his right leg, brushing it.

"I hope you won't drip blood when we get there."

"I can't see anything."

"The sunglasses are for covering your black eye. Leave them on."

He had no clue where "there" was. The cold rain felt extremely uncomfortable. He reluctantly followed Varenka through a well-lit entrance.

"Laugh," she commanded under her breath, his right arm slung over her shoulder for support. Varenka followed suit, a man's voice said something in the background. She nudged him to bench across from the registration desk. He faked a drunken smile and leant against the wall until Varenka returned by his side and helped him up.

Francis felt feverish but forced another laugh. He perceived the world as if seeing it through a long, dark tunnel. He wobbled into the clunky elevator, barely big enough to carry three people, Varenka in tow pretending to be drunk. To him she sounded forced. The hotel employee must have bought the act, though. A drunken couple, soaked by the rain, stumbling into the hotel for a quickie. She held him up.

"We're almost there," Varenka whispered. "Hang on just a bit longer."

The elevator doors opened. Varenka nudged him out and to the left, then gently stopped him when they reached their room. She opened the door and led him in. Francis fell face first onto the floor. He was shivering. The darkness closed in again.

Francis woke with a start. There were two tall shapes in the room. He lay on a double bed, the sheets felt coarse against his naked body. He blinked a couple of times. One was a blonde man, wearing a long camel hair coat and carrying a small briefcase. He was giving instructions to a beautiful woman wearing a gray blouse and a black skirt.

Varenka.

The man spoke patiently in accented English. Varenka nodded.

"He needs plenty of rest, ma'am. As for the sutures, they can be removed in a week or so. Anyone can do that if you don't have access to me."

"What is sutures?"

"These," the doctor gently lifted the sheet and showed her his leg.

"Okay. I understand. Thank you."

"Thank you for your generosity, ma'am," the doctor faced Francis. "Good. Our patient is awake. How do you feel?"

His aches and pains slowly came back to him. His calf throbbed.

"Alive, I think," Francis enunciated in a raspy voice.

"You were very lucky, Mr. Bishop. You were quite beat up but you'll pull through. Ms. Ulyanova told me about your rib. As far as I can tell it's just lacerated. Just make sure that you don't exert yourself."

"I won't."

"And you should eat plenty of iron rich foods, green vegetables, beans, liver, crustaceans. And drink plenty of liquids. You lost quite a bit of blood."

"I will. Thanks."

"I'm glad you're awake. Ms. Ulyanova has a prescription and instructions for your care. When are you leaving Vienna?"

"I... what day is it?"

"We leave two days," Varenka cut in the conversation. "He and I must go work."

"You should be fine for the airplane ride if you rest plenty until then." The doctor grabbed an umbrella standing by the door. "And don't exert yourself when you get back home."

"I won't, doctor, I promise. Thanks for your help."

"Goodbye then," the doctor left the room, closing the door behind him.

Francis tried to prop himself up. His whole body hurt.

"Here," Varenka said, pushing a pillow under his head.

"Where are we?"

"We're staying at the Prinz Eugen hotel, across the street from a train station."

Francis scanned the Spartan room. There was a small table and two chairs by the window. A black telephone. A closet. A door leading to a small bathroom. An old TV. It was quite a step down from the Sacher. "How did we get here?"

"You and I pretended to be party drunks. I got us a room and here we are. You collapsed at the door. I had a hell of a time dragging you to the bed. You had a fever and were hallucinating."

"I don't remember."

"You kept talking in several languages. Babbling, actually. I didn't understand most of it. Finally I decided to get a doctor for you. I called the front desk and told them that you'd taken ill. They probably figured you were having a bad hangover. Anyway, the doctor came. I told him that you and I were lovers, that discretion was a must. He hesitated at first until I paid him off. You know the rest."

"The doctor, he called me 'Mr. Bishop'."

"Yes, I used that name. It's on one of the passports I found in your pocket. Is that your real name?"

"No, my name is Francis, like I told you."

"Who are you?"

"I'm just a fool who accepted a suicidal mission, that's who I am."

"That's no answer."

"I am a freelance agent working on behalf of a government. I was on a mission to recover the documents Fakhri stole from them."

"Which government?"

Francis returned her hard stare, then lowered his gaze. "The United States, if you ought to know."

"And Fakhri stole those documents?"

"That's why I'm here," Francis insisted. "May I have something to drink?"

"I bought water and fruit juices. What would you like?"

"Fruit juice. Anything red."

Varenka walked over to the table. A grocery bag was underneath it. She produced a couple of bottles of juice and handed him a red one.

"It's some berry juice," she said, opening the bottle for him. "I went out earlier to get this and some cheap clothes for me at the train station."

He grabbed the bottle and eagerly drank from it. It tasted like cranberry. Delicious. "Thank you."

"So, what do we do now?" Varenka asked, sitting at the table and looking out the window.

"Well, we better get out of Vienna as soon as we can. It won't be long before Fakhri's hounds come after us. You should head back home, forget you ever met me."

"You aren't thinking, Francis," she chided him. "Don't you remember I told you Fakhri is doing business with my company? I would run into him again in Moscow. For all I know, even my boss is involved."

Francis put the bottle of juice by the bed. He was in too much discomfort to think straight.

"I want to stop Fakhri," Francis said finally. "You can probably help me track him down."

"Oh, I know where he is headed."

"Help me catch him."

Varenka looked at him. Her blue eyes betrayed a hint of sadness. There was no fear in them; just resignation. She asked, "Why would I do that?"

"Because we have no choice," Francis replied. "God knows what he's really up to, but one thing is sure. He'll want to kill you when he finds out that you survived his goons. And I want to get him for my own reasons. We just have to outsmart him."

"You're crazy."

"Do you have any better ideas?"

Varenka stood up and paced the room for several minutes.

"I want to get the bastard myself, but I'm scared. I don't know what to do."

"I think we owe our lives to each other," Francis said almost solemnly. "Let me try to help you."

"What do you want to do?"

Francis grimaced when he shifted position in the bed.

"The doctor is right about one thing. I need rest if I am to assist you. And I'll need the medicine and some clothes. Could you help me get those?"

Varenka looked at him for a long time from the far end of the room.

"Somehow I feel like Faust," Varenka said softly, "choosing between the lesser of two evils. I don't feel there's much of a choice, and what you said makes a twisted sense. I'll help you, Francis."

Francis closed his eyes and leant back. He dozed, feeling a bit better having knowledge that he had a new friend, albeit a reluctant one.

CHAPTER 17

Varenka turned the car engine off. She'd found a parking garage downtown, close to the Sacher. She'd driven the car to the lowest floor, then parked at the farthest spot from the elevators to the street. She used a washcloth she'd taken from the hotel to wipe off the wheel, dashboard, and every surface she could remember touching. She inspected the passenger seat. The floor mat on that side would have to go. It had plenty of bloodstains. The interior reeked of decomposing blood. Fortunately the seat was almost clean. There were just a few streaks of blood on it. She took the rolled mat under her arm when she left the car.

Varenka took the elevator to the street level. She was a block or two away from her former hotel. She walked unhurriedly to the Sacher, feeling like she was being watched. She looked around and dropped the rolled floor mat, the garage claim ticket and the washcloth in a rubbish bin. She kept walking.

The hotel entrance was a mere half a block away. It was a gray mid-morning, a bothersome drizzle hit her face. She stopped at a vending kiosk and bought a cheap umbrella. She opened it and walked the remaining distance to the hotel. She found a grate at the next intersection. She looked around casually, ensuring that nobody watched her drop the car keys through it to become forever lost in the Viennese sewage system.

Varenka entered the hotel lobby. She felt stiff and mannered, and forced herself to act casually. She passed the registration desk, where the clerk greeted her. Anyone who could possibly identify her would be in a conference session at this time. She cracked a fake smile and headed for the lift.

She arrived at her room, feeling high-strung. Her hand was trembling so hard she had trouble opening the lock. Finally she got into her room.

It was almost the way she'd left it. The maid had made the bed, but otherwise her things were the way she'd laid them out the day before. She hurriedly packed her clothes and toiletries. Per Francis' instructions, she spent a few minutes writing a note on a sheet of guest's stationary and placed it in a Sacher envelope along with five hundred Euros.

Varenka took the lift to the third floor. She was surprised to find a work crew changing the carpet by the lift and covering with plaster what looked like bullet holes on the wall. The men ignored her as she walked to Francis' room. She went in, retrieved the backpack, and headed back to the lift.

Varenka emerged from the lift on the ground floor and went to the registration desk. A bellboy saw her hauling the luggage and ran to help her. She thanked him and approached the clerk, still feeling nervous.

"May I help you?" the solicitous man asked in English.

"Yes, I need check out today."

"Of course. May I have your name?"

"Ulyanova, Varvara."

The clerk entered the name in the computer. "Of course, Dr. Ulyanova. Shall I leave the charges on your credit card?"

"Yes, leave on card," she replied, handing her key to the man. "Also, my boyfriend wants check out. He busy, cannot come. He asked me to give you this," she handed the clerk the envelope.

The clerk opened the envelope and read the note. Varenka had written a simple note, in what she hoped was correct English, instructing the man to check Francis out of the hotel. The five hundred Euros were there to cover any gratuities he might have overlooked, the note read. The clerk's eyes reflected a small glint of suspicion which was appeased when she produced Francis' key and handed it over to him. He typed the room number into the computer.

"Your boyfriend's name is...?"

"Bishop, Richard," Varenka said easily. Francis had told her he'd registered at the hotel under that name.

"You're both checked out, Dr. Ulyanova," the clerk said smiling as he slid the envelope into his coat pocket. "Do you need transportation?"

"What is *trenzportayshun*?" She didn't remember that word.

"Do you need a taxi?"

"Yes, please," Varenka said.

The clerk waved at the bellboy and instructed him in German. The bellboy bowed courteously and rushed to fetch a taxi.

. . .

The air in the room felt stuffy. Varenka snuck past the bed, trying not to awaken Francis from his restless sleep and cracked the window open. Fresh, moist air rushed into the tiny room.

God, I need a smoke, Varenka thought. She'd given up that vice eight years before, and this was the first time she'd felt the urge to have a cigarette since. She sat at the small table, opened a bottle of mineral water, and looked out. People came and went from the train station in an early afternoon frenzy. She'd asked the cab driver to drop her off there, then she'd walked across the busy avenue back to the hotel.

"You're back," Francis said softly, startling her.

"I thought you were asleep."

"I was. Don't feel bad. How did things go back at the Sacher?"

"Not a problem. I was able to get in and out in less than twenty minutes. I parked the car and disposed of the keys."

"Good," Francis sighed. "Thanks for getting my medicine earlier. I noticed he gave me some antibiotics and some Naproxen for the swelling. The pain killers make me nauseous."

"What did the doctor give you?"

"Tylenol number 3, prescription strength. I don't think I'll take it anymore. It doesn't ease the pain and it just makes me nauseous and loopy."

Varenka laughed. "Loopy. It sounds strange. Only small children use that word."

"My Russian isn't as good as it should be. I don't practice it that often."

"Your Russian is excellent, actually. Where did you learn?"

"I went to school for it, then I had plenty of practice when I lived in Kiev and Moscow."

"Are those the only two places you've ever been to?"

"Oh no," he smiled weakly. "I've been to many Russian cities. Saint Petersburg, Kazan, Novo Cheboksarsk, Sochi... A few in the Ukraine as well, like Kiev, Odessa, Kherson and Kharkov."

"You've been to more places than me," Varenka said, smiling back. "I couldn't tell where you were from when I first met you. At first I thought you were from one of the former Soviet republics. Your accent is very indistinct."

"Call it linguistic pollution," Francis huffed. "I speak four languages, and none of them well anymore. I've been learning Japanese but haven't had much of a chance to use it."

"You sound fluent in English."

"I am; it's just that I now have a funny accent in all the languages I speak. Everybody I talk to can understand what I say, but will have trouble pinpointing the accent."

"Is that part of your training as a spy?"

Francis smiled. "I'm not a spy," he said, raising an ice pack to his swollen eye.

"I've been thinking about what happened last night, the things you said. I figured you might be some kind of industrial spy."

"You call the police on an industrial spy, not a gang of thugs."

"Yes, I thought the same thing."

Varenka looked at Francis for a long time. His strong naked body was outlined by the sheets. His face was temporarily disfigured by the black eye and a split lip, but he would heal. He was handsome in a rough way, but he wasn't vain. His expression occasionally darkened, betraying a violence lurking just beneath his affable surface. She knew the violence this man was capable of if pushed far.

"Why is Sattar trying to kill you?"

Francis pondered before answering. "As I told you before, Fakhri is involved with Embeaath, the terrorist faction. They stole some-thing that I was charged with recovering."

"The stuff in the container? What was it?"

"It's not important at this point," Francis coughed, grimacing. That must hurt. "I can confirm that Fakhri was directly involved in murdering at least two people. And he wanted you and me dead."

Varenka stared out the window. Sadness and anger fought for precedence. Sadness at the disappointment in Fakhri, anger at the bas-tard for trying to kill her. "Why did he want me killed?" she asked, her voice almost a whisper.

"Because of me. He's been hunting me for a couple of days, since Zurich. That's where we met, by the way. Then he saw us together. He probably thought you and I were on the same team."

"I knew he was going to Zurich. It's hard to believe that was only two days ago."

"He told you that?"

"Yes," images of their last night together flashed through her mind, his touch, the ambiguous tone in his voice whenever he discussed the trip to Zurich with her. "He said that he had to pick up in Zurich the rest of the plans for an oilrig we're working on. I guessed that's what was in the container."

"What exactly are the plans you're talking about?" Francis asked after a pause.

"My company is building a new design, a mobile offshore oilrig. There are a number of electrical machines on board, most of them designed by a separate team in eastern Russia. We estimated that those machines require a tremendous amount of electrical power. My team was commissioned to build an array of coils and transformers that would regulate the electrical current feeding into their machines."

"The container had a number of pages describing some sort of electrical circuit," Francis said, looking at the ceiling as if trying to remember. "Some kind of transformer. The weird thing was, the circuits appeared to run on direct current, not alternating current. There was nothing I could think of that hinted at its use in an oilrig."

"That's strange," Varenka said. "So the plans were in that container?"

"Yes, the plans for something. The documents, however, were extremely old. The pages describing the electrical circuit were dated in the early nineteen hundreds. A couple others of were dated in the nineteen thirties. Old stuff. I didn't have time to look it all up."

"That doesn't make sense," Varenka said, sipping her water. "He claimed that what we're doing is cutting edge, and going by what my team and I guessed, I'd say it's true."

"You said you guys are building a mobile oilrig. What does that mean?"

"Oilrigs can be stationary, moored to the bottom of the ocean. Assembling and disassembling them takes a very time consuming and expensive effort. Others can be tugged around by a large ship, launch it somewhere offshore, anchor it to the ocean floor like a boat, then move it elsewhere when the work is complete. Finally we have mobile oil drilling units; ours is one of the most efficient, latest designs."

"I'd think an oilrig would stay put for a long time," Francis grimaced. He was feeling worse every second.

"Not if you're only beginning to explore an oil field. The oil quality may be low, or there may not be enough oil for commercial exploitation.

In that case, using a mobile rig for initial drilling makes more sense because it's cheaper to deploy. You can then lease or sell the rig to other parties once the project is over."

"Interesting. What is your company's interest in all this?"

"We build the rigs and train the crews, then we lease the equipment to oil companies like Lukoil or Exxon."

"What interest would a terrorist group have in an oilrig?"

"I don't know, but I would imagine they would make good targets. I don't see what use our rig would be for the terrorists. Maybe they plan to legitimately finance their activities by leasing the equipment."

Francis propped himself up against the headboard and painfully reached for his bottle of juice.

"Do you need any help?" Varenka asked.

"No, thanks," he said, swigging some juice.

Varenka smiled. Francis was a stubborn man. She could tell he was very self-reliant, even feeling as much pain as he now did. She had had plenty of time today to think about Francis' request for help. He wouldn't have made it unless he meant it. Sattar's strange behavior, his secrecy, all made sense now. She always felt like he was holding back. Even when they had made love the man seemed as distant as the moon.

Varenka's hand clenched around the pendant he'd given her. She yanked it from her neck in a fit of anger, snapping the delicate chain. She tossed the little golden tree in the waste bin.

"What was that about?" Francis asked, watchful.

"Nothing," Varenka said, fighting back the tears. "I... I don't feel like talking about it."

"Fakhri meant something to you, didn't he?" Francis asked, sympathetic. "I'm sorry you had to learn about him this way. You're a brave and kind woman, Varenka. You deserved better."

"Thanks," she said, wiping an angry tear running down her right cheek.

Varenka stood up and went to the confined bathroom. She looked at herself in the mirror. Her eyes were red, her expression sad. Get a hold of yourself, she urged the image in the mirror. She grabbed a tissue and blew her nose. Francis was right about she deserving someone better. Sattar Fakhri, a man she'd thought would one day be the love of her life, had ordered her killed with the same indifference as someone wiping his shoes clean.

She fought the urge to vomit.

Varenka wiped her nose with another tissue and went back to the room. She asked, "What now."

"He might've been using your company," Francis explained. "We won't know for sure unless we confirm that with your boss. For all you know, he was deceiving everyone involved in your project. You must remember that his only allegiance is to Rebirth. Everyone and everything that impedes his plans he will try to eliminate."

"What about getting help from your people?"

Francis thought for a few seconds before replying. "There is nobody I can turn to for help at this point. Somehow Fakhri and his thugs found me and my exfiltration team—"

"What is exfiltration?"

"My rescue team. They were the ones picking me up at the hotel when I ran into you. Anyway, I believe there is a leak somewhere, or Fakhri and his gang are better organized that we thought. Last night, when we got in the cab, I thought that heading to the American embassy might be a good idea. It probably wasn't. I'm a NOC, a non-official cover agent, a freelancer. Only the people running the operation know of my involvement. I can't just walk up to the embassy and request help. We'll be laughed off the premises. No, I need to recover the original documents first, before Fakhri uses them. Then we can come in."

"We are on a very tight schedule to deliver the oilrig," Varenka said, thinking about the travails back at work. "We have between ten and twenty days to complete the project if we are to meet Fakhri's deadline. I imagine that at least some people in my company know exactly what he's building. I don't think, however, that my boss would willingly participate in a deal so dangerous with Sattar unless there was a big payoff waiting for him in the end."

"Your boss is a fool if he thinks that Fakhri will let him live after the affair is complete," Francis said. "Enbeaath doesn't leave loose ends."

Varenka studied Francis for a few seconds. There was an urgency in his demeanor that she found assuring. "What do you think we should do?"

"We can't do much from Vienna," Francis replied. "We must contact your people and warn them. Do you feel like going out again?"

"It's still drizzling but I'll manage."

"Varenka, there's a Russian passport in my backpack. Could you please get me an airplane ticket for Moscow under the name in it?"

Varenka studied Francis for a while. "Sure," she replied. This was crazy. She had never been involved in anything like this. However, going back to Moscow and blowing the whistle on Fakhri was such a mad idea that it just might work. She also had a score to settle with that murderous bastard.

CHAPTER **18**

NSA Headquarters
Fort Meade, Maryland

Adam Jones trotted along the breezeway connecting the OPS 1 building to OPS 2B, past the photographs of NSA personnel assembled in a collage forming an American flag. It was early in the morning, few people crossed between the buildings. He passed the Russian Technical Library, a relic of the Cold War, and headed for the turnstiles leading to the upper floors. Security had been greatly enhanced since the Manhattan and Maryland terrorist attacks of 2001, and NSA employees and visitors now had to go through multiple security posts even when moving within connecting buildings in Crypto City, as the NSA employees called the sprawling NSA complex. That wasn't a stretch of the imagination either. Crypto City was possibly the largest non-incorporated city in the state of Maryland, perhaps in the whole United States. It had movie theaters, gas stations, convenience stores, even a stadium. The only difference with real world counterparts was that even the newsstand was manned by people with high security clearances.

Jones reached the security post. He pulled the lanyard securing his blue badge over his head and inserted the ID into the appropriate CONFIRM slot by the turntable under the watchful eyes of an MP. A LED indicator atop the turnstile column shifted from red to green. Jones looped the lanyard around his neck as he walked through and headed for the bank of elevators. It was a swift ride to the eight floor.

The elevator doors opened to a long hallway. Jones walked to the executive suite at the end, which included the director, deputy director, and chief of staff offices. General Morgan Helmwood's office was the last one on the left.

Jones approached Margaret, the receptionist. She greeted him warmly and waved him through. She was polite but her demeanor indicated there was no time for pleasantries this morning. Jones reached the door to the corner office and entered. General Helmwood was on the phone.

"Good morning Adam, please have some coffee and sit down" Helmwood said, covering the phone mouthpiece with his hand and nodding to a chair in front of his walnut desk. He swiveled the high-backed, green leather chair around to continue his conversation. Jones walked to the brewing machine atop a credenza, chose a white mug, and served himself some coffee before sitting down.

Jones had rarely been in General Helmwood's office since he became director of the NSA. The executive staff usually met at a large conference room on the same floor. Jones looked around, killing time.

The vast expanse of Crypto City could be watched from the eavesdrop-proof large window to his left. Two TV sets were to the right of the desk, one showing CNN and the other connected to the NSA secret cable network. Both TV's were muted, close captioning was on. There was nothing interesting on either, so he shifted his attention to the room itself.

A dark conference table surrounded by eight green upholstered chairs dominated the center of the room. A green and gold couch stood off to the side. There were few pictures on the walls, all of them bland corporate art. A couple of family photos were atop the desk.

General Helmwood hung up.

"My apologies," Helmwood said, turning to Jones. "We have our hands full. Sometimes I wish I had a direct link to the White House. I'm tired of triangulating all communications when something important comes up."

"I understand, sir," Jones replied.

"So, Adam, what kind of horseshit are we having to deal with now? Any changes?"

"No sir, the situation hasn't changed. The Austrians are cooperating fully, and so far they've kept the events out of the newspapers. I figured they have much to lose in the eyes of public opinion if this whole thing goes out."

"Or they have nothing to gain by making it public," Helmwood countered. "Either way we win. I spoke with Richardson, our SUSLO in London."

"What did the Special US Liaison Officer have to say, sir?"

"There is surprise at the means you chose for recovering the missing DARPA documents. They believe this to be CIA's turf. I understand your motivation for acting the way you did, and fully support you. President Brook's administration can't afford either congressional oversight on this matter or the leaks that the Agency is so famous for."

"Thank you, sir."

"On the other hand," General Helmwood insisted after drinking some coffee, "this might reflect negatively on you unless we recover the documents and keep the operation out of the headlines."

"I understand, sir. The thorniest issue so far is handling the deaths of Captain Paul Adler and Lieutenant Vincent Morrison."

"Their families have been notified. They'll be buried with full military honors. I wrote a commendation for both and letters to their families. These men died in the line of duty."

"Their families will find some consolation in that," Jones said. Like most military personnel, he wasn't sentimental when it came to casualties in the line of duty. "A couple of issues cropped up with the embassy in Austria, sir," he changed the subject. "The ambassador and the local CIA chief of station are raising a stink with State. They're causing a storm in a teapot about jurisdiction, and have used the word 'conspiracy' once or twice in our conversations. J.R., the CIA star analyst, is coming out with all kinds of wild theories regarding operation ZEPHYR. Director Kennedy is on our side, but if you recall, J.R. has the President's ear."

"J.R. should focus on analysis, not on operational issues, especially if the Agency isn't involved. Adam, remember that, in the end, he's just a bureaucrat. The Agency hates sharing information with us because they're more concerned about labels in the org charts than with operational effectiveness."

"What about their cries of a conspiracy?"

"Don't worry about that; I'll talk to Mitch. We'll put an end to it. Besides, every week some nut comes out saying that we, the NSA, are this all seeing, all powerful behemoth. Sometimes I wish it were true. Anyway, one more nut claiming that isn't really going to hurt us. What I would like to know is exactly what do you want to do next."

Jones sipped his coffee. It was lukewarm at best. "Sir, I believe Montagnet is dead. You will receive a full report after I have a chance to proof my current draft. He has disappeared and hasn't contacted me so far."

"And I assume the documents disappeared with him."

"Yes, sir. We're still checking on a couple of anomalies that cropped up. We have intelligence that he checked out of the hotel this morning. That doesn't make sense. His account was settled, the room was vacated normally."

"So, in essence, Montagnet and the documents are missing, possibly in the hands of Enbeaath."

"Yes, sir," Jones took his glasses off, rubbed the bridge of his nose, and put the glasses back on. "On the other hand, the folks at DARPA are rebuilding the cross reference indices as we speak; we must gain an insight into what was stolen. The man guilty of the original theft did too good a job of covering his tracks."

"So we're back to square one," General Helmwood retorted.

"Well, we made some progress in tracking the money wires out of Switzerland and into the world's financial system. It will take time, but we'll eventually trace them to the targets."

General Helmwood spun his chair to look out the window as he rubbed his chin. Jones waited patiently until the General spoke.

"Adam, there is no point in following any of this until we get a solid lead. I want you to focus all your attention on the upcoming UN Anniversary Summit of the Nations. One or two bad apples may want to disrupt the meeting and we would look like fools if they manage to succeed. The President would want our collective heads on a platter."

"Yes sir, I understand," Jones replied. "My team is already working on it. The teams from W Group are routinely scanning the airwaves, the Internet, and every other source for data about disruptions or an attack during the summit. We're watching for threats from all the usual suspects as well as less militant organizations like Green Peace and the White Knights. There will be a significant foreign presence during the summer, but we believe the FBI, ATF and the INS can handle those once we provide them with the intelligence we gather."

"Make sure all the agencies involved are up to speed," General Helmwood admonished. "We're less than a month away from the summit."

"My deputy, Major General Samantha Killpack, is keeping close tabs with the operations group and maintains open lines of communication with all the agencies through the Special Collections Service. M Group, on the other hand, is combing all our communications infrastructure to make sure that we aren't vulnerable in any way before or during the summit."

To Jones' relief, General Helmwood seemed satisfied with the report. "Excellent, Adam. The summit is the most important event this year in the President's agenda. The leaders of every major nation will be visiting our country and we can't afford any snafus. Make sure that your teams remain in a state of operational alert against anything that could threaten the success of this gathering. Forget ZEPHYR and concentrate on this new task. Whatever Enbeaath stole probably isn't relevant at the moment. After all, it's only a bunch of documents that, as far as we can tell, aren't even current. ZEPHYR contacts should be handled by someone in your junior staff so you can focus on keeping the leaders of the free world safe. The final report, of course, will remain highly classified."

General Helmwood closed the folder on his desk, containing the status of operation ZEPHYR. The original Gamma classification had been scratched off and replaced by the letters VRK/DO. The General placed the folder in his out tray for filing.

The new classification for ZEPHYR effectively yanked the operation out of Jones' hands. ZEPHYR was now Very Restricted Knowledge/Director of Operations, meaning that only he and General Helmwood would have access to the dossier. Jones could do nothing about it without the General's prior approval. Not that it mattered anymore. Jones would devote himself to the new fiat.

CHAPTER **19**

Moscow

"What the hell do you mean they were killed?" Fakhri exploded on the phone. "How can that be?"

"We don't know, Colonel," Sheik Dogukan Yavuz replied from Vienna. "The police notified their families. Their wives have come to pray at the mosque, seeking my spiritual advice. All four men were killed at the park. We just received the news this morning."

"Did anyone say anything about a woman?"

"Negative. There is no mention of a woman. Who is that?"

"A Russian whore who was helping Montagnet."

"There is no mention of either one."

"So, for all we know, Montagnet somehow managed to kill these men," Fakhri said, almost to himself. "And he is on the loose."

"That seems to be the case, Colonel."

"They've had a two day lead in which we've done nothing to stop them!" Fakhri shouted. "Idiot! I must assume that he and the woman escaped and are now briefing the Americans!"

"I disagree with that assessment, Colonel," Yavuz replied. "I'm sure that if Montagnet had already spoken to the authorities the Austrian GEK Cobra would be investigating our men's deaths. So far their deaths are being treated as drug-related violence, not terrorism. The vice and homicide squads are carrying out the investigation. We haven't spotted any unusual activity at the American embassy."

"You should know better," Fakhri replied exasperated. "I will yield to your judgment in this matter for now. Keep me informed of new developments."

"So I shall, Colonel." Yavuz hung up.

Fakhri leant back in his chair. He was in his room at the Marriott Tverskaya Yamskaya. He would fly east that evening, again in Kurok's private plane. He was very upset at the news. He was almost positive that bastard Montagnet had killed the men in Vienna. How did this happen? Did he get external help? Had there been a second team tailing them after they'd dealt with the two men at the Sacher? Probably not. They would have intervened earlier, perhaps would have stopped the taxi before it got to the park. Montagnet couldn't be such a trained killer to overcome four expert Rebirth combatants, could he?

More than anything, Fakhri was furious for underestimating his opposition. The man was lethal, as he had demonstrated in San Francisco, two years ago. He should have killed Montagnet himself when he had the chance.

Fakhri stood up and walked to the window. His room faced Tverskaya Yamskaya; he would've preferred a room facing the alley in the back of the hotel. It would be much quieter. He looked out the window. The crazy afternoon traffic was just beginning, men and women rushed to the Byelorusskaya metro station a block away to his right. A few pedestrians entered the arcade across the street, presumably to gamble their change at the slot machines.

How should he deal with Montagnet and Varenka?

If, as Yavuz suspected, Montagnet had not approached the American authorities, it was very likely that he would come after the documents himself.

If Varenka was working with Montagnet, she'd begin filling in the blanks. Varenka represented a loose end that had to be eliminated. Everyone else in the engineering team had already been flown to White Fortress. They would all work under Dr. Volin's command.

If Kurok had a soft spot for Varenka, as Fakhri suspected, and she approached him, development might be stopped until the situation with Fakhri and the orders he had issued were cleared. Moreover, Varenka and Montagnet may offer a deal to Kurok. The greedy pig might betray Fakhri if the carrot they dangled in front of him was juicy enough.

Varenka... Fakhri felt disgusted. He had betrayed his wife's memory by getting involved with such a whore. The anger swelled within him. Why had he even considered the Russian bitch? Why had he had such high expectations of her? He returned to his desk.

Fakhri analyzed the situation once more. Montagnet had failed his mission and would try to recover the documents. Yes, he and Varenka would certainly try something. They would come to Moscow looking for Fakhri. They might try turning Kurok against him. Fakhri decided. He picked up the phone, pressed 9 to get the outside line, and dialed a local number.

Alexis Abdullayev, native of Kazan, the capital of the Russian state of Tatarstan, had lived in Moscow since before the collapse of the Soviet Union. He had completed his military service in the Red Army, where he had the distinction of being one of the few non-ethnic Russians to get promoted to a higher rank. He had been a demolition officer. He had mastered his craft while working for the GRU, the Army Intelligence Service. The rebirth of the Russian nation allowed him to separate from the military and open a successful chain of convenience stores scattered throughout Moscow. He also reverted back to his roots and became an active practitioner of Islam and a vocal member of the local mosque, one of the few in Moscow. The skinheads and the Russian *maffiya* usually left him alone. One local hoodlum had made the mistake of vandalizing one of his stores and later tried to extort money for "protection". The gangsters backed off after learning that the biggest piece of the hoodlum found by the paramedics could fit in a matchbox.

Abdullayev was going over the accounting books when the phone rang.

"*Allo,*" he fetched the receiver.

"The peace of Allah be with you," said a voice in Russian that he didn't recognize.

"And with you," he replied, feeling uneasy.

"Your skills are needed, Abdullayev."

"I'm a simple merchant," he replied. Could this be entrapment by the FSB? The secret police might be on to him.

"We must speak in person," the voice commanded. "Meet me at the *Kitai Gorod* metro station in forty five minutes. Get off the train and wait for me on the platform."

"Who is this?" Abdullayev demanded.

"My name is Sattar, and I will approach you." The line clicked dead.

Abdullayev knew he had no choice. He would rendezvous with the caller and hear what he had to say.

. . .

The meeting had been brief. Abdullayev had spent the next hour shopping for apparently innocuous materials around the city. Commercially available explosives were tightly controlled in the Russian Federation after the bombings at the Mayakovskaya train station of a few years back. He had procured fine aluminum powder from a paint store and six liters of tetrachloroethylene from a dry cleaners supplier. He headed to one of his stores on Basmannaya Street. It had a well-ventilated storage room in the back.

The sales clerk greeted him formally when he walked into his store. He grunted a greeting, then went to the storage room and locked the door behind him. He didn't want any interruptions.

Abdullayev unwrapped a large wooden spatula he found in storage and took mental note to notify the clerk that he'd done so. He found a large bucket, rinsed and dried it, and got to work.

He measured two parts of aluminum powder into the bucket. He then poured roughly one measure of tetrachloroethylene into the bucket, stirring it evenly with the wooden spatula. He stirred the mix into a homogeneous paste until it had the consistency of syrup, averting his face from the fumes.

Abdullayev looked around the storage area for a suitable container for his explosive. He decided on a carton of eight heavy mineral water glass bottles, each holding a bit over a half liter of fluid. He opened all of them, poured their contents down the drain, and then filled them with the mixture he'd concocted. He was careful to not pack the mixture too densely into the bottle; it might not ignite. He tightened the bottle caps closed and returned the bottles back to their carton. All he needed were a few blasting caps, a clothespin and some wire to complete his booby trap. He called one of his employees on his mobile phone and ordered him to bring his car over. Then Abdullayev called Fakhri up.

"The peace of Allah be with you," Abdullayev said.

"And with you," Fakhri replied. "Status?"

"I have a team of three, myself included, who will wait for the quarry to roost. The nest will hold few eggs," he used a euphemism for bombs.

"Very well. That should provide a deterrent."

"I used glass for the outer containers," Abdullayev continued. "The shards will cause maximum damage, yet very little evidence will be left behind. Anyone can get the type of bottle I used anywhere in Moscow."

"Your team must be on the lookout for at least the next seventy two hours," Fakhri commanded. "The woman knows that we're on a tight schedule, so she'll be there soon if she's going to interfere."

"I understand. We'll plant the eggs in the nest within the next hour, then we'll work on eight hour shifts to monitor the situation."

"Report your results immediately back to me. I'm flying out in an hour but you can always reach me at this number."

"I shall," Abdullayev replied. He hung up.

Abdullayev yawned and stretched. Boredom was getting the best of him. It was the second day of surveillance after they'd planted the explosives in Ulyanova's flat. Abdullayev had come on duty forty-five minutes before. The back of the van was cramped and uncomfortable, but he could watch the building across the street through the heavily tinted windows without arousing suspicion. There had been nothing to report.

A black Mercedes Benz was coming up the street. It parked right in front of the building. The chauffeur jumped out of the car and opened the driver's side rear door. A woman got out of the car. A man wearing large sunglasses and dressed in black from head to toe stepped out on the other side.

Abdullayev's pulse raced.

The driver solicitously opened the trunk and took two bags from it. Ulyanova took one, the man carried the other, some kind of backpack. The man paid the driver and limped behind the woman into the building.

There was no lift, and the man didn't seem very nimble. The woman's flat was on one of the upper floors. It would take them a bit to climb up the stairs. Abdullayev waited patiently for the inevitable. The Mercedes left.

The explosion wasn't particularly loud. The building's heavy mortar and bricks had absorbed most of the sound but Abdullayev's ear was tuned to the anticipated bang. He looked up, a shattered window showered glass onto the street. Not bad for a low yield explosive. All eight bottles must have detonated. He waited in front of the building a bit longer, an old babushka wobbled screaming out of the building. Other dwellers soon ran to the street, yelling excitedly about the damage.

Another woman had a wailing infant in her arms. Very few men came outside.

Five minutes passed, then ten. The first ambulances arrived, a police car pulled in. Chaos mounted in front of the building, at least 20 people swarmed outside, blocking Abdullayev's view of the entrance to the building. He had anticipated that. He wore a nondescript jumpsuit, not unlike those worn by the rescue crews. He clasped a stethoscope around his neck, grabbed an empty field case, slipped out of the van, and walked across the street. He must visually confirm that Ulyanova and the man were dead.

Abdullayev broke through the crowd and rushed to the fourth floor. The door to Ulyanova's flat was wide open, a police officer was entering just ahead of him. He entered the flat.

The police and paramedics were inspecting the damage. Glass was everywhere, the foyer was destroyed. The police officer examined the clothespin switch Abdullayev had used for the booby trap.

Abdullayev felt a chill run down his spine. What he found, or rather, what he didn't find, turned his blood to ice. Colonel Fakhri had been adamant about the mission outcome, the punishment for failure would be severe.

Neither Ulyanova nor the man had been outside. He had not passed them on his way up the stairs, and the paramedics had rescued no one from the interior of the building. He had expected to find Ulyanova and the man dragged out of the apartment building in pieces. Instead, they had vanished.

CHAPTER 20

Moscow
From Sheremetyevo Airport to Downtown

Fatigue. The flight from Vienna had felt much longer than it had been. Francis probably shouldn't have traveled just yet, but they decided to move more quickly if they were to recover the documents and stop Fakhri.

Francis and Varenka rode in a black Mercedes taxi, the only reliable transportation Francis would accept for a ride into town. He just wanted to relax after going through immigration. Sheremetyevo was one of the most annoying airports in the world and was probably the most inefficient one. Getting through Russian immigration was an ordeal even when he was feeling well. Nobody respected the lines. People simply mobbed by the booths where the officials gruffly checked everyone's travel documents. And the building was ugly, with its copper-colored cylinders decorating the ceiling, matching the brown/black/gray elongated tiles on the floor. Old bubble lamps looked like 70's relics standing on their chromed bases. The facility had an old and abused look. Arriving or leaving Sheremetyevo always deflated Francis' spirits.

The taxi merged onto the highway to Moscow. Francis leant back on his seat, very much aware of Varenka sitting next to him. Her perfume floated in the confined car. He looked out the window trying to pass the time.

Francis was always surprised at how quickly the Muscovites adapted to the new economic system. He'd visited Moscow for extended periods every year since 1995 and every time he returned he felt like a whole new world had opened in front of him. They passed an IKEA store on the right, a million signs hawking everything from shampoo to automobiles lined the highway. The drab Moscow of 1995 had given birth to a modern metropolis not unlike New York, Los Angeles, Madrid, or

Mexico City, with all the advantages and drawbacks that entitled. Quality of life had gone up for some, hand in hand with a rise in crime.

The taxi wove in and out of traffic. Francis didn't care. He was so tired he barely paid attention to the newly painted, Stalin era buildings, the crowded boulevards, the now pervasive neon signs. Varenka's presence was the only thing he was aware of. He stole a glance at her; she smiled back, her blue eyes livened. Francis felt reenergized by her smile. He suddenly realized he was very attracted to her. Francis smiled back.

The car veered left when they reached the Garden Ring, the avenue that circled the whole Moscow downtown area, with the Kremlin and Red Square at its center.

"We're almost home," Varenka said. "We'll freshen up and get in touch with my boss, Anatoly Petrovich Kuryakin."

"I hope you're right about him," Francis replied. "Let's discuss this later," he said, cocking his head toward the driver.

"I understand."

The taxi driver turned right on Tsvetnoy Boulevard, then made a sharp right onto a side street. Francis was familiar with this part of the city, a mishmash of residential and commercial buildings.

"It's the next building on the left," Varenka instructed the driver. "The one with the red door."

The driver stopped in front of the building and turned the engine off. He courteously opened the door for Varenka while Francis struggled to get out of the car. His right leg throbbed but at least he could put his weight on it without resorting to a cane or crutches.

The driver handed him his backpack. He put his arms through the straps and paid the driver. Seventy-five dollars for a cab ride. Francis sighed. That was Moscow these days, one of the most expensive cities worldwide. You could never pay more, but you could always get better. Besides, if they'd ridden in a standard cab they might have wound up aboard a rickety old Lada or a Volga. Francis was in such pain he'd take comfort wherever he could find it—or afford it.

Varenka led the way into the old, Soviet style boxy building. Francis limped behind her. The stairs were bare. The iron handrails were unadorned. There were two apartments on opposite sides of each landing. None of them had a welcome mat or any of the decorations normally found in western buildings. Even the lighting was poor. While the outside of the building was well kept, the inside probably hadn't seen a coat of paint since before Gorbachev. Francis knew that the outside appearance was deceiving. Each flat was probably luxuriously furnished.

"I'm on the fourth floor," Varenka said. "We're almost there."

"Thanks," Francis puffed. "The going isn't too hard; the steps are wide and not too tall."

"Yes, just like every other building in Moscow from the same era. How does your leg feel?"

"Fine, all things considered. Just don't make me run a marathon, deal?"

"Deal."

Varenka reached the fourth floor landing. Hers was the door on the right.

"I'll open the door as soon as I find my keys," she said, rummaging in her purse.

"Take your time," Francis said, coming up the stairs, one painful step after another.

"There," she pulled the keys from her purse and began opening the locks, Francis was almost at the top of the stairs.

"*Oy, koshmar!* This is so annoying!" Varenka griped.

"What's the matter?" Francis asked as he reached her. She was struggling with the middle lock after unlatching the top and bottom deadbolts.

"This lock is stuck," she replied, frowning. She jiggled the key up and down, fruitlessly trying to turn the lock. "I must have locked it when I left for Vienna. I was late, rushing to the airport. Normally I don't use the deadbolt in the middle because it doesn't work very well. I can open it without hassle only one out of ten times. That's why usually I don't lock it."

"Do you want me to try?"

"No, I've almost got it," Varenka struggled with the lock for a few more seconds. It finally gave in. "There!" Varenka announced, triumphant.

Unease swept over Francis as Varenka opened the door.

Normally I don't use the deadbolt in the middle because it doesn't work very well.

Anything out of the ordinary is a risk, Francis thought, following Varenka into the apartment.

That's why usually I don't lock it.

Varenka let go of her luggage handle in the foyer. She was reaching for the strap holding her Chanel purse to her shoulder. She didn't finish.

"Go!" Francis shouted as he snatched Varenka by her waist and hurled them both through the doorway.

They thudded hard on the floor. Varenka squirmed under Francis' weight with a panicked look on her face. He ignored her; instead, he held her tight and rolled both of them down the stairs, protecting her with his body as best as he could. Her purse whacked his face twice. The hard backpack made a hollow clank as they rolled. They were halfway down to the next landing when a series of explosions detonated inside the confined apartment.

"*Bozhe moi!*" Varenka gasped under him. "My God!"

They stopped at the next landing.

"Are you all right?" Francis asked. Damn! My leg hurts, he thought.

"Yes," Varenka muttered.

"We've got to get out of here," Francis said as they both started to get up.

A woman carrying an infant opened the door next to them.

"What's happening?" the woman asked.

"There was an explosion!" Varenka explained, dusting her clothes off.

The woman didn't have to be told twice. She ran down the stairs, screaming her way to the street.

"Let's go!" Varenka said, tugging at Francis' right hand.

The stairwell carried the sound of more doors opening, women and men left the building. There were shouts of confusion, a hubbub of disbelief.

Francis and Varenka headed down the stairs as fast as his wounded leg would allow.

They reached the second floor. An old lady struggled down the steps ahead of them.

"Hold it," Francis said, holding Varenka's upper arm. "We can't go outside."

"Why?"

"Because there is a chance someone's waiting for us. We won't make it past the corner before someone guns us down."

"What?"

"Think! They found your apartment somehow."

"Sattar knows where I live."

"That's my point. He'd have the place watched." Francis and Varenka went down another flight of stairs. They were on the first floor. Just one more landing to the ground floor. "Is there a back exit from the building?"

"No," Varenka answered. "The main entrance is the only way of entering and leaving."

"Shit. What's behind your building?"

"There's a narrow alley separating us from the next building."

"Does the alley run all the way parallel to your street?"

"I... I think so..."

Francis looked around. There were no windows in the stairwell.

How do we get out?

Francis pushed the door on to his left. It was closed and locked. He tried the opposite door.

It's open!

"Follow me!"

"What...?"

"Whoever lives here was in too great a hurry to lock it," Francis explained. Francis pushed the door closed behind him. The apartments were small. This one smelled of freshly cooked food. His stomach growled. Whatever they'd been cooking smelled delicious. "Where are the windows facing the back alley?"

"In the bedroom," Varenka said, taking the lead. "This way."

They strolled left past the foyer and into a small but cozy bedroom. Varenka opened the first pane in a double window. There was a gap of about a half-meter between the inner and outer panes, built that way for insulation during the winter. Francis went by her.

"Wait!" he said, pulling her back before she opened the outer pane. "You don't know who's out there." Francis squeezed past her, unlatched the window and carefully peered outside.

The alley ran all along the back of several buildings. There were a few garbage dumpsters, a forgotten soccer ball that belonged to a neighborhood kid, a bicycle rack with several bikes chained to it.

"Let's go," Francis said, struggling to swing his injured leg over the ledge. It was a ten foot drop to the ground. Francis gripped the ledge and stretched himself down. He was five-eleven, his feet were two or three feet from the ground. "Follow me!" He let go.

The impact wasn't painful on his wounded leg because, even though it was only a small drop, he executed a sort of parachute landing fall, legs together. He rolled onto his left, distributing the impact over his left calf, hip, and upper body. His wounded leg didn't touch the ground. He got up.

"Come on!" he called Varenka. "We've got to hurry!"

Varenka's shoes and purse fell next to Francis. Good idea, since they had two-inch heels. She then dropped to the ground, gracefully landing next to him in a squat, using her legs as shock absorbers, stumbling a little. She regained her balance.

"What now?" she put her shoes on.

"Now we need to get as far away from here as we can," Francis said, looking up and down the alley.

"Follow me," Varenka started walking to their left. "Bolshaya Lubyanka Street is this way. We can catch a bus, find a taxi, or board the Metro at the Turgenskaya station."

"Let's go, then," Francis followed her.

Service passages ran in between buildings. They reached the first one, between Varenka's building and the next.

"Wait," Francis commanded her. "If they're waiting for us, this would be a good place for a stakeout. Get ready to run the other way if I tell you to." He flattened himself against the wall and carefully looked around the corner. A police car was just arriving to the scene, a few people were gathered in their line of sight, but all were looking up, probably at Varenka's apartment.

"Come after me," Francis said, turning to face her. "Don't run. That will call attention to you. Just walk past the passageway, without looking at the street. If you look that way you risk making eye contact with someone. Understood?"

"Yes," Varenka said.

Francis went first, trying to not limp. Varenka followed.

Varenka took the lead once more. They got to the end of the alley and circled around a concrete barrier banning motor vehicles from turning on to it. Francis looked up and down Lubyanka Street before waving Varenka to follow.

"Here we are," Francis said. "Which way?"

"Go right," Varenka said, grabbing his hand, leading him.

Her touch was like an electric shock, her hand was soft and warm. That's nice, Francis thought.

They trod a busy street. A couple of taxis went by, but they were taken. They got to a busy intersection and turned left.

They entered the station. Francis realized he had no Russian currency.

"I got it," Varenka said, walking to a row of cashiers. There was a brief exchange. She handed him a cardboard ticket the size of a credit card, the instructions printed in blue and red Cyrillic characters, and with a magnetic stripe. "It's good for five trips."

"Thanks," he said, and followed her to the automated turnstiles.

Francis put his ticket in the reader and walked through. The ticket popped up on the other side, where he picked it up. The time and date at this entrance were printed on the ticket.

"Which way are we heading?"

"Prospekt Mira," Varenka replied. "It's a Metro hub. We'll figure out where to go from there."

They hopped onto the escalators. Francis loved how fast they moved. They quickly traveled down.

"You know something?" Francis asked.

"What?"

"Escalators in the United States are excruciatingly slow. Especially compared to yours. The manufacturers and the businesses running them are afraid someone may sue them if they fall."

"Americans are so litigious, and for the most stupid things."

"You're right on that one," Francis smiled. They got to the bottom. Francis hopped off the stairs and stepped aside. The people behind him would rush to the platforms and bump him out of the way.

"There," Varenka pointed as they walked past a newsstand. "We're going toward Chelobityevo. Prospekt Mira is the next stop."

Francis read the signs with a bit of difficulty. It always took him a day or so getting used to reading Cyrillic characters.

They arrived at the platform. A train had just pulled away.

"It will be just a few minutes until the next one," Varenka explained.

"I know. I've been here before."

"Really?"

"Yes, I know the city better than you think. I used to live by the Lenin Library."

"That's interesting. What were you doing here?"

"Oh, some computer stuff," Francis replied evasively. It wasn't time to discuss his past with her yet. "Here comes the train."

The train acted like a plunger pushing the wind out of the tunnel to their right as it zoomed into the station. The doors opened, quite a few passengers got off. Francis followed Varenka inside. They found two seats. He was glad to get his weight off his injured leg.

"*Ostoroshna, dvyere zakrevaytsa*," an automated voice announced. "Be careful, the doors are closing. The next station is Prospekt Mira."

Varenka still held his hand in hers. Francis turned to face her. She gave him an affectionate look.

"Thanks for pulling me out of the apartment," Varenka said.

"Don't thank me yet," Francis replied. "We must still get out of danger. And we're defenseless. My knives are still packed in your suitcase. We're very vulnerable right now."

"You're bleeding," Varenka said, pointing at his leg.

"Damn!" Francis rolled his pant leg up. One of the sutures had burst open. "It isn't too serious." The wound was not so bad, only a thin trickle of blood ran from it.

"We can't stay in Moscow," Varenka said seriously. "We run the risk of getting killed everywhere we go."

"I have some friends here, but I don't want to contact them either. Not yet. We would be putting them at risk for no reason."

"I think... I have an idea."

"What's that, Varenka?"

"You need rest and I need to clear my head. We can't fight Sattar and his people here in Moscow. We'll get killed before we get a chance to speak to Kuryakin. We have about ten days before the situation becomes really critical."

"So?"

"So, I suggest we both take a break to muster our energies," Varenka's eyes glinted with determination. She looked at her watch. "I have a plan, but we don't have much time. I hope you're up for a long train journey."

Francis said nothing. The Metro arrived at the next station. Varenka got up and led Francis out of the train, still holding his hand.

CHAPTER 21

**From Mayakovskaya Train Station, Moscow
to a dacha outside of Volgograd**

The loud whistle announced the train slowly pulling away from the platform. A few people waved goodbye to their dear ones peering out of the windows.

They had departed from the Mayakovskaya Metro and train station. At Francis' urging, Varenka had bought all four berths in the compartment. There was no need for them to share the sleeping car with other people.

Varenka and Francis sat in their first class, sleeper compartment. The upper bunks were folded back, the lower bunks served as seats. It had been a while since Varenka had traveled in one. There was a certain familiar feeling to the cold, red vinyl seat. A small table by the window was stocked with a few items they'd bought at the station: a few bananas, bread, four one liter bottles of mineral water, grapes and plums. Francis watched the city disappear behind, giving way to the countryside surrounding Moscow. Varenka sat across from him.

"How do you feel?" she asked.

"I'm fine, I think. My leg hurts again."

"You should rest. The conductor will bring our bed sheets and blankets shortly. You can then make your bed and go to sleep."

"I'll do that."

Varenka studied Francis. He looked haggard. There were deep dark spots under his eyes. She felt sorry for him. He was injured, tired and, undoubtedly, scared. Varenka didn't know what to think of this man. He had saved her life back at her apartment at a cost of great pain for him. She felt a strange bond with this man, who represented great danger but had twice been willing to risk his life saving hers. She was attracted and afraid of him.

Francis stared out the window with vacant eyes. What was he thinking? Varenka had an urge to hold his hand, to tell him that everything would be all right. But would it? They were running away, both of them scared, both of them wishing that things had worked out differently.

There was a knock on the door.

"Come in," Varenka called.

It was the conductor, a uniformed chubby woman in her early fifties carrying two large bundles of blankets and sheets. She dropped them on Francis' bunk.

"It will be a hundred rubles," the conductor said. "Do you wish to have some tea?"

"Yes, thank you," Varenka agreed, paying the woman. She left the compartment, closing the door behind her.

"Why did she ask for more money? Didn't we pay for the sleeper car already?" Francis asked.

"It's a laundry charge, paid at the train."

"Thanks for taking care of it. I'm feeling a bit woozy."

"Don't mention it, Francis. You just need some rest."

"What will we do now?"

"We're heading to Volgograd," Varenka explained. "My mother lives there. We have a dacha outside the city. We'll stay there for a few days while you recover. We must work on a plan before we engage Mr. Kuryakin and, potentially, Sattar."

"How long do we really have?"

"About ten days, give or take three days. That gives us enough time for you to heal a bit and for me to try to figure out what Sattar is really up to."

"Perhaps I can help," Francis said. "I... I may have access to a copy of the documents that Fakhri took from me in Vienna."

"We'll talk about it later," Varenka said, when there was another knock on the door.

Varenka opened. It was the conductor. She gave her two glasses of tea. She took both by their metallic holder, paid her, and closed the door.

"Now, let's have some tea, shall we?" Varenka said, setting the tea glasses on the little table. "You should probably go to sleep afterward, Francis."

. . .

The train swayed on its tracks as it zoomed across the Russian countryside. Varenka guessed it was past midnight. The moon shone at the zenith. She could see it from her bunk, above the curtains covering the lower half of the window. Its light bathed the small compartment in a numinous, bluish shade. She could feel Francis' warmth. He slept across from her, his features set in a rather cruel mask. It amazed her how cruel he looked when his grayish green eyes weren't open.

Varenka couldn't sleep. She turned in the narrow bunk, trying to make herself more comfortable. It didn't work.

The enormity of their plight had become more pressing once Francis had fallen asleep. She was alone with her thoughts for the first time since Vienna. She was glad to be alive but she took turns at blaming Sattar and Francis for her current predicament. These two men, poised to strike at one another, had altered her life in ways she'd never fathomed. One day she was a successful professional in Moscow. The next she was running for her life, hunted by a maniac whom she'd thought to be her lover. Her orderly life, now shattered, felt like another woman's dream. And perhaps it was so. She turned to lay flat on her back.

Francis stirred on the bunk next to hers. She raised her head to look at him. She was concerned about him since their first night in Vienna, when he'd tossed and turned all night, feverishly talking in his sleep in a mishmash of languages she neither spoke nor understood.

Francis' eyes popped open, alert. That always unsettled Varenka. She'd noticed that Francis didn't seem to go through that groggy stage most people experience while awakening. He was fully alert or sound asleep with no middle level.

"What's wrong?" Francis whispered. It was almost as if he'd heard her thoughts and wanted to confront her.

"I can't sleep. Too many things on my mind."

"Is there anything I can do?"

"I don't think so," Varenka said. "There's just so much going on! I'm scared. My life is going to hell. Too many things happening!"

Francis propped himself up in his bunk. "Varenka, if there was anything I could do to get you out of this mess, I would do it in an instant. You deserve better. The last thing in my mind when I asked for your help was that you would be involved with Fakhri. Believe me, had I known that, I'd have *avoided* you. On the other hand, I'm very happy to have met you."

"So many bad things are happening!"

"Look at it like this," Francis said gently, "worse things will happen if we don't stop Fakhri and his people."

"What can be worse than killing someone? You killed several men."

"And they would have killed you and me first if I'd given them a chance. He would have killed us—and who knows how many others. That's precisely why we must stop them."

"The enormity of the situation just hit me. You killed someone. That's not something you just wink away."

"That isn't something you dwell on either," Francis said. "You are torturing yourself. The best thing you can do after killing someone is to put it out of your mind. What's the point of reliving the experience? Instead, be thankful that you're alive. We can always figure out a way to straighten things as long as we stay alive."

Varenka reached with her right hand over the gap separating them. He extended his hand to meet hers. His hand was warm, his touch gentle. Their fingers intertwined.

"Come to me," Varenka said.

Francis swung his legs off the bunk. He was fully dressed under the covers except for his socks and boots, which were neatly arranged by the door. He sat on the narrow bunk beside her, she turned sideways and flattened herself against the wall separating them from the next cabin. His face reflected a soft, gentle expression.

"Lay down with me," Varenka said. "I want you to hold me."

Francis briefly touched her face but said nothing. He stretched himself along her body, wrapping his left arm over her shoulder. She felt the coarse denim of his black jeans through her pant legs. She rested her head on his chest, listening to his heartbeat, his breathing.

"Good night, Varenka," he said, tenderly caressing her face with his right hand.

Varenka closed her eyes, relishing Francis' warmth. The click-clack of the train continued in the night. She reached up to touch his face with her left hand. He kissed her fingertips softly. Varenka closed her eyes and fell asleep.

...

It had been a hectic day from the moment they left the train station at eight o'clock that morning. It was now one o'clock in the afternoon. She and Francis had taken a taxi to the family dacha in the outskirts south of Volgograd. She'd kept the taxi waiting while she showed Francis around the small cottage, then told him to wait for her until she returned. He'd complied grudgingly. He was a man who liked making his own decisions, but he understood that Varenka had to do a few things alone.

First she had gone to her mother's house. Mama had been exuberantly joyous to see her until Varenka explained, in simple terms, what had been going on. Mama was to answer that she had not seen Varenka for months, that she was supposed to be in Moscow. Her mother was bewildered but quickly stepped up to the challenge once she understood the stakes. Varenka kissed her mother goodbye and pretended to not notice a tear running down the old woman's cheek when she left.

Varenka had bought some groceries for the dacha. There was nothing there for them to eat other than their leftovers from the train ride. She bought fruit, tomatoes, carrots, four two-liter bottles of water, bread, cheese, butter, and so on. They'd have groceries for a few days. She also bought some kerosene.

Varenka went next to her doctor's house. Doctor Sergei Sergeivich Khodorkovsky had retired a few years ago, and still considered Varenka his favorite patient. He'd been her father's friend until his untimely death. Varenka knew she could trust the old man. She needed him now.

Doctor Khodorkovsky, or Sergeivich as people in his confidence called him, had driven Varenka out to the dacha once she had explained a censored version of the situation. The old doctor batted his bushy eyebrows as she explained but refrained from making any comments until she was done. "I hope you know what you're doing," were his only words before he grabbed his beat up leather briefcase and led her to his old Moskvich car. They'd stopped at a local apothecary to procure some medicines and they were off to the dacha.

They parked the car on the shoulder outside the fence. Eight properties shared a common dirt road. Varenka hopped off the car, grabbed the grocery bags, and led the way to the gate into her family's property. The doctor took the heaviest bag from her, then followed her taking his time. He wasn't a man to rush. She led him to the small cottage at the far end of their property, past the birch trees and the lots where her mother and aunt grew tomatoes, cucumbers, corn, and other vegetables.

Varenka held the door open for the doctor and pointed him to a chair by the window. She dropped her bag by the tiny kitchen; Sergeivich did the same. Varenka went to one of the two bedrooms in the back and opened the door. A shirtless Francis slept on the narrow bed.

"Fyodor?" Varenka called, using the name printed in Francis' fake Russian passport. "Fyodor?"

Francis woke up. "Yes?"

"The doctor is here to see you."

"Please let him in," he said, sitting on the bed.

Varenka stepped aside to let Sergeivich in. The doctor flashed an encouraging smile and went into the room, closing the door behind him. Varenka was left alone with her thoughts while the doctor examined Francis.

The dacha was far from luxurious. The cottage didn't even have a built-in bathroom. There was an outhouse at the far end of the property. Visitors normally didn't spend more than a single night there, so even bathing would be a major chore. Water came from a manual pump right outside the cottage. The small kitchen had a wood stove and a sink, and the water had to be brought in from outside in a bucket. Varenka sighed. She unpacked the groceries she'd brought from the city and stored them in the kitchen cabinets. She was washing a fruit bowl when she heard the door to Francis' room open and close.

"There you are," said Sergeivich. "Your friend the foreigner will recover fully. He just needs to keep his weight off the leg for a few days and he'll be as good as new."

"Thank you," Varenka replied, relieved. "He seems a bit distant at times."

"I think that's normal, under the circumstances," the kindly old man explained. "Now, you can tell me to mind my own business, but I'm too old to keep my mouth shut. What are you two up to?"

"I... I'd really prefer to discuss that another time."

"Varenka, I've known you since birth. You can tell me. Are you two involved in anything illegal?"

Are we? Varenka thought for a moment before answering. That had not occurred to her. "No, Sergeivich, we aren't. Please trust me. I can't tell you what's happening yet. I will when it's over, you have my word."

"Are you hurt in any way?"

"No, I'm just tired. We had a long journey."

"Your friend, Fyodor, he is very weak. He should take better care of himself. He's lost a significant amount of blood, and I haven't seen wounds like the one on his leg since the Afghan war. That's a bullet wound."

"I know," Varenka replied simply. "I was there when it happened."

"Who is this man, Varenka?"

"I will explain later, I promise. There is no time right now, and I'm trying to figure this out myself. Don't you trust my judgment?"

"You were always very levelheaded," Sergeivich admitted, "and you were also stubborn as a donkey. I'll let it go for now. Just be careful, do you hear?"

"Why are you so worried?"

"Because while I don't doubt that this man has good intentions toward you, I have reason to believe he's not your best choice for a friend. The scars all over his body, which you've seen I'm sure, tell me he is nothing but trouble. There is an old bullet wound on his left shoulder, and what appears to be a knife wound on his left leg."

"A lot of men get injured throughout their lives."

"During my examination I also discovered something you should know."

"What is that?"

"This man was under constant strain, and I'm not talking only about the fight where he got the leg wound."

"What do you mean?"

"I'm talking about chronic, round-the-clock stress. His hands and feet are unusually cool, a sure sign of stress-induced vasoconstriction. I couldn't tell for sure without running some lab tests, though he doesn't have a blood pressure problem. Stress is the only thing I can blame for his condition. Whatever this man does for a living, I'm sure is extremely dangerous."

Varenka mused about Sergeivich's comment for a few moments. Francis seemed to be very highly strung. There was a certain violence lurking right under his skin, even when he was apparently at ease, waiting to be unleashed. Yes, someone operating under constant stress would react like Francis did.

"I know, Sergeivich. I beg you to trust my judgment. I'm fine, and, for what I know of him, he's a good man. Trust me. I'm making the right decision on this."

"Very well, Varenka," Sergevich sighed. "He's probably sleeping now. I gave him a Percodan and some Naproxen for the swelling." he looked at his watch. "How about making me some tea before I head back into town?"

"For you?" Varenka smiled. "For you I'd prepare a whole banquet."

It was sometime past eleven at night. Varenka sat in the porch, watching the stars and enjoying the chirping of night bugs. She heard the door to Francis' room opening. The only light came from the moon, high above the horizon.

"Good evening," Francis greeted her as he limped to her side.

"Hello," Varenka said, turning around. "How are you feeling?"

"Rested, for the most part. Whatever your doctor gave me sure knocked me out."

"He said you needed rest."

"How long have I been sleeping?"

"About eight hours," Varenka stood up. "Would you like some tea?"

"I'll take some water, thanks. My mouth feels dry," Francis said, following her back into the cottage.

Varenka negotiated her way around the kitchen by feel. She'd refilled the lamps with kerosene. She lit the one in the kitchen and handed Francis the matchbox so he could light the one in the small common area. Francis obliged as Varenka poured him a glass of mineral water.

The yellowish light from the lamps cast long, surreal shadows against the walls. Francis looked rested, though, even in this light.

"Thanks," Francis said, taking the glass from her. "What are we going to do next?"

"The doctor insisted you must rest," she said, sitting next to him.

"Perhaps it's time for us to figure out what Fakhri is really up to," Francis handed her a handheld computer from his pants pocket. "This machine contains a copy of all the documents that Fakhri stole. I need your help to analyze them and tell me what the hell he's planning."

Varenka turned the machine on and pulled a stylus from its side. A set of icons appeared on the screen.

"How should I view this?"

"Click on Graphics. It will give you a list of about seven hundred TIFF files. They are in sequence, from 0 onward, corresponding to the documents Fakhri took."

Varenka selected the first one, page000.tif. The screen turned into a tiny page. A magnifying glass icon appeared on the bottom right corner of the screen. She tapped it. She then tapped an area of the document and it zoomed in. The enlarged digital page was somewhat legible.

"This document is in English," Varenka said. "It says something about the Office of Alien Property. I think... yes, I think it's a receipt. It itemizes a number of crates, put in storage, dated in 1943."

"The first few slides are like that," Francis said. "A few of them have handwritten notes in Cyrillic, but the language wasn't Russian. Do you think you can have these printed?"

"Yes, I think so," Varenka turned the handheld in her hands to inspect the connector on its back. "Do you have the cradle? I may need it to connect this to a computer and dump the data."

"Yes, I do; it's in my backpack."

"This will take quite a while," Varenka guessed at least a day's work. "I'll probably go to the Internet café on the quay by the Volga river and dump the files to disk. I'll print them there."

"Erase all the files from their computer when you're done, regardless."

"That shouldn't be a problem. They wipe out the machines every time a user logs off."

"You may have problems with the device drivers for the handheld cradle. Take the original disk with you and see if you can install it. The disk is in my backpack as well."

"I will."

Varenka leant over to Francis and kissed his cheek lightly. The stubble of a couple of days without shaving felt rough against her lips. "Have a good night, Francis," she said. He was looking at her expectantly. "It's late and I have a lot of work to do tomorrow."

Varenka stood up and blew the lamps off. She walked by Francis on her way to her room. He reached for her arm, grabbed her, and gently pulled her toward him. He kissed her lips. Varenka's heart raced, her hand caressed the nape of Francis' neck. He stood up. They embraced in a long, tender, urgent kiss. Varenka caught her breath and pulled away from him.

"It's not the time..." she said, breathless.

"Good night, Varenka," he said, letting her go.

Varenka went to her room and closed the door behind her. She undressed and got into the small bed. She smiled in the darkness. The memory of the kiss lingered until she drifted to sleep.

D-20

CHAPTER **22**

A dacha outside of Volgograd

"Bullshit. There is no way this will work," Francis said, drumming his fingers atop the hefty binder that Varenka had brought him.

"I find it hard to believe myself," Varenka countered. "But what if it's true? What if it works?"

"Are you really buying this?"

Having been trained as a digital electronics engineer, Francis was familiar with some aspects of Nikola Tesla's discoveries. Tesla had been arguably one of the most brilliant minds of the Twentieth Century, having invented a cart load of electrical machines like transformers, motors, generators, and so on. There were, however, some rumors about the man that were the electrical engineering equivalent of urban legends. Many engineers spoke in hushed tones about Tesla having discovered a new, unheard of source of energy. Others related tales about Tesla having contacted extraterrestrials. This was all nonsense, of course.

Francis was angry because Fakhri and his accomplices had believed these tales and had killed and maimed many people pursuing a madman's dream. More than anything, Francis felt angry at the useless waste of life surrounding them; the documents described a futile fantasy.

Francis and Varenka worked at a table outside the cottage, sipping a cold mint tisane and snacking on a few fresh carrot sticks and tomatoes that Varenka had prepared. It was a warm afternoon. The sun shone on a cloudless sky. Cuckoo birds cooed in the distance, the soft breeze ruffled the trees.

Francis and Varenka studied documents that presented in detail the last important projects by Nikola Tesla. They skipped the first few uninteresting pages. They detailed an inventory of trunks taken into custody immediately after Tesla had died in 1943.

The most important set of papers was a typewritten document from 1937 with many handwritten annotations and a number of diagrams dated between then and 1943. That document began on the third microfiche slide, or around page fifty of the sheets Varenka had printed. The document was titled,

New Art of Projecting Concentrated Non Dispersive Energy
Through Natural Media (rev. 1942)

Francis and Varenka were reading that document in parallel, with Francis occasionally translating for Varenka. Nikola Tesla provided in it specific instructions to build what he called "the machine that will end war." In Tesla's own words, this machine "will send concentrated beams of particles through the free air, of such tremendous energy that it will bring down a fleet of enemy airplanes at a distance of 250 miles."

The papers represented Nikola Tesla's Testament.

"I still don't buy this," Francis insisted. "Tesla talks about what sounds, in essence, like a particle beam defensive weapon. That's the Holy Grail of the Strategic Defense Initiative, the core of the Star Wars program unveiled by Ronald Reagan in the 1980's and resurrected in different incarnations by subsequent administrations. There is no way this... this 'death ray' could work."

"Tesla invented many things in his time that were laughed at by his peers, and subsequently they were proven wrong," Varenka said. "In other instances, Tesla discovered some principle and someone else appropriated it."

"Like what?"

"Like wireless communications. Who invented the radio?"

"Marconi," Francis replied. *Everybody* knew that.

"Wrong," Varenka corrected him. "It was Nikola Tesla. He invented radio transmitters years before Marconi. Tesla eventually sued Marconi for patent infringement and won. Unfortunately the damage to Tesla's memory was already done. History will forever attribute radio and a cartload of other inventions to undeserving people, when in reality they were first conceived by Tesla."

"If I remember correctly," Francis said, scratching his head, "Tesla did a lot of work in the distribution of electrical power over long distances. Didn't he piss Edison off by proving that high voltage, alternating current was the best way to transfer electricity over long distances?"

"Yes, he did. He was also behind the creation of the first hydroelectric plant. People thought he was crazy when he suggested using the Niagara Falls to power giant turbines that would produce electricity. Westinghouse made a fortune from that."

"Still," Francis pointed at the documents before him, "this sounds too fantastic."

"That's the beauty of it," Varenka said. "It's so fantastic it sounds impossible. The more I think about it, though, the more likely it seems."

"What exactly are we dealing with?"

"There are multiple things that Sattar could be building back east. All of them could've been taken from Tesla's inventions."

"Why? I don't understand why Fakhri or anyone else would go back to technology introduced a century ago that was never proven feasible. It doesn't make sense."

"Think strategically," Varenka chided him. "What do all of these things have in common?"

Francis thought for a moment. He didn't want to look like a fool in front of Varenka. She had the benefit of having been exposed, albeit obliquely, to this technology. He mused for at least a minute before replying. "All these things are electrical..."

"That's obvious," Varenka snapped impatiently. "Think harder. What else?"

"They all consume a tremendous amount of power to work."

"And there is no large power plant anywhere on the designs I saw in Moscow. There is just no place atop the oilrig for it. How will it be powered?"

"By..." Francis thought hard, remembering what he'd read, "by using a Tesla power transmitter?"

"Exactly. Tesla claimed that the Earth itself could be used as a generator, using the planet and its magnetic field to produce electricity "

"And that's why I insist this is nonsense," Francis cut her off. "It's the kind of bedtime fantasy geeks tell their children. Nobody has ever proven that."

"The fact that it hasn't been proven doesn't mean that it can't be done," Varenka sipped her tea. "Assume for a moment that this is *possible*."

"Yeah?"

"What would be the advantage of building a weapon with fifty- or a hundred year old technology?"

Francis thumbed through the documents. Transformers, turbines, and a myriad of other engineering diagrams appeared in them.

What is the common denominator...?

"I got it," Francis said. "All of these things are easily available off the shelf. None of the building materials appear on the ITAR lists or have import/export restrictions. They aren't *weaponized*."

"Exactly. If these things work, then Fakhri and his friends will have built a weapon of mass destruction with materials that could pass inspections by the most stringent customs officials."

"That would explain why the documents were kept under custody in the United States," Francis said, putting a tomato slice in his mouth. It was sweet and juicy.

"And that's why Sattar wanted so desperately to nab the documents. He believes these devices will do as Tesla intended. Whether the devices perform or not... only Fakhri and Dr. Volin know."

"Who?"

"Dr. Vassily Volin, a colleague back east who is the technical lead in building Sattar's oil drilling rig."

"Is there any reason why we'd think this... this harebrained contraption would work?"

Varenka paged her set of documents back and forth, stopping to scan a few pages, then continuing.

"Yes, I think there is enough in here to assume that it would work in some form. The documents describe many different inventions, some more credible than others."

"So," Francis asked, "we'll have to plow through the papers and figure out what they mean, is that so?"

"That's exactly so," Varenka said, grabbing a carrot stick. "We'll figure it out. Sattar has limited time and a limited budget. Only a few of these things will be implemented." She ate a carrot stick. "Our job is to figure out which ones."

The next few days were busy.

Francis was regaining his strength. He could almost walk normally, the wound in his leg was barely a nuisance. He exercised every morning, doing sets of pushups, sit-ups, and a walk around the perimeter of the dacha. He couldn't quite jog yet, but he was recovering quickly.

Francis and Varenka had established a routine. They would get up early in the morning, do their respective workout, then take turns to bathe in the back of the cottage. There was a large vat they used for that, where they mixed cold water from the pump and hot water boiled atop the stove. The first couple of times had been uncomfortable but Francis quickly adapted. Some mornings the weather was extra cold so he cleaned himself as quickly as he could, got dressed and ran into the cottage for a hot cup of mint tea. Then they would try to make sense of the documents for a few hours. Varenka had left him on a couple of occasions to get some materials from the local library. Francis would nap in the afternoon, then they'd just talk and get to know each other until early evening, when they took turns cooking dinner for each other. Francis was glad that Varenka was a vegetarian, like himself. That made their lives much simpler.

Varenka had been to town that day. They had just finished dinner and putting the dishes away. Francis was drying his hands with a dishtowel.

"I thought you might like to read this," Varenka said, handing him a book. "It's an anthology of Lermontov's works."

"Thanks," Francis said, taking it. "I've never read anything written by him." He opened and searched for the table of contents. He glanced at it quickly. There were a few novellas, a few plays, some poems. "What should I read first?"

"Whatever you like," Varenka replied. "I just thought you may need some recreation. You mentioned yesterday that you like to read before you go to sleep."

"I do," Francis said. "Thanks for remembering."

"Well, have a good night. I'll see you in the morning." Varenka kissed his cheek lightly. The caress made Francis' heart beat so hard he thought it would jump out of his chest. He was pleasantly jolted every time she touched him, and the kiss had been unexpected, to say the least.

"Good night, Varenka," he said softly.

Francis watched her go into her room. He realized that, even though she was just a wall away, he missed her already. He was developing a crush on her. What was it? Was it her blue eyes, so expressive and full of life? Francis felt alive when they were together, and longed for her when she was away. He sighed. She'd left the kerosene lamp for him. He took it to his room and placed it on a small table, opened a window, and made himself comfortable in his bed. He paged through the book, scanning the poems. He tried reading a few, but he felt too tired to read classic Russian. He placed the book by his bedside, turned the lamp off, and fell asleep.

Today they were working inside the cottage because of rain. Their small table was littered with notebooks, books, calculators and magazines. There was barely enough room on the tabletop for their glasses of water.

"What do we do next?" Varenka asked him, closing her notes.

"We have to report this back to my people," Francis replied. "Although I failed to recover the documents, I'm sure they'll want to learn what Sattar and his guys stole, however crazy it seems."

"How do you propose we do that?"

"We'll get back to Moscow first," Francis took a sip of water. "I'll establish communication with my contact. Then we'll figure out what to do."

"Do we want to go over this stuff once more?"

"Let's do it," Francis said. He was still struggling to buy into all of Varenka's conclusions and the absurd Tesla ramblings.

"First," Varenka closed her copy of the document and paged her notes back, "I think that the team at the White Fortress built a Tesla power transmitter. There are three reasons for that. First, to power everything aboard the rig..."

"Yes," Francis jumped in, "second, to use it as an energy concentrator to discharge a blast of electrical energy at long distances. And third, to power a 'Tesla death ray' or another similar defensive weapon."

"You got it."

"Nonsense," Francis shook his head, refusing to believe.

"Francis," Varenka was on the verge of losing her patience, "what if Tesla was able to build the marvels he describes here, but was also unable to control them at first? This document explains how Tesla overcame the control problem. That's probably one of the reasons why

Sattar wanted it. Sattar and Dr. Volin needed to understand how to focus the energy without blowing themselves up."

"According to the notes," Francis replied, looking at his notebook, "Tesla carried out an experiment in June of 1908 that got out of hand. He used his experimental power transmitter, the one shaped like a tower with a globe on top, to transmit an energy beam at the North Pole from his research site in Long Island. He overshot his target by about two thousand miles."

"Yes, he claimed he hit the region of Tunguska, in Siberia," Varenka said after reading her notes. "It was an accident. Tesla was so awed by it once he understood what happened, that he stopped development of the energy transmitter until he figured out a way to control it. He died before he could implement a solution."

Francis closed his eyes and rubbed the bridge of his nose, trying to remember. Varenka had brought Francis a magazine with an article describing the devastation in the Tunguska region. What happened there was a century-old scientific mystery. Francis shuddered, wondering what Fakhri and Enbeaath could do if they possessed a weapon that could cause that kind of destruction.

"Why couldn't Tesla control the energy output?" Francis asked.

"I have a couple of theories," Varenka replied. "I think that the kind of precision that Tesla needed was not achievable with the tools and instrumentation available a hundred years ago. Tesla, being a genius, was ahead of his time. Controlling the energy output would have required an extremely accurate feedback controller."

"How would it be implemented today?"

"Using some kind of computer. Remember, the Earth isn't perfectly round or perfectly smooth. Tesla might've failed to take this into account, or had chosen to ignore it to simplify his calculations. If you want to be accurate, you have to take into account the variations in the Earth's electromagnetic field due to its shape and the power differentials this would cause. Gravity and the rotation of the planet are probably factors as well. Only a modern digital computer is fast enough to recalculate these variations on the fly. The analog control systems available in Tesla's time weren't up to the task. You would use a digital controller with a feedback loop to channel the power the way you intended."

"He reached that conclusion," Francis passed a page to Varenka. "It's here, in the notes he wrote before he died. There are no details as to the implementation, but there is a non-linear system of differential equations that he claims would solve the problem."

"The solution required a computer, which wasn't available to Tesla at the time of his death. Besides, I think that some of the things that Tesla was trying to do can't be explained by classical physics. Quantum physics theory would better describe some of the effects that Tesla was unable to control, and he wasn't a quantum physicist. Niels Bohr was just beginning his career at the time Tesla caused the Tunguska event."

Francis sighed and leant back in his chair. "Is the technology available for doing this today?"

"It is, though some of the finer controls would have to be built with superconducting materials. Even the vestigial resistance in normal electrical systems would be a problem if you escalate the energy output the way Tesla described in his papers."

"What kind of energy output are we talking about?"

"The plans he revised after 1937 indicate an electrical potential of 100 million volts, that can be discharged with an instantaneous current of 1,000 amps. That would be 100 billion watts of power."

"That's a lot!"

"Remember, the Earth has almost infinite electrical potential. A bolt of lightning is nothing but an instantaneous power transfer that liberates a tremendous amount of energy."

"So a Tesla transmitter would be a way to discharge lightning any-where on the planet that you chose, vaporizing whatever happened to be in its path."

"Yes, and with a great deal higher energy discharge," Varenka said, punching numbers into her calculator. "We're looking at releasing, conservatively, the energy equivalent of ten to the seventeenth Joules. Do you have any idea how much that is?"

"Not really," Francis replied.

"About a ten megaton nuclear blast."

"Jesus!"

"And that's only the power transmitter. This is also how Tesla wanted to generate power for his machine that would end war."

"The particle beam weapon?"

"Yes. However, having a non-nuclear, infinite power source makes creating these 'death beams' a much easier task."

"Of course, all that is speculative," Francis insisted, refusing to believe, "right?"

"Yes, it's all speculation," Varenka agreed, "and these documents are incomplete. It's hard to guess how far Sattar and Dr. Volin got by just going through these papers. I think they already had a set of plans to build their power transmitter before they stole these documents. Based on what I saw before, I would guess that Sattar and Volin were just looking for a way to control the system. I'd guess they are very close to having a fully operational Tesla death ray."

CHAPTER **23**

Byelaya Kryepast former Navy Base
Near Petropavlovsk-Kamchatsky, Russian Far East

The hangar roof slid back on its hydraulic mechanism, exposing the Tesla power transmitter to the heavens. Though they lacked complete assurance, intelligence reports predicted no overhead Russian or American spy satellites during the test. It was a warm day, a sharp contrast to Col. Fakhri's first snowy arrival to White Fortress several weeks before. The metallic globe atop the derrick gleamed like a silvery vision in the late spring sunlight. The Tesla power transmitter was erected atop the almost finished Mobile Oil Drilling Unit. Fakhri had named the MODU *Al Borak*.

Fakhri was on the bridge of the *Al Borak*, his high power binoculars hung from his neck. The first operational tests of the long-range weapons and the Tesla power transmitter were in progress. Captain Akhmar was his second in command in Enbeaath hierarchy, but he was the officer in command of the vessel. The crew would simulate the *Al Borak's* navigational maneuvers since the rig's seawor-thiness wasn't certified yet.

"The rig is in position," Captain Akhmar reported. He clicked his microphone. "All hands, stand by."

The two navigators had a brief exchange with Akhmar. Akhmar went to his command console, tapped a few keys and barked an order. A siren blared on all decks.

"*Al Borak* is in position, sir," Akhmar reported.

Fakhri stood up and walked to the operators. The duty roster consisted of two navigation officers, two radar and electronic counter-measures operators, and two Tesla power transmitter engineers.

"Report," Fakhri snapped.

"Sir, we have an incoming aircraft due west," one of the radar operators said. "ETA four minutes."

"Attention all decks," Fakhri spoke into his microphone, "this is colonel Fakhri speaking. Red Team to combat stations, repeat, Red Team to combat stations."

Fakhri went to the windows and looked down to the rig's deck. Four men emerged from their quarters two floors below, dressed in gray fatigues and wearing crash helmets. Each jogged to a different corner of the oblong deck, where a combat station was built. Each had a cannon mounted on a rotating platform that spun left or right in a ninety-degree arc. All four cannons completely covered them against attack from any air or surface vessel.

Each battle station was fully automated. The operator sat at an anatomical chair in front of a control panel that had a large screen and a joystick. The battle station and the cannon responded to the operator's commands, rotating the platform and swiveling each cannon up or down.

The speakers crackled in the control room.

"Red two, ready," the first man reported.

"Red four, ready."

"Red three, ready."

"Red one, ready," the last voice reported several seconds later.

"Colonel," Akhmar informed Fakhri, "eighty-seven seconds from your command to full state of readiness."

"That's still too long," Fakhri retorted. "They should be ready in less than a minute. Continue the drills after this test is complete."

"Understood, sir."

"Inbound aircraft ETA in two minutes," the radar operator said.

Fakhri spoke into his microphone. "Engage power transmitter."

"Power transmitter engaged," the chief engineer acknowledged.

"ETA sixty seconds,"

"Red Three engaging target tracking system."

The computers aboard *Al Borak* tracked the incoming aircraft in real-time, feeding instantaneous data to the long-range weapons' targeting systems.

A red light blinked on the console to his right. Fakhri knew it was a warning that the aircraft was within a few seconds of attaining visual identification.

"Red Three," Fakhri commanded, "fire at will."

The robotic actuators rotated battle station 3 to align it with the incoming target. The cannon swiveled down as Red Three adjusted its sights and readied to fire.

The globe, or terminal, atop the Tesla power transmitter glowed with a preternatural blue light, brighter than the sun. A single electrical arc jumped from the terminal to a metallic attractor not unlike a lightning rod installed atop battle station 3. The electricity flowed wirelessly between the two devices, ionizing the air.

Fakhri peered through the binoculars. He saw the unmanned aircraft approaching in the distance.

"Target engaged, firing," reported Red Three over the comm link.

The cannon notched right and down, adjusting to the incoming target's changing trajectory. Fakhri knew that each long-range weapon was essentially a long Tesla coil wrapped around a twelve-foot cannon. There was a mercury reservoir at the base of the cannon. The liquid metal stored there was used as ammunition. The cannon chambered a small amount of the liquid metal from its reservoir. The electrically charged mercury molecules turned positive, which instantly shot them away from one another. Red Three pressed the trigger on his joystick, firing the weapon by creating an instant magnetic field in the cannon. This propelled the mercury particles from the chamber's positive pole toward the muzzle opening's negative pole. The particles escaped through the muzzle opening, covering the distance between the rig and the incoming unmanned aircraft at a speed of sixteen thousand meters per second. The unmanned aircraft disintegrated in a flash of light.

"Splash target, distance two thousand meters," Red three reported.

"Congratulations, Red three," Akhmar spoke into his microphone. "Had this been a real attack, you and the rest of your team should've taken half a minute less in getting to your stations. We'll repeat this exercise."

"Understood. Red three out."

"Control," Akhmar turned to the power transmitter operators, "shut main power off."

The operators tapped on their keyboards. The power transmitter returned to its normal, metallic gleam. The hangar roof slid closed, quickly eclipsing the morning sunlight.

"That was a good performance, Akhmar," Fakhri said.

"Sir, we'll practice this until all three teams can get ready in forty five to sixty seconds."

"Carry on," Fakhri said, leaving the binoculars atop his control panel.

Fakhri left the control room. Like all oilrigs, the access ways were as narrow as those in a submarine. Space was at a premium. Fakhri walked past sickbay to the stairs at the other end. He jogged down the steps to the main deck, past two floors of crew's quarters. The delicious smell of freshly cooked food came from the galley at the deck level. Fakhri was pleased. Everyone aboard the *Al Borak* was becoming proficient in their tasks.

Fakhri stopped for a moment to look at the power transmitter atop the derrick. Every exposed surface was painted battleship grey or black. Fakhri was amazed at how well everything worked, just as Nikola Tesla had predicted a hundred years ago. He crossed the deck to the ramp back to the main hangar floor. Dr. Vassily Volin awaited him.

"I take it everything was satisfactory?" Dr. Volin asked with a smug look on his face.

"Everything went as well as could be expected," Fakhri admitted. "Your team did a good job."

"Indeed," Dr. Volin replied, his voice brimming with pride, "we assembled some of the most talented electrical and munitions engineers and physicists in the Russian Federation."

"The beam of light shot from the long range weapon number 3, I've never seen anything quite like it."

"You know that the LRW didn't fire a beam of light," Dr. Volin explained, clearly pleased with himself, "it was a stream of mercury molecules. Each molecule is traveling at approximately fifty-five thousand kilometers—or thirty six thousand miles—per hour. From our vantage point, the destruction they caused appeared instantaneous. It took them slightly over one-tenth of a second to cover the distance to target."

"At that speed... they are faster than any munition I have ever known."

"Indeed they are. By comparison, the fastest projectiles recorded, fired from a .17 Remington rifle or a Kalashnikov Grabityel, top at around one fifteen hundred meters per second or five thousand kilometers per hour."

"That's ten times slower than the LRW."

"It is. The kinetic energy of our particles is such that they'll disintegrate anything in their path. No military shielding can withstand such an impact."

They strolled toward Dr. Volin's office at the far end of the hangar. Various crews worked on different platforms, derricks, and other tools and machines like those aboard the *Al Borak*.

"We're making progress with our own version of the power transmitter and LRW," Dr. Volin explained, pointing at a group of Russians already constructing a new metallic dome. "We learned a lot by building your power transmitter and its weaponry. Of course, adapting the oilrig was also a challenge, considering that both projects require a high degree of sophistication."

"You did an excellent job, and will be rewarded. I'm sure Kurok will be pleased with your progress."

"Indeed. We're all very interested in the outcome of your venture. The *Al Borak* is fully operational. Incidentally, what does that mean? We have a couple of snickering Ukrainians in our team. They think the MODU's name is beet."

"Like the vegetable?" Fakhri was a tad irked.

"Yes. *Borak* sounds very similar to the Ukrainian word for beet root."

"Make sure you explain this to your crew," Fakhri sneered. "*Al Borak* was a fabulous creature, half human, half mare, who took the prophet Muhammad to heaven."

"Indeed... why such a name for the rig?"

"The word *borak* also means 'bolt of lightning' in Arabic."

"Very appropriate."

"I thought so. My men will find it inspirational, and the name, written in Cyrillic on the vessel's hull, will read as vaguely Slavic. That's good enough in case the MODU is monitored after we leave port. Russian flag, name in Cyrillic, and so on."

"Talking about the vessel," Dr. Volin changed the subject as they reached his office, "the propulsion system tests will be completed the day after tomorrow. The nautical engineers are now testing the modifications to the hull. The rig will be capable of doing between twelve and seventeen knots. *Al Borak* is probably the fastest oilrig in the world. Please sit down."

Fakhri sat on a new, comfortable chair while Dr. Volin poured black tea for both of them.

"Like most people," Fakhri said, "I always thought that oilrigs were stationary."

"Oil drilling platforms are stationary. Most rigs are mobile, and self-propelling. Think of them as very stable, navigational, floating cities."

"Like giant motorized rafts," Fakhri replied. "That greatly simplified our mission logistics. At first I thought we'd need a ship to tug the rig to its destination. That would have implied a much larger crew."

"The *Al Borak's* deck is built atop a system of ballast tanks for stability. The ballast tanks, which are mounted on pontoons, the rudders and the propellers were designed for maximum efficiency in the water. Our company will become the leader in semi-submersible oilrig manufacturing worldwide by selling and leasing rigs built around these advances alone. Also, the thirty men you command are more than enough for sailing the rig and handling its weaponry. I must admit that your crew is highly skilled."

"And motivated," Fakhri cut in. "Their passion for this mission comes from a desire to settle a score against the United States."

"How so?"

"They blame the United States for the deaths of relatives, either directly like in Afghanistan, the Philippines and Malaysia, or indirectly like the men from Lebanon, Palestine and Egypt. Or they feel like U.S. influence is corrupting the Islamic way of life. Everyone of us—for I include myself among them—has a score to settle."

"Indeed," Volin reflected, nervously swigging his tea. "I rather not dwell on your politics. I see the creation of the power transmitter, the long-range weapons, and the rig itself as technological challenges. Many people thought that Tesla was mad. My team will be remembered by history as the men who proved right almost every theory and concept discovered by Nikola Tesla."

"I must admit I was more than skeptical at first. Now that we've proven that everything works, we must ready ourselves for the most hazardous part of the journey."

"Moving the rig?"

"Exactly."

"I was wondering how you planned to do that."

"Lukoil deployed a larger oilrig, the *Malvina*, in the Sea of Okhotsk, east of Sakhalin. The *Malvina* is due for maintenance in Long Beach,

California, at around the same time as our rig must arrive at its destination."

"So?"

"The *Al Borak* will intercept the *Malvina* five hundred miles east of Iturup, in the Kurils archipelago, and take its place. As far as the satellites and the U.S. Coast Guards are concerned, it will be the *Malvina* and not our rig that approaches their shore. They won't know we switched until it's too late."

"A daring, cunning plan indeed," Volin shifted in his chair, carefully avoiding Fakhri's eyes. "By 'take its place' you mean..."

"You don't want to know."

"I see." Dr. Volin said, looking at his watch. "I must go now and supervise my team. Feel free to use the facilities." He walked to the group at the other end of the hangar.

Fakhri sensed Dr. Volin's discomfort in asking these questions. He had guessed, correctly, that eliminating the *Malvina* meant an act of piracy. Its crew of one hundred and twenty men would disappear in the high seas. Every battle in every war resulted in collateral damage. It had been a long time since Fakhri had felt any remorse.

Fakhri peered through the window, watching Dr. Volin haranguing his team. What a shame, Fakhri thought. They were good men.

Enbeaath couldn't afford the possibility of anyone tracking down the *Al Borak* to its builders. Fakhri had planned to eliminate Kurok and Dr. Volin's team all along. The first true operational test of the Tesla power transmitter and its associated weapons would be the destruction of the White Fortress compound.

Who had said "loose lips sink ships?" Fakhri mused. It didn't matter. All Fakhri cared about was that his ship sailed successfully to its rendezvous with destiny.

CHAPTER **24**

A dacha outside of Volgograd

Sweat. A single drop ran down Francis' nose. It splashed on the ground in front of his face. "Forty-eight," he counted, pushing himself up, his back and legs straight. Only the palms of his hands and his tiptoes touched the ground. His upper arms burnt with the effort as he lowered himself down. "Forty-nine... fifty!" He finished the set.

Francis jumped to his feet. His wounded leg still hurt under strain but didn't bother him anymore. He continued his pushups, sit-ups and squats until he completed three sets of fifty each.

He felt ready.

For the last several days, Francis had followed a strict routine. Running, shadow boxing using the cottage windows as mirrors, and three sets of exercises to bring his strength back. His reflexes were somewhat off after the long period of inactivity but he felt strong. He'd have preferred training at a gym, perhaps even sparring. He made do with his limited resources.

Francis inhaled the fresh morning air. He grabbed a towel he'd hung on the nearest birch tree branch and headed for the manual water pump. He pumped cold water into a bucket and carried it with him to the back of the cottage to wash himself. He put his bucket on the floor, next to a vat of hot water that Varenka had readied for him.

Francis undressed and poured water over his head and body with a small plastic tub. He shivered while he cleaned himself with a soap bar left on the windowsill for that purpose. A slight draft cut through the trees. He shampooed his hair and washed his face. He reached for the tub to rinse himself.

Dammit, he thought, it stings! Soap got into his eyes. He couldn't open them. He crouched, feeling his surroundings with his right hand, trying to find the water vat. He blindly stepped over and hit his left little toe against the cold water bucket. He cursed in Russian, then bent over to scoop water on his face with his hands. He missed the bucket, losing his balance and knocking the bucket over with his right knee. He slipped while trying to stand up and landed on his butt.

"*Khuynia*," he swore once more.

He first heard the giggling as he struggled to stand up, still unable to open his eyes. The giggling became a hearty, almost musical laugh.

"Here," Varenka said holding his left hand in hers. She guided his hand to the hot water vat, snickering.

"May I have some privacy?" he protested, rinsing the soap off his eyes.

"I heard a racket back here when you fell. I just wanted to check if you were all right."

"I'm fine," he said in mock anger, finally opening his eyes. "Do you mind if I finish rinsing myself?" He stood up.

Varenka was smiling broadly at him. He felt a bit self-conscious, standing naked and wet in front of her. He covered his genitals with his hands and flashed a silly smile back, not knowing what else to do.

"Go!" he laughed, scooping some water in his hand and splashing it at her. She jumped back and sauntered into the house.

Francis finished rinsing. He smiled the whole time. The episode had broken the ice in a childish but refreshing way. For weeks he'd felt the sexual tension building between them. Well, now he no longer had any secrets from Varenka. He shaved quickly, using the window as a make-shift mirror and soap instead of foam. He splashed water on his face, dried himself and wrapped the towel around his waist. He walked to the front entrance and entered the cottage.

Varenka was setting the table for a light breakfast. Cuts of cucumber, watermelon and fresh strawberries were arranged on two plates. She placed two cups by the plates and plucked a dying daisy off a small vase she'd placed on the table center a few days ago.

"Go get dressed," Varenka said as he walked by. "Breakfast is ready."

"We don't want the fruit to get cold, right?"

"You're impossible!" Varenka said, throwing the wilted flower at him. He caught it by the stem in mid air. "Hurry up, though. I'm hungry."

"Don't rush me," Francis said, noticing the glint in Varenka's blue eyes for the first time. The morning light made her eyes sparkled. "You startled me outside."

"Oh, I'm sure you were petrified," Varenka said, coming closer to him. "I'm a grown woman, you know. It's not like this is the first time I've seen a naked guy."

"What will the neighbors think?" Francis asked, stepping closer to her.

"Today is a weekday; everyone is back in town," Varenka stepped closer and raised her right hand to his left cheek. He could feel her warmth as her fingers hovered over his skin without touching it. "Hold still," she commanded, fetching a paper napkin from the table. She gently daubed his cheek with it. "You nicked yourself shaving." She crumpled the napkin into a ball and tossed it across the room and into the kitchen sink.

"You scored two points," Francis said. He thought, Why can't I think of anything smart to say? "I... th—, thanks," he stuttered. She was so close he could smell her fragrance.

Varenka's lips were slightly parted and moist. He leant forward and kissed her softly, half expecting her to pull away. She closed her eyes, the tip of her tongue caressed his lips. Francis closed his eyes and wrapped his right arm over her left shoulder, his left around her waist, gently pulling her body against his. She wrapped him in her arms. Their lips and tongues explored each other urgently.

"Take me," she panted.

Francis led Varenka to her bedroom. They explored each other's bodies while they kissed. Francis' lips fluttered over the tip of her nose, her cheeks, her ears, her neck. He was savoring the dewy taste of her body. He unbuttoned her cotton blouse and pulled it off her shoulders. She wore no brassiere. Her soft alabaster skin had the fresh smell of spring flowers. He unclasped her blue skirt, pulled the zipper down and let it fall around her ankles. Varenka quickly pulled her blue thong off before undoing the towel around his waist.

Francis and Varenka fell on the narrow bed as if in slow motion. Their pale nude bodies were in sharp contrast with the dark sheets. Francis kicked the blanket to the floor. Varenka moaned as Francis kissed her breastbone, working his way to her small breasts. He kissed each nipple, then continued down toward her flat stomach. He smiled. Varenka had a coquettish mole right below her bikini line. Francis relished her taste, her warmth. Varenka separated her legs, he kissed her right inner thigh down to her knee, then worked his way up her left leg.

He kissed her vagina. She was wet. He finally let go and kissed and nibbled at her clit, eagerly lapping at her moisture. Varenka responded by thrusting her hips forward in sync with the flicker of his tongue. She began to moan and pulled his head gently, urging him to come to her.

Francis entered her slowly. They gazed into each other's eyes, their hearts beat quickly in anticipation. Francis was in her, she clasped her long legs around his waist and ran her right hand along his back. Varenka kissed him fiercely. Their bodies moved in unison, the rhythm increased.

They made passionate love for a long time. At times they were gentle, at times rough, at all times they absorbed each other's vital energy. They finally climaxed together, exhausted but happier than either one had been in a long time.

Varenka opened her eyes. Her head rested on Francis' shoulder. She could hear his heart, smell his scent. They were tightly embraced to avoid falling off the narrow bed. That was fine with her. She felt warm and joyful and safe in his arms.

Varenka's feelings for Francis had deepened over the last few days. She saw in him a newfound light. He respected and liked her, all in one, unlike most other men. It was a refreshing change. She sighed, then raised her head to kiss his lips.

He smiled back at her.

"That was fantastic," Francis said, running his hand through her hair. "Unexpected, too."

"I figured it was time for us."

"You figured right," Francis replied and looked at the ceiling. His eyes momentarily clouded with sadness. It was a fleeting moment, but Varenka detected it.

"What are you thinking about?" she asked.

"I'm very happy, Varenka, that's all."

"You were sad. What's wrong?" She propped herself on his chest, cradling her face in her arms. Francis clasped his hands behind his head.

"Nothing. I'm actually quite happy. It's just this crazy world around us. I was just thinking that we'll have to get back soon."

"But not too soon," she stretched to kiss him. "I could get used to this."

"Me, too," he smiled back.

"What happened to you here?" she asked, pointing at a half moon shaped scar under his left armpit.

"It's a long story; I'll tell you all about it some day," he said, evasive. "I'm feeling much better. We will have to return soon. After this morning, though, I don't want to leave. I could get used to this."

"I saw your work out. I'd say your leg has healed."

"Yes, for the most part," Francis' green eyes gazed sweetly at her. "I just had some of the best medicine, though."

She felt herself blush. "You won't have complaints about my bedside manner."

"I have nothing but praise," he kissed the tip of her nose. "Anyway, don't change the subject. We must go back soon."

"The deadline for completing work on the oilrig is this week."

"Then we must go back."

"And do what?"

"I don't know; I'll think of something. Approach your employer, perhaps. We must determine if Fakhri was able to complete the project on time or not."

"How does that help us?"

"Well, you'd said that Anatoly Kuryakin is greedy, if nothing else. Let's appeal to his greed. I'm sure the U.S. government will pay handsomely for any information that helps stop Fakhri and Enbeaath from whatever plan they want to execute."

"Kuryakin won't be easy to approach. He trusts nobody."

"I'm sure. Yet we must start with him. Then we'll contact my people. We must stop Fakhri."

"Why are you so keen on this? Let someone else stop him. You've sacrificed enough."

Francis' body stiffened under her. He averted his eyes to stare at the ceiling once more. "You have no idea how much I've lost to Enbeaath. It goes far beyond the attacks in Zurich and Vienna, Varenka."

"Tell me about it."

"Enbeaath killed the woman I loved two years ago," Francis said. The sad expression returned to his eyes. "The man who killed her escaped and was never caught. I swore I would do anything I could to prevent such a thing from happening again."

"I'm sorry," Varenka said earnestly. "I didn't know."

"Don't be. She's gone," he said bitterly. "Nothing we say will bring her back."

"What was her name?"

"Susan."

"Do you still love her? Do you miss her?"

"I love her, yes, for the priceless few months we shared together. I don't miss her, though. You can't miss a ghost. She's gone forever. You can only miss those who you hope will one day return to you." Francis gazed at her. "I'm sure she'd approve of you and me being together, though. You two could've been friends."

"Do you really think so?" Varenka asked.

"I'm sure. You're very smart and you know what you want. You two would've gotten along just fine."

"I'm honored. I now have a lot to live up to."

"I just wish I could do a better job of keeping you out of harm's way than I did with her."

"I can take care of myself," Varenka said. "What happened?"

Francis sighed. "Let bygones be bygones, Varenka."

"Susan must've been very special."

"She was. Her family never liked me, though. Somehow I always felt that they blamed me for her death. If anything, I did everything I could to prevent anyone from harming her."

"I'm sorry to hear that, really."

"Thanks." His tone of voice became more businesslike. "Which brings us to our problem. I don't want you to get hurt "

"I will be fine."

"Yes, but you know Fakhri and his people are dangerous. I want you to stay in Volgograd."

"I can't do that, Francis. You need me by your side or Anatoly Petrovich won't ever talk to you."

"What if he is in cahoots with Fakhri?"

"What if he is? Anatoly Petrovich trusts nobody. He might listen to me if we approach him correctly. But he won't listen to you alone. And God only knows what nonsense Fakhri has already fed him about you. No, you need me by your side for the initial contact."

Francis gaze turned into a steely stare. "I agree to that, but only if you promise me that you'll come back here when we're done."

"I can't promise you that, Francis," Varenka said, beginning to lose her patience. "Fakhri hurt me too. Did you forget? He was my lover and yet he ordered me killed. I will help you do what you must to stop him."

"Promise me at least that you'll go away if the situation becomes too dangerous. Please."

Varenka raised herself and kissed Francis before replying.

"I'll do my best, I promise."

"Varenka, I don't want to lose you. I couldn't live with myself if anything happened to you."

Varenka realized that Francis' feelings were deeper than he let on. There was urgency in his voice, a pleading in his eyes she had not expected. This man actually cared for her behind the cool, detached facade. That took her by surprise.

"Francis Montagnet, you have nothing to worry about," Varenka said, flashing an encouraging smile at him. "I'll help you stop Fakhri and I'll be fine, I promise. Besides, what guarantee do I have that you won't do something crazy? I don't want anything bad to happen to you either."

"I'll be fine."

"See? You're as stubborn as I am," Varenka laughed merrily, deflating the tension. "We'll be fine, both of us," she kissed him again, passionately. "We'll worry about this later. Right now I have other plans for you."

"Really?"

"Really," Varenka replied and kissed him again. She smiled when she felt him harden. She ran her hand over his hairy chest. It was surprisingly soft. She kissed him, tenderly at first, then with more intensity when she felt his urge to be one with her. She rolled on her side, inviting him to explore her body. Francis took his time kissing every part of her, from the tips of her fingers to the well of her navel. His tongue probed and caressed expertly everywhere it touched her. A playful nibble here, a tender kiss there. Finally she pushed him on his back and straddled his body.

"*Luby menya, dorogoy,*" she said, "make love to me, darling."

Varenka fused with him, their bodies throbbed. She ground her hips against his with ever-increasing intensity, feeling every inch of him deep inside her. The passionate rhythm of their bodies eased the fears in their hearts. Varenka clawed his shoulders in ecstasy. His vital energy permeated her being.

"*Davay!*" she screamed in ecstasy and both exploded as one. She felt like she and Francis were unstoppable.

CHAPTER **25**

The White House
Washington D.C.

To say that Adam Jones felt self-conscious was an understatement. Like most NSA employees, he felt more at home fighting threats to national security than among politicians and Beltway insiders. He followed the aide to a soundproof conference room. They passed men and women who walked the aisles and worked at their desks with serious expressions.

Jones didn't speak to the aide. This was Jones' first official visit to the White House. Unlike their colleagues at the CIA, NSA officers were seldom seen here. Even General Helmwood, the NSA director, only visited the high office once or twice a year, usually for some special event. Today was different. Today they would discuss the security arrangements for the upcoming Summit of the Nations.

They arrived at a large, windowless conference room. The aide opened the door and politely directed Jones to enter. Twelve chairs were arranged around a long table. Six men and a woman had already arrived and sat at their designated places. General Helmwood was already there. Jones crossed the doorway, the aide closed the door behind him. A tray of doughnuts and four large carafes of coffee were placed on a credenza to his left.

"Good morning," Jones said.

"Good morning, Adam," General Helmwood said from the other side of the table; the other attendees greeted him in a dissonant chorus. "Help yourself to some coffee and sit down. You're early, as usual. We'll start in a few minutes."

"Thank you, sir, I'm fine. I ate breakfast before I left the house."

"I'm sure you know everyone in here," General Helmwood said.

Jones greeted the people in the room and sat down. Mitchell Kennedy, Director of the CIA, and Jonathan Davis, his Deputy Director of Operations, sat across from General Helmwood and himself. A female secretary was setting a tape recorder and a stenography machine up. A balding African American man whom Jones didn't recognize sat to his left. Jones read the card in front of him. That was Robert C. Walker, the security adviser to the City and County of San Francisco. The three men getting coffee were from the Department of Homeland Security. The door opened and the humorless directors of the FBI and ATF walked in. Ken Bancroft and Mark Buell were ironically called Castor and Pollux by the media. The two even looked alike. Could they have been twins separated at birth? Jones extracted a yellow notepad and a felt-tip pen from his briefcase and placed both on the table.

The door opened. The president entered. Everyone hushed and stood up.

"Good morning," President Brook greeted and took his place at the head of the table, past General Helmwood to Jones' right. "Please sit down."

The participants obliged. Maybe it was Jones' imagination, but everyone seemed to sit up straighter. Though President Geoffrey Brook lacked a commanding gait, the powers vested by his office made everyone in the room feel his presence like a physical manifestation. The president wielded his power with great restraint; he was too conscious of the polls that guided most of his actions.

"I would like to start this meeting backwards," the president began. "Rather than debriefing you on your respective agencies' plans, I'll start with the end result. The world community steadily pulled away from our shores since the terrorist attacks of September 2001. Tourism has been hurt and important meetings of the economic powers moved abroad. The fact is, aside from the inevitable state visits, the upcoming Summit of the Nations will be the first high-profile meeting of world leaders held in the United States in a long time. Dignitaries from one hundred and ninety nations will gather in San Francisco to celebrate the anniversary of the foundation of the United Nations and its mission. Neither as hosts, nor as a superpower, can we afford any incidents, big or small, marring this event."

The president cleared his throat before continuing.

"This is America. This is the land of the First Amendment. Protesters will take to the streets and express their views. I want to be clear about this: as long as the folks don't endanger themselves or the safety of our visitors, they should have the opportunity to talk, to protest, to march. My concern is that extremists and terrorists may use this chance to bring attention to their causes. We can't afford the risk of anyone instigating an international incident." The President stabbed the table in front of him with his right index finger as he said "I expect you to guarantee the safety of the attendees, the folks, and the nation, during this time." He leant against the backrest. "We can't afford disturbances caused by the Enbeaath, Al Qaeda, or any other terrorist groups that seek to shatter our image and our confidence. Your charter is simple: To uproot all subversive elements from the upcoming legitimate activities. To prevent all terrorist and anarchic actions during the Summit of the Nations."

President Brook paused to look around the table. His gaze stopped at each participant's face. Jones guessed that the professional politician was mentally measuring the effect of his words on this audience.

CIA director Kennedy was the first to speak.

"Mr. President, I think I speak for all of us. We're looking into every possible eventuality. The celebrations of the anniversary of the foundation of the United Nations will not be hindered by any incident. Everyone from the National Guard to the intelligence services will see to that."

"I still think such an event would be better hosted in New York City," Bancroft of the FBI grumbled. "We have better logistic support."

"We disagree," one of the men from Homeland Security piped in. "We suggested San Francisco as the host city for a variety of reasons. The representatives of the original fifty United Nations countries first met there in 1945. The city was originally slated to host the organization. Next, San Francisco is a city ten times smaller than Manhattan. In the event of an incident, collateral damage would be more easily contained. Last, the Bay Area is less densely populated than the New York metro area. Crowd control and emergency services will be far easier in San Francisco in case of an unwanted event."

"Have the facilities been cleared?" Bancroft asked.

"Yes, they have," Walker, the head of security for San Francisco replied in a baritone. "The main event will be held at the San Francisco Opera House on the twenty-sixth, where the original charter of the United Nations was signed. The heads of state of almost every member country have confirmed their attendance, and we're working around the clock with their security detachments to ensure their safety. All vehicular traffic within two blocks of the Opera House and Civic Center will be rerouted from June 24 through June 27. Spot checks will be carried out, and we secured permission from the landlords to deploy snipers and surveillance equipment atop every building surrounding the area. Pedestrian access to Civic Center will be tightly controlled. Nobody can bring bundles larger than a camera, and even photographic equipment will be inspected."

"What about the press?"

"The press are cooperating fully," Walker continued. "News organizations understand the need for security and have complied with our requests."

"Seems like we're running this one by the numbers, Robert," a pleased President Brook remarked to Walker.

"We were able to cut through the red tape, sir. Homeland Security, the FBI and the Secret Service have been most helpful."

The president turned to Bancroft. "How are we doing in terms of suspicious characters?"

"Intelligence is paying off," Bancroft said. "We've had our ears to the ground for months. Our primary concern were the Islamic radicals, and Muslim organizations throughout the country have been of enormous help in weeding out the bad seeds."

"General Helmwood?" the president turned.

"We're monitoring all communications channels, with assistance from the commercial carriers and intelligence branches. The signals analysis and communications intelligence programs developed after 2002 are now paying off," the general turned to Jones. "What's our status?"

Jones inhaled deeply before speaking. "We are running various programs intercepting communications to and from most of the hot spots favored by terrorists, from Europe to Malaysia. We are working with the CMG in Europe and the Australian Defense Intelligence Organization. In addition to tracking the usual communications channels, we also invested our resources in tracking everything from Internet chat rooms to international financial transactions."

"What is your success rate?" The president asked.

"Very high across the board," Jones replied. "The CIA, the military and the FBI receive intelligence extracts on issues related to the summit every twelve hours."

"And the data provided by Jones and his crew has been excellent so far," Kennedy said. "Speaking for the Agency, I can say that they helped immensely to increase our operational effectiveness."

"What we are doing, Mr. President," Jones continued, "is improving our response time once we spot a potential threat. Cooperation from the other agencies and the Bureau is paramount for achieving this goal. We want to respond quickly to legitimate threats. We also want to discard false positives as soon as possible."

"We rely heavily on your mission," the president addressed Jones and General Helmwood. "You and the CIA are our eyes and ears. A quick response to a threat is..."

Jones stopped listening to the president. The Blackberry attached to his belt vibrated insistently. He unclipped the device and glanced at the tiny LCD screen. A chill ran down his spine.

```
XMIT GAMMA QUADRA
PR3D4T0R/CORPOSANT
MSG_FROM: PR3D4T0R@INTERNET.LU?JANAP/299=ZEPHYR
MD5=2BAFA4A1DA4C657F0DF150041775DC47
```

"Is anything the matter?" General Helmwood demanded, exasperated at the interruption.

"Sir," Jones whispered in the general's ear, uncomfortably aware that everyone's attention focused on him, "Permission to return to base requested." He showed his pager to the general.

"Permission granted," General Helmwood barked.

"Mr. President, sir," Jones stuttered a bit, "If you will excuse me, there is an urgent matter that I must attend to." The room suddenly felt hot and stuffy. GAMMA QUADRA meant that the message had the highest classification. CORPOSANT meant it had the highest priority.

"Does this matter warrant interruption of a national security meeting?"

"It does," Jones said carefully. An edgy president was the last thing Jones needed or wanted right now. "I must leave for Ft. Meade immediately."

"Is this matter related to this meeting?" the president insisted.

"No sir," Jones said. "We just completed an intercept that requires my attention. It involves Enbeaath."

Everyone in the room watched Jones with renewed interest.

"You may be excused," the president said simply. "Now, let's get back to business. Stop gawking at Mr. Jones," he scolded the attendees. "we've got matters to discuss."

Jones returned the notebook and pen to his briefcase and went out. Two marines flanked the door on the other side, rigid at attention. Jones walked past them. A female aide dashed from a nearby office, probably summoned by the stenographer in the conference room.

"Mr. Jones," the African American aide said, extending her hand, "I'm Pat Johnson. I will escort you out. Your driver was already summoned; we'll meet him at the east entrance."

"Thank you, Ms. Johnson," Jones said, shaking her hand. She had a firm grip. "Please show me the way."

Pat Johnson led him through a maze of corridors. At first she tried making small talk. She gave up soon, noticing Jones' monosyllabic answers. Jones had other things in mind.

PR3D4T0R/CORPOSANT

Montagnet was alive, and had unearthed something related to the stolen documents and Enbeaath. Now all Jones had to do was retrieve the information and put it to use.

CHAPTER **26**

Moscow
Tretyakovskaya metro station

Varenka felt nervous. Her heart almost jumped out of her chest if anyone simply made eye contact with her. She avoided calling attention to herself. She felt self-conscious. Anybody could be an enemy waiting to pounce. "Pull your hair back," Francis had instructed her, "and go for a more mousy look. Avoid make up. No lipstick or gloss. Dress as plainly as possible. Wear grey, white, black. You want to disappear in the crowd."

So here she was, treading across the Tretyakovskaya station, transferring from the orange Metro line to the green, heading south. She breathed in shallow draws, suddenly aware of how tight her chest felt. It was ten forty-five, too late for the morning commute and too early for the lunchtime crowd. She reached the appropriate platform. A train zoomed in. The doors opened and she boarded after several commuters got off. "Caution, the doors are closing," a pre-recorded voice announced. "The next station is Paveletskaya." She sat by the sliding doors.

Varenka and Francis had arrived to Moscow that same morning past dawn. After a few inquiries, they'd camped out at Konstantin's apartment near the Ostankino Tower. Konstantin was one of Francis' friends. The older, gnome-like man had greeted them at the door, mumbled something about having to leave on business, and had handed the keys to Francis. It was clear to Varenka that Konstantin, if that was his real name, was willing to help but didn't want to participate. The men's demeanor made her think they'd shared some adventure in the past. Francis and Konstantin had greeted one another with familiarity, yet Konstantin had not asked the customary "what brings you here?" It was as if he knew that whatever reason had brought them to his doorstep was none of his business.

Varenka and Francis took turns in the shower before rehearsing their story for Kuryakin several times. Their plan was for Varenka to approach Kuryakin first, then bring Francis in. Varenka left as soon as she felt ready.

Varenka arrived at her destination. She disembarked from the train and exited the station. There was a pay phone by the entrance. She used a calling card for dialing the number.

"Kuryakin's office," a female voice answered after two rings.

"I'd like to speak with Anatoly Petrovich Kuryakin."

"Who is calling?"

"This is Dr. Varvara Dmitryevna Ulyanova."

She was put on hold. Varenka had a white knuckled grip on the handset.

"Varvara Dmitryevna?" Kuryakin's voice boomed when he answered. "You've been missing for over three weeks! The Austrian police are looking for you and "

"Cut the bullshit, Anatoly Petrovich. Sattar Fakhri almost had me killed. I know what our company built for Fakhri, and I know the kind of criminal he is."

"Don't you dare talk to me like that," Kuryakin growled. "Such lack of manners, of respect, from one so young... What is it that you think you know?"

"The Tesla testament, the long range weapon, the mobile oil drilling unit..." The swelling anger helped her rein a nervous stutter.

"What do you want?" Kuryakin hissed after a long pause.

"Perhaps we can help each other to solve mutual problems," Varenka replied; her knees threatened to buckle. "We must meet."

"Who are *we*?"

"You and I, for starters. Then we'll involve other people."

"When?"

"Right now, if you want. No tricks."

"You're treading on dangerous ground, Varvara Dmitryevna."

"And so are you, and we both know that," she snapped back. "I'll be there in five minutes." She hung up.

Varenka took a deep breath. Francis had accurately predicted Kuryakin's reaction; she walked toward the company headquarters building feigning an assurance she didn't feel. She arrived at the building, crossed through the glass doors and walked straight to the receptionist as if she owned the place.

"I'm here to see Anatoly Petrovich," Varenka said, tossing her company badge onto the receptionist's desk.

"One moment," the wide-eyed woman replied.

Two men armed to the teeth and a brusque, toad of a woman closed in on Varenka.

"Follow me," the woman said, leading Varenka to a back room past the elevators.

Varenka's heart pounded against her ribcage. She and the female security guard entered a small, windowless room. The men stood guard outside. The door closed. The woman expertly frisked Varenka. She was neither armed nor bugged, but surely the security guard wouldn't have taken her word.

"Let's go," the security guard said after inspecting the contents of Varenka's purse.

Varenka followed her out of the room, letting out a sigh of relief. Two armed men flanked the women. Nobody spoke on the way to Anatoly Kuryakin's office.

They were somewhat crammed in the lift. The men stared forward with expressionless faces. The female guard picked at her teeth with a fingernail. Varenka looked away, disgusted. The doors opened after what seemed like an eternity.

Varenka's mobile phone rang in her purse. The two men clutched their guns tighter, the female guard stared hard at her.

"I must take that call," Varenka said, reaching into her purse.

"Kuryakin's orders were to bring you up immediately."

"Anatoly Petrovich will be very upset if I don't answer that call," Varenka replied, staring the woman down. The phone rang again. She was motioned by the guards toward a window. Varenka took the phone and answered.

"Where are you?" Francis asked with a trace of anxiety.

"I'm inside, on my way to meet Kuryakin. Everything is fine," she insisted. "I'll call you when we're done."

Francis hung up without replying. She knew he'd not want to hold the line long. Varenka and her guardians arrived at Kuryakin's office.

Kuryakin's secretary studiously ignored them. The heavy double doors opened. Kuryakin sat at his large desk, his dark eyes were trained on Varenka like the double barrel of a shotgun.

Varenka entered the room alone. The guards remained outside. The doors closed. She threw her shoulders back and walked straight to the desk. She wouldn't give Kuryakin the satisfaction of knowing how afraid she truly was.

"I never thought I'd see you again, Varvara Dmitryevna."

"The feeling is mutual, Anatoly Petrovich."

"Please, call me Anatoly. After all, we're dealing as equals now. Sit down."

"Thank you," she replied in a businesslike tone. "We want to make a deal with you."

"What can you possibly offer me that I can't get myself?"

"A chance to live, for starters," Varenka said, noticing the effect her words had on Kuryakin. "What do you think will happen to you once Sattar decides to use the Tesla weapons against a target? It will be only a matter of time before someone figures out who built the weapon for him."

"So what?" Kuryakin's tone dripped contempt. "We're stepping up production of those machines, Varvara Dmitryevna. Did you think we'd build only one? Colonel Fakhri will use the prototype in his suicide mission. I don't expect him to return. I shall use the new weapons we're building to protect my interests."

"What about the Americans? What about our government?"

"You're so naïve. You obviously don't understand how powerful this technology is. I will be untouchable. For the first time since the Cold War someone has the warlike capability to neutralize the nuclear arsenal. What could either one do against me? Nothing. None of the nuclear powers can touch me. Conventional weapons will be useless."

"Thousands of people will die!"

"Collateral damage."

"You're mad!"

"And you're arrogant!" Kuryakin slammed his ham sized fist on the desk. "I didn't invite you here to insult me. You're testing my patience. I thought you had something valuable to offer. Instead you come here and attempt to give me a civics lesson."

"I'm here to offer you a way out of this madness," Varenka insisted. "Can't you see you're living on borrowed time?"

"You are a fool, Varvara Dmitryevna. The MODU sailed already. Colonel Fakhri and his team are aboard. They shall be within the target's range within a few days."

"What's the target?"

Kuryakin laughed. "Do you take me for a fool?"

"I take you for a man who values his life and who I once respected. You could help me stop this madness before it begins."

"Has it occurred to you that I stand to profit as much from this operation as colonel Frakhri does?"

"His motives are political; what about yours?"

"Oh, I stand to profit economically and politically from this operation," Kuryakin said in his deep voice. "What do you think would happen if our president were killed in a terrorist action?"

"Chaos."

"Exactly," Kuryakin lit a cigarette. He puffed on it eagerly before continuing. "The power institutions in Russia, regardless of their definitions on paper, are centralized on the president. Many parties would rush to fill the vacuum, only one will succeed."

"So that's what you're planning to do," Varenka said.

"I plan to do nothing. Colonel Frakhri offered to do all the dirty work. My only advantage will be the knowledge of when and how, but I will have no material participation."

"We have enough information to stop Fakhri now. The Americans have it."

"I don't doubt that you do," Kuryakin replied almost playfully. "However, you wouldn't be here if your information were complete."

"This is your chance to become a hero," Varenka tried to appeal to Kuryakin's ego. "You would go down in history as the man who prevented a catastrophe."

"Heroes must die first to become martyrs. My time hasn't come."

The distant sound of an explosion reverberated throughout the building. The glass windows behind Kuryakin rattled in their frames. Kuryakin sprang to his feet and looked out the window. The muffled crack of machine guns filtered through the closed doors.

Kuryakin snatched the phone from its cradle. His face reddened, fury burnt in his eyes.

"Damn you, Varvara Dmitryevna! Seems like your friends are here."

Varenka was petrified in her chair. Whatever was going on, she knew it wasn't Francis' doing.

The door into the office exploded in a million splinters. Varenka dove for the ground, the shockwave washed over her body as dust and other debris rained all around her. Kuryakin fell back and covered behind the heavy desk. The staccato report of gunfire persisted for a few more seconds, then the whole building became eerily still.

Two men dressed in military fatigues entered the room, aiming their assault rifles at Kuryakin and Varenka. The two guards who had escorted her earlier were sprawled on the floor. A familiar figure entered the room, his eyes glinting with recognition.

"We meet again, Varvara Ulyanova," Sattar Fakhri said unctuously. "You've proven surprisingly resilient. Your presence here greatly expedites our business. We now get to kill two birds with one stone."

"What is this nonsense?" Kuryakin's voice blasted from behind the desk as the man stood up.

"It's a shame our relationship had to end like this, Kurok," Fakhri said, aiming a handgun at the Russian honcho. "You will understand, though perhaps not appreciate, my need for tying all loose ends."

Kuryankin's eyes went back and forth between Varenka and Sattar with a puzzled expression.

"No, she isn't working with me," Fakhri answered the implied question. "I honestly thought she would be dead by now."

"Go to hell," Varenka yelled.

"No Varenka, it is you who is going to hell, escorted by one of its most wretched demons," Sattar looked at his watch and turned to the two men. "Tie them up. We're running out of time."

"Yes, Colonel," the men replied. "Sit down, both of you," one of the men commanded. His Russian had the singsong of the provinces, somewhere in Tatarstan or maybe even Chechnya. Varenka sat down, the other man forced Kuryakin into his chair at gunpoint.

"This will look like an accident, Kurok," Fakhri explained as his henchmen secured their wrists and ankles to the chair's armrests and legs with duct tape. "You, of all people, can appreciate the need for not rocking the boat. It will look like a gas main blew up."

"They're secured, Colonel," one of the men reported.

"Well, it was a pleasure doing business with you, Kurok," Sattar said sarcastically to Kuryakin before approaching her. "As for you, Varenka, I wish we had the time to discuss your friend Montagnet's whereabouts and what you disclosed to him, but I must catch a flight soon." Sattar put his hand under her chin and roughly forced her face up. "Here," he said, forcing his lips on hers, "something to remember me by."

Varenka clenched her jaw and tightened her lips shut. Sattar's mustache prickled against her upper lip like a black caterpillar. Sattar backed away from her, smirking. "Cunt," he muttered, his face just a few inches from hers. Anger swelled in her chest. She spat at him. He jerked back, though not quickly enough to prevent the sputum from landing on his left cheek.

Sattar backhanded her. "Bastard," Varenka hissed, her face burning from his vicious slap.

"Enough!" Sattar barked impervious, wiping the insult off his face. He turned to his henchmen. "Plant the charges. Let's go!"

The men avoided eye contact with Sattar or their captives. They expertly adhered a half a kilo block of orange putty under Varenka and Kuryakin's chairs. A faint smell of almonds rose from the putty.

"How dare you?" Kuryakin demanded.

"What? Use the HMX you sold us against you? You said it during one of our first meetings, Kurok. *Biznis is biznis*," Sattar mocked. "I can't afford any leaks."

The men tested the blasting caps and the radio controlled detonators before attaching them to the blocks of explosive.

"I'll rip your heart from your chest and make you eat it," Kurok said. "Wherever you go, my men will follow."

"Empty threats, Kurok. You won't get the chance. The men and women of your personal army have disbanded or are dead somewhere in this building. Only a Tesla weapon could stop us," Sattar looked at his watch. "the White Fortress compound no longer exists. Dr. Volin and his team, and the next generation of the Tesla power transmitter, have been obliterated. The first operational use of the Tesla power transmitter was a success."

"We're done, sir," one of Sattar's men said. "The radio detonators are ready. They're all set to the same frequency."

"Then lets go," Sattar said. "Goodbye, Varenka." Sattar left the room escorted by his two men.

Varenka tried to pull free from her bindings. The duct tape wouldn't budge. A chill ran up her spine.

"Help me, Varvara Dmitryevna," Kuryakin called.

"I can't... I can't undo the tape."

"We only have a few minutes. Fakhri will blow up the building, and us with it, using a radio transmitter. We must break free."

Varenka squirmed in her chair, tugging stubbornly to break free. Kuryakin was doing the same; neither was successful.

The gunshots from somewhere inside the building startled her.

"You!" she heard Sattar's distant voice, followed by more gunfire. "Get him!"

Boots stomped in the distance, their clack-clack became louder with every passing second. Suddenly Francis dashed into the secretary's anteroom. The wooden wall behind him burst into splinters under the impact of a million bullets. Francis dove to the ground and gracefully slung an automatic rifle from his shoulder. He aimed and fired in short bursts. Varenka couldn't see whom he was firing at. Francis rolled away from the open door, jumped to his feet, and ran into Kuryakin's office.

"Varenka! Are you all right? We got to get out of here," Francis said urgently, pulling a small credit card like gadget from his trousers pocket. He flipped it open to reveal a small knife.

"I'm fine," Varenka said as he cut her lose. "The chairs are booby trapped."

"Both of them?"

"Yes."

Varenka was free. She stumbled to her feet. Francis carefully turned the chair over and inspected the setup. A small black box with two wires leading into a metallic cylinder was attached to the chair. Francis yanked the cylinder out of the orange putty brick and threw it to the far end of the room.

"What about him?" Varenka said.

"What about him?" Francis said, training his eyes on Kuryakin. "We have no time to waste and this fat bastard deserves to die. Fakhri's men will be here soon. We've got to find a way out."

"Fakhri will blow the building up. We have a safe way out," Kuryakin bellowed behind them. "Free me and I'll get us all out of here alive."

"Why should I trust you?"

"Because you have no choice," Kuryakin said almost calmly. "Fakhri's men didn't follow you in here. They must be evacuating the building now."

"I shot one of them," Francis said from Kuryakin's side as he severed his bindings, "but you have a point. You're free. Move!" Francis turned the chair over and pulled the blasting cap and detonator off. "Which way?"

"Here," Kuryakin wobbled to the far wall. He pressed on the rich, lacquered wood paneling. The whole wall slid back with a hydraulic hiss. A dark tunnel sank into the bowels of the building. "My private entrance."

"Lead the way," Francis urged.

Kuryakin crossed into the passage. He pressed a button on the inside after Francis and Varenka entered. A string of lights illuminated a bare, windowless stairwell. The door to the secret entrance slammed back into position.

"It's only four floors down," Kuryakin explained.

"I know—", Francis began to say when a series of explosions shook the building. "Run!"

The building screeched like a wounded animal when its over stressed steel structure began to buckle. Varenka guessed that the explosives had been strategically placed to collapse it. She ran after Kuryakin with Francis in tow. Kuryakin's voluminous mass was surprisingly nimble, perhaps in response to the adrenaline surge. Varenka hoped that Kuryakin wouldn't suffer a heart attack and cost them all precious seconds.

More explosions reverberated throughout the building. A cloud of dust rose from below. The stairs shook as the group hurried downstairs and out of the building.

"Move!" Francis urged behind her. "We've got to get out before the building collapses!"

"We're almost there!" Kuryakin clamored. "One more floor!"

Francis leapt past Varenka, aiming his gun at Kuryakin.

Varenka covered her mouth and nose with her hand. She saw Francis and Kuryakin do the same through gritty eyes. The fine dust swirled everywhere.

They reached the bottom. A single fire door with a metallic handle and a keypad next to the frame separated them from freedom. Kuryakin punched several digits into the numeric pad.

An alarm went off. The numeric pad blinked red.

"What's the matter?" Francis asked anxiously, coughing. The dust was everywhere.

"My code was incorrect," Kuryakin explained. "It won't let me try for another 30 seconds."

"Francis!" Varenka shouted. "The building is collapsing!"

Large chunks of concrete and brick fell from somewhere up the stairwell, shattering at their feet. Varenka was terrified as she huddled closer to the door. She realized they might not make it alive out of there. The walls cracked. She looked up.

The stairwell was twisting in a surreal spiral as the building buckled. Several tons of concrete and metal were about to collapse around them.

"Dammit, Kuryakin, hurry up!" Francis barked, trying to make himself heard above the screeching noises.

Kuryakin punched the numbers once more. The door buzzed, Kuryakin tried to open it.

The door was jammed. Its frame slanted, the walls began to fall around them.

Varenka screamed, impotent. She was sure now they would die.

"Here!" Francis tossed her the gun. She caught it in mid air. "Let me try!" he said, pushing Kuryakin aside.

Francis turned the metallic door handle and heaved. The door was wedged in. He used his right foot to push himself away, desperately trying to open. Kuryakin grabbed Francis' waist and leant back, applying their combined weight and strength.

The door violently swung open, Francis and Kuryakin fell back. They were facing the parking lot.

"Go!" Francis shouted at Varenka as he scrambled to his feet. She saw him help Kuryakin up and they dashed out of the building.

The group ran as fast as they could. The building behind them collapsed in a cloud of debris. Men and women screamed.

"Dive!" Francis shouted, pushing her between a van and a car. The trio thudded on the ground just as bullets hit the spot where they had stood moments ago.

"Give me the weapon," Francis commanded. "Any way out of here?"

"My car is just by the building," Kuryakin said. "If it isn't buried in the rubble, that is."

"Let's hope it isn't," Francis said. "Varenka, you and Kuryakin try making it to the car. I'll keep Fakhri's men busy."

"But Francis—"

"No buts! We don't stand a chance if we stay here. They'll close on us at any moment. Get ready. Go when you hear the shots."

Madness. Varenka crouched at the back of the car with Kuryakin next to her. She saw Francis slip in the opposite direction.

Gunshots exploded in the air, and acrid, burning smell intruded in her nostrils as she made her way crouched to Kuryakin's dust covered Mercedes. It was only a few cars away, but dangerously close to the building, and the shooter was there.

She told herself to focus on the car, to ignore the crack of guns. She knew Francis was alive and possibly fine as long as shots were fired. She dreaded the silence if it ensued.

They made it to Kuryakin's car.

Kuryakin pushed his way next to her and ducked just in time. A bullet shattered the driver side window of the car parked next to his. He seemed oddly controlled as he put his key in the lock and opened the car door. He jumped in, Varenka followed and shut the door.

The inside of the car rattled with the bullet impacts outside.

"Armored car," Kuryakin explained as he turned the engine. "It won't hold forever, but it should get us out of here."

Kuryakin pulled off his stall, bullets smashed against the windshield as they drove in reverse to where Francis had left them. The door locks popped open.

"I'll get his door," Varenka said, turning back in her seat and opening the rear passenger door.

Francis darted into the car, grimacing. Kuryakin slammed the accelerator, throwing Varenka and Francis about the interior. The car skidded past the entrance and drove up Proletarsky Prospekt.

"Are you all right?" Varenka asked.

"I'm fine, *dorogaya*," Francis said.

"What now?"

"Now," Francis said, making himself comfortable in the back seat of the Mercedes, "I think Mr. Kuryakin, you and I must talk."

CHAPTER **27**

A mansion on the outskirts of Moscow

Garishness. The mansion was ostentatious beyond imagination. Reporters swarmed at its gates. Several police cars were parked outside, the officers partly guarded the house, partly managed the mob. The news of the explosion at Teknoil headquarters had traveled fast. The house itself was surrounded by a tall wall and crowned by electrified wire. The monstrous house was erected in the center of a beautiful garden, professionally tended and full of roses and various ornate trees. It's like living in the proverbial gilded cage, Francis thought as he paced on the marble floor, looking out the window. It's beautiful, but Kuryakin can't survive outside and experience real life.

Kuryakin and his attorney were in the library, Varenka was tidying herself in one of the ornate bathrooms. A servant had brought Francis an herbal infusion, something called *shipovnik*. Francis drank it. It was hibiscus laced with some other flower that gave the tisane a dainty aroma. He placed the delicate porcelain cup and saucer on a nearby table.

The door to the library opened. Kuryakin's attorney, a painfully skinny, balding man in his fifties, left without glancing in Francis' direction. Anatoly Kuryakin followed with a determined look on his large face, the pulsating veins accentuated by anger.

"I hope you enjoy the comforts of my humble home, Francis Montagnet."

"I'm fine, Kuryakin," Francis said.

"Call me Kurok. My close friends call me that."

"Since when are we close friends?"

"Since you saved my life."

"I did that for selfish reasons, Kurok," Francis tried the nickname. "I still don't care if you live or die. All I want is the information about the MODU and the Tesla long-range weapon. And I want to get Sattar Fakhri."

"I appreciate your honesty. In time, young one, you will get what you seek," Kurok said. "Follow me. We've got much to talk about."

Varenka came out of the restroom, freshened up. Francis admired her slim figure as she walked to join the men.

"How do you feel?" Francis asked her.

"I'm fine now."

"Come," Kurok insisted and he strolled to the back of the house.

The group arrived at a large game room. A well-finished pool table was located in the center, dartboards and card tables were strategically placed throughout its expanse. A full bar, belonging in a Las Vegas hotel, was set at the back.

"Thank goodness my family is safe," Kurok explained. "My wife and children are at a resort in Sochi, enjoying the sun. The house is ours to talk. What do you drink?"

"Mineral water," Francis replied, "*Borjomi* or *Essentuki-17* if you have it. No ice."

"No vodka for you?"

"I don't drink."

"Suit yourself," Kurok said, shrugging. He turned to Varenka. "And you?"

"Some fruit juice, please."

Kurok summoned a servant rather than fixing the drinks himself. A young man came in, prepared the drinks, and handed them to Francis, Varenka and Kurok. Francis noted the 250 grams glass of Absolut that Kurok drank. The servant left.

"We will discuss this in a civilized manner, Francis Montagnet. Here," Kurok said as he approached the pool table, "we shall play as we talk."

Francis walked up to the wall and chose a well-crafted cue. Kurok was racking the balls on the table.

"What are the rules?" Francis asked, noticing that there were fifteen white balls and a red one. "I've never played Russian pool."

"We'll play a game called *Amerikanka*," Kurok grinned, showing a row of gold teeth. "The white balls are numbered one through fifteen. We'll break with the red ball. You may strike any ball after the break. Whoever sinks eight balls first wins."

"So the red ball is the cue only for the break?"

"*Da.* All balls are fair afterward," Kurok finished racking the balls. He handed the red ball to Francis. "You're my guest. You should break."

This will be a piece of cake, Francis thought. He was good at this game. Francis placed the cue ball across from the pyramid. He put his drink down at a small table, chalked his cue, aimed, and struck hard. The fifteen balls scattered in all directions. A couple came close to sinking in the pockets but stubbornly refused to go in, bouncing off the pocket edges. Kurok circled the table once, studying it carefully.

"Talk," Kurok said, shooting. He shot one of the white balls, which ricocheted against the bands. He sunk no balls.

"I must learn Fakhri's final destination, and what he hopes to accomplish," Francis said.

"Fakhri is aboard a Mobile Oil Drilling Unit identified as *Al Borak*. The ship sailed a few days ago. It's expected to arrive in U.S. territorial waters in two days." Kurok shot a ball and pocketed another one on the rebound. He aimed and struck again. He pocketed no balls on the second shot.

"What's the MODU's cruising speed?"

"It's a new design, one that we're proud of," Kurok replied. "It can do eighteen knots. Up to twenty on calm seas with a tail wind."

"How long will it take him to arrive at his destination?"

"Ten days, maximum twelve."

Francis chose a ball, called it on the far corner pocket and shot. The ball bounced harmlessly against the pocket guard back onto the table. "I can't believe I missed that shot," Francis mumbled. He was feeling frustrated.

"The pockets are only four millimeters wider than the balls. It's not as easy as English or American pool."

"I can see that," Francis huffed. "Your turn. Where did the, ah, MODU start its journey?"

"In the Pacific, north of Japan. Kamchatska peninsula."

Kurok shot trice in a row, sinking balls on two occasions. Three-to-naught.

"And his final destination?"

"He intends to stop the MODU three hundred kilometers off the San Francisco shore. From there he intends to use the weapon."

"San Francisco?" Francis' heart sank. "Why that target? Why not Los Angeles, Washington or New York?" Francis chose a ball, struck it with his cue, and successfully pocketed a ball. He walked around the table, aimed, and struck again. Missed.

"Have you been living under a rock for the last year?" Kurok scoffed.

"More or less," Francis said. He was getting angry. "Can we cut to the chase and stop talking in riddles?"

"Have you seen or read the news?" Kurok hit a ball. Missed.

"No, I haven't for the last month or so. Fakhri's goons did too good a job on me. I was convalescing." Francis aimed his cue at the red ball. He bounced it off the opposite end of the table at an angle. The red ball fell into the pocket next to his hand.

"Very good shot," Kurok praised. "The leaders of all UN member countries are meeting in San Francisco in two days. Most presidents and prime ministers of all the member countries confirmed their attendance. That's Fakhri's angle. He's got everyone in one place at the Summit of the Nations."

Francis chose another ball, aimed, and struck it. "He's mad," he said, as the ball traveled across the table to a side pocket. He scored. "Looks like we're tied now." He struck another ball, number five. The ball hit the edge of the pocket and bounced harmlessly to the center of the table. "Kurok, I need your help to stop Fakhri."

"What's in it for me? I can't afford a leak. If I help you, the Russian authorities will put two and two together. They will arrest me and confiscate my assets. I could be shot for treason, or forever incarcerated on conspiracy charges. Our current government is not one to trifle with." A white ball shot quickly across the table, homing on the far left pocket. The ball sank. He readied to shoot again. He struck ball number seven, which bounced off the pocket.

"We can work better together," Francis said, aiming his cue carefully at ball number eleven. He struck it as number seven coasted across the table. Francis held his breath. Number eleven hit number seven in mid-trajectory, deflecting it so that both seven and eleven were pocketed at opposite ends of the table. He flashed a smug smile at the wide-eyed Kurok.

"That wasn't a legal shot," Kurok protested.

"We're not talking about legal or chivalrous actions here. We're talking about aiding each other to stop a maniac. I can't speak about what the Russian government will or won't do to you if this ever comes out." Francis aimed and struck a ball. It rolled slowly toward a pocket but stopped short of falling in. "It's my job to ensure that it never does come out."

Kurok hit the ball and scored. His chosen cue ball stopped short of a pocket. He scored again. "It sounds like I haven't much of a choice. I could kill you and whatever you know will go with you to your grave," Kurok spoke as if he were describing the weather. "However, I don't know who you've spoken with, what arrangements you made. Or if Fakhri succeeds, he will hound me until he kills me. If he fails there is a chance that the rig and the weapons will be traced back to me." He struck another ball. It was a savage shot. The ball zoomed across the table, bounced back, rolled between two others and fell into the far corner pocket. "So you think we can negotiate?"

"I don't see why not," Francis replied.

"Anatoly Petrovich," Varenka said behind Francis, "you have my word that anything discussed between us shall remain so. You've known me for years. I wouldn't lie to you."

Kurok turned and gave Varenka a contemptuous look. "Why should I trust you? You were assisting this," he pointed at Francis with his cue from the far end of the table, "this *shpion* to sabotage the MODU and the long range weapon. For how long did you share information with the Americans?"

"Stuff it, Kurok," Francis cut in. "She and I met by chance. I knew nothing of the MODU until a few days ago. The only reason we wound up together is that Fakhri assumed she was working with me and I stopped his goons from killing her. Unlike you or me, she was dragged into this without her knowledge. And stop pointing the fucking cue at me before I break it over your head."

"How dare you!" Kurok took a menacing step toward Francis.

"Cut the drama, Kurok," Francis stood his ground. Careful now, he thought. "The theatrics may impress your employees and people like Fakhri, but not me. We have a problem and we need to solve it. Varenka didn't know about this. She spoke truthfully when she said she was loyal to you and your firm. She had every reason to be. Blame me, if you want a target. And use your head. If Varenka had been in touch with me or anyone else, the MODU would've never sailed. We would've bombed it to oblivion by now."

"Anatoly Petrovich," Varenka interjected, "I felt it my obligation to contact you directly once we decided to move forward. Regardless of your intentions, I believe you're a reasonable man, and I respect you. We must stop Fakhri. Everyone wins if we do, everyone loses if we don't."

"Who is being melodramatic now?" Kurok walked to the small table where he had set his glass of vodka. He emptied the glass in a long swig, then looked back and forth at Varenka, Francis and the pool table, sizing it all up. "Can you offer me immunity?"

"Nobody needs to know of your involvement," Francis said. "I have friends in the United States who would like to have you as an ally."

"If my involvement would ever be known I would be ruined."

"You have my word," Francis replied solemnly, mentally crossing his fingers that this deal would be approved by Jones and the NSA. "Nobody will learn of your involvement with either Fakhri or any other plans you had for the Tesla long range weapons," he searched Varenka's eyes. She gazed back reassuringly. "Varenka and I will testify that Fakhri misused your company's resources and know-how. Nobody on your team knew exactly what you were building until it was too late."

Kurok considered Francis' words as he lined up the cue. He struck. The nine ball rolled smoothly across the felt, bouncing off the far band and falling straight into the left, mid-table pocket. "I like your idea. And any surviving members of my staff here in Moscow will swear to that," he said as he walked around the table for an optimal position to shoot.

"We really were in the dark about this whole thing," Varenka addressed Francis. "My team was building components for the MODU on spec, but we had no idea how they fit together. I finally figured it out when we studied our copy of the Tesla documents."

"Only the team at White Fortress had the whole picture. You have a copy?" Kurok asked, his interest piqued. He struck a ball. It bounced off the edge of the pocket he had intended.

"Yes, we do," Francis cut in. "Of course, any documents that you have and can facilitate to us will be part of our bargain." Francis struck the two ball. He'd aimed for its lower half. The ball had backspin. It jumped over the ball in front of it, bounced off the edge of its intended pocket and, luckily for Francis, struck number five and sank it into a corner pocket.

Kurok's deep voice boomed, his laughter sounded almost like a bleat. "Oh, but most of the information we have is publicly available!"

"What do you mean?"

"The Americans were too stupid to realize the treasure trove they held. They turned almost all of Nikola Tesla's papers to Yugoslavia after the Great War. All we had to do was ask the Tesla Museum in Belgrade to show us its whole collection."

"Just like that?" Francis took his shot. He hit ball two and sent it spinning in a gentle arc to the end of the table. "Looks like we tied the game, Kurok. Next one to sink a ball wins."

"Admittedly, I had to make a donation to accomplish this," Kurok explained as Francis circled the table, studying the two remaining balls. "It evolved from Fakhri's idea, by the way. He approached us because he needed the rig to launch his attack and because he knew of my contacts with Russian intelligence. So, we went to the museum, handed them a check, and we had Dr. Volin photocopy every sheet relevant to the project." He took his shot and missed.

The two remaining balls were together close to the center of the table. "I'm not buying that story. It's too easy."

"Granted, there was an additional piece of information that we got from our friends in the former KGB."

"What was it?" Francis struck the ball closest to him. It bounced off the other, propelling it toward a mid table pocket across from him. It didn't sink.

"Tesla was labeled a lunatic by the American establishment sometime in the 1920's. Among other things, Tesla found a way to do of wireless distribution of electricity—and for free!—throughout the world. Of course this would be bad for *biznis*. The electrical companies mounted a smearing campaign against Tesla. Even institutions like the Smithsonian went along with it, crediting others for Tesla's discoveries. Tesla became an embittered man, but he had an ace up his sleeve. Early in the 1930's, as the drums anticipating the Great War began to beat, Nikola Tesla approached the United States government with a proposal to build, in his words, a weapon to end war. In modern terms, Tesla invented an accelerated particle beam. The Department of the Army snubbed him." Kurok shot a single ball, aiming for the pocket, and missing. "This game is harder when there are so few balls on the table."

"I have more than enough balls," Francis said, smirking. "So what did Tesla do?"

"He went to the press and announced the weapon as a Death Ray. It was highly publicized, but the stunt didn't sway the Army's opinion. Unfazed, Tesla put his invention on the market. England and the newly born Soviet Union became interested. Nikola Tesla received a payment of twenty-five thousand dollars from the Soviet Union to produce a prototype. He delivered. By then the FBI realized that maybe he wasn't a quack, and he was ordered to stop his research. He didn't stop, but never completed the Soviet project. Tesla was, after all, a patriotic American. He loved his adopted country."

Francis chalked his cue, readying for what he hoped would be his final shot.

"The original plans for the Death Ray were kept under wraps until the fall of the Soviet Union," Kurok continued. "They were declassified a couple of years ago, probably by mistake. Tesla's Death Ray eventually evolved into a secret project to counterbalance the American Strategic Defense Initiative."

"Reagan's Star Wars," Francis said.

"Yes. Anyway, the plans were incomplete, as we had anticipated. Circumstantial evidence, such as the FBI appropriating some of Tesla's documents after his death, indicated that the rest of the documents existed. Those were the documents from DARPA that you successfully intercepted in Switzerland. What DARPA didn't get was shipped to Belgrade years after Tesla's death. You know the rest of the story."

Francis aimed his cue to the center of the ball. He struck. The ball rolled smoothly across the felt, bouncing off the far band, then the right, then across the table toward a corner pocket. The ball went in smoothly. "Looks like I won," Francis smiled. "Too bad we didn't have a wager riding on this game."

"Looks like you did," Kurok approached Francis and slapped him hard on the back. "Not bad, for a rookie. I could tell you never played Russian pool before."

"I can't say I had," Francis wasn't sure about the sudden show of camaraderie. "Can we count on you, er, facilitating all the information on the MODU and the Tesla power transmitter?"

"Only if I can count on keeping my involvement secret. You may even tout my new found patriotism and willingness to help."

"Consider it done," Francis put the cue back in its holder and offered his hand to Kurok.

"It's a deal," Kurok said, shaking his hand with Francis. The fingers felt like sausages wrapped around his. Kurok applied enough strength to make the gesture feel genuine without being exaggerated.

"There is something I don't understand," Varenka said. "Tesla's discoveries indicate that the power transmitter could focus its destructive energy on any point on Earth. Why go through all the trouble of building the MODU and sailing to the American coast? Why the exposure? He could have built the power transmitter in Iran or any other safe haven and fired from there."

"Physics," Kurok said, releasing Francis' hand and facing Varenka. "Tesla's mathematical model works in a perfect universe. We could probably iron out the kinks if we had enough time, but Fakhri was on a time table."

"What does that mean?" Francis looked from Kurok to Varenka and back.

Varenka spoke first. "It means that Tesla didn't take into consideration air, the varying density of the Earth at various latitudes, the magnetosphere, and so on."

"Precisely," Kurok continued. "If the power transmitter were operating in a vacuum, and if the Earth were a perfect sphere, then quantum fluctuations wouldn't affect the effectiveness of the weapon over a long distance. In the real world, however, the electrical power can only be discharged at a maximum range of 700 kilometers, or about four hundred nautical miles. An attempt to do it from farther away from the target decreases the accuracy with the square of the distance."

"I see," Francis said, and now he understood. That was why Tesla had missed his target in the North Pole in 1908 and instead created the Tunguska event.

"So, at three hundred miles, the MODU will be just over the horizon," Varenka finished.

"Yes, it will," Kurok poured another half glass of vodka and gulped it. "That also means that the *Al Borak* MODU will be outside American territorial waters when Sattar Fakhri snuffs out the world leaders gathered at the Summit of the Nations."

CHAPTER **28**

Moscow
The United States Embassy

Haste. Francis and Varenka arrived at the embassy gates red-faced and sweaty. Francis pressed the intercom button. They stood by a side door a few yards away from the entrance to the consular section.

"State your business," a tired female answered in Russian.

"*Eto Fyodor Goristyi i Varvara Ulyanova.* We have an appointment."

The employee hung up without responding, the door buzzed open. Two marines flanked it. Francis and Varenka crossed inside. A tall, pleasant man dressed in an off-the-rack brown suit and wearing an ugly, cheap tie awaited them past the security station and metal detector.

"This way, Mr. Montagnet," the man said.

Francis emptied a few coins from his pockets. He carried no weapons anyway, since he had ditched them in Austria, almost a lifetime ago. He crossed the metal detector under the watchful eyes of a security guard. The marines stood at attention flanking the door, their weapons ready. Varenka followed him after placing her purse on the X ray machine conveyor.

"Mike Gunn," the man introduced himself, "International Trade Administration."

"Francis Montagnet," Francis said, handing him his Russian passport, "traveling as Fyodor Goristyi. This is my partner, Dr. Ulyanova."

Mike examined the passport with a clinical expression. "We did a good job with this one." He turned to Varenka. "My pleasure, Dr. Ulyanova. Please follow me."

Varenka picked her purse up and they rushed to a secure room. It was furnished with a small, rectangular table surrounded by six chairs. Two 32 inch TV sets, one with what looked like a camera on top, dominated the far end of the room. A grey telephone and phone conferencing station with omni directional microphones were at the center of the table.

"Please, sit anywhere you want," Mike instructed. "Washington contacted us less than a half hour ago and appraised me of the importance of your arrival. You caused quite a stir."

"I can imagine," Francis said, assuming that Mike was really the CIA chief of station in Moscow. He took his leather jacket off and hung it on his chair's backrest. Varenka sat next to him.

Mike fussed with the secure video conferencing equipment. The TV on the left, the one with the camera on top, came to life. It displayed a view of the room. The other screen was black except for a line of text giving a network address and a stand by notice in green characters above a yellow progress bar that steadily increased to one hundred percent. The screen flickered to life, showing a different conference room somewhere in the United States. Adam Jones sat alone, facing the camera. There was a small notebook computer next to him. A man left that room, closing the door behind him.

"It's good seeing you again, Francis," said Jones. "I thought you were dead."

"There was a time when I thought that myself."

"Who is your friend?"

"This is Dr. Varvara Ulyanova," Francis turned to her. "She's helped me piece this thing together."

"Nice to meet you," Varenka said in English with her delectable Russian accent.

"Pleased to meet you, Dr. Ulyanova," Jones smiled and turned to Francis. "You understand she has no clearance. I may ask her to leave the room."

"We both understand that. However, she's the one who put it together, and she probably understands more about the kind of trouble we're in than we do. You want to hear what she's got to say."

"Let's go on the record. Mike, whenever you're ready."

Mike pressed a few buttons on the remote control. A red dot flashed on the screen. "We're all set, Mr. Jones."

"Let's hear it."

Francis and Varenka spoke for the next forty minutes. Francis gave an account of what had happened after the exfiltration operation had failed in Austria, omitting no details. Mike was looking at him the whole time with a blend of respect and disbelief. Then Francis and Varenka talked about the Tesla testament. Jones asked a few questions to better understand the discussion. Francis aided a couple of times to translate for Varenka or to clarify something she said. Finally they told the story of that morning, leaving out some of the details regarding Kurok—and the fact that Francis now had obtained a copy of Kurok's set of the documents before coming to the embassy.

"So that's where we stand," Francis concluded. "I find some of it hard to believe. Yet it must be true, if Fakhri and Enbeaath are willing to go through all this trouble."

"This is worse than we thought," Jones said, rubbing his bearded chin. He tapped on his keyboard. "Well, here is what I found in our records, which confirms what you said.

"Nikola Tesla died in 1943 in a hotel in New York City. He left behind a number of trunks packed with documents. A secret memorandum, signed by J. Edgar Hoover, ordered that the trunks be secured at once. Hoover feared that these documents would fall into the hands of Nazi spies. The memo was directed to the assistant director of the FBI New York office."

"What about relatives?"

"Tesla's nephew, a guy named Sava Kosanovic, was present when the trunks were removed. He did not object at first, but eventually sought legal help. Of course, this led him nowhere. Kosanovic eventually became the Yugoslav ambassador to the United States."

"Hard to spar against Hoover's FBI."

"Brawn over brains, even today," Jones shrugged. He continued. "The FBI in New York urged the Office of Alien Property to cooperate in hiding the documents. The OAP was to appropriate the documents and make them available to the FBI and other authorities immediately. The OAP protested that Tesla had been a naturalized American citizen since the beginning of the century and thus they had no jurisdiction. Hoover himself overruled them."

"Wow. So the documents were taken illegally?"

"Let's say that they were seized under dubious circumstances. The threat of war, German espionage and all that."

"So in a way this was done in a climate much like today's," Francis said. "Hoover was stomping on a citizen's rights."

"That was business as usual while he was in charge," Jones shrugged. "Several subsequent memos traced the itinerant documents as a portion of the originals were transferred to the Office of Scientific Research and Development, a branch of the National Defense Research Committee, a precursor to DARPA. A Dr. Trump, commissioned with analyzing Tesla's writings, recommended immediate appropriation by the NDRC of all technical documents found in Tesla's suite. The originals became highly classified information and were studied by various teams between 1943 and 1999. Copies were summarily destroyed after review. Whatever wasn't in the NDRC's or DARPA's hands eventually turned out in what became the Tesla Museum in Belgrade."

Varenka and Francis exchanged glances. "That is confirm what we know," Varenka spoke. "This is DARPA documents that Francis got in Zurich."

"Hoover's zeal in trying to prevent the Nazis and the Soviets from snapping Tesla's writings backfired," Jones said. "Ambassador Sava Kosanovic recovered the documents from the OAP in 1952 and created the Tesla museum."

"And that helped the Soviets expand on the plans they had from 1937," Francis said. "The documentation was still incomplete but—"

"—but the soviets had enough to start their own weapons programs based on Tesla's documents," Jones cut in. "Most people think that particle beam weapons and other exotic technologies were a product of the Reagan years. In fact, we were playing catch up. The soviets had been working on such programs since the 1960's. Fortunately nobody had the complete set of documents to finish a Tesla death ray or a power transmitter."

"Nobody had them until Fakhri and his people put them together." Francis leant back in his chair. He looked at Varenka and at Mike. Varenka seemed quite calm. Mike, on the other hand, stared at the screen vacuously, unbelieving. Francis continued. "Our only advantage is knowing that neither the so called death ray or the power transmitter work over long distances."

"Why is that? What do you mean?"

"Propagating beam or focusing energy discharge over long distance is..." Varenka's voice trailed. "*Trudnyi*?" She looked at Francis.

"Difficult."

"Difficult, yes. This is why weapon cannot locate more than seven hundred kilometers from target."

Jones leant forward in his chair. "We don't have time to waste then. The Summit of the Nations begins in two days. You and Dr. Ulyanova should brief the troops here."

Francis swallowed hard. Return to San Francisco. He had not been back since Susan died two years ago. "What can we do that isn't done yet?"

"Well, Dr. Ulyanova can brief us on the capabilities of the oilrig, for starters. You can return the documents. Besides, you'll be safer here."

"If you say so," Francis said. "What do you think, Varenka?"

"I want go, if it helps stop Sattar Fakhri," she said flatly. She switched to Russian. "I'm not sure I want to be in San Francisco when Fakhri attacks the city."

"So be it," Jones turned to Mike. "How soon can you get the appropriate paperwork ready for these two?"

"Do you have your passports with you?" Varenka nodded. "I can get the visas authorized right away. I'll have to check on flight information, but I think I can get you out of Moscow today."

"I'll get a military transport to bring them in if necessary," Jones said. "We have lots of work to do. Francis?"

"Yes?"

"It'll be nice seeing you again in person."

"Same here, Adam."

"I'm going off now," Jones said and clicked his end of the conference off. The TV screen went black.

"You two follow me," Mike commanded. "I'll find you a nice place to wait."

"We've got to get our stuff from my friend Konstantin's house," Francis said, getting up from his chair and grabbing his jacket. "That ought to take us less than an hour. Can you facilitate transportation?"

"Yes, we can. How far?"

"By the Ostankino Tower."

"Not a problem."

Varenka and Francis followed Mike out of the room. They trod the maze like corridors to a waiting room. Mike took Varenka's and Francis' passports with him. "Help yourselves to some coffee or whatever," he said as he walked away. "Be back soon." The door clicked locked after he left. Francis had the distinct feeling that they were more than prisoners and less than guests.

"Varenka," Francis said, holding her two hands in his and gazing at her. "Are you ready for this? This will be dangerous."

"Yes, I am," she gave him an earnest, loving look. "We must stop Sattar. Besides, you will be there to protect me, right?"

"Right," Francis said with a conviction he did not feel. His heart skipped a beat, his resolve wavered momentarily. He inhaled deeply before he leant forward to kiss her cheek. "I won't let anything happen to you."

"I'll be right down," Francis instructed the driver as he inspected the building through the bullet proof glass. They parked their armored VIP Chevy Suburban in front of Konstantin's apartment. Varenka would remain in the vehicle escorted by their security detail. Two marines, CJ and Zebulon, were armed to the teeth and sat by the vehicle's doors. The driver's eyes darted to the mirrors.

"Sir, we have instructions to escort you at all times," Zebulon informed him.

"You can wait for me here, though. I won't be a minute."

"With respect, you ain't goin' nowhere without me."

Francis didn't feel like arguing. This jarhead might actually beat me if things get physical, he thought. He sighed. "Do your worst, Zebulon. Don't you have a nickname or something?"

"No, sir."

Zebulon jumped out of the vehicle. Francis followed and then took the lead. They climbed to the sixth floor apartment up the dark, narrow stairwell. It was as quiet as a tomb. Francis opened the door, they entered.

"First time in a Russian apartment?" Francis asked.

"Yes, sir. Seems kinda small. How many people live here?"

"Just one, but this apartment is intended for a couple and maybe one child. Probably built during the Stalin era. I won't be long. Have a look at the rest of the rooms."

"Yes, sir."

Francis went to the bedroom to gather his and Varenka's belongings. His backpack and leather jacket were on the bed, Varenka's small carryon was on the floor.

A chill ran down his spine when he spotted the package.

Their belongings were neatly packed, just as they'd left them earlier. Francis inspected them with an expert eye. They had been moved. A gift-wrapped package had been carefully placed beyond the backpack.

What is this? Francis thought, handling the package carefully. A small, engraved envelope was propped against the backpack itself. Francis tore it open.

Francis,

Thank you for saving my life. The roads to Moscow are many, and perhaps our paths will cross again. Make good use of the Tesla files I shared with you. Good luck in your quest, and don't forget our bargain. Enjoy this present.

Anatoly Petrovich Kuryakin

Is this a bomb? Francis thought, carefully weighing the package in his hands. How the hell did Kurok find us here? How did he know we were staying at Konstantin's apartment?

Francis tore the wrapping open, revealing a gift box from a fancy delicatessen. He opened it with caution. A bottle of Krug Rosé champagne and two large tins of black caviar were nested inside. Interesting. Francis closed the box and strapped his backpack on. He left the box with the champagne and caviar on the bed for Konstantin to enjoy, grabbed Varenka's carryon, and left the bedroom. He took Kurok's note with him. Konstantin would enjoy the impromptu present.

"Zebulon? Let's go."

"Yes, sir," Zebulon led the way out of the apartment.

Francis locked the door and kicked the keys underneath it while Zebulon scanned the stairwell.

"After you," Francis said, and both men walked down the stairs.

I have to admit this is one hell of a present, Francis thought on his way to the Suburban. The caviar is a nice touch. Kurok is far from being a friend, though. On the one hand he delivered this gift. On the other he's letting me know that he could track us down. It's like slap in the face delivered with kid gloves. I'm glad that all the Tesla Testament files are actually in my pocket, carefully kept in my Palm computer's encrypted memory.

"The peace of Allah be with you," said the voice on the phone in heavily accented Russian.

"And with you," Sattar Fakhri replied. "I'm on my mobile phone. Be brief."

"The man and the woman were sighted. The foreigner and the Russian woman that you—"

"Montagnet and Ulyanova!" Fakhri exploded. How could that be? "Where are they? Speak!"

"They are at Sheremetyevo airport. I saw them from my taxi as I waited for a fare. They were escorted by three men. Americans. Possibly military. They were taken to the diplomatic waiting area."

"Can we get a team in place?"

"Not... not at Sheremetyevo," the voice stuttered. "It would be suicidal."

"Quickly! Is there any way we could intercept them? Put someone on their flight?"

"Not in such a short time."

"Hell and damnation! Where are they going?"

"To the United States. San Francisco."

"You served well." Fakhri finished the call without waiting for a response.

Somehow they had figured out Fakhri's plan. Kurok had to have helped them. Montagnet and Varenka were on their way to ground zero. Fakhri was sure that they were there to try to stop him. Only Kurok knew Rebirth's final destination and objective. Montagnet and possibly the Americans had forged an alliance with the *maffiya* kingpin.

Why take Varenka? Fakhri paced in his room, pondering. Of course! The Russian whore had become a technical adviser of sorts. She had designed much of the basic oilrig technology, and had been instrumental in developing some of the machines driven by the Tesla power transmitter.

How could he have been so careless? Montagnet had proven many times how resourceful and dangerous he really was. Montagnet and his puppet masters were resolved to stop Rebirth from completing its mission. It was Fakhri's duty to see this through to completion, and this time without mistakes. Fakhri himself was scheduled to depart within a few hours. He would travel to the United States under his Spanish citizen cover. The countdown to Enbeaath's highest achieve-ment had started.

D-2

CHAPTER **29**

San Francisco

"How far are we going?" Varenka said, snuggling against Francis. The taxi smelled of cheap air freshener. She looked out of the taxicab window. There were very few cars on the road.

"My flat is only twenty minutes away from the airport," Francis replied. "We'll be there shortly."

"It's dark outside. I thought American cities were lit up at night like Christmas trees."

"They are; San Francisco summer nights are almost always shrouded in fog, though. That's why you can't see much. And the climate is always cool in the summer." He turned to the driver and said something in English.

"I asked him to take the long route home if the sky is clear when we get to the city. You'll have something more to see than the signs by the freeway."

"What time is it here?"

"Around ten-thirty."

"I'm tired."

"I know. Come here," Francis gently pulled her toward him.

Varenka leant against his body. She felt warm and protected by him. While the confined back of the taxi was hardly the most romantic place to cuddle, Varenka relished Francis' proximity. They were both silent, lost in their own thoughts. The driver ignored them. She was in America. It was a strange, somewhat anticlimactic feeling.

The car took a secondary freeway and Varenka straightened up. They were approaching the city. The fog gave way to a majestic view. A long bridge was lit up on her right, the downtown skyscrapers welcomed them ahead.

"Is that the Golden Gate Bridge?"

"No, that's the Bay Bridge. We can't see the Golden Gate from here."

"That's very beautiful."

"Oh, that's our ugly bridge; you'll get to see the pretty one later," Francis bragged.

Varenka kissed his right cheek lightly. His face felt prickly against her lips. Francis had not shaven since early morning in Moscow, more than thirty hours ago. He flashed a weary smile and gently kissed her back. Probably he was as tired as she was.

The car left the freeway and entered the city. They drove through a maze of streets.

"This is Market Street," Francis said at the intersection while they waited for the light to change. "Downtown is to the right. We're going all the way up north, close to the bay, where I live."

She looked out the car window. An electric train traveled on their right down the well-lit but slightly hazy street. San Francisco fog. Several homeless men and women were clustered at the nearest corner, on their side of the littered intersection. She noticed how clean the street was on the other side.

"There are so many derelicts..." she muttered, almost to herself.

"Yes, that's one bad thing San Francisco is known for, especially here on Sixth Street." Francis shrugged. "It's been a problem in the city for as long as I can remember. It's a very touchy political issue."

"I thought there were no poor people in America."

"There are quite a few, and it seems most of the homeless sooner or later wind up here."

The light changed, they drove forward. She tried to read which street they were on. Taylor Street. All the traffic lights were synchronized to green. The car worked its way up a very steep hill. The driver said something to Francis when they reached the summit.

"He's apologizing for going this way," Francis explained. "The streets we'd normally take are closed around Civic Center because of the Summit of the Nations. That's further that way," he pointed to their left. Varenka noticed three helicopters circling in the distance; their powerful searchlights swept the ground underneath.

"Is it much longer? I'm really tired."

"Not really. Besides, you get to see a few more things this way. That, to our left, is Grace Cathedral..."

Varenka looked at the Gothic church with interest. It looked like a scaled down version of Notre Dame de Paris. She realized that Francis pointed out the landmarks in an effort to distract them both from their mission.

Their car went down hill. They had entered a much nicer neighborhood. The Victorian buildings lined the streets, a few well-dressed people walked home from various restaurants and bars. Varenka caught a glimpse of the bay illuminated by a lighthouse from an island peeking through the fog; she couldn't remember its name and Francis was directing the driver so she didn't ask. The taxi turned left and finally stopped. Francis paid the driver, who helped them unload their belongings from the trunk.

Varenka followed Francis into a courtyard flanked by two Victorian buildings. The air smelled of the fresh grass as they walked past the fountain to his flat. The entrance was on the far left. He fumbled in his jacket pocket for a single key and opened the door. Grey carpeted stairs led them to the second floor flat.

"Welcome home, Varenka," he said simply, dropping his backpack in the living room. She did the same.

Francis showed her around. All the rooms were spacious. The living room and bedroom windows faced the courtyard. The carpet only covered the stairs up, and the rest of the flat featured polished hardwood floors. The living and dining rooms had raised ceilings and beautiful brass light fixtures on the walls.

Varenka was surprised at how Spartan the flat was. She shivered. It was a bit cold, regardless of the heaters in every room. There was almost no furniture, and what was there was all black or grey. The only conceit was several paintings on the walls. Even the bedroom was decorated purely in black and white. The bed covers and sheets were black, as were the headboard, the dresser, the night tables, a television, and its stand. The curtains were white, like the bathroom and the toilet room at the other end of the flat. There were no plants or anything that showed a personal touch. No family photos. No pillows on the sofas. No trophies. A corner of the living room had four large bookcases.

"You must read a lot," Varenka said as she scanned the collection of books with English, Spanish, Russian, and French titles. There were works of fiction and non-fiction, biographies, technical books. "I like that in a man."

"I try," Francis said, leading her to the kitchen. "It gives me something to talk about."

The kitchen was as large and sterile as the rest of the flat except for the first touch of color Varenka had seen so far: The gold and red flower patterns on the black lacquered finish of a set of Russian, *Khokhloma*-style tray, cups, and spoons. All the appliances were black or white, from the stove to the refrigerator. A white vase held a few orange and yellow marigolds. It was on the large, bare table in the center of the kitchen. Francis read a note attached to it.

"It's from the housekeeper. She left food in the refrigerator. I can make some tea. Make yourself at home. Are you hungry?"

"Not at all, thanks. I just want to take a bath and go to sleep," Varenka said. "We have a long day tomorrow. May I have a glass of water, please?"

"Of course," Francis said. He poured water in a tumbler from a pitcher by the sink and handed it to her.

They went to the large bathroom. Varenka drank while Francis rummaged in the closet for a large, fluffy, white towel that he set on the towel rack. He began to fill the enormous porcelain tub before handing her a bar of glycerin soap, a washcloth, and a bottle of lavender scented Roger & Gallet bath gel. He left her alone.

Varenka immersed herself in the hot tub, pondering their dangerous future after washing the trip and the stress off. She closed her eyes. She was enjoying the bath and, for the first time in weeks, she allowed herself to relax.

The black sheets felt fresh when she got into bed. She wore a long T-shirt in guise of a camisole; she'd forgotten to pack one. She heard the running shower while Francis readied to join her. She sighed. She felt safe for now.

A buzzing sound broke through the stillness of the apartment. She opened her eyes, realizing she'd dozed off. The buzzing sound continued for a few minutes, then stopped with a loud click. What had that been? She was still puzzling over it when Francis walked in with a towel wrapped around his waist. He had clipped his hair to a crew cut. His face was clean shaven.

"Hi," he said, smiling. "How do you like my new look?"

"It's different. And I'm cold here. Are you coming to keep me warm?"

"Of course," he smiled, letting the towel drop to his feet before getting in bed beside her. His naked body felt good against hers. She pressed herself against him and he put his arm around her.

"So what's with the haircut?"

"It's a long story," Francis said after kissing her tenderly. "It's a ritual I picked up from the Thai kickboxers. They always cut their hair really short prior to an important fight. It's part of their mental preparation."

Varenka ran her hand over his head. The bristles felt like a soft brush. "I like it," she decided.

She kissed Francis' lips. He responded immediately. She pushed him down, straddling him. She removed her T-shirt and pinned his arms against the bed above his head. He didn't resist; he simply lay there, his eyes sparkled with anticipation.

She kissed his face, his neck, his chest. She positioned herself so that he could penetrate her. She swayed slowly, their bodies instinctively matched their rhythm. She let go of his arms. He pulled her closer to him and nibbled on her left ear as he ran his hands up and down her body. His breathing quickened. Varenka moaned.

"Slow down," Francis said. "We have all night."

He ran his hands along her body, finally resting them on her waist. He propped himself up to kiss her hard nipples, first the right, then the left, sending a shiver through her body. She turned her face to him, panting, searching for his mouth. They kissed.

Varenka couldn't wait any longer. She ground her hips against his, dug her nails into his shoulder leaving a trail of fiery red half moons. His member was buried deep inside her; she increased the tempo, dragging him along to her explosion in ecstasy. They came together, Varenka collapsed on top of him. She lay there for several minutes, enjoying his caresses and soft kisses on her shoulder. She could feel his heartbeat against her own chest. She looked up.

"Promise me we'll always be together," Francis said, meeting her gaze.

"Forever, my love," Varenka replied. "Nothing will ever come between us, I promise."

Varenka rolled off his body and gently massaged his temples. There was a lot of tension there, accumulated from their weeks on the run. She soon realized that Francis had fallen asleep in her arms. She shifted to lay beside him. Francis stirred and unconsciously wrapped a protective arm around her. She cuddled against him and drifted off to dreamless sleep.

CHAPTER **30**

A mosque off Van Ness Avenue, San Francisco

"The peace of Allah be with you," Fakhri's amplified voice reverberated in the packed room.

"And with you," the voices of a hundred followers chanted back in Arabic.

Fakhri looked around the room. The men knelt on their mats, their feet bare, their presence at the mosque explainable as nothing more than attendance to a morning service. Most of the men were dressed in casual, nondescript clothes. All of them listened to Fakhri in rapture.

"We followed giants to reach this point," Fakhri spoke into the microphone. "From the first, wobbly steps of Al Qaeda to the wars in Malaysia and Afghanistan, the groundwork was laid for us to lead the world away from its heretic ways to an age of enlightenment. We, the disciples of *Enbeaath*, of Rebirth, will bring the love and wisdom of Allah to the heretics who have defied His wrath. When our children go to bed tomorrow evening, they will know that a new world is reborn for them. It is only through the efforts of everyone in our organization, our *brotherhood*, that we'll finally eliminate the enemies of the faith and the exploiters of our people. We've been chosen by Allah to carry out His will against the heretics, here in San Francisco."

Fakhri studied the men before him during his pause. There was a look of awe and respect on their faces, a look of anticipation mixed with anger waiting to be unleashed.

"Tomorrow night the world will look up to us with newfound respect. The humiliation we suffered at the hands of the United States and the rest of the world will be wiped from history, the arrogant nations will be brought to their knees, the men who branded us criminals will bow before us and beg for forgiveness. Tomorrow we'll see the birth of a new age of peace and prosperity after the wrath of Allah is unleashed on the infidels and oppressors. Tomorrow we shall see the blinding light of

Allah strike them down. Tomorrow we shall be free of tyranny and oppression."

Fakhri paused when the thumping sound of a low-flying helicopter broke through the mosque's walls. It soon faded away. The men were oblivious to it, their feverish eyes were focused on him, their hearts and minds were absorbed in the message he preached. Like many men recruited as fighters for Enbeaath, they were largely uneducated and fanatical. Fakhri didn't share their religious fervor, but nevertheless he understood what made them tick. He needed them to accomplish his goal, they needed him to help them regain their dignity. These men were willing to sacrifice their lives for a cause they fully understood. Only Fakhri and his top lieutenants truly comprehended the geopolitical implications of things to come.

Fakhri nodded at four men almost directly in front of him. They stood up and promptly joined him. They respectfully saluted Fakhri before turning to face the audience. Fakhri spoke again.

"These four brothers volunteered for a most important task. They are the harbingers of Allah's punishment. These men will help direct His wrath to the very place where mischief breeds. Remember them in your prayers, for their task ahead is fraught with peril," he turned to the group, "May the peace of Allah be with you, brothers."

"And with you," they chanted in unison.

"Now, my brothers, we shall turn to another important matter. Many will try to stop us. We must thwart their success. In particular, there is an evil woman who has the means to derail our quest. She's from the godless land of Russia, and her escort is a very treacherous man. We must find them and stop them before they impede our quest." A man quietly entered the room and handed several sheets to the attendees. Photos of Varvara Ulyanova and Francis Montagnet appeared in them, with a brief description of each. "You must stop at nothing. They are here in San Francisco, lurking in the shadows and abetting our enemies. Find them. Bring them to me." He paused for a few moments while an old man joined Fakhri at the front of the room.

"Let us pray," the old man said.

One hundred men prayed in unison, their fervor almost as palpable as a physical entity. Fakhri left the room.

. . .

The journey was almost at an end. Captain Akhmar consulted the computer screen. They were at the correct latitude and longitude. It was time.

"Engines at ten percent," Akhmar ordered.

"Ten percent, aye," his navigator answered.

The *Al Borak* came to stand still in the middle of the open sea. It was cold and cloudy, but nothing compared to the unbearable chill of the Kamchastka peninsula they had left ten days before. The sea was calm, there were no birds or any signs of land on the horizon.

"Sir, we're in position," said the navigator after consulting his GPS screen.

"Shut engines down and flood the ballast tanks," Akhmar ordered.

"Flooding, sir."

"What's the pitch?"

"Four degrees, sir, and stable."

"Commence flooding the pontoons."

"Aye, sir."

"Report our position,"

"Sir, we're within position with plus minus one twentieth of a degree."

Akhmar consulted his charts. "Engage turbines and maintain position."

"Aye sir."

Akhmar noticed the obvious reduction in elevation above the sea level. He knew that the *Al Borak* would displace roughly 30,000 tonnes of water once the ballast tanks and pontoons were filled to capacity. This elevation, or draft, would be no more than twenty meters after the ballast tanks were full, from almost forty while they were cruising.

"Ballast tanks filled to 85 percent," the navigator reported after a long pause.

"Prepare to deploy sonar cubes," Akhmar ordered.

"Aye, sir."

Akhmar marveled at the set up. Unlike boats, the oilrigs were not anchored nor tethered to the bottom. That was too inefficient and prone to positioning errors. They used either a geosynchronous satellite feed for positioning, or a sonar mechanism. After much deliberation, they had decided to use the sonar cubes because they were more independent than the GPS. If the *Al Borak* was discovered after positioning, it was plausible that the GPS signals could be shut off, sending the MODU adrift.

"The positioning program passed the test," the navigator replied. "Standing by to deploy sonar cubes."

"On my mark," Akhmar checked the data pouring onto his screen. "Deploy."

The sonar cubes were deployed by a Remotely Operated Vehicle, or ROV. The ROV was a robot controlled by an umbilical, commonly used for salvage operations. A typical ROV provided video and remote manipulation capabilities to its masters aboard an oilrig. The ROV used for deploying the *Al Borak's* sonar cubes was an electrical and hydraulic vehicle. The machine provided up to 200 Hp for thrust and tooling, more than enough to handle the sonar cubes and the cement blocks they used for ballast. Two operators manipulated the ROV for a long time, adjusting the depth and location of the vehicle and its payload until each had been properly set up.

"Cubes deployed," the navigator announced after a long pause. "They will reach the bottom shortly."

There was another long pause while the sonar cubes settled on the bottom and the diagnostics software tested them. Finally the test was over and all cubes operational.

"Engage thrusters," Akhmar said.

An operator consulted his computer screen and flipped several switches. "Electric thrusters engaged. We're off position by one tenth of a degree."

The oilrig was completely still. Akhmar's crew tapped on their keyboards and checked their screens repeatedly.

"Sir, we are in position. The rig is now stable. Maximum deck pitch is less than one degree." The operator tapped his keyboard. "All systems nominal."

"Well done, Eyman," Akhmar praised his navigator. He clicked the PA system on and spoke into the microphone. "All hands, this is the captain speaking. We are in position. We are entering condition red. I repeat, condition red." Akhmar knew that somewhere in the crew's quarters this news was received with joy. The men would finally apply their skills after weeks of grueling training.

Akhmar looked out the bridge. Quicker than he expected his construction crew erected the derrick. In a few hours, after the liquid nitrogen was pumped through the superconducting coils and the various systems engaged, the Tesla power transmitter and the long-range weapons would be fully operational.

Fakhri had summoned Amin Fayad to his private chamber. Fakhri poured tea for both of them before he began explaining the mission ahead.

"Amin, this Francis Montagnet is the same man who foiled the action in San Francisco two years ago," Fakhri told the man with him. "He killed our mission leader. The other members of the group were killed or injured, many by this man."

"I remember that," Amin said, clearly nervous in Fakhri's presence.

"We commissioned you to find Montagnet and kill him."

"Yes, I was in charge of that. After the mission failed we assumed that he was a local. The news sources never mentioned him, a strange thing considering it was such an explosive event. We searched for many weeks, until we unearthed him. His name. His address. We trained a fighting squad to go after him but he disappeared without a trace until today. We can find him again soon if he is in San Francisco."

"I'm sure he is now," Fakhri said, pacing. "He surfaced in Zurich almost two months ago. He probably left San Francisco shortly after the incident. Perhaps he feared retaliation, perhaps he was just lucky. In any case, I want you to gather your squad."

"We shall not rest until he's dead, Colonel." Amin paused before continuing. "During our investigation two years ago, we discovered something you may want to know. How well do you remember those events?"

Fakhri sipped his tea before answering. "Well enough. Talk!"

"A woman was shot during the scuffle. She was on the stage when that happened."

"Yes, I remember. What of her?"

"We discovered that she was Montagnet's fiancée."

Fakhri stood up to pace the room. So that's another reason fueling Montagnet's quest! They had botched the mission and he regretted not having shot Montagnet back then. His life would be much simpler now if he had. Well, his chance would come soon enough. Montagnet had first tarnished the success of that first Enbeaath operation. Next Montagnet had almost derailed the construction of the *Al Borak*. Finally, Montagnet had corrupted Varenka, the woman Fakhri had loved. That pig! Yes, Fakhri would see that Montagnet paid for all his transgressions.

"Amin," Fakhri spoke softly, trying to control his anger. "I want the Russian woman alive, if possible. But this man I want dead—and I literally want his head. Contact me when you find him. Be careful. He's evaded us too many times. I want to take his head with me when I leave, and use it as an example for those who defy us." Fakhri dismissed Amin with a wave of his hand. "May the peace of Allah be with you."

"And with you," Amin replied as he left.

The four men had taken their positions in different parts of the Bay Area. Each carried a custom made device that combined the features of a mobile phone and global positioning system. One was in San Francisco, the others in Sausalito and the suburbs of Walnut Creek and San Mateo. Each took readings with their device and compared them with the known latitude and longitude of a given location in each city. Each device might carry a slight error, but correlating all four identical devices would render accurate data. On D-Day, the men would station themselves at various points around the United Nations Plaza and Civic Center, as close to the Opera House as possible. They did not know this, but in less than twenty-four hours Fakhri and his crew would use their readings for providing the exact coordinates of the United Nations Plaza and the San Francisco Memorial Opera House to the *Al Borak*.

Fakhri received the reports and entered them in the computer. The data was analyzed and retransmitted, including a digest, to the *Al Borak*. The crew in the modified oilrig would use it for adjusting the power transmitter's focal point and range.

Fakhri readied his equipment for departure. Time was running out and Montagnet and Varenka were still missing. He shrugged; soon it wouldn't matter. Fakhri was due aboard the *Al Borak* before nightfall. He snapped his aluminum case closed and methodically removed all evidence of his visit.

"Sir! We found them!" the shrill voice announced, jolting Fakhri to attention.

"Montagnet and the woman?"

"Yes, sir!" The speaker was a young recruit born in the United States of Palestinian parents. "They were sighted when a police escort took them into the Federal Building just a few minutes ago. They opened the barriers set around the Civic Center perimeter to allow them in."

"Are you sure it's them?"

"Yes, sir."

"Alert Amin and his squad!" Fakhri roared and looked at his watch. Perhaps Varenka and Montagnet were too late. Perhaps security around them was such that Amin, Fakhri and their team would not be able to breach it. Perhaps Fakhri himself would pump a bullet into Montagnet's head before he was due aboard the *Al Borak*. Killing Montagnet and recouping Varenka would give immense pleasure to Fakhri. The next twenty-four hours would mark the final success of Enbeaath, a victory crowned by a string of personal victories for colonel Sattar Fakhri.

CHAPTER **31**

Havoc. The FBI offices in the San Francisco Federal Building were a whirlwind of activity. Francis watched through the conference room windows how the resolute men and women performed their duties. He was taking a mental break from the drilling he was getting. Kenneth Bancroft, Director of the FBI, sat across the narrow table, his doll-like eyes fixed on Francis. Bancroft had been confrontational from the moment they had met.

"Where are the documents?" Bancroft insisted.

"How many times do I have to repeat it?" Francis retorted; he felt close to losing his cool. "We destroyed all the printed and digital copies before we left Volgograd, just in case we got caught. I didn't want to carry them with us."

"Do you realize that you destroyed stolen classified documents?"

"I did what I thought was appropriate," Francis said.

"I can't believe this!" Bancroft slammed the table with his fist. "You're a goddamn loose cannon, Montagnet. I'll have your ass for this!"

Varenka flinched at the impact. She was standing by the white board, marker in hand. She had drawn a detailed diagram of the Tesla power transmitter and how it would work. She had finished her presentation and was ready to field questions. Bancroft ordered the other ten men and women from the room and insisted on Francis producing the documents. Varenka looked at Montagnet, confused.

Don't say a word, Francis thought, gazing back at her. He hoped she wouldn't say anything about the copies of the documents being stored in his handheld computer. He tried to reassure her with his gaze. Things would be fine as long as she kept quiet. Her translator was too anxious to convey to the room whatever Varenka had to say.

"Look, you're learning whatever Dr. Ulyanova and I know," Francis said. "That was the whole purpose of getting us to San Francisco. Now, we can argue about bygones all afternoon, or we can get on with the program."

"Let me get this straight then," Bancroft leaned forward in his chair. "We have no plans, no hard data that we can use to build a defense. We have only your suppositions based on a document you read days ago, and some other intelligence you gathered in Moscow. This is a waste of time! Your mission was to bring the damn documents back. Instead I'm being lectured by a punk and a geek."

Francis bit his lip before spewing a reply he would regret. The translator, a dowdy Jewish Russian woman, told Varenka what Bancroft had said. She stepped forward.

"You," Varenka said, flustered. "You are not *kulturny*. Don't be insulting. If you think this is waste of time, we can go home." She and Bancroft glared at one another. "I can explain what weapon does better than only Sattar Fakhri. If you don't want hear it I want leave now, because when Fakhri activates it everyone will die within at least a one kilometer radius."

"My apologies, miss," Bancroft said. "I heard what you had to say. It's of no use to me or to my mission. You'll both be debriefed at the Alameda Air Force Signals Intelligence station in," he looked at his watch, "two hours. A vehicle is waiting for you. My problem is recovering those files, and determining whether we must evacuate this area or not, and when."

"The timing is anyone's guess," Francis interrupted. "For all we know, Fakhri and his goons are aiming the weapon at us right now. We could be pulverized any minute. I would evacuate."

"We don't think so," Bancroft countered. "Enbeaath would want to make a political statement. The only victims, if they fired now, would be the same protesters whose support they want to garner. They don't want that. Their best time will be tomorrow, during our President's keynote address. We believe we have about eighteen hours to stop Rebirth. The armed forces are in full alert, patrolling our shores constantly. Recovering the documents, though, is a matter of national security."

"I can't help you with that anymore," Francis insisted.

"Then I will make sure the Attorney General presses charges against you. Treason, for starters."

A youngish man entered the room. He went to Bancroft and spoke into his ear. What is he saying? Francis fruitlessly strained to hear.

"Well," Bancroft said, "we'll have to continue this conversation later—"

"You mean interrogation."

"Don't be a wiseass, Montagnet. Your ride is here. Follow agent Simons to the first floor. We aren't through, Montagnet."

"Whatever you say," Francis shrugged. There was no point in arguing with Bancroft.

Varenka gathered her purse while Francis put his leather jacket on. It was a custom garment, made of tough leather and with insets in the shoulders, back, and sides. The insets were made of a light rubber compound used in motorcycle racing suits. They could withstand a fall from a speeding motorcycle while preventing serious injury by spreading the shock over their surface. Francis figured that his attire by itself was enough to rub Bancroft the wrong way, from the steel-toe combat boots to his mirrored sunglasses. He wasn't armed.

Well, I'm not here for a modeling session. And I will protect myself.

He had urged Varenka to wear walking, rubber-soled shoes and comfortable clothes. He'd handed her a leather jacket as well, but it had been too big for her so she wore a simple wool jacket. Francis hoped she wouldn't need the extra protection.

Francis and Varenka followed Simons. None spoke until they were on their way down in the elevator.

Francis put his Gargoyles mirrored sunglasses on. "So, Mr. Simons, where are we going?"

"You will be escorted to a secret facility in Alameda, about thirty five miles from San Francisco."

"I know where Alameda is."

Simons shrugged. "The facility is managed by the Navy. NSA Director of Operations Adam Jones awaits you there. A control center was set up there and you're summoned. Various experts are flying in as we speak."

"Interesting," Francis translated for Varenka. She nodded. "You seem to be very well informed, Mr. Simons."

"I'm the FBI liaison, Mr. Montagnet."

"Call me Francis."

"I'm Joe."

The elevator doors opened. The group walked to the white car parked on Golden Gate Avenue, in front of the building. The street was eerily deserted, all pedestrian and vehicular traffic held back on Turk street. Joe Simons took the passenger seat; the driver was already there, his expression obscured by aviator glasses. Francis opened the rear door for Varenka and they both went in. The car took off before Francis slammed the door shut.

"We have to go up one block," the driver said to Simons. "We can't go across Civic Center or through to Van Ness. We must either leave down Gough or Jones streets."

"Take Gough," Simons replied. "That will put us right on the freeway."

The car reached the barrier at the intersection of Polk and Turk. Several hundred protesters brandished signs there, mounted SFPD officers controlled the crowd with the mass of their horses. Two police officers pushed the crowd back to open the barrier for the car to go through. Francis heard some of them chanting, others shouted at the FBI car. Simons and the driver stared forward, pretending to ignore the crowd. Francis exchanged looks with Varenka and squeezed her hand reassuringly. They'd be gone shortly.

The Molotov cocktail flew from somewhere in the crowd and crashed on the windshield, startling them. The fire spread and splattered with the shards of the exploding bottle.

"Don't panic!" Simons called as the driver stepped on the gas. The car lurched forward, parting the mass of people in its way like a wounded dragon. The fire licked the car hood and windshield. The acrid smell of burning paint and rubber floated in the confined interior.

"Crack a damn window!" Francis barked and pressed the button on his door without result. The driver had disabled the rear compartment's windows.

"We must get out of here!" Francis urged.

Varenka tried to lower her window. The driver cracked all windows a bit and tried to increase the speed. The fire and black smoke obstructed his view of the street and he was forced to slow down.

"We must abandon the vehicle or we're dead!" Francis shouted.

"Not here," Simons said, grabbing for the radio.

A horse neighed in panic somewhere behind them. Francis turned back in time to see both horses dashing away, one knocking its rider off, both trampling the protesters in their wake. The crowd panicked. They began running in all directions. Why had the horses panicked like that?

"Varenka, get ready to jump out of the car," Francis urged in Russian.

"I'm ready!" she said, fear in her voice.

We are trapped...!

Francis couldn't finish his thought. A Middle Eastern man in his early twenties had approached the vehicle and shattered the driver's side window with a heavy hammer. He then pulled a gun from the folds of his clothes and aimed it at the driver, whose eyes widened in disbelief before he stepped on the accelerator. The car shook when another Molotov crashed against its roof.

The window next to Simons exploded in pieces. Francis heard a gunshot and Simons' body doubled over the dashboard. The impact splattered blood and tissue all over the front of the car.

He's hit! We've got to get out of here! Francis was on the verge of panic. He knew the attackers were from Rebirth. They had to flee as quickly as possible.

I've got no weapons and they have us surrounded.

"Step on it!" Francis barked to the driver. "Varenka, duck!"

Francis saw Varenka huddling on the floor of the car as he reached to the passenger seat and pulled Simons up. Just in time! Something had shattered his window. He desperately patted Simon's blood soaked body. There! Francis pulled Simons' revolver out of its holster. He released the safe with his thumb as he slid back to his seat. He pointed the revolver out the shattered window and fired before consciously registering the form of a man aiming a gun at him. The man fell back.

The car picked up speed and finally broke free of the crowd after an endless half block. They drove north on Polk street, people gawked at the fireball on wheels. Finally the driver pulled over when they got to Eddy Street.

"Are you injured?" the driver asked, kicking his door open.

"We're fine! Get the hell out of here! Unlock my fucking door!"

The locks popped up. Francis swung his door open and jumped out of the car, dragging Varenka behind him. The reek of burning hair reached his nostrils when the tips of her hair were zinged by the flames. They rolled on the ground away from the car. Francis propped Varenka against the tires of a parked car. She was scared, but seemed otherwise all right.

"Stay here," Francis urged her. She nodded. "I'll be right back."

The driver was out of the car, his face and white shirt were darkened with soot. Francis strode to the car and pulled the passenger door open to yank Simons out. The unconscious man was heavy, but Francis managed to drag him out before the fire enveloped both of them. Luckily Simons had not been wearing a seatbelt.

Many people had stopped to gawk at the burning car. Francis looked down the way they came. Seven bearded men were jogging up the street toward them, their expressions resolved, their pace precise. Francis guessed the bundles in their arms were some kind of weapon.

"Varenka, get up!"

Francis crouched low next to the car, desperately looking for cover. He inspected the revolver, a Ruger .357. Four shots left. He turned to Simons and patted him. There! He reached under Simon's body and pulled a revolver speed loader with six more bullets.

"Put the weapon down!" the driver ordered, aiming his own gun at Francis' head.

"See those guys?" Francis said, cocking his head. "They're after us! Cut the bullshit and help me get the hell out of here!"

"My orders are to escort you at all times. Drop the weapon!"

Francis couldn't read the expression behind the sunglasses. He put his left hand up and slowly crouched again to drop the gun on the ground. "Okay, nice and easy." Francis turned to look at the men. They were taking positions down the street, preparing for the attack. "Damn you, agent, can't you see those guys?"

Sunglasses finally turned his head. The three men in front dashed in between two cars. Someone screamed. A shot was fired. A bullet crashed against the door of the car between Francis and Varenka.

"That was an AK-47!" Francis roared. "You're gonna have to kill me to carry your orders!" He dragged Varenka with him in between their car and the next. "Varenka, don't move until I tell you to. Be ready to run on my signal. Got it?" She nodded.

Francis recognized the dry cough of the Russian built weapons. The bullets caught Sunglasses somewhere in his mid body. He slammed to the ground close to where they were huddled.

Francis reached for the fallen man and tried to pull him closer. He picked up his gun after giving up; Sunglasses was too heavy.

Think...

He looked around. People screamed, others took cover on the sidewalks and between the vehicles. The Enbeaath death squad was closing in.

Think...

A young man came out of a store holding a helmet in one hand, oblivious to the happenings on the street. He mounted an old, aqua colored scooter. He was only ten meters away from them.

"Get ready," Francis whispered to Varenka.

Francis dashed to the sidewalk, crouching low, toward the scooter two cars away. The attackers opened fire when they realized where he was. Plaster exploded off the wall to his right, windows were shattered. The situation dawned on the guy in the scooter; he fumbled with his keys, trying to get the machine going.

Don't go yet! Francis thought. If he could get the engine going, Francis and Varenka were doomed.

"You!" Francis finally made it close to him. He aimed the revolver at the rider. "Get off the scooter and toss me the keys!"

Fear washed over the guy's features. He was just a kid. He dismounted and handed the keys to Francis, who was next to him by then.

"Now on the sidewalk, face down!" The kid complied.

More explosions. The attackers knew what Francis was trying to do.

"Francis!" A shrill call cut through the air.

Varenka!

Francis turned in time to see one of the attackers no more than two cars away from Varenka, and making progress. Francis slid toward him and fired two shots. He missed! The man took cover.

"Varenka, run!"

It's now or never.

Francis hopped onto the scooter and turned the key to unlock the handlebar. The old machine had a crank pedal on its flank. Francis kicked it down and was glad that it caught the first time.

Good!

Varenka straddled the back of the scooter and held onto his waist. Francis pushed the scooter off its center stand an rode down the street in between the cars. Fortunately the burning FBI car was blocking the traffic in their direction. Bullets buzzed by their side, crashing against the parked cars. Francis zigzagged as much as he could while gaining speed. They were just a few yards from the intersection.

Turn!

Francis banked the scooter to the left and tried to merge with the traffic crossing the street. The vehicles rode down the street at roughly the scooter's top speed. Varenka's weight in the back made it hard to maneuver and they came precariously close to being run down by an oncoming truck.

Move!

Francis throttled the scooter all the way down. The light turned yellow at the next intersection. Francis went for it.

We made it!

The scooter crossed Van Ness at its top speed just as the cars began to move. A couple slammed their breaks, most of them blared their klaxons in anger. Francis ignored them and turned right at the next intersection.

The scooter wasn't going to take them very far. Francis needed the cavalry fast. There was only one place he would feel relatively safe for now. He sped up Franklin Street, over Pacific Heights and down to the Marina district. He'd taken that route because the traffic lights were synchronized. As long as they cruised at a constant speed they wouldn't have to stop.

"Where are we going?" Varenka asked.

"Home. We're far enough ahead of them. I'll call for help from there. We also need something to defend ourselves."

"I trust you, *dorogoy*."

Francis smiled bitterly. He better not screw up.

They rode the remaining blocks in silence. Francis turned right onto his street. A taxi was parked outside his building, waiting for a fare. Francis stopped the scooter on the sidewalk and put the center stand down after Varenka dismounted. They walked toward the entrance to the courtyard.

What...?

Francis saw the driver talking furiously into his mobile phone. Their gazes met. The Middle Eastern man's eyes sparkled with fury. Francis instantly pulled the gun he'd taken from the FBI agent and aimed it at him.

"Get out of the car!" he yelled. "Varenka, take the keys from my pocket, get inside, and dial 911. That will summon the police." Varenka did as instructed. Turning back, he yelled "you, get out of the car!"

The man didn't move. Francis fired a shot at the windshield. It shattered in a macabre spider web. The goon flinched at the impact but still didn't move. Francis walked slowly to the driver's side, his gun raised. The driver side window was rolled down. "Open the door," he commanded. "Slowly. And let me see your hands."

The driver inched the door open. Francis could see his feet underneath it as he stepped off. Still, he couldn't see the man's hands.

The driver aimed a gun at Francis.

Now!

Francis fired his own revolver without thinking, catching the man in mid-body. One, two, three shots, then the empty click. The impacts sent the driver to the ground. He was still alive, but not for long.

Self-defense, Francis thought darkly.

Francis knelt by him and took his gun. It was a GLOCK, Rebirth's sidearm of choice. Francis patted him and then looked into the cab. It was a real taxi, not some kind of decoy. The guy probably made a living that way. Francis picked up the mobile phone and put it to his ear. The line was still on. He clicked it off and ran to his flat.

"The police are coming," Varenka said, hanging up the phone when he arrived. "I didn't understand but they will be here soon."

"Good," Francis said, picking the phone up. "Now we need to take care of business." Francis dialed a number.

"Identification?" the emotionless voice answered.

"Zephyr. This is Predator. Patch me up to Guardian Angel."

"Authentication code?"

"Ninety nine, twenty, zero eight."

"Just a moment."

There were a few clicks on the line.

"Predator?" Adam Jones came on the line. "Where are you?"

"I'm in San Francisco and I have Rebirth after me."

"We know."

"I need to know where to go in Alameda. It isn't safe for me here. I found one of their goons outside my house. They'll be here any minute. Fortunately, so will the police."

"We're in Alameda, off 880. Do you think you can make it?"

"The traffic will be a bit heavy. Can you arrange for the police to take us there?"

"Yes."

"I recovered one of the bad guys' phones. It's a regular mobile, so someone can track the numbers this bastard called."

"Good job. Now, get off the line." Jones hung up.

Francis went to his bedroom.

"What will we do now?" Varenka said.

"We're going to the COMINT/SIGINT post in Alameda. Now give me a few seconds and we'll be on our way.

Varenka was truly afraid now. Sattar's people seemed to be everywhere. She sighed. Francis seemed to know what he was doing, and she tried her best to trust him.

Varenka sat on the bed to watch Francis. He had pulled a large metal case from the closet. She peered inside after he opened it. Francis took a shoulder holster from it, removed his jacket, and strapped it on. He then retrieved a large automatic gun from it and holstered it.

"Do you want some help?" she asked.

"No, just let me get ready."

Varenka watched him remove his belt and add a number of small holsters, each containing what looked like a magazine for the gun. He finally strapped three knives, one on each forearm and one on his right calf. He was completely absorbed putting his jacket back on.

Then she heard them.

Quick steps tapped in the courtyard, followed by shouting and gunshots. Francis went to the window and peeped through the curtain.

"They're here! And they're fighting with the police!"

"What do we do now?"

"We'll leave through the back door," he replied, digging into the case for the last time. She stiffened. He took two grenades out. "Don't look at me like that, it's just tear gas to cover our exit."

Something heavy smashed the entrance door in pieces, the cacophony of broken glass and splintered wood sent an ominous message to the upper floor. Varenka felt her pulse quicken.

Francis ran out of the bedroom toward the entrance stairs. He popped the tear gas grenade and rolled it down the stairs.

"Go, go, go!" Francis said, running toward her.

Varenka grabbed his hand and they both ran to the kitchen.

"This will slow them down," Francis closed the door and locked it. "These old flats have locks in the weirdest places."

They ran together to the back of the kitchen. Another door—and another lock leading to a pantry. Francis locked that door behind him as well, and finally opened the back door out of the flat. They dashed down the stairwell toward the first floor, past a garbage chute.

Varenka's heart felt like it was trying to break out of her chest. They got to the ground floor and Francis stopped before going to the service aisle in the back of the building. They flattened their bodies against the wall, opposite to the dumpsters.

Francis peeked around the corner, then waived her to follow. They walked toward an iron gate. He unlocked it and they both went in. They were under the building. Gunfire exploded in the courtyard, people shouted. Varenka tried to focus on following Francis past the washing machines.

They were in the garage. Of course! She had read that American buildings almost always had a place for people to park their cars. Several parking stalls flanked the main access lane leading from the main automatic door. They jogged to a stall with two covered vehicles. She guessed them to be a car and a motorcycle.

"Help me get this off," Francis said. "They'll figure what's going on soon."

"What do I need to do?"

"Just pull it off the car on your side," Francis said. "That's all."

Varenka reached under the car and pulled the elastic rim of the car cover. They unveiled the car, some kind of black, small vehicle, low to the ground and sporty. The car faced the access lane.

"Get in and fasten your seatbelt!"

Varenka entered the car. It was cold inside. She sat with her legs almost completely stretched forward. She reached for the seatbelt; it wasn't the standard mechanism. It was one of those four-point deals she'd seen on television for racing cars. She figured out how to strap herself in as Francis slid into the driver seat next to her.

"Let's go!" Francis said, turning the key in the ignition.

Nothing happened.

Varenka's fear grew in her like a physical presence.

"What's wrong?"

"Let me think…" he looked around the car, then he smacked his forehead with his hand. "Of course! I'll be right back." He pressed a grey button on the dashboard and jumped out of the car.

Varenka saw the engine cover rise behind her, followed by some mechanical noise. A few seconds later the digital clock in the car stereo blinked to life. She realized that the battery had not been connected. The rear of the car slammed shut.

The sound of screeching metal interrupted her. What was that? She feared the worst. Sattar's men had found the back entrance to the garage and were forcing their way in!

Francis returned, closed the door, and turned the ignition. The loud engine growled, Francis strapped his seatbelt on. The instrument panel glowed red, nine dials jumped to life. Other than the speedometer she didn't understand what the others were.

"What the hell is this, an airplane?" Varenka yelled.

Francis studied the dials. He seemed satisfied. "Be ready to go when I open the door!"

"What…?"

Francis pressed a button on a remote control clipped to the sun visor. The cavernous garage was lit when its automatic door opened. Francis stepped on the accelerator and the car jolted forward. Three men eclipsed the light from the entrance. Varenka braced herself as the car barreled toward the silhouettes.

"Hang on!" Francis yelled.

The tires screeched. The customized Fiero GT ate the distance to the entrance in one second that felt like ages. The men aimed their weapons at Francis and Varenka, then thought better of it and cleared the way.

A terrorist aimed his gun at Francis.

Go, go, go!

The rush of suppressed rage finally unleashed, injecting Francis with renewed hatred. He stepped on the fuel, forcing the man to clear the way or be run over.

The car skidded when it reached the street. There were two doubleparked cars to his left, two other police cars were blocking the far intersection to Francis' right. Another police car raced toward them from across Van Ness, its siren blaring, its lights flashing. Francis yanked the steering wheel to the right, then slammed the brakes. The car would crash against the incoming police vehicle if he continued.

Fools! They've caged us in!

Francis stopped the Fiero. Gunfire erupted behind them. The car shook when the bullets hit it. The police car in front of them screeched to a halt, its bulk blocked the intersection. Two police officers, a man and a woman, jumped off the vehicle, weapons ready, and took cover behind their doors. Francis and Varenka were caught in the crossfire.

"Duck!" he said, pushing Varenka's head down instants before gunfire shot through the car's rear window.

Think... Are these men a Rebirth suicide squad?

Francis was sure they were. That made them more dangerous. They had nothing to lose.

More shots were fired behind them. The police and the terrorists had engaged one another. He ventured a peek on the rear view mirror. At least he and Varenka weren't their focus now.

Francis' heart pounded hard against his chest. He saw movement on the rear view mirror. Old memories from Susan came suddenly to him, the old hatred for the bastard who killed her was re ignited. Some son of a bitch was working his way toward them, covering among the cars parked between the garage entrance and them. He had some kind of grey box in one hand, a gun in the other.

Was it a limpet mine?

"Hold on, Varenka," Francis said to her. "It'll be a close one."

"What are you going to do?"

Francis ignored her. He shifted the car into reverse. It was time for justice, with him playing the part of the executioner.

Come on...

The terrorist was just a few meters behind them. Francis waited until he saw the top of his head above the hood of the car closest to them.

Now!

Francis slammed the accelerator; the tires screeched, grabbing onto the pavement. The Fiero shot back in reverse.

Did the bastard have time to remove the arming pin? Francis thought. Is the mine activated by a timer, or by gyroscopes? Probably not by gyros or it isn't armed. He wouldn't be running around with it.

The rear of the car hit the corner of the parked vehicle, shattering its headlight, bending its fender. The Fiero's force slammed the other vehicle onto the sidewalk, forcing the terrorist to jump clear. Francis switched gears and rolled the car forward. The terrorist was momentarily stunned—and without cover.

Die, motherfucker!

Francis put the car in reverse and floored the accelerator. The car sped backward. He turned his head to watch through the car's rear window.

"Hold tight!" Francis yelled at Varenka. She shot him a terrified look.

The Fiero caught the terrorist in mid body and pinned him against the brick wall. His body jerked back in an unnatural way, his mouth let out a scream followed by a geyser of blood, saliva and mucus, forced from his entrails by the impact. He let go of the limpet mine, which bounced off the rear of the car and onto the sidewalk. Francis pressed the clutch without releasing the accelerator. The car rolled forward, then Francis let go of the clutch. The car slammed against the dying man once more. The man toppled to the ground like a broken doll.

"Francis, stop it..." Varenka muttered, gently touching his right hand. He looked at her. Her eyes pleaded at him with a mix of fear and compassion.

The gunfire on the street stopped. The police officers aimed their weapons at Francis and Varenka. The remaining terrorists had capitulated and came from behind their cover, their hands up.

"Get out of the car!" the police officers to Francis' right yelled at them, their guns raised.

"Put your hands up, and do what they say," Francis instructed Varenka.

They opened the car doors and slowly came out of the car with their hands up. The next few minutes passed by in a flash. Francis and Varenka were roughly forced to the ground before being handcuffed. The cops frisked them and seized Francis' weapons. Someone later instructed the incredulous law enforcers to let them go after a few radio exchanges.

Francis sat in the back of the squad car, saying nothing. He had-half expected some closure after killing the terrorist. He felt drained. He vaguely noticed Varenka saying something to him, but whatever she'd said didn't register.

"We have instructions to take you over the bridge to Alameda," a female officer instructed, undoing the cuffs.

"It's about time," Francis said, slowly coming back to his surroundings and rubbing his wrists where he'd been bound. "May I have those back?" he said, pointing at his knives and his Beretta.

"No, you can't. They're illegal, particularly the knives. You have no license to carry concealed weapons."

"Look," Francis wasn't in the mood to deal with her, "do you want me to escalate? You know who we are up against," he pointed at the emergency crews all over the street. "Let me contact your commanding officer. He'll clear me."

"Wait here," the officer instructed, waving him and Varenka away from the police car. She had a heated exchange over the radio. Finally she turned to Francis. "Take them," she said after hesitating.

"Thanks." Francis gathered his weapons and strapped them to his body.

Two new squad cars pulled in, their lights flashing. People gawked from the open windows, a small crowd had formed at both intersections. Ambulances and fire trucks crowded the street.

"That's our escort," the female officer explained. "Please get in the car and—"

Someone in the crowd screamed. A gun was fired. Francis saw a black, round object flying at them.

"Incoming!" someone yelled.

Won't the Rebirth lowlifes ever give up?

People dove to the ground. Francis recognized the object almost too late. He grabbed Varenka by the waist and pulled her along with him over the hood of the police car and onto the pavement.

The grenade exploded, sending shrapnel in all directions. Francis' ears rang, and he quickly took inventory of his body. He wasn't hit. His car was close by, its doors open.

"Go!" he urged Varenka.

They got into Francis car. The shooting started once more. Another grenade was thrown at them, but it bounced off the car's hood and rolled away from them. Francis fired the engine when the grenade exploded, rocking the car. The passenger side fastback window was shattered by the grenade. Francis pressed the gas and they fled.

The drivers in the police cars sensed their cue and pulled away from the intersection, making way for Francis' car. The Fiero shot through. The police escort joined in formation, one leading, one tailing. More gunfire chased them as they turned left on Van Ness and then right on Bay Street.

"This is madness!" Varenka shouted, on the verge of hysteria.

"We're clear now. All we have to do is stay with these guys. We'll be safe soon!"

They zigzagged between the traffic, zooming their way down to the Embarcadero. There were police vehicles blocking traffic at almost every intersection, making a clear way for them to the Bay Bridge. They finally got onto the bridge's empty lower deck. The authorities were holding the traffic behind them.

They crossed the span at almost a hundred miles an hour. Francis glanced at the dials. Oil pressure was a bit low, the battery was charged. He began to relax.

"You... you killed that man in cold blood," Varenka murmured.

"It was either him or us, Varenka. It was self defense."

"You didn't have to run him over with the car twice. Why didn't you let the authorities take him?"

Why didn't I, Francis asked himself. "Because he deserved it. He was going to kill us."

"You are not some avenging angel, Francis. You might become like them."

Francis looked at her briefly. She held his gaze with her sad and expectant blue eyes. "I did what I thought was necessary to save our lives. I don't like it anymore than you do, but it had to be done."

"I saw the hatred in your eyes. You were like a rabid animal."

"Look, I'm not happy about this, but I believe what I did saved us."

"You're rationalizing."

"And we would all have been blown into the bay if I hadn't stopped him."

"Francis, I love you," she touched his hand. "Don't let this hatred consume you. Don't become like Sattar."

"Don't worry, Varenka," Francis said, sighing. "Everything will be fine."

The three cars took the freeway exit to Alameda. The traffic was light, cars and trucks made way for them as they approached. They would reach their destination soon.

A white van pulled to the right lane as they approached it. It accelerated as soon as Francis' car was aligned with it. Alarms went off in Francis' mind.

Damn!

The driver was aiming a gun at Francis and Varenka. Francis slammed his brakes, the Fiero skidded on the pavement. Francis could barely regain control of the car, the police car behind them accelerated. The van cut in front of the Fiero and the driver hit the brakes. Francis swerved to the right, trying to avoid it.

Another car pulled forward from the right lane. It was some old American car, maybe a Cadillac. Three tons of Detroit's old-fashioned steel whammed the Fiero's black composite flank.

Francis sped up, trying to escape the heavier vehicle. He was sure they were faster, but the bigger car had the initial torque advantage. The police car in the front pulled back to the Fiero's side. The other police car pulled behind them, a CHP patrol joined them. Francis floored the accelerator, inching his way past the Cadillac.

A shadow washed over the Fiero.

Francis glanced through the glass sunroof. A low flying helicopter had joined the chase. Was that a news crew? He focused on the road ahead as he finally cleared the Cadillac. The helicopter flew past them. A hand stuck out of the helicopter, dropping black objects onto the pavement.

Oh, SHIIIIIIIIT!

The bombs exploded in their path. The windshield cracked, the car shook. This wasn't like in the movies, with flashy but relatively harmless gasoline fueled fireballs. These lethal explosions were sending bomb fragments in all directions.

The driver of a green SUV on the right panicked. Her truck strayed directly onto their line of travel. Francis yanked the steering wheel, desperate to avoid a collision.

He lost control of the car.

He tapped the brakes, trying to tame the runaway machine.

There is no room!

He looked for a way around the SUV and past the helicopter. Their police escorts pulled back. The Fiero bucked all over the road.

Death joined Francis and Varenka like a third passenger in the car's cockpit.

Francis took a deep breath and released the brakes in time to prevent the car from rolling over. The car careened perpendicularly to the road. He felt Varenka's body stiffen next to his, bracing for impact.

They hit the guardrail at eighty miles per hour. The seatbelts tightened around their bodies, saving them from shooting through the windshield. The incoming police car on the left lane hit the Fiero and spun it around, slamming the car's driver side against the rail. Francis and Varenka bounced inside the cockpit. His head hit the frame around the window. He heard Varenka scream before a velvet darkness engulfed him.

CHAPTER **32**

**The *Al Borak*
37°36'35.1" N, 126°5'43.2" W**

The *Al Borak* rose from the steel-grey ocean against the setting sun. Purple and orange clouds decorated the western sky. The helicopter approached the oilrig, skimming the wave crests with its landing skids. They had flown to the open ocean after confronting the police and the subsequent escape.

And what an escape that had been!

Confusion had reigned on the ground after Montagnet had crashed the car. Fakhri's pilot had expertly landed on the shoulder, giving Fakhri precious seconds to pull Varenka out of the car and to throw a gel grenade inside the vehicle. A fireball had exploded inside the car just seconds after dragging Varenka with him. The police officers had opened fire. Sattar had thrown a smoke grenade at them, sending them scurrying behind their squad cars. He laughed out loud. Getting aboard the chopper and leaving with his prize had been easier than he'd expected.

The pilot had maintained a low altitude to avoid detection. They'd been sighted by a few vessels and other aircraft, but that couldn't be avoided. The confusion reigning on the ground had eased their escape.

Fakhri and Varenka sat in the back. He glanced at her. She was unconscious after the car crash and a generous dose of chloroform. The woman he'd known in Moscow had changed. The new Varenka knew no fear. She was untamed. He understood that a relationship between them would've never worked out. She was too headstrong, too independent. She had been an excellent colleague and a convenient, even skilled, lover, but nothing more. Fakhri felt like a fool. He couldn't conceive having harbored feelings for this betraying whore.

They landed on the helipad next to the now erect power transmitter. The crew had almost completed assembly. The metallic dome reflected the last sunrays. Fakhri disembarked after the pilot, crouching low. An armed detail was waiting for them.

"Get the woman from the back and confine her to storage room five. Set a cot for her. Post a sentinel by the door and call me the moment she wakes up," Fakhri commanded.

"Yes, sir," the men acknowledged and roughly dragged Varenka from each arm to pull her out. Her head bobbed drunkenly. Fakhri watched them half carry, half escort her away, then shrugged her off his mind. He had other concerns.

Fakhri had not been aboard the *Al Borak* since they set sail ten days before. He surveyed the platform. Men were posted at the four battle stations; the power transmitter was almost fully assembled; the radar dish spun atop the bridge, scanning the sky. They were defenseless until the power transmitter was operational because the *Al Borak* carried no conventional weapons. It had been captain Akhmar's tactical decision in case they were boarded. The only conventional weapons on board were the handguns and automatic rifles issued to the men.

Fakhri entered the main quarters and climbed the stairs to the third floor. He felt proud when he entered the bridge, witnessing for the first time how his crew executed their tasks.

"Commanding officer on the bridge!" captain Akhmar called. The men stood up at attention.

"Carry on with your tasks," Fakhri said, pleased. The men returned to their consoles. "Akhmar, what's our status?"

"The power transmitter will be operational at 2100 hours. All systems are nominal. They began pumping the liquid nitrogen through the coils just prior to your arrival."

"Did all the systems checks pass?"

"Affirmative. We had to address few issues. The Earth's magnetic field readings varied significantly at this latitude, since we're closer to the equator and the power transmitter depends on it for correct operation. We fed the discrepancies to the computer and we have new parameters for adjusting the power transmitter and focal point. We're calibrating the equipment with the new values."

"Will these variations affect our defensive weapons?"

"Negative, sir. They affect only the energy transmitter. The long range particle beam weapons will be fully operational."

"Very well. What about air traffic? Coast Guard?"

"Nothing unexpected. We spotted a few commercial aircraft. So far the Coast Guard has ignored us."

"That won't be for long. They might have picked up the helicopter."

"We've tracked no unusual traffic."

"The Russian whore probably told them all about this rig. It's only a matter of time until they attack. Make sure that the power transmitter and the long range weapons are operational so we can defend ourselves when that happens."

"Yes, sir."

Frakhri turned to leave. "I will be in my quarters if anything needs my attention."

"Yes, sir." Akhmar saluted, clicking his heels. Fakhri acknowledged him before leaving the bridge. He wanted to change out of his civilian clothes into his uniform to carry out an inspection. This would be Enbeaath's first military operation. He wanted every detail to be perfect.

Fakhri went down the steps to the storage rooms in the lower deck after finishing his inspection. Captain Akhmar's crew was running the final tests before engaging the Tesla power transmitter. Other matters occupied Fakhri's mind now.

It was imperative that Fakhri found out what Varenka had revealed to the American and the Russian governments about the capabilities of the *Al Borak*. Kurok had surfaced alive in Moscow after the destruction of Teknoil's headquarters, publicly blaming Chechen rebels for the attack. Fakhri was sure that Varenka and Montagnet had acquired vital information from Kurok after escaping the collapsing building. All that remained was determining how much potential damage was caused by Varenka's disclosures.

Two Rebirth Alliance soldiers guarded the entrance to storage room 5. They saluted when he approached.

"Open the door," he instructed. The young man to his right unlocked it. "You," Fakhri spoke to the other one, "Get me two large bottles of carbonated water from the galley, some nylon rope, a chair, and an extension cord."

"Yes, sir." The man saluted and rushed to fulfill the order.

Fakhri entered the room and closed the door behind him. The vast storage space was empty except for a cot by the far wall and a bucket that one of Fakhri's men had left behind for Varenka to use for relieving herself. A single, naked light bulb illuminated the room. Varenka was laying down on the cot, completely immobile, her eyes fixed on the ceiling. She did not acknowledge Fakhri when he approached her.

"Hello Varenka," Fakhri said in Russian. "I never thought we'd meet again. In a way I'm happy to see you. Perhaps we can resolve our differences and continue where we left off."

Varenka clenched her teeth and said nothing. She squinted. Fakhri figured she had a headache.

"You know, I never had any intentions of hurting you. I was shocked when I discovered that you were helping the Americans all along."

"You're mad," Varenka replied without looking at him. "I never helped them until after you ordered me killed in Vienna."

"Your association with Montagnet tells me otherwise. I think you were a snake in our bosom all along. You betrayed Kurok and me while you hid behind your facade of professionalism."

"I'm not a liar."

Fakhri sighed. "Varenka, we don't need to make things more unpleasant. Don't waste time arguing your innocence. I don't believe you. You may still save yourself if you simply tell me what the Americans know about the Tesla power transmitter and this oilrig."

"I have nothing to say to you."

Fakhri grabbed Varenka's jaw and roughly turned her to face him. "You will talk or you will die."

Stupid bitch, he thought. Varenka's eyes widened. Was it fear he saw in them? No, her previously vacant eyes now burnt with hatred. She tightened her lips and held his gaze. Fakhri swelled with anger and grabbed her by the neck and bodily lifted her, then slammed her back against the wall before dropping her on the bed, sitting upright.

"How much do the Americans know about the power transmitter?"

"Go to hell, Sattar."

Fwap!

Fakhri slapped her face so hard that she reeled to the floor. He stepped closer to her and kicked her ribs twice. The kicks were hard enough to mean business but not enough to cause a fracture.

"We'll be here all night, Varvara Dmitrievna. What exactly did you tell the Americans?"

She wheezed but said nothing.

Fakhri lifted her by the collar and the waistband and threw her on the cot. She was very light. He felt disgusted. Why was she clamming up on him?

Someone rapped the door. "Enter," Fakhri ordered.

The soldier entered the room, carrying the items Fakhri had requested.

"Where do you want the chair, sir?" the soldier asked in Arabic.

"Place it by the cot."

The soldier set the chair and placed the rest of the items on the floor by it. "I took the liberty of bringing you a pocket knife and a lighter, sir, for the rope, in case you want to cut segments off it."

"Well thought. Now give me a hand."

Fakhri and the soldier hauled Varenka off the cot and forced her on the chair. They tied her ankles to the chair's legs and her wrists to the backrest frame.

"Leave us," Fakhri ordered.

The man saluted and left.

"So, Varvara, are you ready to talk?"

"Never!"

It would take time, but he would only get the answers he sought after destroying Varenka's character and personality. He paced around the chair, studying his captive. He would cause her extreme physical and psychological pain. He was maddened by her defiance.

"For the last time, how much do the Americans know about this oilrig?"

She tightened her lips and looked straight at him, angering him even more. He pushed her chest, knocking her and the chair backward. She grunted when she hit the ground, her face twisted with pain.

"If that's what you want, that's what you'll get."

Fakhri grabbed Varenka, chair and all, and placed them on the cot with her head hanging over the edge. He then loosened his collar, rolled up his sleeves, and opened the two-liter bottle of carbonated water. He took a couple of swigs, then approached his captive. It would be a long night for both of them.

. . .

Varenka felt a mix of fear, pain and anger. She was very uncomfortable, lying on her back with her head hanging back. She fruitlessly strained against her bindings. The nylon rope dug into her wrists. Her face and chest hurt where Sattar had hit her. She saw Sattar drink from the bottle, realizing for the first time how parched her lips were.

"Would you like some water, dear?"

She met his gaze but refused to answer. She wouldn't give this bastard an inch.

"Here, let me give you some."

He walked behind her. Instead of pouring water on her lips, as she had half-expected, he put her head between his legs and held it tight, using his knees like a vise. She struggled but he was too strong for her. She panicked.

Sattar covered the bottle opening with his thumb and shook it vigorously before lowering it and putting it right against her nose. He let go.

The high-pressure carbonated water shot up Varenka's nostrils. It was cold and it hurt. She tried to open her mouth but Sattar used his free hand to shut it closed. Varenka struggled against her bindings, tried shaking his head, tried to exhale and release the water with all her might. It was no use. She panicked. The pain spread through her sinuses and down her throat. Sattar was looking down at her impassively. The water kept flowing; she choked. Finally he stepped back. Varenka shook her head, struggling to breathe. The cold fluid was in her lungs. She coughed once, twice, three times. Finally the water was expelled out of her respiratory passages. She gasped desperately. Her chest hurt when she inhaled, so she took shallow breaths. Her heart pounded hard against her chest.

"Aren't you tired of this? I can make the pain go away. All you have to do is tell me what the Americans know about us."

Varenka said nothing.

Sattar set her down on the floor once more. Sitting up eased her breathing. Thank goodness for that.

"You know, Varenka, I always respected you. Sometimes I even admired you. I don't want to hurt you anymore. Why did you betray me with Montagnet? Why don't you tell me what you and Montagnet know?"

"There is nothing to tell, Sattar."

Sattar crouched in front of her, placing his hands on each side of her head. He wasn't hurting her. His hands were just there.

"For your sake, I hope you're speaking the truth. Montagnet, by the way, died during the crash. And, if he didn't die of that, he died when I squashed him like the dog shit he was." He paused. "If you answer me we can simply carry on as before."

Francis was dead? The memories from the car crash and her abduction were very vague. She remembered Francis' unconscious body next to hers before Sattar pulled her from the wreck. No, it couldn't be!

"So, what did you tell Montagnet? What possessed you to leave me for such scum? Why did you betray me?"

She was only half listening. Too late she realized that Sattar misinterpreted her silence. He clapped both hands simultaneously against her ears. It hurt! Her ears were ringing, her pain was intense, she felt disoriented. Sattar repeated the procedure once more. She screamed. He did it a few more times, ever harder, until she lost count. Her abused body finally gave up. She fainted. The last thing she remembered was Sattar's sneer and the hatred in his eyes.

How long have I been here?

Varenka opened her eyes. Her eyelids felt heavy, her body hurt. She shivered. She was laying nude on the dirty cot. Hot angry tears rolled down her cheeks. At last Sattar had left. Her breasts, pubic area, and knees hurt where he'd applied the electrical current. Her nose was runny. Countless welts blemished her skin. She felt abused, dirty. At some point she'd realized that more than information, Sattar wanted her to atone for what he thought was a betrayal to his manhood. Bastard. This was not about the oilrig or the weaponized power transmitter. She rubbed her wrists. Her struggle against her bindings had left ugly red burns around them. At least her hands and feet were free.

Varenka scanned the room. Her clothes were crumpled near the bucket they'd left for her. An almost empty bottle of carbonated water remained by the cot. She took it with trembling hands, unscrewed the top, and drank the last drops. Even her larynx hurt.

She sobbed.

Varenka was too proud to feel self-pity. She was physically hurt, but Sattar had failed to dent her soul. Her head spun, her vision blurred. She felt the vomit rising up her esophagus and barely made it to the bucket. She collapsed by her bucket, holding on to it like a lifesaver. She felt a bit better. She stood on shaky knees and stumbled to the pile of clothes. Everything but her underpants. Sattar had perversely shoved in her mouth to muffle her screams, then took them with him when he was done.

She felt revolted. What had she ever seen in that pig?

She dressed slowly, mustering whatever dignity she could. When she was done she lay back on the cot, her mind racing. What would they do to her? It wasn't hard to guess. The men would probably rape her before tossing her overboard. The only reason she was still alive was that Sattar wanted his crew to remain focused. Would she have the strength to fight them when the time came? Would Sattar have the decency to kill her before submitting her to such fate? She didn't think so.

Varenka looked around the windowless storage room. She didn't know if it was day or night. Grief washed over her. She was a caged animal, Francis was dead, and Sattar was free. Had they fired the power transmitter yet? How many people had they killed?

Francis! The thought of him dead was more than she could cope with right now. She felt pain, despondence, loss, guilt. Francis had loved her, had risked his life for her, and she'd insisted on putting herself in peril by coming along for this mission. He would have taken different actions had he been by himself; she would be safe. She and Francis had failed to stop these maniacs because of her pigheadedness. She cradled her face in her arms, closed her eyes, stifled her sobs, and awaited her fate.

Sattar Fakhri and Enbeaath had won.

CHAPTER **33**

Somewhere in Northern California

Twilight.

So this is what being dead is like...

Francis stirred, summing up his sensations. He was laying flat on a soft surface. He panicked. Am I in my coffin? No... there is plenty of room to move.

He swung his legs to the ground to sit up. He'd been laying on some kind of gurney. He was in a room bathed in a blue light. He blinked, trying to focus his vision; eventually he made up the shapes of a long counter and a door. The walls were bare, a row of featureless cabinets hung above the counter. He stood up and took a few tentative steps toward the door. A wave of nausea hit him. He stumbled to the rubbish bin by the counter just in time to retch into it. The bitter taste of bile flooded his mouth. He stood up. The counter had a sink. He cupped some water with his right hand to rinse his mouth and splash his face, noticing for the first time the bandage over his left temple. The skin on the back of his right hand hurt. He touched it. It was completely devoid of hair. He felt better after a while. He opened the door.

Francis walked into a well-lit, crowded command center. He squinted. There were rows of terminals, radar equipment, communications stations, large map projectors, glass plotting panels. Several uniformed men and women peered at him curiously.

"Well, the Sleeping Beauty is finally awake," a familiar voice said.

"Adam!" Francis turned, glad to meet the bespectacled face of Adam Jones. They shook hands.

"How do you feel?"

"Like a truck ran me over. What's going on? How did I get here?" Uh, oh. "Where... where is Dr. Ulyanova?" Francis looked around.

"She's not here," Jones replied. "She was abducted after you crashed on the freeway—"

"How?" Francis yelled. Several people turned to look at him.

"Shush! A helicopter."

Madness! They had succeeded in taking her!

"Where... where was she taken?"

"We don't know for sure, but we believe she's aboard the oilrig."

"Have you located the rig? Where is it?" Francis ran his hand over his head. He had failed her! "Come on, Adam! Where is it! We must get Varenka out of there!"

Jones replied in a soothing voice, "Calm down, Francis."

"Dammit Adam, her life is in danger!"

"So are the lives of the President, the attendees to the Summit of the Nations, and several thousand inhabitants of San Francisco. We have time. Rebirth needed Ulyanova alive or they would've never abducted her."

"Yes, but for how long?"

"You must assume that she's still alive. Meanwhile, we need your help for figuring out how to stop the threat."

Francis rubbed his chin, noticing the stubble on his face. He also realized that he wasn't wearing his leather jacket, nor the sheaths for his throwing knives or his shoulder holster. "How long was I out?"

"About twelve hours. The paramedics gave you a sedative before they brought you in. Your car was wrecked."

"Where is my stuff?"

"I don't know, but we'll get it back to you. Your jacket was burnt in a few places. Someone threw an incendiary gel bomb into your car. The jacket and the car took the bulk of the damage. You were very lucky."

"Are we in Alameda?"

"Yes. This used to be a Navy base; we use it now for COMINT and SIGINT ops. This command post was set up after you signaled us from Moscow. Follow me," Jones led the way past a bank of maps and computer screens. An officer with a chest full of decorations was giving instructions. Francis wished he knew the meanings of the insignias on the various uniforms. Jones stopped by the officer. "Captain Bruce Grady, this is Francis Montagnet."

Grady was a tall man, somewhere in his fifties. "Nice meeting you, Mr. Montagnet. They tell me you're the expert on this thing we're after."

"The pleasure is mine, sir," Francis replied, a bit at a loss as they shook hands. "I'm not the real expert, though I did have a chance to study the Tesla testament in detail for several days."

"Very well, Montagnet. Mr. Pallone!"

"Aye, Skipper," a burly man about Francis' age but in extremely good shape answered.

"Get your team in the conference room. Jones, you come with us. Mr. Montagnet, I hope you're ready for debriefing "

An alarm blared. Lights and screens on several consoles flashed red.

"Sir, we've lost contact with the *Hammerhead*!"

"Our meeting will have to wait," Captain Grady said, turning to his men. "Report."

"Sir," a young communications officer reported, "the *Hammerhead* was five miles from the target, periscope depth. They were transmitting the next set of night photographs of the *Al Borak* when all communications were cut off."

Francis and Jones moved by the wall, out of everyone's way. "What the hell is going on, Adam?"

"The *Hammerhead* is one of our subs," Jones explained. "It's been keeping tabs on the oilrig since we identified it yesterday."

"Yesterday? Why didn't they board it or sink it or something?"

"Frankly, there was a lot of skepticism in some quarters regarding what they considered outlandish claims of its capabilities."

"What?"

"They had some scientists from DARPA make a case against the power transmitter. It was deemed non-functional."

"They should have boarded the rig anyway. Better safe than sorry. What the hell is the Coast Guard doing?"

"I wish I could tell you there is some good reason why it didn't happen, but it all boils down to shortsighted bureaucracy. Nobody wanted to take responsibility. All resources in the area were diverted to protecting San Francisco against more conventional attacks. An unarmed oil rig almost three hundred miles off shore isn't considered a threat. The *Hammerhead* crew provided intelligence that the rig carried no missiles or other conventional weapons. No action was mounted against the rig because analysts dubbed it a decoy to divert resources from the real target, San Francisco. If anything, they strengthened patrols close to the coast and in the bay."

"And so they decided to sit it out." Francis was appalled. How could these people think that way?

"Exactly."

"And now they've lost contact with a submarine," Francis leant closer to his friend. "It will be too late by the time they realize the extent of their foolishness if the power transmitter is functional."

"Colonel Fakhri, the submarine's depth is 150 meters and sinking," the sonar technician reported.

"Did it flood its ballast tanks?"

"Negative sir. It banked to starboard and then began to sink."

"The power transmitter is operational, colonel," Akhmar commented.

Fakhri looked south through the window. "How did you find the submarine in the first place?"

"Since we don't have sophisticated sonar equipment on board, I got the idea from Dr. Volin back at the White Fortress. We have very sensitive equipment to measure the earth's magnetic field; we need it for calibrating our instruments."

"So?"

"It was rather simple. We detected fluctuations in the nearby magnetic field. We ran it through the computer and determined that they could be caused by a large metallic object," Akhmar pulled a computer printout. It plotted several vertical lines along a scale. Some of the lines turned to squiggles near their mid section. "These lines are mostly straight, except for this set of four, showing the fluctuations. They told us about the submarine."

"Congratulations, Akhmar," Fakhri said, pleased with the results. "Not bad for an army crew with no operational experience in the high seas. How did you stop the submarine?"

"We localized an electromagnetic blast on it. It fried its instruments, including its comm gear, and certainly breached the hull. We're tracking it on sonar. The submarine is sinking."

"Its disappearance will encourage others to look for it," Fakhri said.

"We'll deal with them in the same manner, colonel, if and when they decide to show up."

. . .

Captain Grady spoke urgently on the phone. He slammed the handset down after barking more orders, then walked toward Francis and Jones.

"You better be ready, gentlemen," Grady said, his brow creased with concern. "It seems we have a live one in our hands."

"We're ready, sir," Jones answered, nudging Francis forward.

"Ensign," Captain Grady called over his shoulder, "escort the oilrig civilian expert to the conference room and arrange for refreshments and coffee. We'll be there a while."

Francis and Jones followed Grady to the conference room past the control center. Pallone and seven equally strong men already sat around the table, their backs straight. All wore fatigues. Their conversation hushed when Francis and his companions walked in.

"Gentlemen, we have a situation," Grady said somberly. "We lost contact with the *Hammerhead* a few minutes ago."

"Accident?" Pallone asked.

"We don't know what happened. The boomer went silent in the middle of a transmission."

"Maybe they're having communications problems. Otherwise they'll be in a hell of a pickle. Any blips from its rescue beacon?"

"None. The Coast Guard is checking into it as we speak. I hope you're right. If, on the other hand, this was a hostile action, we'll have to overcome the *Al Borak* before we can mount a rescue operation."

"That's what we're here for, sir."

The door opened. A tall, tanned man of around forty-five walked in. He was dressed in jeans and a cotton shirt, and looked in reasonable shape. He had dark hair, bushy eyebrows and a mustache. The newcomer took a chair across from Montagnet. He had a competent, professional air about him. A young man in uniform had trailed him and pushed a cart with coffee, water, soft drinks and doughnuts to the far corner of the room before leaving and closing the door behind him.

"Well, we can start now that we're all here. We have lieutenant commander Andrew Pallone and his team. They are assigned to assist us in neutralizing the platform if other means of engagement fail."

"SEALs," Francis said, a bit too loud.

"Yes, Mr. Montagnet," Grady glared at him. "I would appreciate if you don't interrupt me." He paused before introducing the civilian. "We also have here Dr. Thomas Silva, considered the world authority on the design of fully automated offshore drilling equipment. He's known among his peers as Robot Tom," Grady exchanged a friendly smile with Silva. "Robot Tom was the lead automated systems designer of the *Odyssey Sea Launch*, a floating oilrig modified for launching satellite rockets from its decks. Finally, we have colonel Adam Jones and Mr. Francis X. Montagnet, who will provide us with the latest intelligence regarding the suspected defensive and offensive capabilities of the *Al Borak*."

"Thank you, captain Grady," Robot Tom spoke in a rich baritone. He went to the whiteboard. "Gentlemen, what we have here is a fairly standard setup carrying non standard equipment." Captain Grady passed a stack of photographs to each attendee as Robot Tom spoke.

"What are the dimensions of this platform?" Pallone asked.

"This isn't a platform, commander Pallone. A platform is stationary. This type of vessel is called a Mobile Oil Drilling Unit, and commonly referred to as MODU or a rig. Judging from the photographs and some information I received as background for this meeting, I estimate its deck surface at about 115 by 30 meters, or about 31,000 square foot. Roughly half of that is dedicated to the bridge, crew's quarters, mess hall, and so on."

"What's that tower on the deck?"

"That's what these gentlemen," he nodded at Francis and Jones, "will explain. Normally the rig would have a drill and other machine tools in that area, not a derrick that tall. The derrick, including the globe on top, is about 60 meters tall."

"And that is your target," captain Grady said.

"If we approach it by sea we'll have to climb up to it," a man with a scar from his left eyebrow to the right corner of his mouth said. "How high is it above sea level?"

"The rig's draft, after the pontoons and ballast tanks are full, must be around 50 feet, maybe lower. The Pacific is calm at this time of the year. We're expecting good weather for the next few days. The waves won't wash over it; it might even be as low as 30 feet." Robot Tom rattled other statistics of importance to the SEAL team. Francis took a few notes.

"Do we know how many men they have on board?" Pallone asked. Robot Tom hesitated, then looked meaningfully at captain Grady, who turned to Jones.

"Adam, do we know that?"

"Unfortunately we aren't sure at this point," Jones replied. "We identified between twenty and thirty men on board in the satellite photos. The *Hammerhead's* mission was to clarify that point before it became silent."

"A rig like that could accommodate up to eighty men," Robot Tom said. "The crew quarters are large enough."

"So we'd have to worry about as few as twenty and as many as eighty men. We can handle that," Pallone said with bravado. His men nodded in agreement.

Robot Tom continued explaining the layout of the crew's quarters and operational areas. Essentially half of the deck was occupied by a four floor structure. The top floor was probably the bridge and control room. There were observation towers at each corner. The crew's accommodations were on the next level down, including showers and closet space. The galley and mess hall were below the accommodations. "I can't be sure, but I'd imagine that sick bay is sandwiched somewhere between the bridge and the accommodations. It might also be on the deck floor, but that's usually reserved for tools, controls, and storage space."

"Are we supposed to take the bridge, Skipper?" Pallone asked Grady.

"That's your secondary target. You must first neutralize the tower, then secure the rig."

"What kind of training do the bad guys have?"

"Most of them were professional soldiers," Jones replied. "Their leader is colonel Sattar Fakhri, a deserter from the Iranian army. He provided all the technical know-how to turn Enbeaath recruits into more professional, focused troops. They aren't amateurs. We believe that most of the crew aren't your garden variety terrorist, long on idealism and short on skills. They were trained in Malaysia, possibly the Middle East, and Russia."

"Arabs?" asked another man in Pallone's team.

"Probably, most of them."

A young officer burst into the room, went to captain Grady and handed him a piece of paper. Grady's expression darkened when he read it. "I'll be damned," he said, after dismissing the messenger. "The Coast Guard sent two helicopters and a boat to have a look. Communications with all of them are lost. A brief transmission on the emergency band got cut off. The Navy is officially in charge of an attack operation."

"What's the protocol, Skipper?" Pallone asked.

"We're sending a destroyer its way, and four Hornets just took off from San Francisco Airport, bound for the rig. You're going next if their mission doesn't succeed."

Pallone shifted in his chair, but said nothing.

"Your turn, Montagnet," Grady instructed. "What exactly are we dealing with?"

"Sir," Francis walked to the white board while Robot Tom took his seat, "they built what is known as a Tesla power transmitter. Tesla intended to transmit electricity without wires to every point in the world with it."

"Bullshit," Pallone said.

"There is circumstantial evidence that he succeeded," Francis said, ignoring Pallone. "However, while Tesla discovered a way of doing it, he miscalculated and instead wound up creating a very destructive force."

"Tesla's discoveries have been clouded in mysticism and speculation for a hundred years," Robot Tom said. "Some of them have just recently been confirmed and explained satisfactorily. Wireless energy transmission might be one of them."

"What do you mean a hundred years?"

"The basic technology that resulted in the power transmitter was developed by Tesla in the early 1900's," Francis explained. "Other weaponized components were developed in the 1930's. Tesla spent the last years of his life trying to perfect them. Anyway, the power transmitter has several functions aboard the rig. It provides power to operate the rig's equipment. It garners enough energy to power four Tesla death ray guns mounted at each corner of the deck. It can garner electrical energy from the Earth's magnetic field, accumulate it in the dome, and then discharge almost anywhere on earth."

"What do you mean by 'Tesla death ray'?" Grady asked.

"Tesla invented what we now know as a particle beam weapon. He had a flair for drama, so he called it a death ray. This particle beam weapon consists of electrically charged particles, possibly mercury, shot at high speed from a canon-like device. Each particle consists of only a few atoms. These particles are shot at relativistic speeds, and dissipate enormous energy on impact."

"Such a weapon has been demonstrated theoretically, under laboratory conditions, but not in the real world."

"My now missing partner, Dr. Ulyanova, could've explained this better, captain, but I'll give it a shot. The biggest hurdle was the transmission of energy through air. Laboratory conditions require a vacuum. Tesla figured out a way of creating that vacuum in the death beam canon using a Tesla turbine. The particles are accelerated by a high-powered magnet. That's not the biggest problem, though. The weaponized power transmitter itself is our main worry. Once fired, effectiveness of the weapon and accuracy diminish with the square of the distance. The Russians who built the *Al Borak* figured out how to overcome that by readjusting the distance to target through complex computations. Those computations were first proposed by Tesla himself, but seventy years ago he lacked the control systems to implement them in real-time."

"How do they control that amount of energy, assuming it could be done in the first place?" Robot Tom asked, clearly interested.

"A combination of superconducting materials not available in Tesla's lifetime, and modern control systems."

"What does that mean to us?" Pallone asked.

"It means that, if hit, a conventional airplane or ship will immediately lose all its electronics. Any personnel on board will most likely be killed. Depending on the amount of energy released, metallic parts may instantly melt."

"So the *Hammerhead* and the Coast Guard might've been hit by this," Pallone commented.

"Hopefully not, commander," Grady said. "Montagnet, in her briefing to the FBI, Dr. Ulyanova mentioned another potential threat involving the, ah," he checked his notes, "Tesla power transmitter."

"Sir," Francis said carefully. "We just don't know for sure what Rebirth and the Russians accomplished. Dr. Ulyanova and I speculated that the death ray would be used for defensive purposes, in case the rig was attacked. The power transmitter is really our main concern. It will power all tactical weapons aboard the rig. Assuming that the calculations are correct, an energy discharge would dissipate as much energy as a small nuclear blast."

Francis looked around the quiet room.

"What is the range of this power transmitter?" captain Grady asked.

"Sir, I don't know that for sure; only Fakhri and the Russians who built it know. I would assume that San Francisco must be within range."

Robot Tom thumbed his notes. "How does it harness the energy in the first place?"

"They probably have some kind of pipe dug into the bottom of the ocean. That's their ground. The difference in potential between various segments of that rod, the dome, and the Earth's ionosphere is what generates the electricity."

"It sounds almost like they're using the Earth as a giant capacitor."

"Yes, that's a good way to describe it."

"Captain," Pallone asked, "so how do we stop it? How do we get ourselves on board?"

"Your team's intervention may not be necessary, commander," captain Grady said. "We're confident that the attack in progress will succeed. They can only fight so many fronts at once—"

"Sir," Francis said, ignoring the annoyed look that Grady shot him at the new interruption, "I think you should start implementing the contingency plan. Nobody has ever faced a threat like this. Making assumptions about its capabilities is like speculating about how many angels can sit on a pinhead. Remember your submarine and the Coast Guard. Enbeaath and this technological monster were underestimated before. Please don't make the same mistake again."

"Sir, we're under attack!"

Fakhri jumped to the control console. He scanned the screens to assess the incoming threat. "What is it?"

"Sir, we have four aircraft approaching from different directions," the radar man reported and pointed at a different screen. "That ship changed its course in the last fifteen minutes and it's also inbound."

"What's the airplanes ETA?"

"Five minutes, sir."

Fakhri grabbed his microphone. "Battle stations, this is not a drill. We're under attack. Prepare countermeasures." Fakhri knew that each man was entering its distance to target data into their target computers, governed by radar.

"ETA four minutes, sir."

"Plot a solution and fire when ready," Fakhri commanded.

An alarm sounded throughout the bridge.

"What is it?" Fakhri barked.

"Sir, they're jamming us! We can't aim our weapons in their direction."

"Akhmar, actions?"

"Sir, I suggest that we use the power transmitter."

"Carry on!"

Akhmar and his team focused on inputting the Tesla power transmitter coordinates. "Report?" Akhmar said.

"Focal point adjusted to new coordinates."

"Wait!" Fakhri snapped. "That's our location!"

"Sir," Akhmar looked at Fakhri, "we're at the epicenter of the event. We should be fine."

"We're firing the power transmitter unto ourselves!"

"No, sir, we're firing it *around us.*"

"Fire!" Fakhri ordered after a moment's hesitation. He held his breath, hoping that Akhmar knew what he was doing.

The crew aboard the *Al Borak* was blinded by the blue column of light. The heavens parted, the energy beam shot upward from the dome of the power transmitter. The air crackled and smelled of ozone. A dull bang rocked the rig; Fakhri and his crew watched in amazement how the energy of the blast spread in a perfect sphere enveloping the oilrig. They watched the shock wave travel outward in all directions, like being in the center of an expanding bubble. The waves were flattened in its wake, the clouds were swept in its path.

"Report!" Fakhri said, realizing they were fine.

"Sir, we won't have readings until the energy bubble dissipates."

"What's their estimated ETA?"

"One minute sir."

"Blue team, do you have visual contact?"

There was a pause before each of the men at the battle stations reported. "Negative sir."

An alarm beeped.

"Blue four, we have an inbound bird!" Fakhri's palms were sweaty. He looked at the console. The computer reported an inbound AGM 65D air to ground missile. The old and effective Maverick, used successfully against oilrigs and other targets in the Persian Gulf.

"Target acquired sir!"

"Fire!"

A flash of lightning and a loud boom followed as the particles shot at high speed out of battle station four. Almost instantly, a bright orange explosion flared above the horizon, five kilometers north of the *Al Borak*.

"Report!"

Captain Akhmar and his operators ran various tests. "All targets neutralized, colonel Fakhri," he had spoken over the rig's PA system.

The whole crew cheered in unison. Fakhri allowed himself to smile and shook hands with every man within reach, praising their effort. He had the confidence of knowing that nothing stood between Rebirth and its objective.

"I won't allow a civilian to participate, Montagnet," captain Grady insisted. "You've done your part. Robot Tom did his. Let the professionals deal with this. We seem to have lost a submarine crew, several Coast Guardsmen, and four pilots and gunners. You'll remain on this base."

"Balls!" Francis said, his frustration mounting. "Dr. Ulyanova might still be alive aboard the rig. I want to get her out of there."

"Don't speak to the captain like that," Pallone said. "You ain't coming with us, boy. You'll jeopardize the mission."

"My apologies, sir," Francis said to Grady before turning to Pallone, "Look, we don't have time to argue! I'm going in on my own recognisance. You guys *owe* me."

"Listen," Pallone replied, taking a step toward Francis, "we don't owe you squat. You were brought here to provide intelligence and your job is done. You are an operational liability." Pallone stabbed the air with his right index finger as he spoke, insultingly close to Francis' face. "I won't allow you to risk the lives of my team or jeopardize the mission, boy."

Now!

Francis parried Pallone's hand with his left as he stepped sideways with his right foot. He caught Pallone by surprise, who countered immediately by shooting his left hand at him, aiming for his throat. Francis leant back and push-kicked Pallone with his left foot. Pallone recovered and stepped in to pivot on his right foot as he shot a roundhouse kick at Francis' body. Francis instinctively tightened his right arm against his head, elbow down, at the same time that he snapped his right leg up with his toes pointing down, in classic Muay Thai block. His shin, elbow, forearm, and hand formed a shield against Pallone's kick. The SEAL's leg connected with Francis' shin with a dull thud. Francis stepped in and immediately shot a right kick as soon as Pallone put his leg down, catching him in his upper thigh, numbing his leg.

"Don't you ever call me boy, you condescending son of a bitch," Francis hissed, regaining his fighting stance, ready to counterattack with a right punch to Pallone's face. The hard kick had helped Francis vent some of his frustration.

"Enough!" captain Grady growled.

Pallone snapped back to combat pose, while Francis went to his fighting stance. Francis felt his blood boil with anger and tensely awaited Pallone's next move. Surprisingly, Pallone relaxed.

"You got spunk and some interesting moves, Montagnet," Pallone said, his palms up in mock surrender. "I could take you if I really wanted to "

"Try," Francis dared.

"No, you're right, we have more important things to worry about. Besides, neither one of us wants to spend the rest of this caper in the brig."

Francis relaxed, lowering his guard but still keeping an eye on Pallone, just in case. Let's try again, he thought. "Sir," Francis turned to Grady, "I request permission to join commander Pallone's party."

Grady exchanged looks with Pallone, who shrugged as he spoke, "This ain't going to be a party, skipper, but if Montagnet can jump out of a plane without killing himself, and then stays out of our way once we're aboard the rig, he can come with us."

Francis smiled, reading the other man's mind. Pallone was betting that, like most people, Francis would be put off by this. "I hold a USPA D-class license." Pallone returned the smile. Francis turned to Grady. "I'm a skydiver, captain."

"This is crazy," Grady said, shaking his head. He turned to Jones. "Adam, what do you think?"

"Well," a bemused Jones replied, "as long as Montagnet leaves behind all identifiable items he might be carrying about his person, and as long as he understands the risks involved, I see no reason why he shouldn't go, especially since commander Pallone seems to have no more objections. They may have use for the extra pair of hands."

"Montagnet, be careful what you wish for because you might get it. You're under commander Pallone's command. You do what he tells you, do it fast and efficiently. Understand?"

"Yes, sir."

"Mr. Pallone, gear up. We don't have time to waste." Grady looked at his watch. It was almost 0800 hours. "The main event will begin in two hours in downtown San Francisco. The President is already on the way to the summit."

"Aye, sir," Pallone turned to Francis. "Follow me. We need to brief you on our methods."

Francis followed Pallone out of captain Grady's office and out of the building. The SEAL team was assembling in a hangar across a tarmac.

"Montagnet?" Pallone stopped, beyond earshot from the hangar.

"Yes, commander?"

"You're coming with us because I think you might actually make it and provide some support."

"Thank you, commander," Francis said earnestly.

"I'll make one thing clear," Pallone's cold, hazel eyes honed on his. "If at any time I feel like you become a problem for me or my men, I will personally put a bullet in your skull and toss you in the ocean." He paused, as if expecting a rebuke from Francis. "Let's go."

Pallone turned to stroll to the hangar. Francis shrugged Pallone's threat off his mind. He would stay out of the way. The SEALs mission was to neutralize the Tesla power transmitter; his was to rescue Varenka and, if she was harmed in any way, to even the score with Sattar Fakhri.

D-Day

CHAPTER **34**

Aboard the *Al Borak*

Varenka paced in her lockup. She no longer had her watch but she guessed it was around 9 o'clock in the morning, judging from the sunlight coming through the portholes. She still felt sore and scared. She was thirsty. Her joints hurt. She was not sure of what to expect anymore. She had heard the explosions earlier and felt the oilrig pitch and roll under her feet. The men had cheered, then an eerie quietude fell over the rig. There had been no noise other than a soft, electrical humming for several hours.

A man's voice spoke in Arabic over the PA system. She heard steps above and on the stairs leading to the bridge. She guessed the crew was readying for their mission of destruction. She had figured a way to stop them if she could escape from her prison.

She went to the far wall. The portholes were way too small for her to squeeze through. She unlatched one, and was surprised that it opened. Her plan began to shape up. There were a thin blanket and a pillow on her cot. She scratched her head. It was a long shot, but it might work.

Duyal Sivaslian felt cold, thirsty, and stiff. More than anything else, he felt bored. He'd stood guard by the storage room turned prison cell since 0200 hours, and it would be another hour before he was relieved. The last few months had been a drag, first in the cold Russian base and now in the ocean. He missed the warm coast and waters of the Mediterranean, a mere hour drive from his Turkish hometown. The wind and the ocean here were cold and unpleasant. His only consolation was that the weather here wasn't as harsh as it had been in Russia. Sivaslian lit a cigarette. He couldn't go back to Turkey anyway; he was a wanted man. He inhaled deeply, relishing the strong tobacco flavor. Being here in the middle of the ocean, stuck with guarding a prisoner instead of actively pursuing the goals of Enbeaath like his comrades, gave him too much time to reminisce.

A loud bang and a muffled scream from within the room jerked him back to reality. What was that? Should he report to the bridge? Captain Akhmar had just given the general alert. They would begin the attack any minute. He risked Akhmar's or even colonel Fakhri's wrath if he interrupted now.

There was another sound, this time more like a whimper.

Sivaslian made the decision. He opened the fire door. The damn bitch was trying to escape! He knew colonel Fakhri would have his head if he let her escape. She was already halfway out of the porthole at the far end of the room, with only her right leg and part of her rump to go through the opening. The porthole was so small she was probably stuck.

Sivaslian rushed into the room to pull the woman in. He grabbed the leg, which felt strangely soft to the touch, more like padding...

There was a metallic blow to the back of Sivaslian's head. He saw spots and felt the sharp pain spread through his cranium. He turned around, staggering, to discover the woman, nude from the waist down, and swinging a bucket at him.

The bucket wasn't as heavy as Varenka had hoped. The guard was still on his feet. The second blow caught the guard's face and somewhat stunned him, but he still posed a threat. He would probably recover quickly. What had Francis said while he was shadow boxing back at the dacha?

The best place to hit someone is straight on the chin. Your opponent will drop to the ground, out cold. Never punch with your fist. Use the ball of your hand.

The guard stumbled forward, his face flushed with anger. He extended both arms, trying to grab her.

Wait... she told herself.

The man vaulted toward Varenka. She stood her ground, tightly curling back the fingers of her right hand. One moment the guard was atop her, the next she swung her arm up, catching him by surprise on the chin. The impact snapped the guard's head back and sent him back before his knees buckled and he fell to the floor.

Varenka wasted no time tying the guard up. Her right hand hurt a bit, specially her palm, where she'd connected with the guard's chin. First

Varenka took his side arm. She removed his shoes and shoved his socks into his mouth before using his belt to gag him. Next she used her own stockings to tie his hands behind his back, then tied them to his ankles. She strained to drag her hogtied captive onto the cot. Once she more or less laid him there, she retrieved her pants from the porthole and pulled the blanket from the leg to cover the guard. She put her pants and shoes on and pulled her hair away from her face. She sighed. The door was open, and she had achieved her goal with a minimum of racket.

Would she make it to the bridge or the control panels before Fakhri or his men spotted her? She picked up the pistol and shoved it in her waistband like she'd seen men do it in the movies; it felt quite uncomfortable as she walked to the entrance. She carefully peered out the door. The service corridor was empty. She stepped out, closing the door behind her and fastening the hasp over the staple. She clicked the padlock locked and broke the key in the keyhole.

She wished she felt more confident. While she'd worked on designing oilrigs, she'd never actually been on one. Calm down, she told herself. She needed to figure out how to proceed; how was this rig different from the ones she'd worked on? After a few minutes of hiding in the doorway, Varenka took a deep breath and began sneaking her way around.

The television set seemed somewhat out of place in the control room, but Akhmar had insisted that one be installed. A TV and a home satellite dish had made it on board.

Fakhri watched elated as the President of the United States walked to the podium. The Summit of the Nations keynote address was about to start. The applause continued long after the president, all smiles, reached the podium and acknowledged his welcome. Fakhri had feared that the president wouldn't show up, or that the event would be canceled and the San Francisco Opera House evacuated. They had continued, betting perhaps that Enbeaath posed no threat being so far away, or betting that an attack against the rig would be successful.

The arrogant Americans had failed.

"Captain Akhmar, what's our status?" Fakhri spoke softly.

"We have fourteen surface ships and two submarines converging on us. None is closer than 100 kilometers. They seem to be waiting for something."

Fakhri pondered about this. The President was addressing the gathering, yet a massive military buildup had begun. Perhaps the Americans were not taking the threat seriously, or perhaps the President had overridden objections and gone forward anyway, trusting their armed might to overcome the *Al Borak*. Fools. "What do they have in the air?"

"Nothing unusual, sir," Akhmar checked his screen. "Two airplanes, using the airline corridor to Hawaii. A third aircraft is approaching."

"Altitude and configuration?"

Akhmar punched the keyboard before replying. "33 thousand feet, sir. Something big. It's an Airbus A-320 or a Boeing 747, cruising at around 300 knots. It'll fly overhead in a few minutes."

"Are you positive it's a commercial aircraft?"

"Sir, if it was something else its electronic footprint would be different. The airplane is using the IFF transponder for commercial traffic. Sir," Akhmar paused, "shall we take the airplane down?"

Fakhri glanced at the screen. The airplane was where it was supposed to be, another airplane was approaching following the same corridor. "No, Akhmar, let it go. No point in distracting our troops with this. We'll need full firepower after we attack San Francisco." Fakhri grabbed the microphone and flicked a switch on his console. "Red one? This is colonel Fakhri."

"Yes, sir?"

"Keep an eye on an inbound aircraft, bearing 250, altitude 33 thousand feet. Open fire if it deviates from its path or changes its altitude. It will fly almost straight overhead. Acknowledge."

"Bird heading 250, acknowledged."

Fakhri clicked the radio off and turned to his subordinate. "The speech has begun. Prepare power transmitter."

The President was speaking to his audience; no one on the bridge heard the words because Fakhri had turned the volume off. Nobody cared about what he had to say anyway. The camera panned across the audience. Fakhri recognized the faces of several Middle Eastern leaders who had ignored Rebirth's warning. Their lives would be the price of their defiance.

The tapping on keyboards was the only sound heard on the bridge. A few of the men were mouthing silent prayers as they worked in otherwise total concentration. They were bringing *Al Borak*, the lightning from Allah, to life.

The dome atop the Tesla power transmitter glowed. The television wasn't properly shielded like the command consoles on the bridge, so the image began to distort because of the strong magnetic field building around the rig. The sour smell of ozone prickled the crew's noses, a soft hum came from the dome.

"Power transmitter charged, sir. Ready to enable the long-range weapon at your command."

"Engage power transmitter," Fakhri said calmly.

"Power transmitter engaged."

"I'm entering the target coordinates," Fakhri consulted his notes and tapped on the keyboard: 37°46'48.4" north, 122°24'45.4" west.

"Adjusting focal point to target. Distance is 410.3 kilometers... focal point adjusted."

A button under a plastic cover changed from yellow to green.

"Sir," Akhmar reported, "the long range weapon is armed."

Fakhri had waited for this moment for years. He had prepared a speech but decided to squelch it. No words could describe what he felt. The endless humiliations suffered by his people at the hands of the Americans and their lap dog, the United Nations, would be avenged. He looked about the bridge. His crew—his men—all looked back expectantly. He felt sure they shared the triumph.

"Target confirmed and acquired," Fakhri flipped the button cover open. "Fire!"

Fakhri pressed the button. A flash of bluish light burst from the power transmitter, momentarily blinding everyone aboard the *Al Borak*.

Jon Yee had parked his car across the San Francisco baseball stadium on King Street. He carried his double non-fat latte—with a splash of vanilla flavoring—in one hand and he dialed his mobile phone with the other. King Street was busy that morning. Most people in the neighborhood had avoided going downtown. Traffic was gridlocked because of the Summit of the Nations. The loft dwellers were instead enjoying a brew at the trendy cafés. Most men and women wore business casual attire. San Francisco was either treated to thick fog or unnaturally blue skies during the summer; there was no middle ground. There were seldom any cumulus clouds. Today was a beautiful, cloudless morning. People enjoyed the otherworldly blue skies seen only in the Bay Area.

Yee put the mobile phone to his ear. The line rang twice before the connection crackled. That was strange. He looked at the phone's display. Characters and icons were rolling off the tiny screen in rapid succession. He turned it off, then tried again. The phone didn't work.

Somebody laughed.

There were several women and a couple of men whose longish hair was standing on end, just like during that science experiment Yee remembered from high school. It was funny until the St. Elmo's fire formed around every lamppost along the sidewalk. The preternatural electrical luminescence twirled quickly around the shafts, shifting from blue to purple. Yee's amusement became foreboding. He stopped in his tracks. The cars on King and 2nd Street stalled, their engines died. The fluorescent lamps under the café's sign flashed brightly before burning. A transformer mounted on a light post two blocks down exploded with a loud bang. People exchanged looks of confusion and fear.

The explosion killed every living being in a two-block radius. The energy release was instantaneous. Fortunately, everything happened so quickly that none of the victims even felt pain; men, women, children, animals and plants were vaporized in the blink of an eye. The baseball stadium was instantly flattened; the shockwave shook the buildings in the financial district, ten blocks away and further, as if they were made of cardboard. Cars melted into amorphous pools of liquefied metal. All the buildings in a six-block radius were knocked down like dominoes. Clouds of dust swirled from the destruction, a sonic boom cracked through the air. Most of the city of San Francisco lost its electrical power.

The Bay Bridge connecting Oakland and San Francisco snaked precariously as the shock wave passed through it. Drivers on the upper deck had seen the column of blue light cut through the heavens and unleash its wave of destruction when it hit the ground. Cars, trucks, buses, and motorcycles piled up in countless wrecks when drivers panicked and jammed their breaks. A cloud of smoke and vapor rose from where the stadium had been. Fortunately it was early in the day and no events had been in progress at the stadium, or thousands more would have died. The electrical and electronic systems aboard half of the city's cars and trucks were fried. The Fire Department and emergency crews were unable to aid the legions of victims in the area surrounding ground zero. The explosion pulverized the police headquarters on Bryant Street. The survivors suffered a variety of injuries, from ruptured eardrums to third degree burns, and that did not include the countless victims of car crashes throughout the city.

Enbeaath had wounded San Francisco.

"Report!" Fakhri barked.

"Sir, we have no signal from San Francisco yet."

"How long until the satellite phones work again?"

"Ninety seconds, plus or minus fifteen."

The television signal had died upon impact. Fakhri paced in the control room. The wait for the team atop Twin Peaks, the highest point in the city, to report was excruciating. Fakhri wanted to confirm the results.

"Sir, we've got contact from Twin Peaks in San Francisco," Akhmar said.

"On speaker, captain."

There was a pause. The transmission was very noisy. There were a few seconds of static, then a voice in Arabic said: "The Peace of Allah be with you."

"And with you," Fakhri said into the microphone. "What's the status?"

"Impact confirmed, sir," there was a certain reluctance in the voice. Fakhri tensed; the man from Rebirth continued. "However, we missed the target."

"What?"

"Sir, we're calculating the variation. It appears that we hit Bayside Village... the topographer is taking notes and recalculating now."

"Hurry up!" Fakhri clicked the microphone off. "Akhmar, ready to fire. Eyman," he told the operator, "prepare to input new coordinates."

"Sir, the coordinates are correct," the man named Eyman replied. "We had a small error because we never fired after adjusting the focal point for a distance longer than 50 kilometers. That's why we registered variance."

"Colonel," Akhmar said, "we'll be ready to fire 60 seconds after the new data is input."

"Colonel Fakhri?" the man in San Francisco said.

"Yes?" Fakhri clicked his microphone.

"Sir, our topographer reports that we had a discrepancy of 2.3 kilometers east and 430 meters south of the designated target."

Fakhri watched as Eyman input the values into the computer. The digital gauges changed as the new focal point was selected. Dr. Volin had warned Fakhri something like this might happen, due to differences in the Earth's magnetosphere related to latitude and to lack of data when aiming the long range weapon at distant targets.

"60 seconds to fire. Adjusting focal point."

Fakhri flipped the button cover open and placed his thumb on it. He could imagine the evacuation crews getting the president out of harm's way now. "Increase output by 30 percent," he commanded.

"Output adjusted. 45 seconds to fire."

Varenka was hiding among the various machine tools, cables, and electronics cabinets on the main deck, right under the bridge. She felt exposed for the first time since her escape. She moved slowly, trying to avoid notice as she worked her way to the controller closets.

A common oilrig has a number of industrial robots that perform various tasks associated with drilling, laying the pipes, and extracting the oil. The robots used to be governed by bulky programmable logic controllers, or PLC's, in old rigs, or by self-contained, reprogrammable industrial controllers in newer rigs like the *Al Borak*. An average rig would have between ten and twenty controllers, plus something called a Central Management System that orchestrates the others' operations. The CMS was a controller of controllers.

The command consoles on the bridge were connected to the CMS for system status and configuration. They could also use the CMS as a proxy for configuring individual controllers. Varenka was betting that the operations of the Tesla power transmitter depended on precision adjustments governed by four or more industrial controllers, and that the system design wouldn't be all that different from the ones she'd worked on.

Varenka made it to the large metal cabinet housing the controllers. She sighed with relief; the cabinet wasn't locked. She was about to open it when two of Fakhri's men ran across the deck to the battle stations at the opposite corners of the rig. Varenka barely had time to crouch between the base of a crane and the cabinet when they went by. She remained there, counting down from one hundred to zero, trying to remain calm. She was about to move when the power transmitter came to life. The dome glowed and hummed, hinting at the high currents circulating through its innards. Then the glow and the sound stopped suddenly after the humming increased its pitch.

Varenka shuddered; she guessed that they might've already used it as a weapon. She had to stop them! She stepped out of hiding. The men were gone, absorbed in their duties. Nobody was looking in her direction. She opened the metallic door.

The cabinet resembled a large, commercial refrigerator. A number of electronic components were plugged to it. Input/output cards were plugged into the backplane; endless cables snaked from the back to each component. The industrial controllers were all neatly arranged in the middle shelf. Each was encased in a grey, featureless metallic box with I/O and power connectors plugged in the back. She scanned the row of labels until she found the CMS. She unfastened the controller from its rack. A power supply, a Profibus interface, and an Ethernet cable led into the controller. She unfastened another controller. She took a deep breath and yanked them both lose, leaving a mess of dangling cables behind.

"15 seconds to fire," Akhmar announced.

A siren blared. Various screens flashed warnings.

"Sir, we have a malfunction in the control systems!" Eyman yelled.

Fakhri looked at the screen while Eyman typed furiously next to him, running the diagnostics programs. "What happened?"

"Sir, we lost the CMS and the variable capacitance controller."

"Could we have overloaded the system?" Fakhri tried to subdue the tone of desperation creeping in his voice. "Did we have some kind of feedback?"

"Negative, sir. All systems are normal. Both controllers just went off line."

"Do we have a defective power supply?"

"Negative, sir."

Someone shouted excitedly on the main deck. Fakhri and Akhmar rushed to the panoramic windows to look down. Four of his men were chasing someone running across the deck.

It was Ulyanova, holding a controller in each hand!

"*Ya gangbah!*" Fakhri swore. How had this whore escaped? He turned to Akhmar. "Do we have replacements?"

"Yes sir."

"Install the replacements, bring them back on-line as soon as possible, and fire!" Fakhri pulled his GLOCK out. "I'm going after that whore. Stop gawking and get moving!"

Fakhri ran down the stairs with Akhmar in tow. Once on the main deck each split in different directions. Fakhri ran out of the main structure, gun in hand, in time to watch Varenka hurl both controllers into the sea.

Varenka's heart beat so hard she was afraid it would break through her breastbone. She didn't stop to see the controllers splashdown. She turned to her right and bolted along the edge of the deck, not daring to turn back. She knew it would be only a matter of time before they caught her. Should she jump into the ocean? She probably didn't have a chance of survival. Sattar would send his men after her, or they would shoot her from the decks, or the sharks would have their way with her.

Bozhe moi, Bozhe moi, Bozhe moi!

Varenka turned right again, this time heading straight for the crew's quarters. Sattar was coming right at her, gun in hand.

She slipped on the deck as she tried to evade Sattar and her pursuers by going through a narrow passage between the main quarters and the crane. A gunshot reverberated on the deck. A bullet zoomed past her like an angry hornet. Varenka panicked.

Where to go? Where...?

A hand groped her. She screamed and turned around. Almost without thinking she jammed her knee into her would be captor's groin. He doubled over, tearing her shirt. She ran again, glad that the man's prostrated body blocked her pursuers. She dashed across the main deck. She'd made up her mind. She'd jump off the rig if she could make it to the other side. Sattar was resolved to kill her. The ocean offered her a better chance of survival, however slim.

Several men, seven or eight, came from the other side, converging on her. The ones in the front had drawn their pistols. It was only a matter of time before either group caught her.

In a panic, Varenka sprinted toward the derrick. She began climbing the structure as fast as she could. Its material eased the climb—it wasn't very slippery, even in the ocean spray. She kept climbing, not daring to look down, even after two bullets crashed into a beam precariously close to her chest. Sattar shouted something below. She ignored him. She had to stop for a moment. Her breathing was shallow. She was close to collapse. She looked down. Her four pursuers were following her up the derrick. She looked around. She took cover behind one of the thicker beams and jammed her body in a sitting position on a V in the truss. She realized that Sattar didn't want anybody firing at her while she was perched on the Tesla power transmitter. Could she use that to her advantage? Varenka remembered the gun, tucked in her waistband. She pulled it out, studied it for a second, then released what she thought was the safety and aimed at the men climbing the derrick. She pulled the trigger. The gun jumped in her hands, startling her so that she almost dropped it. The men flattened themselves against the derrick, but they'd stop climbing. They exchanged shouts in Arabic, then they slowly went down.

She sighed with relief. She was safe for now. They wouldn't dare come after her as long as she was armed, and they wouldn't dare shoot her. She snuck a peek. The men regrouped below, Sattar was talking to them. Six men broke away from the group and posted themselves around the derrick but didn't attempt to climb it. The waiting game had begun.

Varenka figured her scarce options. It was cold up there; a chilly wind beat her body. She might freeze to death if it got colder. She swore. They would have to come and get her. She would rather die cold and alone up there than surrender to that bastard and his men.

A strange whistling sound, followed by a flapping noise stopped her dark musings. Several shadows glided over the main deck. She looked up but couldn't see through the glare; the sun was in her eyes.

A man shouted above. There was a loud bang and then hell broke loose.

CHAPTER 35

A C-17 flying over the Pacific

"ALERT!" Pallone announced over the comm link. "We're cleared to proceed by CINCPAC."

Francis glanced out the window on the right side of the aircraft. A beautiful aurora borealis, so bright it could be seen in daylight, hung from the sky. A few scattered clouds swirled slowly in an unnatural, counterclockwise pattern around a point northwest of the aircraft. Francis' heart skipped a beat. The spiral clouds had long stringy arms, yet there were no other signs of turbulence.

I've got to stay focused, he told himself. I shouldn't worry about the oilrig until I get there.

Francis and his assigned partner, a SEAL who had introduced himself only as Jason, were giving each other a final gear check. The parachutes weren't very different from Francis' own gear. The containers looked like Quasars. Three ring riser system, but the rings were made of some resin, instead of metal, to further reduce their radar footprint. BOC release for the main. Black (instead of red) main parachute cut away handle in case of malfunction. The harness had a special container with ordnance and a small first aid kit mounted on the jumper's back, above the reserve parachute. Francis wore a waterproof, tight-fitting black jumpsuit with zippered pockets for weapons, ammo, and tools; a load bearing belt and flotation device, Vietnam style combat boots and leather gloves completed the setup. His wrist altimeter was marked in meters and feet. His helmet was a full-face model, specially manufactured for the armed forces, with a self contained respirator. They would need oxygen down to 16,000 feet, or about one minute of free fall. They would not open their parachutes until they were 2,000 feet above the target.

Every member of the team wore a similar helmet, which for now was hooked to the airplane's oxygen supply. The cargo bay was not pressurized.

"Okay Montagnet, what is this handle for?" Jason asked over the comm link, pointing at a special handle on his chest strap.

"It's a cut away that will dump the container and reserve off my back," Francis clicked his neck mike on to reply. "It will also release my main parachute, so I'll have freedom of movement. The belt and the small backpack with my gear will stay in place."

"Good," Jason said, tapping Francis' helmet. "You're good to go."

Francis thanked him and leant to peer through the window again. His equipment was different from the SEALs'. He wasn't carrying as much ordnance as the others, only being allowed to take his sidearm and his knives. That was fine with him, since he wasn't used to jumping off an airplane carrying an extra 100 pounds, like the SEALs and Special Forces did. "We're on jump run," the pilot announced over the speakers. "Three miles out."

A yellow light flashed in the cargo compartment.

This is it, Francis thought, checking his leg straps for the last time.

"Door!" someone shouted.

The rear ramp of the C 17 opened with a hydraulic hiss.

Francis checked his altimeter once more. 33,000 feet, give or take about 250. He and the SEALs unhooked their helmets from their respective oxygen umbilical. They arranged themselves on the exit ramp.

"One mile out, gentlemen; stand by," the pilot announced.

Francis took a deep breath. This was it. He felt this adrenaline rush every time he jumped after a long hiatus without skydiving. It had been a bit over two months since his last jump.

A sudden flash of dazzling light flooded the cabin through the open ramp.

"What the fuck was that?" someone asked over the comm link.

"We're almost there," Pallone scolded him. "Don't get distracted."

"Exit," the pilot commanded. "Good luck!"

The men stepped to the edge of the rear hatch ramp. "Ready... set... go!" Pallone gave the count.

Francis and the rest of his group dove off the plane, going into a flat track. Francis clenched his teeth. The windblast at 300 miles per hour felt like being swatted by a giant hand. It almost knocked the wind out of him. During the briefing he was told to prepare for a controlled tumble instead of an elegant exit, as he would normally do during a sport jump in which the aircraft flew at a mere 80 miles per hour. Also, unlike a sport jump, he was *decelerating* to terminal velocity, not accelerating.

Francis was disoriented for a couple of instants before taking inventory of his sensations. He'd tumbled on exit. He arched his back, pushing his hips forward, to flip his body belly down. He went to a neutral position, hands by his head, legs slightly open, and made a full turn. He found the rest of the team, already tracking toward the target, directly underneath the swirling, wispy clouds.

Francis adjusted his body position. First he extended his legs and pointed his toes, then brought his hands to his side. His arms and legs formed a double V. He cupped his shoulders and pushed against the wind with his hands. He felt his body accelerate at first, then gain some lift. He and the SEALs were delta tracking, their bodies turned into airfoils to build speed and distance.

Commander Pallone led the human flock toward the target. They were so high up that Francis had trouble finding the rig, a mere grey speck in the blue green immensity of the Pacific.

A minute went by. Pallone finished his track and went to neutral flying position. Francis and the rest of the team followed. The oilrig was almost directly underneath them. Francis checked his altimeter. They were at 16,000 ft. Halfway there.

There was a brief flash of light; the swirling clouds dissipated, the aurora vanished. Francis guessed that these strange phenomena were related to the Tesla power transmitter. What did their disappearance mean? Were they about to open fire?

Francis looked at his altimeter. 7,000 feet. Just a few more seconds.

The 9-way team members formed a large circle.

3,500 feet.

Pallone pointed with both hands outward. The group turned around and all the men tracked away from the center, to gain separation.

3,000 feet.

Francis slowed down, went back to a neutral body position again, belly down, hands by his head, legs slightly opened.

2,500 feet.

Francis looked around. There were no skydivers above or below him.

2,000 feet.

Francis grabbed the soft handle on his back, under the container, pulled the pilot 'chute out, and threw it into the wind. The pilot 'chute pulled the main out of the container. He checked over his shoulders, ensuring that his main parachute was inflating. Two seconds later his blue grey parachute was fully deployed, its slider down. It was a 9-cell parachute, almost twice as big as his own. A Manta 260, he'd been briefed. He immediately cleared the steering toggles and veered toward the target.

Eight other parachutes popped open around him. They would try landing on the main deck or atop the bridge. They would touch down in just a few seconds. They could make out the shapes of the men running about the deck.

What...?

Francis flipped his helmet face shield open. He was getting claustrophobic in it anyway. The visor was fogged up. And he wanted to confirm what he was seeing.

Four men were chasing a familiar form across the deck, past the base of the derrick.

Varenka!

He watched her make it to the edge of the deck, pause momentarily, then begin running again as the men chasing her opened fire.

Hang on Varenka! He wished she could hear his thoughts. We're almost there!

Three of the men spiraled down to the derrick faster than the rest of the group. They'd agreed that Francis would not be in the first landing group. One of the SEALs had dropped a smoke canister so they could figure out which way the wind blew. The three men turned their parachutes into the wind and prepared to land. Someone threw a flashbang at a group of armed men coming toward the derrick.

An alarm sounded on the rig. The two closest battle stations aimed their canons toward them but did not fire. The rest of the SEALs and Francis were barely two hundred feet above the deck and approaching fast. This huge parachute was much slower to turn than the smaller canopies Francis was used to. The first group of men landed.

Francis realized too late that his line of flight took him directly behind the derrick with respect to the wind. His parachute shook violently in the turbulence created by the derrick as he approached the deck. He steered gently, trying to fly in a straight line and into the wind. He succeeded as he was barely ten meters above the deck. He descended quickly and pulled on both toggles at the same time to flare his canopy and stop.

The deck was somewhat slippery. He came in a bit faster than he wanted and was forced to run during landing. He put his left hand fingers through the chest strap quick-release handle and pulled. His parachute and containers fell off and he broke into a run, looking for cover. Someone opened fire at him as though on cue. He dove for cover at the base of the derrick. Gunfire erupted all around him.

A man was climbing down from the derrick almost directly overhead. Francis strained his eyes and realized that Varenka was perched up there, about two thirds of the way up. He fired at the man, who dropped to the ground and didn't move. The SEALs dealt with three others. Francis saw an enraged Fakhri barking orders at his men, firing his gun as he dashed for the relative safety of the bridge.

Two SEAL team members joined Francis at the base of the derrick. One provided cover as the other prepared the explosives for blowing it up.

"Dr. Ulyanova is atop the derrick!" Francis shouted at him.

"Then she better get down fast," the man replied, sticking the detonators into the plastic explosive bricks.

"Give her a few seconds!" Francis shouted. The man either didn't hear him or ignored him. Damn! Francis began to climb the structure. "Varenka!" She didn't hear him. He kept going, as fast as he could. "Varenka!"

"Francis…?" she called back, incredulous. "*Bozhe moi!* Sattar told me you were dead!"

"Quick, get down here! They're blowing up the tower!"

"I'm coming!"

Francis began to descend, somewhat relieved. He looked for the demolition expert. He was placing the charges at the base of the derrick. As Francis watched, a bullet struck the demolition expert somewhere in his mid section. His cover man immediately returned fire, but it was too late. Not all the charges had been planted.

Francis let go of the derrick and fell the last twelve feet. He rolled on the ground to break the fall, then dove for the fallen man. "Can you proceed?" he asked.

"I'm hit," the man said. "Here, do the rest! Hurry!"

Francis grabbed the remaining two plastic explosive bricks and placed them at different points of the base of the derrick. He looked back. Varenka was almost on the ground.

"Varenka, quick! Watch out!"

"I'm here," she ran to his side. "Oh my God, I'm so glad to see you! I disabled the Tesla power transmitter."

Bullets flew by them, thudding into the deck around them. They were being attacked from all sides.

"Later! We have to get out of here." Francis snapped. The gunshots had stopped. "Where can we take cover?"

"The control cabinets, next to the engine room," she said. "There, see them?"

"Yes. Get in there and take cover. I'll be with you shortly. We've got to take the wounded out of here. There is no time to lose!"

"Francis, you better hurry then," Varenka said as she turned to leave. "They've already fired the weapon once."

"Go! Stay low. I'll cover you."

Varenka was momentarily exposed before breaking into a run across the deck. Francis fired at a terrorist taking aim at her. He missed, but she made it to the cabinets.

Good!

Francis went back to the fallen man. The other SEAL, the one providing cover, was already pulling the demolition experts' arm over his shoulder to drag him to safety. Blood seeped through the jumpsuit where the man was injured. Francis put the other arm over his shoulder and they dragged him together from under the derrick.

Jason had landed atop the bridge and provided cover fire as Francis and the demolition team headed for the control cabinets. The fifteen meters felt like running a marathon, the smell of blood and gunpowder mingled with that of the ocean. Several Rebirth men lay wounded on the deck.

Just a few more meters...

Something snapped with a sharp, metallic sound. Francis recognized it: some kind of relay. A soft humming sound came from the globe atop the derrick. A metallic shaft ran down the derrick from the center of the globe through a hole in the deck and into the ocean. The shaft slid down with the sound of heavy machinery.

"Francis, they repaired the controller for the power transmitter! And they locked the cabinet. Help me." Varenka screamed. She was pulling at the control cabinet door, trying to break its lock. "Look, they're adjusting the focal point. They'll be ready to fire again in a matter of seconds!"

Bancroft of the FBI stood stupefied. Now he knew from the briefing during the previous day that they'd all better get away from there or they wouldn't survive. Too late he'd come to believe that the Tesla weapons were operational. Pandemonium had broken out at the San Francisco Opera House. The attendees began evacuating as fast as possible. The lights had failed. Six Secret Service agents whisked the president away.

Panicked men and women rushed to the emergency exits. They all realized they were under some kind of attack. Only the President of the United States and a few other U.S. officials knew that the whole city of San Francisco wasn't safe. The president could get away if he and his escort made it to the helicopter waiting by City Hall, and only if the helicopter itself escaped before it was too late.

The crowd poured steadily to the street. Electric arcs were jumping between lampposts along Van Ness Avenue. Some of the lamps on the Opera House facade exploded. The air itself felt electrified. St. Elmo's fire formed around the City Hall spire. The helicopter's flight instruments fluctuated wildly, its engine sputtered.

"Clear!" the injured demolition man grunted. They all huddled together behind the control cabinet.

"Cover your ears!" Francis told Varenka, covering her body with his, just in case, as he covered his own ears with his hands.

The demolition expert pulled a small, oblong transmitter from his TAC vest. He clicked his neck mike. "Take cover!" he notified everyone on the SEAL team and pressed the button.

The explosion wasn't as noisy as Francis expected. Some debris clattered against the cabinet, the deck shook under them. Francis looked over the cabinet.

Yes!

The glowing, humming Tesla power transmitter was toppling over, gaining speed on its way to the deck. The metallic globe atop it glinted in the morning sun.

Francis ducked again, trying to protect himself and Varenka against a potential torrent of debris. The power transmitter slammed against the deck like a wounded Leviathan. The cacophony of crashing metal reverberated throughout the whole oilrig. Metal plates popped from the dome and skidded all over the main deck. At least one terrorist was crushed under the dome as it rolled across the deck to fall off the end and splash into the ocean.

Gunfire could still be heard in various parts of the oilrig, mainly in the main quarters.

"Are you all right?" Francis asked Varenka in Russian as he stood up.

"I'm fine," Varenka hugged him tightly. "I can't believe you're alive! Sattar said you were dead."

"He came close to achieving that," Francis said. He looked at her as she released him. What was wrong with Varenka? For the first time he noticed dark circles under her eyes, and bruises on her cheek and neck. "What happened to you?"

Varenka lowered her eyes, "Don't worry about it now."

"What happened to you?" Francis said, feeling the rage swelling. "Did Fakhri do this to you?" Varenka said nothing and closed her eyes. A tear ran down her left cheek. "I'm going to kill the son of a bitch!" Francis growled.

"No Francis! Stay here, with me. The others will get him."

Francis shook himself free of Varenka's grip. "No Varenka; I personally want to send the bastard to hell." Francis shoved a fresh magazine into his Beretta and chambered a round.

"What are you two saying?" the other SEAL, the one who'd provided cover, asked Francis.

"I'm going after Fakhri; he's the big guy with the mustache and the bad temper."

"We have orders to capture the leaders alive."

"You can have the remains after I'm done with the son of a bitch." Francis stood up.

"Dammit, Montagnet, stay where you are!"

"Catch me if you can," Francis countered and broke into a run toward the bridge.

The oilrig was almost secured. There were a number of dead and wounded Rebirth Alliance men scattered throughout. Francis guessed about twenty. The battle stations were empty, useless now that the power transmitter was destroyed. Several men were tied down on the deck and guarded by alert SEALs. Francis saw Jason checking the deck.

Shots were fired somewhere above. Francis ran up the stairs, his gun arm extended. He passed the empty crew's quarters. The residual OC prickled his nose. Apparently Pallone or his men had used tear gas grenades to flush whoever had been there. After climbing the stairs two steps at a time, Francis made it to the bridge. Pallone and another man were by the hatch into the bridge.

"What's the situation, commander?" Francis asked.

"We're flushing these shitheads out in a few moments, as soon as my team on the roof is ready."

"Anything I can do to help?"

"Just stay the fuck out of our way, Montagnet," Pallone warned. "You did well down there. Don't spoil a perfect record."

"I want Fakhri."

"You will adhere to mission orders, is that understood? We want to capture the leaders." Pallone held Francis' stare.

The other man had finished applying explosives to the hatch. He nodded at Pallone. Francis followed behind Pallone after the other man blew the hatch open.

Pallone's man threw a flashbang into the bridge. There was a long pause followed by an explosion and screams in Arabic. Pallone and his man went in just as two other SEALs blasted the windows from the outside and entered the room from the ceiling. Francis followed. Pallone opened fire against a Rebirth alliance man who wore a military uniform of sorts and pulled a gun on him. The man fell back with the impact of Pallone's automatic fire. Francis approached the fallen man, thinking it was Fakhri at first. He realized that the man was too short. To his surprise, the man had a nametag written in Cyrillic: *Kapitan Akhmar.*

Fakhri's gone!

Francis frantically searched the room. He was nowhere to be found. A door into a closet swung back and forth almost imperceptibly. He dashed there, vaulting over the body of a young Rebirth recruit. He yanked the door open with his left hand, aiming his gun inside.

The closet was empty. Francis peered in cautiously. The back of the closet had a hinge. He pushed against it and cursed under his breath.

A firemen's pole! Fakhri had *escaped!*

"Commander! The big fish is gone!"

"What?" Pallone ran to Francis' side.

"I'm going after him," Francis said. He holstered his gun and jumped on the firemen's pole to slide to the ground floor. He landed somewhere in the back of the rig, opposite to where Varenka and the SEALs were. There was nobody in sight.

"Dammit Montagnet!" Pallone screamed from above before sliding down the fireman's pole.

Four explosions in rapid succession rocked the oilrig. The deck rolled precariously to the north. It was pitched at least 20 degrees. Anything that wasn't fastened on the main deck rolled down toward the ocean. Francis struggled to keep his balance. Pallone landed beside him.

Where did Fakhri go?

Francis scanned the deck. All the battle stations had been blown up, possibly booby-trapped. Of course! If Rebirth didn't have them nobody could have them. Were all the SEALs alive? He hoped so.

Where is Fakhri?

Francis flattened himself against the wall, trying to offer the smallest target possible as he worked his way back to the main deck, gun in hand. He squeezed between a crane and some debris from the fallen derrick, scanning the rig for Fakhri. Pallone was providing cover from under the bridge.

Oh, NO!

Fakhri was aiming an AK-47 at the control cabinets. Francis fired three tap-tap bursts at Fakhri, who was well-concealed between the remains of the derrick. Fakhri ducked and aimed his weapon at Montagnet, who was out in the open.

Francis raced across the deck, chased by Fakhri's fire. He jumped behind three spools of cable, each at least five feet in diameter. Bullets rained on his hideout as Fakhri continued fire. There was a pause, and when Francis looked to see what was happening, Fakhri was aiming again at the control cabinets.

At Varenka.

"No!" Francis ran from behind the spools, drawing fire from Fakhri once more. Francis tripped on some debris and fell hard on his side.

Move!

Francis rolled on the deck, trying to get away from Fakhri's aim as bullets impacted all around him. He scrambled to hide again behind the spools. The bullet spray finally stopped.

"Dammit Montagnet, you're going to get killed!" Pallone yelled. "Stay down!"

Fakhri fired twice after a pause, then ran from his hideout to the control cabinets. A burst of fire from one of the SEALs in either the bridge or the roof followed him, but it was too late. Fakhri had a hold of Varenka after wounding or killing the men with her. Francis couldn't tell.

Francis watched horrified when Fakhri put his arm around Varenka's neck and a gun to her head. Fakhri flattened his back against the control cabinet and used Varenka as a shield. He said something into her ears, her eyes widened and she began to fumble with the lock. There! She'd opened the cabinet under Fakhri's watch.

Francis came from behind the spools, aiming his gun at Fakhri's head. "Let her go!" he shouted.

"Montagnet, when will you give up on your pathetic heroics? She isn't worth it," Fakhri pressed his gun against her temple and whispered something in her ear.

Francis closed the distance to them. Two SEALs were coming to his aid, their automatic rifles raised and aimed at Fakhri. Francis stepped forward. Fakhri pressed the gun to Varenka's head; she reached into the cabinet and manipulated something.

"You can't win, Fakhri," Francis insisted. Fakhri was in his sights. Come on Varenka, get out of the way!

"No Montagnet, it's you and the Americans who can't win. You won't take me alive, and you shall not have these weapons!"

As if on cue, an alarm shrieked and red lights flashed across the remains of the deck. There were more explosions, one of them above—possibly on the bridge! The SEALs were momentarily stunned. Fakhri took this opportunity to shove Varenka forward and drag her with him past the main quarters.

Where are they going?

Fakhri fired back before turning around the corner.

What is on the other side of the rig?

Francis and the two SEALs chased Fakhri and Varenka until they reached the edge. Fakhri forced her to pop a metal grate open and pull a lever. The whir of machinery came from somewhere underneath them. Fakhri was at the edge of the rig, alternatively looking down into the ocean and pressing his gun against Varenka's temple.

There was another explosion. The rig pitched even further, the deck was now steeply slanted. The bridge had blown up. Glass and debris fell all around Francis. Two SEALs were coming closer, aiming their weapons at Fakhri and Varenka. Francis approached.

"That's far enough, Montagnet! One more step and I kill her!"

"Let her go!"

"Shut up!" Fakhri looked behind him once more. "Drop your weapon!"

Francis judged the distance. He was about four meters away from them. He sighed. He knew what was coming next.

"Think Fakhri," Francis said, his gunsight steady on his enemy. "You know she's important to me, but these guys don't care. They'll shoot you both if they must."

"You don't care well for your women, Montagnet," Fakhri said, a mocking smile on his face. "I will kill Varenka just as we killed the woman who was with you two years ago. Remember her?"

"What?" Francis shouted, furious. What was Fakhri talking about? Then the memories overcame Francis. The same cold eyes from two years before. Francis' head throbbed. He was stunned, paralyzed. He faced an opponent just like the terrorist who had killed Susan two years ago. He saw Susan's chest pierced by a bullet fired by an assassin again. Francis felt again the same powerlessness of letting the man escape while he had coddled his dying, loving Susan. Susan's face juxtaposed itself with Varenka's in his mind's eye. Had he failed both of them?

"No!" Francis almost squeezed the trigger. His hands trembled with rage, his heart beat loudly against his chest.

"Shut up! Kick the gun away from you!" Fakhri kept using Varenka as a shield. Francis dropped the gun and obeyed. "Good bye, Montagnet!"

Fakhri pulled his gun away from Varenka's temple and aimed it at Francis. Francis clenched his teeth, waiting for the inevitable. Then he saw that Varenka jam her right elbow into Fakhri's gut. Fakhri pulled the trigger but his aim was off, missing Montagnet by a wide margin.

Now!

Fakhri let go of Varenka momentarily. In one fluid motion, Francis pulled a throwing knife from the sheath on his left forearm and threw it at Fakhri. The knife whistled through the air, burying itself in Fakhri's shooting arm shoulder. His gun clattered on the deck.

Varenka is free!

Francis jumped and knocked Fakhri away from Varenka, who scrambled away from him. Another explosion upset the rig. Francis lost his grip on Fakhri. At least the man wasn't armed anymore.

Two shots were fired at Fakhri and Francis; they missed. It had been one of the SEALs firing! Francis saw for the first time what Fakhri had been doing. There was a boat below!

"You can't win, Montagnet! I will kill you with my own hands if I have to!"

"Fuck you!"

The two men circled each other like pit bulls. Francis knew that at least one SEAL was aiming his rifle at them, and that there was a good chance he'd get caught in the crossfire. Fakhri closed the distance between them, his arms and legs in some sort of fighting stance, like a wrestler.

Francis snapped to fighting stance himself. Fakhri tried to jump him and Francis jammed his right knee into the man's solar plexus, leaning back to keep his face and neck away from Fakhri. Fakhri stumbled back but quickly recovered.

Damn, he's strong!

Francis stepped in and tried to kick Fakhri's leg. The terrorist anticipated the move and stepped back, then quickly recovered and counterattacked. Francis barely had time to cover himself against a blow from Fakhri's hand. Fakhri was quick. He immediately grabbed Francis' shoulder and neck to throw him to the ground.

Attack!

Francis knew that the best way to prevent Fakhri from doing more damage was to close their distance, so he shot his right arm up and pulled Fakhri closer by his neck. Fakhri was surprised, and instinctively tried to upright himself. Bad move, asshole! Francis slipped his left hand between Fakhri's arms and grabbed his neck. He now clenched Fakhri by the back of his neck, with both hands.

Fakhri was significantly taller; this worked against Francis' advantage. Francis slipped his fingers to the base of Fakhri's skull and pulled his head down. He straightened his back and stood on tiptoes, legs slightly apart, measuring the right moment to attack. Fakhri was punching his body as hard as he could, trying to free himself. Francis felt a rib crack; Fakhri almost knocked the wind out of him but he held strong.

Now!

Francis' left knee shot forward and connected with Fakhri's liver, followed instantly by the right one into his ribs. Francis repeated this four, six times, knocking the breath out of Fakhri. Finally the terrorist's arms relaxed from around his neck, and Francis pushed him away.

Fakhri wasn't defeated yet.

To Francis' surprise, Fakhri slipped back, grabbed his left hand and twisted backward. Francis tried to free himself, but it was impossible. Francis closed the distance again, ignoring the pain, and jammed his right elbow into Fakhri's irate face. A nasty cut opened on Fakhri's cheekbone but he didn't let go. The two men struggled with each other, each trying to gain an advantage over the other.

He's stronger than me, Francis thought, panicking. Francis' left hand was numb. He tried pulling it loose but something snapped. Ice-cold pain ran up his left arm as Fakhri's right arm closed around his neck. Francis knew he was just a few seconds away from having his neck broken.

A gunshot reverberated throughout the now quiet, sinking oilrig. Fakhri's grip relaxed somewhat, his face was twisted in a furious grimace. Francis struggled to free himself in time to see Varenka, white faced, fire two more shots into Fakhri's body. Fakhri stumbled back, still trying to strangle Francis. One of the SEALs—Jason?—tackled Varenka to the deck and Pallone made a run for them. He didn't make it.

Another explosion shook the oilrig. The deck pitched downward almost instantly. The guardrail was slightly higher than Francis' waist. Fakhri and Francis struggled to maintain their footing to no use. Fakhri's wounded upper body went over the guardrail; the man's weight dragged Francis along. Both men crashed into the ocean, missing the boat by mere inches. Francis barely had a chance to gulp some air before sinking. The water was cold. The struggle resumed. Fakhri was a dead weight around him, dragging him into the deep.

My right arm is free!

Francis reached down to his right foot with his free hand. He pulled his boot knife from its sheath and stabbed Fakhri's arm. He twisted the blade. Finally Fakhri uncurled his arm from around his neck, just as

Francis' ears began to hurt. The ocean surface was farther away, the light dimmed.

He broke free.

Francis felt like his lungs were about to burst. Fakhri kept sinking below him, his dead eyes stared back without seeing. Francis' knife was still buried to the hilt in Fakhri's arm. Francis shuddered and sought the surface. He couldn't move his left arm—it was probably dislocated. He tried kicking with his legs and his only good hand. He couldn't. The boots were full of water, weighing him down. Exhausted, he couldn't hold his breath any longer. He inhaled the first gulp of salty water.

Francis had heard that dying people see important moments in their life in playback, like a movie. He saw images of Varenka, of Susan, of his family and friends. He saw some of his happiest memories as the darkness swallowed him.

I must still be alive, he thought. Pain shot through his dislocated arm when he brushed it against his load-bearing belt.

The belt!

Francis gulped more water, sunk deeper. He ran his right hand desperately along the tube around his waist as he vainly tried to push the water out of his lungs.

There!

Francis' fingers clawed the small D ring and pulled. The floating device inflated and dragged him to the distant, unreachable surface.

Francis Xavier Montagnet didn't care anymore. A strange, peaceful feeling overcame him. At least Varenka was safe. He relaxed and welcomed death.

CHAPTER **36**

37°36'35.1" N, 126°5'43.2" W

The Pacific Ocean was claiming the *Al Borak*. Varenka limped to the guardrail; the water was rising fast and lapped parts of the tilting main deck. She strained forward to scan the ocean for signs of Francis. The two military men, the one who had tackled her and the one who tried to stop Francis and Fakhri from going overboard, spoke English to one another too fast for her to understand.

How long had Francis been submerged? One minute? Two? Francis and Sattar had fallen about five meters. Had Francis lost consciousness with the impact? Oh, God! Please let him live!

The oilrig buckled. She estimated that the deck would be completely under water in twenty minutes at the rate they were sinking. Perhaps sooner. The pontoons and the ballast tanks were probably gone. Were there enough lifeboats for everyone? The military men were herding the surviving terrorists, hands bound behind their backs, to the far end of the rig. She was sure that Francis would be left behind if he didn't surface soon. Please Francis, come back up!

The turbulence created by the sinking oilrig foamed and bubbled all around. Sattar's escape boat, almost directly below her, bobbed out of control. Its tether tightened and collapsed in sync with the turbulence. Varenka kept scanning the surface with a knot in her throat, to no avail...

There he was!

Francis was floating face up about twenty meters away from the rig.

"Francis!" she yelled, trying to get his attention. She got no response. Her heart sank. Francis floated face up but wasn't moving. The wave crests washed over him as his body drifted away from the rig.

"Help!" Varenka begged the two men, pointing at Francis. "Francis it is in *vater*, he's hurt!"

One of the men nodded and turned to speak with his partner, then into his radio. They were wasting time! Francis drifted farther away in the current while these men argued how to proceed.

She kicked her shoes off and dove into the ocean.

Her dive had been better than she'd expected. Varenka had never dived off from such a height but she was a good enough swimmer. She emerged on the surface and vigorously swam toward Francis.

The water was cold though not enough to faze her. The Volga river was much cooler in the spring. Her urge to reach Francis fueled her kick and stroke to close the distance quickly. Two, six, eight more strokes and she'd be by his side.

"Francis!"

She made it. He was still floating on his back, his green unblinking eyes were turned to the sky, his mouth was half open. Varenka slid her left arm under his chin and began to swim back, keeping his face above the surface.

"Don't die on me, Francis!" she whispered at him over and over as she towed his limp body. "Come on, you can do it!"

A monstrous military airplane flew overhead and dropped something by the oilrig. It was flying so low that for a heart stopping moment she thought it would crash into the ocean.

Varenka was beginning to tire. She stubbornly fought the current. She was barely the length of a swimming pool away from the rig, yet it felt like she made no progress.

An engine roared to life. The man who'd been next to her on the deck before she dove after Francis had taken Sattar's boat and was approaching.

Varenka pushed Francis close to the boat as soon as it stopped, just a few feet away from them. The man hoisted Francis on board and laid him on the flat bottom. She watched the crew aboard the rig. The airplane had dropped inflatable rafts for evacuation. The Americans were readying them.

The man was done with Francis and offered his hand to her; she grasped it. He was so strong that he lifted her bodily out of the water and into the boat.

"Thank you," she muttered and turned her attention to Francis.

"Ma'am, I'll take care of him," the man said, gently pushing her aside before leaning over Francis to start CPR.

Varenka shivered. She watched their rescuer pump Francis' chest, pushing the water out. Once, twice, three times he pressed. Water squirted from Francis' mouth and nostrils.

Varenka knelt next to Francis, frustrated. He had come back for her, had risked his life to protect her, and there was not a damn thing she could do for him now.

"Is there things I can do?" she asked their rescuer.

"No, ma'am," he replied. "I gotta get his breathing going before it's too late. Just leave me enough room to work."

Francis' head twitched; his expressionless face suddenly twisted in pain, a panicked look brought life back to his eyes. Francis expelled water from his lungs with a sickening, gurgling noise. His body writhed. He turned on his belly, coughing. He got on his knees, still forcing water out through his mouth and nose.

Francis gulped air, to Varenka's relief. He was clutching his chest with his right hand. His limp left arm dangled by his side. His face contorted in pain. The military man checked Francis' pupils over before sitting behind the wheel and steering the boat back to the oilrig.

"Montagnet, you should thank this lady. She saved your life."

Varenka understood what the man had said and smiled. Francis reached for her with his right hand and pulled her closer. He was clammy but she didn't care. He was alive!

"You need a doctor, Montagnet," the man said.

"Thanks Jason," Francis groaned. "We'll get a doctor when we're back on land."

Varenka assisted Francis to prop himself against a seat. He winced. "What's wrong?" she asked.

"I think I have a broken rib. Breathing hurts like hell. And I can't move my arm. I can't feel it either. I must be in shock." Francis and Jason engaged in an English conversation so fast that Varenka barely understood. They were back by the rig, or more accurately, halfway across the sinking deck.

"Varenka, Jason's commanding officer wants to know how long do you think it'll be before the rig sinks."

"Well, no more than ten minutes at this rate."

"Is there anything we can do to save it?"

Varenka appraised the wreck before responding. "I don't think so. The ballast tanks and pontoons are breached. Structural integrity is compromised."

Francis translated for Jason, who idled the motor and jumped onto the rig. The water now reached his waist and was still rising. "I'm reporting that to commander Pallone. You two stay aboard this boat and prepare to evacuate. I've got to help my team to move the wounded and deal with the prisoners. And... Montagnet?"

"Yeah?"

"Stay away from the commander. He didn't like you or the missus taking on the leader on your own." Jason trod off in the waist-high water.

"Varenka?"

"Yes, Francis?"

"Let's get the hell out of here."

"Shall we wait for the soldiers to move?"

"They aren't soldiers," Francis wheezed. "They're called Navy SEALs. Think of them as seabound *Speznats*."

"Seals," she asked in English, "like the animal, *tyulyen*?"

"Yes. Come on, *dorogoya*, let's go."

Varenka took the pilot's seat and studied the controls briefly. The speed control lever was to her right. She had never piloted a boat but this did not seem complicated. She pushed the lever one notch. The boat gently moved forward. Varenka steered toward the horizon.

The SEALs boarded their grey inflatable boats, the kind she always saw in Jacques Cousteau documentaries... Zodiacs, she thought they were called. The prisoners were piled on motorless boats tugged by the SEALs. Five Zodiacs and their boat peeled away from the wreck and reassembled about fifty meters away. Varenka maneuvered close to the group and killed the motor.

Varenka and Francis watched solemnly as the rest of the *Al Borak* sank to its final resting place.

"There was so much destruction, so much pain. So many people died because of the Tesla power transmitter. It's ironic that he had called it 'the machine that will end war'. People would have to change first. No machine will end war unless people want to end it first." She sighed. "Is it over, Francis?"

"Not yet," he tugged at the zipper on his left sleeve pocket. "Help me?"

Varenka unzipped the pocket and searched it with her fingers. She caught her breath when she recognized the contents: Two Flash memory cards, the kind used in a handheld computer. She handed them to him.

"I always kept them with me," he explained, holding them on the palm of his right hand. "The complete plans for the Tesla power transmitter. The documents from DARPA and those that Kurok facilitated to us. The last complete set." He put each memory card in his mouth and bit hard until it cracked. Varenka peeked at the SEALs; they were tending their wounded, keeping an eye on the prisoners, hailing for help, or otherwise occupied. Only she saw when Francis casually reached overboard to drop the crushed memory cards into the sea.

"Varenka," Francis spoke softly, "it's over now. And we made it."

He gazed at her for a long time, then reached to caress her face. She was reassured by his touch. She slid next to Francis and offered her shoulder so he could rest.

They were stranded in a small boat in the middle of the ocean, the flotsam was the only evidence left of what had been the most fantastic, lethal and improbable weapon in history. The morning sun climbed toward the zenith, bathing them with its warmth. The last remains of the Tesla Testament sank slowly, drifting in the currents. The memory cards would be forever lost in the unfathomable depths.

"*Ya tebya lublyu*," Francis whispered in Russian, his voice raspy, "I love you. Thanks for coming to get me."

"I love you too, *dorogoy*," she replied before kissing his lips.

Varenka smiled and snuggled closer to him. Francis shut his eyes and slept.

Acknowledgements

Lots of people helped in making this book a reality. Their contributions went far beyond anything I would have expected. You're all important and unique in your own way. Thanks to Barbara Rose Brooker for her coaching. Stuart Dodgshon and his magic 3D touch. Jennifer Hamblen taught me lots about selling books. Thanks to Olga Isaicheva for her support. Charles Kiene made a hell of a nice book cover. Rick Kraft: your amazing CAD work on the Tesla tower rules. Marketa Kroupova and her infinite patience; cheers! Carin Kunz—you're pure inspiration. Carlos Maitret is the engineering genius that first told me about Tesla's amazing life and inventions. Chris and Janet Morris taught me how to do, not tell. Marybeth Riggs is the best editor in the world. Tom Shibel deserves all the credit for bringing the MODU to life in Francis' universe. Diana Silva... you rock!

Deb French: thanks for hauling all those books around—and thanks for enriching my life.

Special thanks to Pincheat Arunleung, David Blaikie, J.R. Boyens, Guillermo Castro, Jason Essington, Jens Frabricius, Bunkerd Fapimai, Maj. Maurice H. Fisher (USAF), Jurrel Forlenza, Nick Heudecker, Margaret Leber, Justin Lee, Andrew Lombardi, Stéphane Meslin-Weber, Tanya Nagar, Joe Ottinger, Lise Pflug, Trevin Rard, Brad Schaefer, Irina Serbina, Tracy Snell, Bruno Tourelle, and Michael Zogg.

I got a lot of semi-anonymous advise from the technical geniuses at irc.freenode.net #xjava; many of them I never met in person, or I never learned their names in real life. Best wishes to doc|work, jp9, Logi, UncleD, and ThunderChicken. Thanks for enduring the banter, the chapter drafts, and the occasional rant.

An extra token of gratitude goes to the folks who educated me about the inner workings of the three-letter agencies who selflessly defend this country and who donated some of their precious time to this project.

Last, for Cary Macias: I hope you enjoyed the story and I give you all my love.

This book was written using OpenOffice.org under Linux/KDE. The final edits were completed under OS X 10.4 Tiger using Microsoft Office:mac.

The text was set in Adobe Garamond 11 points, a Renaissance-family serif font designed by Robert Slimbach and based on a font by Claude Garamond. The book was converted to Adobe portable document format (PDF) using a combination of GNU ghostscript and Adobe Acrobat 7.0 Professional.

The Tesla power transmitter on the cover was designed using Autodesk Inventor. The tower textures and lightning effects were rendered with Autodesk 3DStudioMax. The final layout involved heavy use of Adobe's Photoshop and InDesign software.

I'd love to hear from you if you have any comments or ideas about this story. There are lots of ways of contacting me:

Eugene Ciurana
c/o CIMEntertainment BV
San Francisco, CA USA
+1 415 387 3800
novelist@teslatestament.com
http://www.teslatestament.com/site.php?page=contact

irc://irc.freenode.net – channel ##java

By the way, if you want your book autographed, please send me a message through the contact page so I can give you a mailing address. I will sign your book and return it.

Printed in the United States
97304LV00001B/302/A